LONGSHOT
AN ASTRA MILITARUM NOVEL

T0019510

LONGSHOT
AN ASTRA MILITARUM NOVEL

ROB YOUNG

BLACK LIBRARY

A BLACK LIBRARY PUBLICATION

First published in Great Britain in 2023 by
Black Library, Games Workshop Ltd., Willow Road,
Nottingham, NG7 2WS, UK.

Represented by: Games Workshop Limited – Irish branch,
Unit 3, Lower Liffey Street, Dublin 1,
D01 K199, Ireland.

10 9 8 7 6 5 4 3 2

Produced by Games Workshop in Nottingham.
Cover illustration by Miklós Ligeti.

A CIP record for this book is available from the British Library.

ISBN 13: 978-1-80407-050-5

See Black Library on the internet at

blacklibrary.com

Find out more about Games Workshop
and the worlds of Warhammer at

games-workshop.com

Printed and bound in the UK.

For Mum and Dad, whose kindness knows no bounds.
Thank you, for everything.

For more than a hundred centuries the Emperor has sat immobile on the Golden Throne of Earth. He is the Master of Mankind. By the might of his inexhaustible armies a million worlds stand against the dark.

Yet, he is a rotting carcass, the Carrion Lord of the Imperium held in life by marvels from the Dark Age of Technology and the thousand souls sacrificed each day so his may continue to burn.

To be a man in such times is to be one amongst untold billions. It is to live in the cruelest and most bloody regime imaginable. It is to suffer an eternity of carnage and slaughter. It is to have cries of anguish and sorrow drowned by the thirsting laughter of dark gods.

This is a dark and terrible era where you will find little comfort or hope. Forget the power of technology and science. Forget the promise of progress and advancement. Forget any notion of common humanity or compassion.

There is no peace amongst the stars, for in the grim darkness of the far future, there is only war.

PROLOGUE

Shon'saal stared in wonder as the sky fell over Miracil.

He'd long since removed his helmet to see the spectacle with his own eyes, free from the colour-dulling filters and flashing warning sigils. It was against protocol, but so far from the front there was no danger – so long as the *shas'ui* didn't catch him, of course. He had been caught in his daydreams too many times already, and had been reprimanded more than once for straying beyond the confines of his caste.

But even if he was caught, Shon'saal knew that he wouldn't regret his decision.

Explosions rocked the low city to the west of the river, briefly casting the outlines of tenement blocks in sharp relief, the towers of flame blossoming like the crimson lilies of his distant home world. The flaring light played across the dense clouds of the slate-grey skies above, creating an inverted mountain range that ceilinged Attruso's polluted atmosphere, framing the burning city beneath. Columns of blinding white lights lanced down through the clouds from the *gue'la* ships in the heavens above, so bright that they hurt his eyes to watch, followed by the delayed thunder of a distant waterfall.

It was beautiful.

Shon'saal knew that each detonation was another potential death, every echoing rattle of distant gunfire a warrior that would never see their loved ones again. Flights of enemy dropcraft swirled beyond the city's edge, murmurations of migratory avians that brought death to Miracil. Shon'saal found it hard to reconcile the breathtaking spectacle and the wave of heartbreak it drove through the city. He would write a poem about it later when his watch ended, and try to find a deeper understanding in the carefully composed hexameter.

The scuff of a foot on plascrete drew Shon'saal from his reverie for a moment. He turned, tension rising in his chest as his mind conjured images of the shas'ui's face, angry and reproachful. But the street was empty, the azure light of the Tidewall barricade's energy panels colouring the primitive gue'la stonework in shades of cold blue and black. Shon'saal was alone, watching for enemies that were too far away to be any threat to him or his team. Staccato gunfire echoed over the river once more, and he turned back to watch.

The gue'la were miles from the River Spatka, and thousands of fire warriors and *gue'vesa* stood between them and the stinking, polluted torrent Shon'saal guarded. There was no honour in holding a bridge so far from the enemy advance, but it was safer. When he'd tried to explain this to the shas'ui to help calm his rage, he'd been told that he could have the first watch.

He stepped down from the Tidewall barricade's firing step, sighing as his view of the burning city was lost behind the shield's azure haze. The barricade was one of hundreds erected throughout Miracil as soon as the invaders had entered the system, fortifying the city and barring the thoroughfares in anticipation of the enemy advance. The smooth alloy almost glowed in the light of the energy panels, a stark contrast to the brutish stone of the gue'la city.

His post overlooked a monolithic bridge that spanned the Spatka river, an overdecorated monstrosity of plascrete and adamantine that was encrusted with the gue'la's morbid iconography. He disliked looking at it too long, at the cog-rimmed gue'la skulls and grotesque cherubim that kept an imperious watch over the bridge's deck, wide enough for three Hammerheads flying abreast.

But he had to admit that the crossing was a better sight than the Spatka itself – its grimy orange waters polluted to the point of toxicity, the fast-flowing torrent creating a stinking brown foam that clung to the banks of the river and collected around the vaulted stanchions of the bridge. Even in the dim twilight the river was the dark brown of congealing blood, the darkness doing nothing to disguise the rancid smell.

A particularly loud explosion drew his attention from the river back to the battle raging in the lower city. Honoured Mui'el said that they would throw the invaders back into the void, that their resolve would break in the face of the united defenders. Shon'saal wasn't so sure. He'd seen the gue'la troop ships as they thundered down from the heavens that morning, still hundreds strong despite the planetary defence grid and the fleet in orbit above. No, these gue'la were different to the people they had met on Attruso. They were more determined, more belligerent. The gue'vesa had been openly fearful when they learned the name of the enemy that had come to face them, though the word had meant nothing to Shon'saal.

Then came the noise again, a foot scuffing the plascrete surface of the road, and his stomach clenched tight.

'I had to see it with my own eyes, shas'ui,' he said, turning and making the gesture of apology with his hands as another explosion shook the ground.

He barely had time to register the prone forms of his squad before a flash of light consumed him.

From a third-floor window of an abandoned building overlooking the t'au barricade, Sergeant Darya Nevic watched the xenos warrior pitch to the dirt as it joined its compatriots in death.

'Kill confirmed. It's down.'

With a silent prayer of thanks to her long-las' machine spirit, Darya lifted her eye from the scope and took in the view.

Ten dead t'au littered the street between her and the barricade, killed by her team of six snipers concealed along the street overlooking the rear of the xenos position. The Cadians had carried out the plan with ruthless efficiency, using the arrhythmic thunder of the Imperial bombardment to mask the sound of their shots.

'Any signs of movement?' Darya subvocalised into the short-range vox.

'Nothing, boss,' Ullaeus' voice fizzed.

'Good. Frantt and Kadden, get down there and set up the charges along the barricade. Ullaeus, take Bellis and Arfit and scout the route to the emplacement to the north. Yanna and I will keep watch here. Move.'

Her team replied in a series of vox-distorted acknowledgements and set to their tasks; Ullaeus, her second-in-command, orchestrated his scouting team as the figures of Frantt and Kadden appeared on the street below.

Both ran in a crouch to minimise their silhouette, using the shadows and their cameleoline cloaks to move from cover to cover on their way to the barricade; they knew their work well, which is why Darya had selected them for the job. They would have the t'au position sabotaged faster than anyone else in the team, as sure as Bellis and Arfit were the best scouts that she could have sent with Ullaeus.

Kadden was the first to finish and took up a defensive position, while Frantt stowed the last of his explosives out of sight beneath the barricade's firing step. Darya flexed her grip on her long-las' forestock, the rough cloth wrappings damp with her sweat and water from the Spatka. Their infiltration across the rough, stinking waters of the river had been challenging, but they'd managed to cross beneath Trackway Span itself without being discovered.

So far.

The risk of discovery increased every minute they stayed in one place, and they had too many objectives left to complete to get bogged down in a firefight.

'Frantt, what's the hold-up?' Darya asked over the vox, as her trooper struggled with something at the base of the barricade.

'Two seconds, boss,' Kadden said, his voice barely understandable beneath the heavy static that choked his signal.

'Damned vox-blunt,' Darya cursed. 'Yanna, get ready to move.'

Frantt extracted himself from the firing step and flashed a thumbs-up signal – he was done, and it was time for the team to move on.

Darya pushed herself to her feet and held her long-las at the ready as she worked her way through the abandoned building back down to street level. The overhead lumen strips were long extinguished, covered in a thick layer of dust and grime, which left Darya's route in almost complete darkness. She stepped carefully over the prone form of the t'au sentry she'd silenced on the way to her chosen sniping position, its hands still clasped around its slit throat.

'Ullaeus, how's the route looking?' Darya whispered into the vox as she reached the bottom of the stairwell.

'Minimal con… far. We're at the… of vox range, boss.'

'Hold position, we're coming to you. Street team, regroup on me.'

Darya moved quickly out from the building and onto the street, ignoring the subtle feeling of exposure as she moved from an enclosed space out into the open air. Darkened windows looked down on her from all sides, each a silent threat that set her nerves on edge even after she'd found some cover.

Within moments, Frantt and Kadden had taken a knee nearby whilst Yanna appeared in a doorway further down the street.

'Good shot that last one, boss. Kasrkin couldn't have done it better,' Kadden said.

'Kiss-arse,' Frantt replied.

'He moved at the last second, didn't you see?'

'I'm not sure there are any Kasrkin left,' Yanna said as she approached and knelt alongside Darya. 'Do you want me to send an update to Captain Kohl?'

'No. We'll stay on the short-range vox until dawn to keep the risk of detection down. We have our orders – the rest of First Company are going to roll across that bridge in the next two hours and we still have three more positions to neutralise. We just need to get it done – for Cadia.'

'For Cadia,' the other three chorused back.

'Good. Let's move out.'

1

The city of Miracil burned.

Its red-bricked cathedrals of industry blackened and crumbled alongside broken hab-blocks, all long since abandoned by the city's indentured classes. Manufactoria that had stood undaunted beneath Attruso's corrosive atmosphere for millennia were felled by shells, orbital lance strikes and the grinding tracks of war machines. The Astra Militarum didn't stop to consider the provenance of their enemy's defences – they belonged to the enemy, so they must fall.

And fall they did, turning the air into a barely breathable haze in the perfectly gridded order of the manufactorum city, the fingerprints of the Adeptus Mechanicus clear in the obsessively ordered design of each street, plaza and thoroughfare. The empty-eyed skull emblem of the Mechanicus watched as acrid black smoke billowed out of shattered windows like blood into water, but with no breeze to carry it away it lingered in the air, drawing a false night over the western fringes of the city. Ash and dust mingled with the first flurries of filthy snow, carpeting the path of the Imperial advance with a murky grey slurry.

The Astra Militarum ground onward beneath it all, soldiers bleeding for every yard they clawed back from enemy hands. Their cries of anger and pain were lost beneath the constant barrage of artillery, drumming a staccato beat that seemed to shake the planet itself. Acts of individual heroism were so common that they went unremarked. A trooper armed with a flamer breaking cover as his fuel tank was punctured by a stray shot, saving the lives of his squadmates as he was immolated alone in the middle of the street. Another soldier diving in front of his commanding officer, taking the superheated plasma bolt that was meant for her and dying in agony as he fought to breathe through liquified lungs. A soldier dragging his oldest friend back to cover under withering enemy fire, honouring a promise not to let them die alone.

Amidst it all, a lone officer knelt in the scant cover offered by a tenement's rubble-strewn roof, the southernmost corner of the building torn away to reveal the meagre lives once lived by its inhabitants. He held a pair of magnoculars to his eyes, straining for a better view from the building's eastern edge.

The vox-bead in his ear crackled with a nearby signal, but he ignored it. His view finally settled on what he had been waiting for – the heat haze and smoke from the east cleared for a few tense heartbeats, revealing a distant bridge over an unseen river. Human forms were on the nearest bank, springing out of improvised cover to fire at glowing blue barricades set along the bridge's length, their defenders holding their ground with bright bursts of fire from their own weapons.

He sighed as his vox-bead crackled again and ground his teeth. Keeping low, he stashed the magnoculars inside his jacket and crawled back over to the roof's southern edge and began to work his way down to the ground.

'Anything, sir?' a pale trooper asked as the officer navigated the last few feet down a rubble incline, spraying dirt and fist-sized rock fragments as he slid to a stop at the foot of the rise. The trooper was still sitting astride his dirtcycle in an alley between two hab-blocks, the engine inactive as he waited for the officer's return.

'Keep your voice down,' the officer hissed as he cleared the ruin and swung his leg over his own dirtcycle, which had been leant up against the next building's wall.

'I'm sorry, sir,' the trooper said, moving to remove the vox-bead from his ear.

'It doesn't matter,' the officer grunted, checking a dull steel chronometer on his wrist. 'Get back to headquarters, let them know that the vox-blunt is stronger in the city. It doesn't look like Third Company have taken the Glazer's Gate bridge yet. I'm carrying on to Saintsbridge to see how House Gyrrant are progressing, then I'll look for First Company.'

'Understood, sir,' the trooper said, kicking his dirtcycle into growling life. 'Lieutenant Eridan?'

'Yes?'

'Emperor be with you, sir.'

'And with you, trooper. Now get going,' Eridan said, making the sign of the aquila as the trooper roared off out of the alley and out of sight.

Eridan kicked his own dirtcycle back into life and took a deep breath before accelerating towards the sounds of gunfire.

He sped through the maelstrom of war without any sign of hesitation. He sloughed his battered dirtcycle through the slurry of ash and blood that caked the rockcrete, weaving between advancing troopers and fallen masonry as he fought for every ounce of grip. Where the terrain was most uneven he was forced to stand using the bike's pegs, before dropping back into the saddle when he needed a burst of speed.

Eridan gritted his teeth with every tortured note from the engine, wringing yet more speed from his tired and battered mount. Most troopers dived out of his way as he raced through, the bike's exhaust baffles long since disengaged, the sound warning his comrades that he was coming, which lessened the risk of being shot by a jumpy Guardsman.

'Don't fail me now, old friend,' Eridan said to the bike.

A Leman Russ powered through the wall of a refectorum hall less than half a block ahead, followed closely by a ragged band of flak-armoured Cadians, the dusting of ash and powdered stone giving them the look of spectres that haunted the tank's shadow.

Lights ignited in the building opposite the Leman Russ, blinding in their intensity, as the enemy peppered its inches-thick armour with their plasma weapons. Eridan heard the tell-tale delayed snap-crack reports a moment after he saw the shot, and clamped down on the dirtcycle's brakes as the troopers ahead scattered for cover.

The Leman Russ reacted with arrogant slowness, slamming to a halt and slowly traversing its battle cannon to aim at the offending building.

Not this way, Eridan thought, swinging the bike around in the opposite direction as the Leman Russ fired, the shockwave violently kicking up the loose ash and dust for a hundred yards in every direction. He could hear the building collapsing behind him and the unmistakable barrage of las-fire as the troopers strafed the ruin with their weapons.

He darted down a side street half choked with the detritus of war: abandoned possessions that the city's wayward citizens had abandoned to the coming inferno, meagre trinkets whose sentimental value had been outweighed by their owners' desire for survival. Charred papers floated through the air, disturbed and given animus by the battle raging nearby.

The alley opened out onto a street that looked remarkably like the one he had just left. Its blackened and broken buildings were silhouetted against the sickly magenta light of the Cicatrix Maledictum, still faintly visible through the columns of smoke hazing the twilight sky. Occasional lance strikes flared down from the heavens like pillars of lightning, briefly illuminating the broken spires and shattered manufactorum halls as they cleared the way for ground troops to advance.

Clearly, the new orders hadn't reached the fleet yet. He patted his chest pocket out of habit. The order packet was still there, and he offered up a prayer to the God-Emperor to see it safely to its destination.

Eridan raced through tight alleys and clouds of stinging embers beneath the thickening smoke above, a false ceiling that capped the heavens and made each street seem smaller and more claustrophobic.

He whipped past the myriad tableaus of city war, catching glimpses of Cadians breaching glowing energy barricades and firefights of dazzling light as lasguns traded fire with t'au plasma weaponry. He rushed past it all, a blur of featureless Cadian fatigues and promethium fumes, before he was waved down by a squad from Third Company.

'Stop!' one cried, breaking cover to leap into Eridan's path. Enemy fire stitched his footsteps in the ash as he dashed out of cover towards the mounted messenger, coming to a sliding stop in the cover of a fallen aquila, blown clear of a manufactorum spire high above. Eridan skidded to a stop just in front of the other Cadian, the dirtcycle's engine barking as it was forced into idleness.

'This way is blocked,' the trooper explained quickly, pointing a gloved hand up the street in the direction of the enemy fire. 'Enemy firing line, we're waiting for armoured support.'

'Understood,' Eridan said, nodding his thanks. Enemy shots carved scorching rents in the fallen masonry, forcing both to duck a little lower as splinters of stone scattered between them. The Cadians' lasguns barked out their response, the exchange of fire intensifying momentarily as the air was stitched with blue-white lights of pure energy.

'Lieutenant Markas Eridan, under Major Wester,' Eridan said, extending a hand to the other man.

'Lieutenant Bamber, Third Company of the Two-Hundred-and-Seventeenth,' the other man replied. 'You here to tell us why the vox is down?'

'Vox-blunt,' Eridan said. 'Deployed just after dawn to maximise the confusion.'

'It's working,' Bamber said. 'Have you got some new orders for us?'

'Not exactly. Your primary objective is still to take the bridge at Glazer's Gate and establish a beachhead on the eastern bank.'

'Is that all?' Bamber was half-shouting over a sudden crescendo in the fighting along the street. Behind him, a soldier primed a shoulder-mounted rocket launcher and counted down on his fingers. On three, his fellows sprang from shelter to provide covering fire as he stepped out and loosed the missile up the street and out of sight. The Cadian was back in cover before the smoke trail cleared, and a distant boom was met with ragged cheers.

'Those are your orders, straight from the top,' Eridan shouted back over the noise. 'Second wave will be coming up from behind to reinforce you before nightfall. What's your disposition?'

'I'm down to four squads, two flanking this position whilst we wait for some armour,' Bamber said, pointing up the street towards the t'au barricade. 'Captain Lowes has the main bulk of Third Company pushing on the bridge, but we've not heard from him in a few hours.'

'Understood.' Eridan pulled a folded map from his pocket and started making notes with a red wax pencil. 'Have you heard from House Gyrrant?'

'Nothing. Just the occasional explosion.'

'Thank you. I've got to get to First Company. Relief is on the way, just keep pushing forwards,' Eridan said, shaking the other officer's hand once more.

'I wouldn't know how to do anything else,' Bamber said, laughing. 'For Cadia.'

'For Cadia,' Eridan replied. He wheeled his dirtcycle around and pointed to the west. Bamber's eyes followed, and he smiled.

'Your support has arrived, lieutenant,' Eridan said, pointing towards the distant sound of squealing tracks chewing their way across rockcrete. The enemy guns increased their fire as a Leman Russ rounded the corner at the far end of the avenue and unleashed its battle cannon with a deafening roar. Dust and rubble seemed to leap up in the shell's wake as it flashed down the street, before exploding against the t'au emplacement with an earth-shaking blast of earth and alloy fragments.

The Cadians were up and charging before the debris had cleared, their roars blending with the sound of Eridan's engine as he accelerated away.

Eridan raced south at speed, trying to ignore the uncomfortable heat that the dirtcycle's engine was radiating the further he rode.

The bike was old, tired and in dire need of refitting and maintenance. Attruso was the fourth planet on which Eridan had ridden it in as many years as the primarch's crusade barrelled headlong through the galaxy, retaking worlds in the name of the God-Emperor of Mankind.

Eridan still remembered the day that news of Cadia's fall had reached the 217th as they had raced back to defend their home world. The anger and shame at not being there to defend Cadia still burned hot; it didn't matter that word had reached them too late, that the regiment had been too deeply entrenched against their foes to leave immediately. Cadia had fallen and they had been too far away to help it, and the entire regiment mourned as the Cicatrix Maledictum had torn its red route across the sky.

The Imperium had reeled from that blow like none before. The tenuous hold that so many worlds had on order and civilisation failed, seeing them fall to Chaos and ruin as the empire of humanity tore itself apart. Its citizens rose up against each other and the Emperor, embracing the Ruinous Powers or giving themselves willingly to xenos dominion. Worlds like Attruso.

That was, until *he* returned. The primarch Roboute Guilliman, who strode boldly from the jaws of death and assembled the greatest crusade since the Emperor Himself had walked the galaxy. Guilliman had returned order and civilisation to the worlds of the Imperium, either with long-needed aid or by lasgun and bolter.

The sound of both lasgun and bolter rose to a crescendo as Eridan sped across the cleared floor of a refectory hall, its high walls and damage-pocked ceiling echoing with the sounds of approaching battle. He headed for a huge gap smashed through the opposite wall, a sixty-foot high wound in the building's side that opened out onto a street flooded with smoke and dust.

With a deep breath he plunged through the cloud, and emerged into the centre of a battle between giants.

Imperial Knights in the blazing orange livery of House Gyrrant duelled with flights of white-alloy Crisis suits, each side fighting for dominance in a raging exchange of solid munitions and energy rounds. Ion shields flared and force shields shattered in blazes of light, overpowering all other colours so they appeared to momentarily fight in shades of black and white.

Eridan gritted his teeth and dropped a gear in his dirtcycle, fighting for grip as the titanic footfalls of the Knights shook the earth beneath his wheels. This was exactly where he didn't want to be, caught between two forces deep in the heat of combat who would barely notice if they stepped on him. But that insignificance was also the best protection he had – with luck and no small measure of speed, he might be able to escape before they noticed that he was there.

He kicked out the rear wheel and scythed his bike to the right, raising his weight on the dirtcycle's pegs for better manoeuvrability – he knew he was going to need it.

Eridan darted beneath the nearest Knight, *Ignatius*, as it swivelled at its waist to swat a Crisis suit from the sky in a shower of sparks and scrap alloy. It reached out to grasp at another battlesuit with its Thunderstrike gauntlet as a third hurled a barrage of plasma into the Knight's ion shield, distracting it long enough for the first to take to the air once more.

Then Eridan was clear of the first melee and dodging the second, as an Imperial Knight lurched backwards towards him. He pressed himself to the dirtcycle's fuel tank as the war machine fell over him, catching on the facade of a hab-block in a spray of dust and stone fragments just long enough for him to escape before being crushed. He barely had time to reseat himself before an ion blast scoured the air overhead, fired by a descending XV104 Riptide to shatter the shield of a Knight further down the street.

The shield broke with an apocalyptic thunderclap, the tamed lightning stripping the shoulder assembly from *Relentless Defender* in a screech of tearing metal that Eridan felt deep in his bones. The limb fell slowly through the air, the Avenger gatling cannon still spitting death as its barrels slowed their lethal spin and Crisis suits descended from the sky to swarm the maimed Knight.

Eridan barely had a moment to process the spectacle of a

god-machine being brought low by xenos artifice before the air around him shimmered and howled as gatling rounds screamed past. The backwash of pressure almost tossed him from the saddle but he held on with a hissed curse – his luck was running out.

Three Imperial Knights turned the corner at the end of the street, announcing their arrival with a chorus of war-horns and raising titanic chainswords in challenge to the xenos assaulting their battle-brothers.

Eridan shot past them as they tilted forwards into a charge, the Knights forming into a spear-tip led by a Knight festooned with blessings and wax seals. He swerved out of the way of the orange-garbed men-at-arms who followed their liege lords into glorious battle, and left the clamour of renewed combat in his wake.

Trackway Span was a freight zone which had once ferried the heavy machinery manufactured at the heart of Miracil out towards the space port on the city's edge.

In order to pass out of the city, it first had to cross the river Spatka.

The river's brackish brown water cut a meandering path through the city's edge, a hundred yards wide at its narrowest points. It was a raging torrent, with both sides of the bank thick with hydromotive plants that had harnessed the energy of the river for the Mechanicus.

Of course, that had been before the planet's fall.

Now both banks were a ragged ruin, the raw edge of a wound that bled men and tanks into the roiling tide. Bodies floated down the river from upstream, carried by the current like so much flotsam to be disgorged and forgotten in the oceans of Attruso.

The span itself was a rail bridge of grey stone over adamantine-veined rockcrete, designed to carry the heaviest freight over the water safely. It was buttressed and reinforced to near invincibility, each stanchion blessed by arch-magi of the Mechanicus for strength in spite of Miracil's acidic rain and the corrosive waters of the Spatka. That wasn't to say that the enemy hadn't tried to bring the bridge down: deep gouges pocked its support columns to expose the reinforcement bars within, where t'au energy weapons had assaulted the unyielding frame. The baroque artifice that had created the bridge was strong enough to withstand it all, which made it an essential objective for the Imperial forces.

Unfortunately, it was clear that the enemy were well aware of its importance and weren't letting the Astra Militarum take it without a fight. Cadian heavy weapons teams traded fire with t'au positions across the river, the bark of heavy bolters mixing with the hissing snap of plasma rounds blasting chunks from the Cadians' improvised cover.

Eridan rode in the shadow of the bridge for almost half a mile, streaking past squads of Guardsmen as they cleared each building along the western bank with flamers, grenades and lasgun fire. He was only stopped as he neared the rear of the Cadian position, as a trooper stepped out from an improvised barricade that blocked the approach to the bridge. He walked towards Eridan with his lasgun raised, covered by several others in his unit as he called out to the messenger.

'Identify yourself!' the soldier yelled over the nearby gunfire. Eridan slowed to a careful stop, the dirtcycle's engine coughing and misfiring as it idled beneath him.

'Lieutenant Eridan, Cadian Signal Corps,' Eridan called back, raising both hands from the handlebars to show that they were empty. 'I need to speak to your commanding officer immediately.'

The soldier stopped a few feet away from Eridan. His features were drawn, with dark shadows developing in the hollows under his eyes, his bone-deep fatigue clear as he performed the familiar glance at Eridan's eyes to check their colour.

'He's Cadian born,' the soldier called out. The men behind him lowered their rifles and turned back to watching the road. 'This way please, sir.'

Eridan dismounted and walked his bike into a shelled-out building that the Cadians had fortified with improvised barricades. It was roofless, the building's high fractured walls framing the smoke-black sky above, sheltering the soldiers within as they dressed their wounds or took a moment to wolf down rations from dull grey sachets.

'You'll have to forgive the security measures, sir,' the trooper explained as they walked past grey-faced soldiers and a Munitorum priest who ministered to a dying soldier. 'Captain Kohl has suspended saluting too, since Lieutenant Neames got himself sniped.'

'Where is the captain?' Eridan asked, as they reached a narrow doorway that looked out over the bridge.

'He's on the beachhead, sir, other side of the bridge,' the trooper explained. 'You'll have to leave that here,' he added, nodding at the dirtcycle.

With a clear view of the bridge, Eridan agreed with the soldier. Whilst the structure seemed almost untouched by the enemy bombardment, the bridge's deck had been chewed into an almost unpassable morass of shell craters and spurs of twisted metal. There would be no way across for a rider, not whilst the enemy still held firing positions on the opposite bank.

'Have you had any word from the other side?' Eridan asked, pointing at the Imperial beachhead on the eastern bank.

'Some, but long-range vox is down so we're limited to

short-range vox and messenger runs. There should be a supply run heading out soon. We'll see if we can't get you across, sir.'

A shout rang out for covering fire, and the Cadians arrayed on the riverbank let loose a withering firestorm of las-bolts and heavy-bolter rounds which curbed the enemy fire as three battered Chimeras sped into view and onto the bridge.

There, they were forced to slow as they navigated the deep craters and jutting spars of slagged rails, their turret-mounted multi-lasers laying down punishing sprays of suppressing fire through their own exhaust fumes.

But slowly, inevitably, the enemy volleys began again, focused on the troop transports on the bridge instead of the bridge itself. Searing white energy beams flashed into momentary existence, most missing their targets to plough through buildings on the western bank. Shouts of alarm and pain began to rise up through the sounds of gunfire across the Cadian position as fresh ruins were cast down on the Imperial side. Eridan grabbed a lasgun from a nearby soldier who was too badly wounded to wield it himself, and added his own shots to the Cadian fusillade.

The first Chimera hit the fractured rockcrete on the western bank and was met by cheers from the Cadians, followed by the second, which trailed bluish smoke from its overheating exhausts. The third almost made the western bank, but was hit as it rose out of a high-lipped crater. The shot's report was audible for a millisecond before the vehicle exploded, the turret shearing free of the vehicle's chassis to fly through the air as if it were made of paper rather than thick metal armour. The Cadians' cheering ceased as the boom echoed through the streets, and Eridan couldn't help but watch as flames gouted through the turret hole and driver's slit.

The other two Chimeras didn't stop until they were out of sight of the opposite bank across the street from Eridan. The rear ramps dropped with a shuddering clang, their hydraulic motors long since exhausted, and an officer emerged from the lead vehicle with a wounded soldier by his side.

'Get these men to the medicae!' he roared as troopers rushed forwards to retrieve the injured from the transport.

Eridan was already moving towards the officer, his escort in tow.

'Sir, a Lieutenant Eridan to see–'

'Are you Captain Kohl?' Eridan interrupted, moving aside as another injured Cadian was carried past on a stretcher, her face a mass of bloodied bandages.

'Lieutenant Munro,' the officer said with a scowl, waving forward more men to clear the wounded. 'You're Major Wester's man.'

'I am,' Eridan said, nodding. 'I have orders for Captain Kohl, if he still lives?'

'The captain's alive all right,' Munro said, 'but I'm a transport down for this run and I'm not sure that I have space for you. Give me the orders and I'll make sure he gets them.'

'You'll find space, lieutenant,' Eridan growled. His hands tightened around his borrowed lasgun, which Munro noticed with narrowed eyes.

'Frag it,' he cursed. 'Help us load up and I'll see what I can do.'

Eridan shouldered the weapon and set to helping unload the last of the wounded alongside Munro, then filled the Chimera's bloodstained interior with crates of munitions, medicae supplies and casks of chem-cleaned and sanctified water. The rest of the space was taken up by a squad of Cadian troopers from the rearguard, who were being sent in to replace the wounded at the front. It was a tight squeeze, but they all made it into the two remaining vehicles.

Eridan held tight to the Chimera's roof webbing as the rear hatch closed on him and six other Cadians, and the vehicle lurched forwards and back into the line of fire.

Inside, the only light came from the firing slits set into each side panel, and a dull red lumen positioned on the dividing wall between the troop bay and the driver's compartment.

'Hold on tight,' a tense voice crackled over the vox, before the Chimera's occupants were thrown forwards, then backwards violently enough that several lost their grip on the webbing and tumbled on the blood-slicked floor. They'd secured the crates to hooks set into the walls and floor with thick canvas straps, but even they strained against the weight as their contents were thrown about over the rough ground of the bridge.

The smell turned Eridan's stomach: warm, clotting blood mixed with the days-old sweat of the occupants, whilst the fumes of burning promethium saturated everything with their clinging actinic stink.

Then the transport came under fire, and there was no time to feel nausea at all.

Plasma rounds hammered the walls and roof of the passenger compartment, and they hunkered down as far as they could in the belly of the Chimera, where the armour was thickest. A trooper defied his comrades' shouts to stay low as he pulled himself up to a firing port.

Two titanic thuds rocked the Chimera in quick succession as a t'au heavy weapon caught the vehicle in the flank. It blasted a neat circular hole in the right wall and exited through the left, splitting the standing man in two with a spray of blood and viscera. His squadmates cried out as he fell, but there was little time to do anything before choking smoke filled the passenger compartment and the transport turned sharply.

Eridan felt his way forward through the press and hammered

his fist desperately against the rear hatch release, but it didn't open. Panic rose unbidden in his chest as the last of the lumen's light was smothered by the smoke, and he dropped to his knees as a coughing fit racked his chest. Someone shouted for them to be let out, before their voice failed beneath their own barking coughs.

The Chimera slammed to a sudden halt and the rear hatch released, spewing forth a cloud of greasy black smoke, and five choking and bloodstained Cadians fell into the shelter of a massive manufactorum building.

Eridan crawled clear, his breath coming in shallow gulps as booted feet rushed past.

'Get the supplies out! Clear these men out of the way!'

Eridan felt a strong hand grab his collar and drag him from the burning transport.

He looked up and found himself in the shadow of a looming black spectre, his knee-high boots polished to a mirror sheen, his black leather greatcoat untouched by dirt, ash or dust. He was broadly built and intimidating just for his size, and doubly so for the peaked cap and garb of the Commissariat that he wore.

'On your feet, lieutenant,' he ordered in a deep, resonant voice. 'Officers shouldn't show weakness in front of the enlisted.'

Eridan pushed himself to his knees and coughed again, before standing up in front of the commissar. Behind him, soldiers were running to retrieve the supply crates from the burning transport, each spluttering as they emerged from the billowing smoke within.

'Munro voxed ahead as soon as the Chimeras came within range,' the commissar said, raising a dark eyebrow as he looked down at Eridan. 'The captain is expecting you. This way.'

2

'You'd better repeat that, lieutenant, because I'm praying to the primarch himself that I heard you wrong.'

Eridan had been escorted through the manufactorum complex to the captain's forward command post, which was little more than a few vox-operators busy at their portable workstations and a map of the area stretched across a dust-covered conveyor belt. An inactive servo-skull sat holding down one corner, its eye-lenses dark and dormant, whilst the opposite corner was pinned beneath a couple of lasgun charge packs.

Captain Kohl had greeted Eridan with little more than a grunt as he took in urgent reports from short-range vox-operators, and relayed orders bluntly in return.

Kohl had been an officer in the Cadian 217th as long as Eridan could remember, a respected veteran long before the primarch's crusade had pushed the regiment to the front of its grinding advance. A battered red-lensed augmetic had taken the place of his left eye decades before, and the rest of his face was a craggy ruin of scars, burns and pockmarked skin. His remaining eye was framed by the same deep shadows as his men, though he showed little fatigue as he rounded on Eridan.

'You are to cease your advance and hold your position, sir,' Eridan said, standing at attention despite the remnants of the Chimera's smoke clawing at his lungs and the rockcrete-ground flesh that cried out for rest.

'Why in all the fragging hells would we do that?' the captain growled, waving away a vox-operator who had turned at his outburst. 'You don't beat the t'au by keeping them at arm's length, you do it by getting up close. General Matliss' orders are pretty damned clear – we keep pushing forwards whilst the second wave clear up any stragglers in our wake. When they catch up they take the lead on the advance, keeping the momentum up so we end this war before winter grinds us to a full, and very cold, stop. God-Emperor above, none of us want a grinding winter siege against the t'au.'

Eridan's stomach turned as he looked meaningfully at the vox-operators, then to the commissar, and back to Captain Kohl.

'Perhaps we should have a little privacy?' the commissar said with a nod towards the vox-operators.

'Fine,' Kohl grunted. 'You three, go and help unload the supplies,' he said to the troopers, who all stood smartly and removed their headsets before striding off to the still-smoking Chimera. 'Fat lot of good they're doing if no one's answering anyway... If this is more bad news, I'm going to blame you, Tsutso. Sigma, give us some privacy.'

The servo-skull on the map whirred into the air, the backwash of its gravitic motor disturbing the paper as it took up position between the command centre and the rest of the room. The noise of gunfire and shouted calls were instantly muted, as if a heavy curtain had been drawn around the three men.

'Carry on, lieutenant,' Commissar Tsutso said, his expression sombre.

'General Matliss is dead. May the Emperor bless and keep her.' As Eridan spoke the words, a sharp twist of grief spread from his stomach through his chest. He clenched his jaw and forced the feeling back down, burying it beneath the weight of his duty.

'Do we know how?' Commissar Tsutso asked as he clasped his hands behind his back.

'Sniper, sir,' Eridan said stiffly. 'Took out the general and two of her command squad as they disembarked their shuttle. It was a damned long shot from outside the landing zone's perimeter cordon.'

'Well, shit. Matliss was a damn fine woman, and an even better general,' Kohl said sadly.

General Hildegarde Matliss had been the battle group's talisman, an ageing relic of Cadian glory who had more victories under her belt than the rest of the battle group's officers combined. After so many years of ceaseless campaigning, she was also the lynchpin of the complex political strands that held the battle group together. All present knew that her absence would have consequences that reached far beyond the battlefield.

'We can't communicate that to the men. Not on top of the order to halt the advance,' Kohl said as he looked to Commissar Tsutso.

'I was about to suggest the same,' Tsutso agreed. 'It is in the interests of the men that we protect morale. Perhaps news of the general's death can wait until a more... official announcement is made?'

'Agreed. I'll brief the officers so they know what's coming,' Kohl said, before turning back to Eridan. 'Who's taken command now then?'

'Colonel Wassenby from the Cadian Four-Hundred-and-First has assumed command for the time being.'

Kohl and Tsutso shared a look.

'The order to hold position makes more sense if it came from Colonel Wait-and-see,' Kohl muttered, ignoring Tsutso as the commissar cleared his throat reproachfully.

'We are not privy to the Emperor's plans for us – the faithful can only trust that He has given us the tools we need for success,' Tsutso quoted.

'And the faithful will prevail,' Kohl said with a nod. 'Has the colonel sent any news about this blasted vox-blunt, lieutenant? If we're to hold this position then I'm going to need reinforcements.'

'Not from the colonel, but Major Wester did ask me to relay some additional information. For your ears alone, sir,' Eridan said, doing his best not to look at the commissar.

Captain Kohl's augmetic eye whirred as his natural eye narrowed, the violet iris seemingly blazing brighter than the augmetic's lens for a heartbeat.

'Commissar Tsutso is a member of my command staff. Out with it,' Kohl said with a reassuring nod.

Eridan approached the map and picked up a red wax pencil that lay on its surface.

'The vox-blunt has been more effective than Colonel Wassenby understands,' Eridan explained, drawing a line from the northern edge of the map to the south along the Spatka's western bank until it reached Trackway Span, where the line crossed the river to encompass the positions that the Cadians held on the eastern bank.

'Major Wester had me take a circuitous route to you as your left flank is too obscured to receive accurate information from orbit – we had no idea how far Third Company or House Gyrrant had advanced. From what I've seen, they have almost reached their bridges – their primary objectives – but almost certainly haven't reached the far banks.'

'That's a damned long way,' Kohl breathed as he took in the line that traced the Imperial front.

'It was, sir,' Eridan agreed, as his every ache and scrape showed how hard the road had been. 'The fact is that Trackway Span is one of only three bridges to have fallen into Imperial hands out of the thirty that still stand. Command have no solid lines of communication to the front, and the combined smoke and cloud cover is too thick for the fleet to give us any useful orbital support. We need to re-establish lines of communication if the advance is to succeed, which is why the Adeptus Mechanicus have supplied a number of vox-relays to cut through the enemy's jamming.'

'Good. When is ours arriving?' Kohl asked.

'You're not receiving one,' Eridan said apologetically. 'Colonel Wassenby isn't deploying any to the front lines. If the t'au get their hands on one they could move to counter the relays with a new vox-blunt, putting us on the back foot again. Instead, select units in the second wave will set them up in cleared areas, with each relay creating a node in the signal chain that will span the entire front, giving us at least some communication between command and the front lines.'

He drew several circles well back from the river on the western bank, deep in Imperial-held territory.

'Your position is covered by the relay that's meant to be here, with the Kintair Rifles.'

'Meant to be?' Tsutso asked. 'Are they not in position?'

'We have no idea where they are, sir,' Eridan said, tossing the pencil down on the map. 'They left their staging point for the advance, but we've not heard anything from them since.'

'Could they have been wiped out?' Kohl pressed.

'Maybe, but we haven't had any reports from the area at all. Could be that they've just been held up, but we can't be sure from what little information we have. What we do know is that under the vox-blunt, the advance is becoming disjointed – your salient is an example of that.'

Eridan pointed to the bulge in the Imperial line that showed where the Cadian 217th had pushed deeper into enemy-held territory than the rest of the advance.

'The issue at hand is that you've advanced far beyond the line, captain, and command is struggling to coordinate the advance to support you. The second wave of troops have made slow progress and almost certainly won't have reached this position in the next twelve hours.'

'I'm not sure that I like what you're heading towards, lieutenant,' Commissar Tsutso said. Eridan felt the threat behind the words.

'We fought bloody hard to take Trackway Span, lieutenant,' Kohl said. 'We've set up the next stage of the assault on Miracil, just as General Matliss planned. Don't tell me that command, or Colonel Wait-and-see, is about to tell us to pull back over the river.'

'Colonel Wassenby doesn't know that I'm here, captain,' Eridan said. 'Major Wester sent me to get a view of the line and to apprise you of your situation, not Colonel Wassenby.'

'Then Major Wester is acting out of turn,' Commissar Tsutso observed.

'Not at all,' Kohl said, smiling as he realised what was going on. 'He's just doing his best to re-establish the lines of communication. Isn't that right, lieutenant?'

'Absolutely,' Eridan said, nodding. 'Once the Kintair Rifles have their vox-relay in position, it will give this entire section of the line the ability to coordinate over long-range vox, and better access to support from the rear and from orbit.'

'Hypothetically speaking, it would be in our best interests that their vox-relay reach the objective zone intact, even if the Kintair Rifles do not,' Commissar Tsutso said. 'Not that we could assist in such an endeavour, since our orders are to hold Trackway Span.'

'Hypothetically, yes,' Kohl agreed. 'But we'd be more likely to hold Trackway Span with reinforcements and fleet support.'

'Undoubtedly,' Commissar Tsutso said. 'Didn't you say that you came under fire as you approached the bridge, lieutenant?'

Eridan looked from the commissar to the captain, who gave him a meaningful look.

'Er, yes, sir,' Eridan replied, a little confused as to the game that the other two were playing.

'Then we'd better send some men to scout our rear on the western bank,' Kohl said with a smile.

'A prudent course of action,' Tsutso agreed, 'Speaking of which, I believe that it's time I walked the front lines, ensure that our faith doesn't give way beneath our fatigue.'

The commissar made the sign of the aquila and strode away past the servo-skull and out of sight. Eridan watched him go, a look of surprise on his face.

'They're not all sadistic executioners,' Kohl said as he looked over the map, as if reading Eridan's mind. 'Some are, but most understand what's necessary on the front lines.'

'I don't think I've met a commissar like him before,' Eridan said with a soft shake of his head. He unclasped his chest pocket and pulled out the bundle of papers inside. Kohl raised a questioning eyebrow as he took them.

'From the major, sir. He specifically said that they're for your eyes only,' Eridan said.

'Then they'll have to wait,' Kohl grunted, picking up the bound sheaf of papers and stuffing them into his own pocket. 'Sigma! Disengage privacy.'

The servo-skull pipped an acknowledgement and buzzed through the air back to the captain's side, its glowing eyes fixed, unblinking, on Eridan. He shuddered.

Kohl seemed not to notice, and shouted for his vox-operators, who appeared a moment later, jogging into view and standing to attention before the captain.

'Get Lieutenant Eridan to a medicae, the man looks like he lost a fight with a grox. Then someone find Sergeant Nevic. I've got a job for her.'

3

Fio'la's breathing was slow and measured, the calming rhythm keeping his rising panic at bay.

He clutched his pulse rifle close to his chest as he jogged forwards in a stoop, the low wall to his right covering him as he moved into a better position.

'What do you see?' Horesh hissed far to his right, his own pulse rifle held high and tense.

'Nothing,' Fio'la said, the targeting hexes of his helm scanning the freight yard before him.

He had worked in a space just like this one, a lifetime ago. He knew the sound the short, boxy cranes made as they swung cargo onto waiting carriages, the cables reverberating almost musically as they were pulled taut by impossibly heavy loads. He could almost taste the polluted rain on his skin as they worked through the harsh Attruso wet season, or the taste of blood as his cracked lips split during the long droughts. Clearest of all, he remembered the feel of electro-scourges on his skin as the red-robed masters flogged him for some imagined infraction, exhorting their labourers to work ever harder and faster despite their growling stomachs and sleep-starved limbs.

Fio'la took a deep breath and pushed away the memories, forcing them down into the dark and forgotten places of his mind. That was another life, when he had lived under another name.

That man was dead. Only Fio'la remained, and he had a mission to complete.

He raised his rifle to his eye and surveyed the freight yard through the scope.

There was little evidence of the Imperial presence on the rail yard. Ancient wheeled carriages and wagons stood waiting on their tracks, the ground beneath yet to feel the touch of the enemy artillery, whilst a forest of cranes loomed overhead as if poised to resume their labours. It all provided ample cover for him and his team to move through, all the way to the warehouse that dominated the yard's far end.

Fio'la looked back at his squad of fellow gue'vesa, men and women that he had known and bled beside since long before the saviours came, back when they had no one to care for them but each other.

'Spread out and look for the drone controller,' he ordered. 'Keep your eyes on the warehouse, I don't want any surprises. Stay safe and stay alive. For the Greater Good.'

'For the Greater Good,' they said as one, then rushed forwards out of cover.

'Contact.'

Darya didn't react as the voice broke through the constant low-level static that crackled in her ear. She'd seen them too, a squad of t'au soldiers scattering into the square – or, at least they wore the blunt grey-plated armour of the xenos. She didn't need to see beneath the sleek plates of their helmets to know that they weren't true t'au. She could see all the evidence through her scope: the angle of their legs, the broadness of their shoulders, and the number of fingers on their hands.

Humans, she thought with disgust, and resisted the urge to spit.

'Hold fire,' she whispered, relying on her throat mic to carry the order across the close-range vox to her squad. 'Let them see the prize.'

'Anyone see anything?' Fio'la asked, the helmet transmitting his voice to his entire squad as he spoke. It was unbelievable technology, one of so many wonderful advancements that the saviours had brought to Attruso, much like the long, boxy rifle that he held in his hands.

'I see it, near the warehouse. Grey-black crane, with the lifting jaws.' Sor'sal's voice spoke into his ear, as if she were standing next to him. Unbelievable.

'Take up positions around the controller,' Fio'la ordered.

'Head count,' Darya breathed.

'Twelve,' Ullaeus' voice replied.

'One heavy. Confirm?' Darya said.

'Confirmed.'

Twelve troopers and one heavy weapon, Darya thought. *Hardly seems fair.*

Fio'la crouched behind a stack of plastek crates, their contents long since picked over for anything of value. The controller was less than twenty yards away in the lap of a saviour who sat with his back against the low plascrete footing of a clawed crane. Behind him loomed the imposing presence of the warehouse building, its red-brick walls pockmarked with windows, air recirculation vents and the gaping maws of empty-framed doorways. He strained to look inside, to spot any indication of the enemy who had come to burn their world, but could see nothing.

'Is he alive?' he asked as he scanned the saviour's blue-grey skin for any sign of life. The nasal slit didn't flare with breath, nor did the chest rise or fall beneath its armour.

'No sign, Fio'la,' one of his men responded.

He looked about at his squad, all labourers playing at soldiers. Several had taken cover together behind a low wall, too nervous or afraid to find their own positions. He was the only real soldier amongst them, the only one who had fought for his freedom. With this mission's success, he would earn the saviours' favour.

But the warehouse loomed over him, fuelling the dark memories of what he had lived through in a yard just like this one, the pale existence he'd been able to scratch between the hours of endless labour, then the terror when the red scar had torn apart the sky. The starvation when the supply ships had stopped coming. The uprising and the coming of the saviours, and the new life of meaning they had offered.

Fio'la took a long breath and forced down the anger.

'Sor'sal, retrieve the device. We'll cover you,' he ordered in as calm a voice as he could manage.

His heart was hammering as his second-in-command broke from cover and moved forwards, carefully scanning the ground for the traps that they had all been told to expect. Fio'la scanned the windows of the warehouse through his rifle's scope, each flickering shadow playing tricks on his mind, the distant gunfire pulling at his already frayed nerves as his sight settled on the fallen saviour propped up against the crane's base.

That wasn't right. Where were the rest of the saviour's squad? They wouldn't just leave his body out in the open like that.

'Sor'sal, come back. There's something–'

'Now,' Darya said, and pressed the button on her detonator.

Fire and shrapnel ripped through half of the t'au squad, who had all cowered together behind a low wall facing the warehouse – the best piece of cover available so close to the t'au corpse.

That was why Darya had ordered Bellis to conceal a krak charge there.

Before the first clap of the explosion's echo, she had fired her first shot. The enemy sergeant dropped to his knees, hands pawing numbly at the neat, smoking hole in the centre of his chestplate.

Her next shot pitched a female from her feet in a boneless heap as the las-beam split her helmet in a spray of grey splinters and red mist.

Then her crosshairs settled on a burly male warrior, but two long-las shots thumped into his torso before she added her own. His legs failed him as her shot took him high in the chest; he fell back, his heels gouging shallow furrows in the gravel as he flailed and slowly went still.

The gunfire stopped, replaced only by the sound of distant dying soldiers. It had taken less than ten seconds, but Darya's team had picked off the entire t'au squad. They'd barely had time to react, no time to fight back, just a sputter of ineffective shots fired off in a panic.

Darya pulled away from her scope to take in the sudden calm of the rail yard, breathing through the rush of adrenaline that stretched every second into a miniature eternity.

Below her, twelve t'au bodies lay in various states, all unified in death. Several were barely even recognisable as anything but charred and ruined flesh from the explosion, the rest lying dead in their meagre cover. Ordinarily, she'd hold position long enough to ensure the dying were really dead then order her team to move, but they didn't have the luxury of patience in this war. They would have to confirm their kills the old-fashioned way.

'Good work, everyone. Let's clear up.'

The crane door shrieked as she pushed it open, rust from the boxy cabin clinging to her fatigues as she slid down the ladder to the loose gravel below. Around her the other seven members of her squad did the same, emerging from crane cabins to secure the area before they moved on.

The t'au were as low on patience as the Cadians, and had prioritised retrieving the xenos device over their own safety. Their haste, combined with the skill and experience of Darya's squad, made the rail yard the perfect ambush site. It was unlikely to work again, however.

Darya made for the man with the red-striped helmet. He still lay where he had fallen, where he had struggled ineffectually to drag himself back into cover that was no protection at all from the snipers hidden around him. She dropped to her haunches and pushed the man's helmet up and off his head, revealing the strong, blunt features of the genehanced Attruso labour class.

Corporal Iago Ullaeus whistled. 'Now that's a big bastard.' His long-las was held loosely across his chest as he approached. 'They breed them big on Attruso, eh?'

'I've seen smaller aurochs,' Darya said, pushing herself back to her feet and making for the body of the t'au warrior they'd used as bait. They'd come across him and his squad less than an hour earlier, silently wiping them out until only this one remained, seemingly unaware of the Cadians. That was until he had removed the strange visor that he wore and tried to flee.

Iago stooped to pick up the headset that they had left on the dead t'au's body. They knew from past experience that the enemy would seek to retrieve the device if they could. Despite their seemingly endless resources it still held some value for them, which gave Darya's team all the advantage they needed.

'What do you think? Set it up and go again?' Iago asked.

Darya looked about, at the fallen t'au and the smoking crater that her squad were giving a wide berth. The device was valuable enough that the enemy might send another squad to recover it, or send another squad to find out what had happened to the others... But resetting the ambush was too much risk. It would take too much time, leaving them vulnerable as they cleared the bodies, not to mention it meant the team clearing up the ruined flesh created by the mine. She wouldn't put her people through that.

'No, we move on,' she said, raising a finger and drawing a circle in the air. 'I want a full gear and ammo check. Ullaeus, trap the device. If they send anyone else to collect it, I want them to pay for it.'

'Yes, sergeant,' Iago said, pulling a frag grenade and a length of wire from his belt.

'Yanna, see if you can get a signal to Captain Kohl,' Darya continued. Yanna nodded her assent, swung her pack off her shoulder and began to set up the portable vox-unit in the cover of a nearby rail engine. Her tattooed features creased in concentration as she worked, the geometric designs masking her features as well as any camo paint. Yanna could not hide where she came from, but Darya did not believe she would if she could – she was a transplant, like Darya, but drawn from the vicious tribes of the death world Episca.

'No signal yet,' Yanna said, her sharpened teeth lending her words an extended sibilance.

'I'm not surprised, but keep trying,' Darya said. Long-range vox had failed not long after the attack on Miracil had started, but that hadn't slowed the Cadians. They always seemed to find ways to adapt, and the ancient flare pistol on Darya's hip was testament to that.

'Arfit, Bellis – scout the north end of the yard, find us an exit towards the refineries but stay in vox range. How are we all for ammo?'

Darya waited until everyone in her squad had signalled that they had enough ammo and had no gear issues before checking her own.

She'd had the long-las since Cocleratum, but didn't like to dwell on thoughts of how she'd earned the weapon. There had been a mission. Her friends had died and she had survived by doing what needed to be done. No more than that.

The barrel was still usable, cloth wrappings around the stock and grip were still tight, and she had four more hotshot lasgun packs. That was all she needed to know in that moment.

Iago laid the trapped headset back on the dead t'au and carefully stepped away, giving Darya the thumbs up once he'd picked up his rifle.

'It's time to move, Yanna,' Darya said to her kneeling trooper, 'wrap it up. Vox must still be down.'

'Yes, sergeant,' Yanna replied, and set about packing away the portable vox-set.

'We're going north, to the refinery district,' Darya said to her squad. 'Bellis, Arfit – what do we have?'

'Blown wall on the northern perimeter, maybe a hundred yards. Looks like old damage,' Arfit replied, his voice crackling. They were at the very limit of the vox range, and if they moved much further the distortion of the vox-blunt would make their words unintelligible.

'*Opens up on a storage complex, sarge,*' Bellis said, his words barely recognisable over the interference. '*We can cut north or back west by the look of it.*'

'Hold position, we're coming to you.' Darya waved the rest of her squad forwards. She hung back so that she fell in alongside Yanna at the rear.

'No one's blaming you for the vox being down,' Darya said quietly as they passed over the thick metal rails and between long-rusted cargo trolleys.

'I know,' Yanna said, 'but when I was drafted into a renowned Cadian regiment I assumed they'd at least have gear that worked.'

Darya smiled at the other woman's joke. Even though Yanna was no more a pureblood Cadian than Darya or Ullaeus, the Cadian black sense of humour seemed to have infected them all.

'Well, you must pray harder,' Darya told her, slapping Yanna's shoulder as she moved up closer to the front of her squad.

They were on the very edge of the black cloud that smothered the western boundary of Miracil, and Darya was glad to finally be at least partially under a clear sky. For days they had fought their way east beneath a pall of ash and smoke, losing all sense of time as the sun was blotted out. The only real indication of the passage of hours was the fatigue that grew heavier in their limbs.

It had been hard fighting, close and brutal, with little chance for her squad to wage their patient war. She was glad to have been given the order to scout the enemy lines, harassing the t'au where they could. They had finally been freed to do what they did best: observe, calculate and execute.

The squad caught up with Bellis and Arfit at the very edge of the rail yard, where a fallen section of wall gave way to an open-topped storage facility stacked high with Munitorum containers.

'Through or round, boss?' Bellis asked, his violet eyes almost glowing in the fading light. Darya looked up to see that the heavens were darkening beyond the thin tendrils of the smoke-cloud, the bruise-like light of the Great Rift growing clearer by the moment.

'We go round,' she said, pointing off to the right. Whilst it would take longer to reach the refinery district, the clear avenues of fire and minimal cover offered by the containers didn't suit the snipers. By keeping to the edge of the space, they maximised their defensive options.

Bellis and Arfit moved off quickly, covering one another as they darted forwards to the nearest container and cleared each avenue in turn. Darya didn't need to turn around to know that the rest of her squad would be in cover themselves, watching every direction for the enemy's approach.

'Sarge,' Ullaeus hissed from behind. He was kneeling down, watching the western approach to their position and pointing at something Darya couldn't see from where she was in cover. When he didn't explain what he had seen, she moved over to him at a crouched run, her mind racing with the possibilities. *Please don't be a battlesuit,* she prayed silently. Facing even a lone xenos flyer would be problematic: without heavy weapons there would be little her squad could do to damage it, and the encounter would almost certainly cost the lives of several of the team. It was a price she wasn't keen to pay.

Darya reached Ullaeus' position and edged around the empty wagon he was using for cover.

She saw it: a red flare hanging in the sky, just visible between the warehouse roof and a tall exhaust stack.

'Damn,' she cursed, just as a whipcrack explosion echoed through the rail yard. 'Everyone on me, double time. We're being called back.'

4

Attruso was meant to be a short stop to rest and refit after years of campaign, a chance for the unaugmented troops of Battle Group Tartaros to reset their strained morale before they were thrust into the next warzone on the primarch's crusade.

But within hours of entering the Carrodan System, as the troops shook themselves free of the lingering nightmares of warp transit, word reached the barrack decks: xenos ships were in orbit around every planet in the system.

Darya had known then that there would be no rest. Briefings were hurriedly given, contradictory orders navigated, and the first Cadians made planetfall within twenty-four hours of arriving in-system. And so the battle for Attruso began.

Far from the equatorial paradise they'd been promised, the Cadian 217th landed in the wasteland steppes outside Miracil on the northern continent, with orders to retake the city.

Three days on from planetfall, Darya felt every single hour of the deployment dragging on her like a physical weight. From the headlong assault through the hab-zones on the city's edge, through the refineries that choked the Spatka's western bank and beyond. Darya's squad had been at the leading edge of the Cadian 217th's advance, crewing the first rafts to cross the river on the third night, when they had taken the eastern bank of Trackway Span under the cover of darkness.

Their route had led them through the warrens of artillery-shattered manufactoria and refineries that crowded the Cadian front lines, on to a wide thoroughfare half blocked with waist-high rubble barricades of bulldozed rubble and dirt-filled sandbags.

Darya shouted a call sign as they approached, and waited for the returned signal before breaking cover with her squad and running, hunched low, through the forward barricades and into the relative safety beyond.

'Friendlies coming in!' the watch sergeant shouted back down the line as they passed, and Darya nodded her thanks.

'Still alive, Hortzo?' she asked jokingly, shaking the sergeant's hand as the rest of her squad filed past.

'Just about,' Hortzo said with a weary smile that didn't quite reach his violet eyes. 'Good hunting out there?'

'Some. The xenos have pulled back, but the next mile is a warren.' Darya looked back the way that they'd come. There were interweaving paths that intersected with hundreds of others, each providing a score of covered routes through the shattered remains of Miracil. The t'au could be advancing on the Cadian positions through any number of paths without being seen until they were on top of the Imperial defences.

'Tell me about it,' Hortzo sighed. 'I can feel them watching us, waiting… They're waiting for us to push on, but they'll have to wait a bit longer.'

Hortzo raised his eyebrows and inclined his head towards the nearby figure of Commissar Tsutso, his burly frame looming over the sheltering troopers as he prowled the forward defences.

'What's going on?' Darya asked.

'New orders, we're holding position.'

The two sergeants shared a look before Darya moved on with a nodded farewell, working her way back towards the command post through the layers of improvised defences.

The soldiers she passed mirrored her own fatigue, their pale faces almost glowing in the thin light that broke through the smoke-clouds above. Darya and her squad exchanged friendly words with troopers they knew as her team passed safely through their positions, the Guardsmen hunkered down behind hastily assembled barricades or in puddled craters left by the now silent Imperial artillery far to the west. Some slept with their lasguns held tight in their arms, watched over by their comrades who resisted the call of sleep to give their squadmates just a few minutes of stolen rest.

God-Emperor, they're all but spent, Darya thought as she passed a trio of Guardsmen who were asleep behind a lascannon emplacement, a fourth keeping watch with the embers of a lho-stick between his teeth.

'Make sure that's out by sunset, trooper,' she whispered as the rest of her squad filed past. 'Makes you an easy target for bastards like me.'

She held up her long-las to the trooper, who nodded and pinched off the end of the lho-stick with callused fingers, then slipped the remaining inch behind his ear.

'Just trying to stay awake, Sergeant Nevic,' he mumbled apologetically.

'You're doing a good job, just keep your eyes on the front,' Darya said with a nod of encouragement.

If that's what they look like, how bad do we look?

Darya caught up with her squad and realised that they were in similar condition. Every single member of her squad had deep shadows beneath their red-rimmed eyes and hollows in their pale cheeks. Their fatigues had lost all colour to the ash and soot they had crawled through over the last two days, with Yanna's blue facial tattoos the only sign they hadn't become bystanders in a monotone propaganda pict.

'Get them some hot food and somewhere for them to bed down if you can,' Darya said to Ullaeus as she caught up to her corporal. 'I'll go and find out what's going on.'

The two shared a look before they parted, silently acknowledging the tension that had risen in the squad as they were called back. After fighting so hard to push into Miracil, after losing comrades and friends as they broke through the t'au lines, they feared the call to pull back – and having to do it all over again in a few days' time.

'Hortzo says we have new orders – hold position,' Darya said.

'Throne knows we need the rest, but this doesn't feel right,' Ullaeus replied, looking around at the static positions taken up by the rest of their company. Darya shared his misgivings; it was the first time that the Cadians had stopped to create such well dug-in defences – for the last three days they'd only been on the attack.

'I know what you mean. Try to see what you can find out from the ground whilst I get the official line from the top.'

Both snipers spun round as a warning came up from the lascannon position, a call that was carried down the line in startled voices.

'Drones!'

Domed silhouettes dotted the sky to the east, jinking and zipping through the air as they effortlessly avoided the first shots from the Cadian defenders. They replied in kind, blazing at the Cadian positions with their underslung plasma weapons.

Sleeping troopers jerked into consciousness and took up their weapons with quick, practised motions. Within seconds, gunfire stitched the sky with white las-beams and glowing tracer rounds from heavy stubbers, the air in the Cadian positions reverberating with sudden action as they fired on the approaching airborne targets. Darya's squad dived into cover, as plasma shots cracked into the Cadian defences, fighting shoulder to shoulder with their comrades to repel the enemy attack.

Plasma fire whipped over the Cadian positions like buzzing insects, chewing through the thinnest barricades and spraying the defenders with shards of plascrete, but few troopers ducked out of the way. They used the tell-tale muzzle flashes of the drones' weapons to sight their guns, their grizzled experience holding firm where less experienced troops might have shied away. Officers rallied their squads, directing volleys of accurate fire from exhausted troopers who barely needed the encouragement – they were Cadian, and they knew what was expected from them.

'Any eyes on the controller?' Darya said into her vox-bead. Her squad had quickly learned that drones were rarely deployed without a controller to direct them, and were easily taken care of if the controller was eliminated.

Flames erupted in the sky less than fifty yards away as drones were picked off, smoking trails tracing their path to the ground. But more came, emerging from behind buildings and blazing plasma fire as they swooped towards the Cadian positions.

Darya's squad called back negative responses one after another. Ullaeus swore as a nearby trooper was caught in a plasma fusillade and cut down, his own reply sandwiched between hissed curses. In the middle of it all, Commissar Tsutso darted from barricade to barricade, his bolt pistol roaring as loud as his shouted litanies as he loosed shots at the advancing drones.

'We need eyes high,' Darya said, looking up over the Cadian

positions to the flat-topped buildings on either side of the street. 'Ullaeus, hold the street level. Yanna, with me.'

Darya broke from cover and ran in a low hunch, crossing the street to a mostly intact red-bricked administrative block. It had already been cleared, and several of the Cadian defenders were firing from empty upper windows.

Yanna followed behind Darya, through the double doors and into the empty halls within. The gunfire from outside rang through the stripped corridors and rooms, their contents buried in the barricades outside.

'Lose the pack,' Darya ordered, pointing to the vox-pack as she made for the stairs to the upper floors. Yanna didn't hesitate, looping the pack's strap over her head and dropping it at the foot of the stairs as she sprinted up after her sergeant.

As they passed onto the second floor, a Cadian fell back past them clutching his arm, the wound in his bicep still glowing where the plasma round had burned through the limb. Darya didn't stop, rushing up towards the roof access as the trooper fought for the breath to scream.

On the roof, the clamour of gunfire from below was an all-consuming maelstrom of noise and heat beneath the cloudless skies. A dead Cadian lay in the lee of the wall's edge, several blackened scorch marks across his torso leaking white steam in lazy plumes.

Darya darted forwards to take cover next to the body, whilst Yanna ducked behind the roof access door.

'Look for the controller!' Darya shouted through the vox, scanning the rooftops in every direction through her scope. In the dim twilight it was hard to make out anything clearly, so she flicked the low-light filter into life. She would have used the night-vision filter, but the t'au's plasma-based weaponry would have been blinding.

A drone crossed her vision as she scanned, and she took the opportunity to shoot through its twin underslung plasma weapons. It exploded in a white-hot blast of raw plasma and melting plastek.

'North-east, white building,' Yanna shouted from the doorway, her voice carrying across the short distance and echoing in Darya's vox-bead. 'Third window from the right!'

Darya thanked the Emperor for the tribeswoman's sharp sight, and that she'd ended up in Darya's unit at all; whilst Yanna wasn't the best shot in the unit, she had by far the sharpest sight, which made her one of the best spotters in the regiment.

'Do you have an angle?' Darya asked, ducking down as a drone sprayed the rooftop with plasma fire, then springing back up to land two shots in its anti-grav plating. She didn't watch as it dropped like a stone through the open air, already resetting for a shot on the controller.

'Not a kill shot,' Yanna said. 'I'll move– Aargh!'

Darya whipped round as Yanna fell back, clutching her face as a drone sprayed her position with full-auto fire. Darya shot the drone from the sky as she ran back to the staircase, ejecting her empty powercell and slapping a new one in place as she reached Yanna.

The tribeswoman was writhing on the floor, her weapon forgotten as she held both hands over the right of her face, stained with blood and dust from the staircase wall she'd been behind. Darya grabbed her collar and dragged her out of the line of fire into the stairwell.

'Yanna!' Darya had to shout, unclipping her water canteen from her belt and pushing it into Yanna's bloody hands. 'Wash the wound with this – it will hurt, but you need to wash it down. I'll be back, I promise.'

Darya tore herself away, turning back towards the gunfire

outside and emerging onto the rooftop to see that most of the remaining drones were pulling back, regrouping away from the Cadian position for the inevitable counter-attack.

Darya ran across the gravel of the roof to the north-eastern edge, sliding to a stop on the loose surface. She raised her scope to her eye and took aim on the window that Yanna had called out, just in time to see a wounded t'au warrior pull the headset from its eyes with bloody fingers before rolling out of sight, clearly aware that they were now being hunted.

'You'll have to try harder than that,' Darya breathed, exhaling as she tracked her rifle left to the very end window.

Less than a heartbeat later, there was a flash of movement in her scope, and she fired. The rifle spat a white-hot beam of pure energy, focused by the techno-artifice of the Adeptus Mechanicus to deliver death to the Imperium's enemies.

The t'au pitched back from the window, staggering as it lost its footing and slumped to the floor. Darya's second shot obliterated the controller device that the t'au still held in its dead hands.

In the skies above, the drones stopped momentarily as they lost connection to their controller and reverted to their base programming. It was all the invitation that the Cadian defenders needed, and they blasted the motionless drones from the sky with bursts of accurate fire.

Her comrades erupted in cheers, but Darya did not join them. She pressed herself lower to the ground and kept her vigil through the scope, scanning for more threats as she whispered into the short-range vox.

'Ullaeus. Yanna, top-floor stairwell. She's been hit.' She shifted, knuckles white as they tightened on the long-las. 'Get her to the medicae. I'm on overwatch on the roof.'

'*On our way,*' Ullaeus replied.

It was an agonising wait as she scanned the horizon, watching for any sign of the next flight of drones whilst listening to Yanna's laboured breath over the short-range vox. It felt like an age before the breathing was joined by low voices as her squad arrived, followed by quick crunching footsteps that told her Ullaeus was coming to join her.

'Anything?' he asked as he knelt beside her, pulling his own rifle close and taking aim at the white building.

'Nothing yet,' Darya said, fighting to keep her rifle still. God-Emperor, she was tired. 'Yanna?'

'Looks like shrapnel, small mercy that is. She'll have a scar like yours,' Ullaeus explained. 'Arfit is taking her back to the medicae post now.'

'Good,' Darya said, her own scar itching as she was reminded of its existence.

It only ever itched when she remembered that it was there, a long-forgotten injury that she only noticed on the rare occasions she saw her own reflection. It had faded over the years, but was still a ragged white line of scar tissue that ran from the corner of her eye, across her cheek to her chin. Like her rifle, it was a souvenir of a mission that she would have given almost anything to forget.

They waited on the rooftop in a wary but companionable silence for several minutes until a voice from the street announced the all clear.

'They must have been alone,' Darya said finally, wincing as her tired muscles protested the change in position after being held tense for so long. Ullaeus sighed as he did the same, putting up his weapon and following Darya towards the stairwell. They stepped over the spotted pools of watery blood that slicked the stairs without comment, and Darya scooped up her empty bloodstained canteen.

As they emerged from the double doors at ground level, they were met with cheers from the defenders – and the imposing figure of Commissar Tsutso.

'Praise the Emperor for your heroics, sergeant,' he said in his deep, rich voice. Darya made the sign of the aquila over her heart to the commissar.

The commissar of First Company was an unknown quantity to Darya. His eyes radiated with an inner light that was more given to mischief than discipline, and likewise his expressive face seemed more given to smiling and laughter than the stern expression he so often wore, and was wearing then.

'Thank you, sir.'

'Thank the Emperor,' he corrected, raising one dark eyebrow. 'Follow me. Captain Kohl is waiting for you.'

'We just need to get the squad rounded up and–' Ullaeus began, but Tsutso silenced him with a motion of his gloved hand.

'Your squad will remain here and help to hold this position,' he said. 'You will both accompany me. Now.'

5

Eridan's wounds itched under the medicae's tight dressings, but the feeling was far preferable to the hot sting of the counterseptics that had been used to clean his scraped and scoured flesh. A Cadian in a bloodstained plastek apron had used a rough cloth doused in chemicals to scrub the rockcrete from his skin, before dressing the worst of them in gauze that still smelled of smoke.

He sat in Captain Kohl's improvised headquarters as he had been ordered, awaiting the return message when Commissar Tsutso entered with two haggard-looking troopers in tow.

Both wore rough cloaks of urban camo-weave over drab khaki tunics, forgoing the flak armour worn by everyone else bustling around the ruined warehouse. The first was a man a full head shorter than the commissar, with curling blond hair and eyes the colour of open, clear skies.

Not a pureblood Cadian, Eridan thought.

Neither was the second, a woman that Eridan recognised from the rumours that swirled around First Company's pathfinder sergeant, the so-called Ghost of Cocleratum. She was of average height for Cadian troops, but radiated a sense of lethality that wasn't just down to the long-las cradled in her arms. Her dark eyes swept the room as she walked, constantly searching for threats until they landed upon Eridan.

'Sergeant Nevic, I presume?' Eridan said, getting to his feet and offering his hand.

'Sir,' Nevic replied, saluting before shaking the officer's hand. Her grip was strong, and the skin of her hands rough. Eridan found his eyes drawn to the long scar that traced a white line from her left eye to the corner of her mouth.

'I've heard a lot about you,' Eridan said, a little abashed. 'It's an honour to finally meet you in person.'

'Thank you, sir,' she replied in a tone that approached disappointment.

'Nevic, Ullaeus, nice of you to finally turn up,' Captain Kohl barked from the improvised map table. The broad grin on his face blunted the venom behind his words, and both Nevic and her companion saluted.

'Captain,' Nevic said, moving forwards to the table. 'Sorry for the delay – we were ranging pretty far beyond the line when we saw the signal.'

'We shouldn't have to rely on ancient tech for much longer if all goes to plan. How's it looking out there?'

'The xenos due east of us had pulled back to new defensive lines half a mile from the river,' Nevic explained, leaning over the table to trace a line far to the east of the Spatka.

'Our little manoeuvre on the river caught them off guard, I think,' Ullaeus added.

'Agreed, but they're already pushing forwards. We've encountered several squads of their scout troops in the last few hours, and they're getting bolder with their drone attacks.' Nevic sighed.

'We've seen that too. Probing attacks mainly, but they appear to be building the pressure on us,' Commissar Tsutso added.

Eridan watched as the captain took in all of this information with little visible reaction. It was a practised dance where they all knew the steps, presenting Kohl with the information they'd gathered so he had everything he needed to find their best way forwards.

'With all due respect, sir, why are we hunkering down instead of pushing on?' Nevic asked. 'The longer we wait, the more time they have to prepare. Winter's setting in, it's going to be hard to break through the t'au lines whilst we're freezing to death.'

'We have Lieutenant Eridan to thank for that,' Kohl said, nodding at Eridan. 'New orders from command – we're holding here until the vox-blunt is dealt with.'

'Holding, sir?' Ullaeus glanced at Nevic.

'Those are our orders,' Kohl said. 'Several missives from Major Wester have confirmed that the second wave of the advance have been bogged down in the low city, dealing with pockets of t'au elements that we bypassed on the way to the river.'

The earth rumbled with distant explosions, shaking dust from the roof that settled on the map and everyone present. Kohl leant over the map and brushed it away, ignoring the fine powder that dusted his armour and uniform.

'As we know, our orders were to take Trackway Span in order to facilitate the next stage of the invasion – our new orders don't change that, but mean that we're holding rather than pushing on. To help secure our position, I'm sending a taskforce back to link up with the second wave, which should make reinforcing and resupplying much easier.' Kohl drew a line through the last of the powdery dust with his finger, tracing a route back from Trackway Span through the low city to the landing zone beyond the city limits.

'Do you need us to scout the route, sir?' Nevic asked without hesitation. By the way that Ullaeus suppressed a laugh, he'd been expecting his sergeant to say something like that.

'No. Lieutenant Munro has that job. I need you on something else – just the two of you, since speed is of the essence. Lieutenant Eridan, if you would?'

Eridan approached the map, stepping in as Kohl made room for him at the improvised table. He was aware of everyone's eyes on him as he spoke, the combined attention suddenly intense as he laid out Colonel Wassenby's plan. A lesser man might have been intimidated, but Eridan was a Cadian, and Cadians didn't show fear.

'The Adeptus Mechanicus have sanctioned the use of vox-relay pylons across the Attruso front. It won't be a perfect solution, but will enable limited encrypted communication channels between ground troops and the rear,' Eridan explained. 'Yours is with the Kintair Rifles, a conscript outfit who were meant to be part of the second wave of the advance. But we've not heard from them in over twelve hours, and the reliable orbitals show that they haven't yet made their primary objective. In truth, we don't have any idea where they are.'

Eridan pointed to a red circle on the map, centred on a point half a mile away from Trackway Span that covered almost half a square mile of warehouses and industrial buildings.

'You need us to find them?' Nevic asked, looking from Eridan to Kohl.

'Exactly,' Kohl said, scratching at the scar tissue beneath his augmetic eye. 'We need to make contact with them and get them to their primary, intact if possible.'

'Can't the sergeant and I take the vox-relay to the objective?' Ullaeus asked.

'No, it's too heavy. It's mounted on a Chimera chassis for

portability, but in any case we can't leave it unguarded. If the enemy capture it then they might be able to knock out the relay system, and then we're really on the back foot,' Eridan said.

'Which is why your orders are firstly to find the Kintair Rifles. If they're alive and in any fit state to fight, get them to their objective and get that vox-relay up and running as soon as possible,' Kohl said, his voice low and powerful.

'And if they can't reach their objective for any reason, sir?' Nevic asked.

'Destroy the vox-relay so it doesn't fall into enemy hands,' Eridan cut in.

'Then use a flare to let us know the operation has failed,' Kohl said. He pulled two thick shells from his pocket, one the vibrant green of autumn grass, the other the red of blood, and failure. 'Green to tell us you've been successful and are on your way back, red for anything else.'

Nevic took the offered flare shells. Neither soldier flinched at the whining reports of lasguns flaring nearby, echoing around the empty rafters of the warehouse.

'Anything else, sir?' Nevic asked, her expression impassive.

'If you have to scrub the mission, then get back to the bridge as fast as you can. We'll need all the help we can get to withdraw back over Trackway Span,' Kohl said.

'We'd give up the bridge, sir?' Nevic asked, clearly shocked by the notion.

'It's pragmatism,' Commissar Tsutso cut in, his arms folded over his black-coated chest. 'The price of our own success.'

'We're isolated. We're the only outfit to take the eastern bank for miles in either direction, and with no artillery or air support we're looking pretty damned lonely... But it's not all bad news. Lieutenant Eridan will be heading back with Lieutenant Munro to report our position to command,' Kohl said with a slight smile. 'There is a chance – a slim chance – that we can consolidate our position here before the order comes through to withdraw. That only gives us a few hours to reinstate the vox-link and commit our artillery and reserves to holding this position. We won't be pushed back over that river. We are Cadians, damn it. We do not take a backward step.'

That fierce light had returned to Kohl's organic eye as he spoke, an infectious energy that seemed to reinvigorate both Nevic and Ullaeus. The Cadians stood a little taller, their fatigue receding.

'Good, I wasn't looking forward to taking that bridge again,' Darya said with a wide, wolfish grin, and Kohl chuckled, despite the precarious position of his outfit and how close they were to disaster.

'You have until dawn. May the grace of the God-Emperor be with you both,' he said solemnly.

6

Darya fought the creeping weight of the last few days as *Thunder of Might* idled, her eyes fixed on the hastily repaired hole in the Chimera's opposite bulkhead. A patch of scavenged metal covered the gap in the layers of thick armour plating, the interior paint scorched away to leave the purple, blues and yellows of heat bloom on the bare metal. The repairer had been attentive during their labours, and she could see the rainbow glimmer of sacred oils and unguents pasted over the thick welds to calm the transport's machine spirit.

Even our vehicles are bruised, she thought, as Ullaeus ducked his head under the hatch lintel and took a seat beside her. He had a steaming cup of recaff in his hand, which he offered to Darya.

'Where did you scrounge this up from?' she asked, taking the cup and enjoying the warmth that soothed her aching fingers. God-Emperor, she was tired.

'C'mon, boss,' Ullaeus said with a grin, 'you know better than to ask questions like that.'

The drink was hot, grainy and bitter, just how the Cadians always made it. Nothing like the smooth, rich and smoky recaff from Cocleratum, but in that moment it was just as welcome.

'Hells, that hits the spot,' Darya sighed, passing the cup back. It was the first thing she'd eaten or drunk since making planet-fall that didn't taste of purifying tabs or preservative-laced grox biltong. It was much needed, the warmth of the drink somehow soothing her aching muscles. Ullaeus drained the rest of the cup down to the dregs, then stowed the cup in his satchel.

Darya nodded down at the bench and tapped a black pack with a dusty boot.

'The fail-safe charge. It's not exactly light, so we'll have to split the carrying time,' she explained.

'Understood. Did you manage to see Yanna?' Ullaeus asked.

Darya nodded with a sigh. The young Episcan's face had been a mess of drying blood and bandages when Darya had stolen a few minutes to check on her. The improvised medicae station was little more than a sterile tent of plastek sheeting surrounded by the wounded and the shrouded forms of the dead. Hollow-eyed troopers sat staring at the dirt, their feet or into the space where their limbs had once been, bloody bandages littering the floor like discarded lho-stubs. It had been quiet there, quiet enough that it was all the wounded could do to stifle their moans lest they betrayed their own weakness.

'I did,' Darya said. 'She apologised for getting hit. Said she felt like she'd let us down.'

Darya left out the tears in the younger woman's eyes as she'd cried, half from the shame and pain of her wounds and half from the mind-dulling pain meds she'd been given.

'Sounds like her,' Ullaeus said with a thin smile. 'What did you say?'

'I told her that if she wanted a rest there are easier ways to go about it.'

'Of course you did.'

It had been hard to leave Yanna there in the midst of the dead, the dying and the wounded, with nothing to do but watch as those worst off around her waited for help that wouldn't come. She'd held Yanna's hand tightly as she told her to stay strong, that she'd be back in the fight before she knew it.

Darya stiffened as several other Cadians stepped into the Chimera. She greeted those she recognised with a nod, but Ullaeus apparently knew each of them by name and spoke to them all in turn.

Lieutenants Eridan and Munro were the last to enter, taking the last seats available opposite Darya and Ullaeus as the ramp closed and blocked out the dim light of the warehouse. After a couple of seconds, a red lumen buzzed into life, casting everyone in shades of crimson and black.

Munro unhooked a small corded vox handset from the forward bulkhead and clamped down on the activation stud.

'*Thunder* is ready,' he said into the vox, then released the stud as he waited for a response.

'*Acknowledged*, Thunder,' the response grated from the other Chimera, the other man's voice thin and warbling over the speaker. 'Saint *stands ready.*'

'We'll take the lead over the bridge and to the first drop,' Munro said, his eyes flicking to Darya and Ullaeus as he spoke. 'Then *Saint* will take over until we hit the rendezvous.'

'*Understood*, Thunder,' the vox burbled.

Munro hooked the vox handset back onto the bulkhead and slammed his hand on the thick plating separating the driver's compartment from the troop bay.

The Chimera's engines roared as they lurched forwards, but

the Cadians inside were braced for the sudden movement. Promethium fumes mixed with the lingering chemical tang of sacred unguents applied to the wounded transport's damage, creating an acrid stink that burned the occupants' eyes and throats for the first few moments.

'No heroics!' Munro shouted over the engine's roar, standing up with the help of one of the roof handholds as the Chimera jerked and shook over debris and fallen masonry. His attention lingered on Darya as he spoke, the red light from the lumen giving him a sinister profile.

'Stay away from the firing slits. We're no use to anyone on the bridge, so if we come under fire you stay down. If the transport gets knocked out you get to the western bank, is that understood?'

'Yes, lieutenant!' everyone else chanted in unison.

'Coming up on the bridge,' the driver's voice fizzed through the vox-grille.

'For Cadia! For the Emperor!' Munro roared.

The shouted reply was lost beneath the hammering of rounds against the hull as they rolled out onto the exposed bridge deck. The noise reminded Darya of the sudden cloudbursts back on Cocleratum when she was a child, when downcast servants would appear to hold stiff plastek shields over her and her mother as they walked the sandstone streets. It was in that moment Darya also realised that the servants had never stood beneath the shields themselves, exposed to the full power of the downpour. The shame washed any warmth from the memory.

The Chimera rocked on one side as it took a glancing blow from one of the t'au heavy weapons. It had only narrowly missed hitting the transport directly, and the sharp ring of solid stone joined the plasma fire peppering the hull.

'I thought your team had cleared the heavy-weapon

emplacements?' Munro shouted, still on his feet at the centre of the troop compartment.

Darya's grip tightened on her long-las as she bit back on a venomous response.

'That was this morning,' she retorted. 'They've had more than enough time to retake those positions since then.'

The transport rocked on its axles as it took a heavy blow on one side, the suspension shrieking as the Chimera's full weight was taken on a single track for a few heartbeats.

And then, as suddenly as it had begun, the gunfire stopped. The Cadians visibly relaxed, some letting out curses of frustration, others simply sighing with relief.

Thunder of Might slewed around a sharp corner and came to a bone-rattling halt, the engines ticking as they were restrained by the driver.

Munro stepped past his men and pressed the hatch-release rune. The rear hatch lowered jerkily on tired hydraulics, revealing that they had come to a stop well clear of the western bank of Trackway Span, under the harsh light of elevated stab-lumens.

'This is your stop,' Munro said, stepping aside to give Darya and Ullaeus room to pass. Ullaeus led the way, making a one-handed salute as he passed the lieutenant. Darya followed, shouldering the fail-safe charge pack and her long-las.

'I don't have to remind you of what the captain is risking by sending you both back here,' Munro said, half sneering the words as he looked down on Darya.

'You don't, sir.'

'Good. Don't let him down,' Munro said, then pressed the rune to close the rear hatch. Darya stepped nimbly off the stiff alloy plate as it rose beneath her, and set foot in the low city for the first time since setting out to take the bridge that morning.

'Bastard,' Ullaeus breathed as *Thunder of Might*'s engines let out a throaty roar. The transport chewed up the rockcrete as it sped away to the south, followed by an equally battered *Saint*.

'Just another trueborn,' Darya sighed, looping the straps of the fail-safe charge over her shoulders. 'Come on, we've got a lot of ground to cover.'

Eridan exhaled as the Chimera hurtled south, juddering across the rough ground of Miracil.

The troopers around him weren't making much conversation, and several appeared to be asleep in their seat restraints, heads lolling with the arhythmic jolting of the transport. Others were sharing lho-sticks, and Eridan caught the warm glint of a golden lighter being passed back and forth between the benches.

But it was Munro that Eridan was most interested in. He'd taken Sergeant Nevic's vacated seat, and glared absently at the closed hatch at the rear of the vehicle.

Eridan leaned forwards in his seat, declining an offered lho-stick, and caught the other lieutenant's attention.

'Lieutenant Eridan,' Munro said with a curt nod, his eyes focusing on the other man.

'A credit for your thoughts?' Eridan asked as the other man's gaze finally left the pocked and grimy metal of the rear hatch.

'I'm fine, lieutenant. It's just been a long few days is all,' Munro said, turning back to scowl at the plasteel.

'Are you worried about Sergeant Nevic and her man Ullaeus?' Eridan pressed.

'Worried?' Munro snorted, dragging his hands down his face as if he were waking from a long sleep. 'No, I'm not worried about Sergeant Nevic. She can look after herself.'

'I've heard,' Eridan said with a smile. 'She's made quite the name for herself in the battle group. I've heard that some have taken to calling her the Ghost of Cocleratum.'

'I've heard that too,' Munro said, non-committally. Eridan blinked, surprised at the other officer's indifference, and realised that several of the other troopers were watching the conversation with quiet interest.

'You're not a fan, I take it?' Eridan went on, leaning further forwards in his seat.

'She's one of our best soldiers, and I admire any man or woman who is willing to place themselves in harm's way in the name of the God-Emperor,' Munro said evenly, leaning back in his own seat and putting a little more distance between himself and Eridan.

'As is only right and proper,' Eridan replied. 'But Sergeant Nevic–'

'She's not a Cadian,' one of the troopers interrupted. His eyes were on his hands as he picked dirt from around his fingernails, a lit lho-stick dangling loose between two fingers.

'That's enough, Gosht,' Munro said sharply.

The man, Gosht, looked up at Eridan. He could see the violet tint to the man's eyes, even in the dim light cast by the red lumen bulb. Gosht held his gaze, and Eridan nodded for him to continue.

'She's one of them transplants,' Gosht said, his eyes flicking to Munro. His commanding officer was glaring at him openly, the muscles in his jaw rippling as he ground his teeth.

'Wouldn't be much of a regiment left without us transplants,' another trooper added from near the bulkhead.

'You know I'm not saying it like that,' Gosht said with a shake of his head. He took a drag from his lho-stick, the blue-grey smoke forking out from his nostrils a few moments later. He looked back to Eridan, his features defiant.

'You know how she got that name, sir? Ghost of Cocleratum?'

'She infiltrated a city on Cocleratum and assassinated a warlord and his squad of Heretic Astartes. Broke an entire city's worth of heretics on her own,' Eridan said carefully, watching as several of the troopers shook their heads and looked away. Only Gosht and Munro held his gaze.

'We were there, on Cocleratum,' Gosht said. 'At the Siege of Elborescum – that was the name of the city. Except that's not what happened.'

Gosht went to take a drag from his lho-stick, but it had gone out. He shrugged, and slipped the half-smoked stub behind one ear before continuing.

'She infiltrated the city all right. Only, she wasn't alone – she was the junior member of a team. Went in with Corporal Anders Mir, and First Sergeant Ilya. We knew him as Uncle. They were both Cadian born and bred.'

'Uncle was a good man,' one of the troopers cut in.

'A damn good man,' Gosht agreed. 'But they're both still dead, despite being the best snipers in the regiment. And they were my friends.'

'I'm sorry. I'm sure they both rest in the Emperor's grace,' Eridan said.

Gosht nodded, his expression solemn. 'I hope so. She still carries Anders' rifle. Think that's as good a tribute as any.'

'Still damned impressive,' another trooper said.

'Never said it wasn't. But it didn't go down like the stories say, that's all I'm saying,' Gosht said, leaning back in his chair.

'How did it happen then?' Eridan asked.

'She was taken along because she's from Cocleratum,' Munro said, his voice cutting across everyone else, an irresistible force pulling everyone's attention to him. 'She was the guide as much as an assassin. She managed to kill the enemy warlord, a witch by the name of Speccius, and his Heretic Astartes bodyguard – that much is true.'

Eridan resisted the urge to curse. To do either of those things alone would have been impressive, but to do both was nigh on unbelievable.

'You think she's exaggerated her legend?' Eridan asked, raising an eyebrow at the other lieutenant.

'Hardly,' Munro said.

'Who do you think told us the real story of what happened?' Gosht said.

'Sergeant Nevic is playing it down, then?'

'She doesn't talk about it,' Munro said. 'I doubt she'd have told you this much, other than to say the mission went wrong. She was the only survivor, after all.'

Eridan sat back in his seat, the metal hot against his back as the Chimera's engines ground onwards, a tense silence falling within the transport as Gosht accepted the golden lighter from another trooper and relit his lho-stick.

'What about the stories about her from Klodden? The Faustus spire? Are they true too?' Eridan said, looking between Gosht and Munro.

Gosht's wide smile was illuminated by the amber glow of his lho-stick, his features underlit by the falling embers.

'Two minutes to rendezvous!' the driver's voice barked suddenly, and the last of the sleeping troopers jerked awake with a snort.

'Stories for another time,' Munro said, before turning to his troopers. 'I hope story time didn't put you all to sleep, because harsh reality is waiting! Get ready to disembark, you slovenly dogs!'

Eridan unclasped his seat restraints and pulled himself to his feet with one of the ceiling handholds, the dressings on his legs twinging sharply as he moved closer to Munro.

'Sergeant Nevic has earned her legend, making her one of the best soldiers in the regiment if not this entire war theatre,'

Eridan said as softly as he could, so only Munro would hear his words. 'And yet you still foster some dislike for her. Why is that?'

Munro glared back at Eridan as the Chimera slowed to a heavy stop, his expression thunderous. He drew his laspistol and hammered the butt of the weapon against the opening rune.

The hydraulics squealed as the ramp lowered, letting in the sounds of nearby gunfire and shouted orders. Munro didn't speak, but simply stepped from the transport and barked orders at his men. The other troopers disembarked behind their officer, darting out in a running crouch with their lasguns at the ready, making for a nearby building alongside the troops from the other Chimera.

Then it was just Eridan and the trooper Gosht, who was drawing in the last dregs from his lho-stick. He flicked the glowing stub out of the transport and stopped in the doorway, just as Eridan was about to close the rear hatch. Eridan's orders were to take the Chimera all the way back to the landing grounds outside the city and report back to command.

'You know, I already said why Munro doesn't like the Ghost,' he said with a wolfish grin. Up close the man stank of stale lho-smoke and sour sweat, his breath almost as noxious as the waters of the Spatka.

'You did?' Eridan said. Gosht grabbed Eridan's hand and slapped something into it, before turning to leave.

'It's because she isn't Cadian,' Gosht said, ducking out of the Chimera towards where Lieutenant Munro knelt, shouting orders to his men.

Eridan pressed the hatch-close rune and stepped back into the depths of the vehicle, unhooking the vox handset from the front bulkhead. He held up what Gosht had given him in the light of the red lumen, and realised that it was the golden lighter that the squad had been passing back and forth.

It was small but weighty, a cuboid of simple milled brass worn to a golden shine by long use. On one face was a name engraved into the metal surface in a passing attempt at a flowing script: *Anders Mir*.

'*Permission to depart, sir?*' the driver's voice fizzed through the vox-grille.

'Yes, let's get going,' Eridan replied into the handset, hooking it back onto the bulkhead as the tracks squealed over rough rockcrete.

He ran a finger over the other words etched into the lighter casing, in the same halting hand that had carved the name on the reverse side. They were words he'd heard shouted a thousand times since the death of his home world, a battle-cry that united his regiment in their anger and grief.

Cadia stands.

7

Darya held out her hand, three fingers extended, then pointed out of the empty window beside her. Ullaeus nodded silently, taking up a position on the other side of the opening.

Darya and Ullaeus had left the safety of the Cadian 217th's defences around the western bank a couple of hours before, working their way south into the area where the Kintair Rifles should have been. But, instead of Imperial troops, they'd spent their time avoiding disparate groups of t'au fire-teams and human traitors.

They were on the second floor of a long warehouse building, its long-destroyed innards bared to the night sky above. The low city was filled with similar buildings, each providing ideal cover for two infiltrators trying to move unseen through hostile territory.

In the street below, two humans in the slate-grey armour and clothing of t'au auxiliaries were tending to a wounded comrade. He was making a lot of noise, crying out whenever they tried to move him or apply pressure to the wound.

Ullaeus moved slowly, inching an eye around the window frame to get a view of the street below, before moving back into the shadows. He raised a hand to his neck and drew a thumb over his throat, asking a silent question.

Eliminate?

Darya shook her head and pinched her ear.

Too loud.

Ullaeus nodded and relaxed his grip on his rifle. Darya knew what her friend was thinking, because she was thinking the same. There was an urge deep in her gut to kill the enemies of the Imperium, stronger still as these targets weren't xenos. They were *humans*, people who'd turned their back on their own kind. Years of training, Ecclesiarchy sermons, Imperial edicts and litanies of hate left little mercy in the minds of most Imperial soldiery.

But she had a job to do. Two human auxiliaries and a wounded third weren't worth being discovered for.

Darya ducked low beneath the window ledge and led Ullaeus away into the depths of the warehouse, careful to stay out of sight of the street below. Whilst they wouldn't be putting down the xenos-lovers, the wounded man's cry could attract attention, and she didn't want to be around when it arrived.

'This place was gutted long before we got here,' Ullaeus sub-vocalised into his throat-mic.

Darya grunted in agreement, using her rifle's scope to sweep the darkest shadows that clung to the warehouse's depths. She'd noticed the same as the Imperial advance had swept through the low city. All of the old working buildings had been gutted, emptied of any valuable contents and left derelict long before the fleet had arrived in orbit. Only the hab-blocks showed any signs of recent life, but the only citizenry they'd seen had been wearing t'au colours, bearing t'au weapons.

Darya took a knee as they reached a point where the second floor had collapsed, the reinforcing alloy lattice warped by an intense heat.

'Promethium,' Darya said softly, running her hand around the edge of the charred plascrete floor panel. It came away black with soot that gave off a pungent fume smell.

'They tried to burn it down,' Ullaeus observed.

'What was it they did in Miracil before the Rift?' Darya asked.

'Component manufacture and material refinement,' Ullaeus said. 'An industrialised feudal system under a planetary governor.'

'Seems the populace seized power by force. Come on, we have a lot of ground to cover.'

Darya slipped the backpack charge off her shoulders and passed it to Ullaeus, then took a tentative step onto the warped metal of the reinforcement lattice. It didn't give under her weight, nor did it creak or groan. Carefully, she reached down to grasp the last protruding spar then lowered herself out into the yawning space below.

The bottom floor was clear, except for a few empty half-slagged promethium barrels. She dropped the last few feet to the floor below in a crouch, sweeping the empty space with her long-las.

'Clear,' she breathed, and stood back to catch the fail-safe charge as Ullaeus lowered it over the edge.

But when Ullaeus crouched to lower himself down, a resounding crack shot through the warehouse.

Darya dropped to one knee, long-las already pressed to her shoulder as she looked for a muzzle flare. Nothing moved in the inky blackness of the warehouse's depths, her rifle's night-vision filter rendering the shapes of broken crates in grainy greys and greens.

More dust trailed down from above her, and she swore.

'Jump!' she hissed.

Ullaeus dived through the air as the flooring gave way beneath him, smashing into the ground floor with thunderous force. Darya threw herself backwards away from the falling plascrete and tangled reinforcement bars, landing heavily in a spray of stone chips and a rolling cloud of dust.

A boom echoed through the empty warehouse as a few smaller lumps of grey stone crumbled and fell, clattering against the fallen plascrete slab in fist-sized lumps.

Darya's heart hammered as she tried to breathe through the thick dust, coughing as she pushed herself to her feet and looked for Ullaeus.

'Iago?' she croaked, 'Iago, where are you?'

A shape pushed itself clear of a blanket of dust and debris, coughing and spluttering as it regained its feet.

'I can't see a damned thing,' he said between hacking coughs.

Darya stumbled forwards over debris hidden by the blinding dust and grabbed her corporal's arm.

'Move, just move,' she said, dragging him forwards. If the wounded man's cries hadn't attracted any attention, their narrow escape almost certainly would.

Ullaeus tried to rub the dust clear of his bloodshot eyes, tears staining the thick covering on his cheeks, but he didn't stop.

'I'm good,' he said as they cleared the edge of the debris field. He was covered from head to toe in thick grey powder, the urban pattern of his cameleoline cloak lost entirely. Darya knew that she would look almost exactly the same, an unwelcome spectre haunting the abandoned low city.

Distant shouts rang out behind them, their warnings echoing down through the warehouse to where Darya and Ullaeus choked out the last of the gritty powder. It left an unpleasant, rough feeling in her mouth, but there was no time to stop and wash it out.

A pair of double doors loomed out of the darkness ahead, both hanging crooked in their frame like loosened teeth. The raw-edged hole around the lock showed where they had been blasted in years before, the steel blackened by fire and age.

Darya and Ullaeus took up positions either side of the door, treading the steps of a well-rehearsed dance. Darya led, darting left through the door with her long-las held tight in a firing position, immediately followed by Ullaeus doing the same to the right.

'Clear,' he grunted.

'Contacts,' Darya replied in a hoarse voice. Tiny figures were approaching in the distance down the long street that ran the length of the warehouse, all in the urban-grey armour of the t'au.

The street divided the warehouse from a large industrial building opposite, which must have been ten times taller, its remaining chimney emblazoned with the double-headed eagle of the Imperium as it stretched into the open air above. A second chimney had collapsed into the building below, leaving a spur of fractured brickwork stabbing into the sky like a broken tooth.

'On me,' she whispered, mastering herself and darting across the street towards an empty doorway that led into the industrial building.

She stopped at the doorway to cover Ullaeus, both leaving wisps of dust in their wake as they ran. Ullaeus didn't pause, running straight past Darya into the building to clear the room beyond.

'Clear... I think,' Ullaeus said a few moments later, his voice crackling through Darya's vox-bead.

Darya slipped back into the building, her breath catching in her throat as she did.

The interior of the building was a massive open space, the edges of the ceiling lost against the polluted sky where the fallen chimney had crashed through it. The floor was dominated by sweeping assembly lines that disappeared beneath the leviathan of fallen brickwork in the centre of the space. Overseer platforms interspersed the tangle of conveyors and lifts, overlooked by black iron gantries suspended from what remained of the high roof, they in turn overlooked by higher levels of stairways and walkways that accessed goods lifts and snaking cooling ducts.

'God-Emperor,' Ullaeus swore, looking about in wonder.

'I've been in smaller cathedrals,' Darya said.

She moved over to the nearest conveyor belt. It was covered in a thick layer of dust and grime, the autogun barrels upon it pitted with spots of rust. The workstation was cramped by trays of parts, powered hand tools and an ancient drill press. It was only when she stood directly over the conveyor that she noticed the alcove beneath.

A thin grey blanket puddled in the cramped space beneath the conveyor, stained with sweat and other effluvia. It still stank, the tang of stale urine lingering on the edge of her senses as she realised what it was. An ancient chain was attached to a loop beneath the conveyor, the thick manacle at the other end dented and shattered.

'I think the workers lived here,' Darya said, pushing at the blanket with her boot.

'I've heard about the conditions on manufactorum worlds,' Ullaeus breathed, standing at the next station on the conveyor. It too had an alcove beneath it, complete with thin blanket and a small effigy made from twisted wire. He picked it up and showed it to Darya – it was the double-headed eagle of the Imperium.

'Come on, we can use the chimney as a high point,' Darya said. Despair hung heavy on the air like cloying perfume, even long after its occupants had left their stations behind.

Ullaeus placed the effigy down reverently on the conveyor,

then followed. Neither of them commented on the black pools of dried fluid that pockmarked the plascrete floor, nor the bundles of empty red robes at the feet of the overseer platforms.

Darya led the way to a dull metal stairway that led up to the higher levels of the manufactorum, far from the unsettling atmosphere of the factory floor. They moved carefully, measuring the weight of each step as they ascended through landings and staircases that shook on long high-tension cables.

They were almost halfway to the highest level when Darya saw a lone figure come through the same door they'd used to enter the building. She stopped at once, pulling her cameleoline cloak tight about her. Ullaeus did the same, though he was caught halfway up a staircase and couldn't bring his weapon to bear.

Darya held a finger to her lips, then held the finger up, then pointed back to the factory floor. Ullaeus nodded his understanding.

One target below.

Darya moved slowly, pulling her rifle in close and pressing her eye to the rubberised eyepiece cover.

The lone t'au figure was helmeted and carried a long, boxy rifle in its thick-fingered hands. Darya grimaced in revulsion as she took in its reverse-jointed legs, and the hooves that capped its bare feet.

Filthy xenos. The thought sprang into her mind, like the answer to a sum learned by rote in the schola.

It moved into the empty space of the manufactorum, looking over it with the single lens of its helmet. Nothing about the creature's posture betrayed any tension or fear as it approached the conveyor line nearest the door.

Then, to Darya's surprise, the t'au laid its rifle down on the belt and removed its helmet.

Through her scope Darya could clearly see its wide, dark eyes as it looked about the space, the olfactory cleft in the centre of its face flaring as it breathed in deeply. It winced then, its brow furrowing as it took in the space before it.

Darya watched the xenos as raw emotions crossed its face, displaying the same feelings that she and Ullaeus had experienced only a few minutes before. That sense of being somewhere that was layered with deep anguish, as if the sadness and grief saturated the building itself.

'Boss?' Ullaeus breathed from the stairway below, dragging Darya back into herself.

She suddenly felt angry, a knot of white-hot rage burning in the depth of her being. That xenos stood on an Imperial world, somewhere it had no right to be. The litanies of the commissars rang in her ears, as if she were back on the lander as it screamed into Attruso's atmosphere. She knew that it hated all humans and wanted nothing more than to tear down the Imperium. It was her duty to kill it, to reclaim the planet through war and tides of xenos blood. And yet she watched, her finger loose on the trigger guard.

Then the xenos picked up the effigy that Ullaeus had left on the conveyor belt, the twisted metal looking so fragile in its thick hands. It studied the handmade trinket, turning it in the dim light cast through the broken roof, with a gentleness that Darya didn't think possible.

Her heart thundered as the xenos looked around the room with an unreadable expression, its eyes lingering on the thick shadows that clung to the upper reaches of the manufactorum, even seeming to stare at where Darya and Ullaeus knelt for a few breathless seconds.

Then the t'au placed the effigy carefully back where it had found it and strode away, scooping up its helmet and rifle as it passed, disappearing out into the night without a backward look.

'Close one,' Ullaeus said softly, moving up the staircase to kneel next to Darya.

'Yes,' Darya agreed, a strange sense of dissonance taking hold.

'What was it doing?'

'It was odd... It picked up that effigy you found. It seemed unsettled by it.'

'These places give me the shivers too,' Ullaeus said. 'Kind of reminds you that people were here once.'

She forced herself to focus on the mission ahead by breaking down the impossible into reachable steps, refocusing her mind despite the growing fog of fatigue and confusion over what she had just seen.

Get to the roof.

Find the Kintair Rifles.

Get them to their objective.

Darya looked up at the great chasm in the manufactorum's roof, where the great mass of the falling chimney had split it in two. There was a route to the roof across the walkways and gantries; if they could get to the roof, they would have a better view of the surroundings. It was a long way up, but it would be worth it – they could search the sector for days and find no sign of the Kintair. A higher vantage point would be a huge advantage.

'I know you won't take a stimm, so how about I carry the bag for a bit?' Ullaeus said, holding out his hand for the fail-safe charge.

Darya shrugged out of the pack's straps and handed it to Ullaeus with a nod of thanks, and tried to ignore the worry lines on his face, visible even under the thick layer of dust that still clung to his features.

8

Thunder of Might ploughed deep furrows in the grime-soaked mire of the outer city, churning up clods of stinking grassy mud with its steel tracks as its engines spewed oily smoke into the Attruso night.

Inside, Eridan sat bent almost double on the bench seat with his elbows on his knees, swaying with the lurching movements of the transport. His battered and scraped skin had long since given up its stoic numbness and now burned in the fume-laden air of the Chimera. He still held the lighter in his hand, idly circling the smooth brass with his thumb.

'*Coming up on the perimeter, sir,*' the driver's voice burbled through the vox-grille.

Eridan reached up and took hold of one of the roof handles and pulled himself to his feet, unhooking the vox handset with his free hand.

'Signal them if you can. I need to get back to command as soon as possible,' Eridan ordered and waited for the response.

'*We're being waved through, sir,*' the driver said a few moments later.

Eridan stepped onto one of the benches to look out of the viewing slits cut into the side of the Chimera's thick hull, and watched as they passed through queues of waiting Chimeras and cargo-8s and into the defensive perimeter.

Reinforced ferrocrete dragon's teeth pockmarked the ground approaching the landing zone, each spur half the height of a man and capable of gutting any tank careless enough to try to drive over it. Beyond them were the great grey pillboxes prefabricated by the Adeptus Mechanicus, their broad firing slits brimming with the barrels of heavy weapons.

These defences should have been all but impenetrable, the might of the Imperium writ large as they had secured several square miles of terrain to land thousands of troops in the opening hours of the invasion of Attruso.

But the t'au had shown that the Imperium's infallible might was an illusion – General Matliss' death had been proof of that. He took a seat and brooded on that thought until the transport rolled to a halt a short while later.

The 217th's command hub was deep in the heart of the Cadian landing zone, consisting of several Chimera command vehicles arranged so they were back to back, their rear hatches lowered to create a solid floor that officers could use to pass between them without stepping into the mud.

Major Wester was standing over a vox-station in the centre transport, one hand clutching a wired vox handset whilst the other held a headset to his ear. He only had the one – half the major's head was a patchwork of scarred grafts and waxy skin, the spoils of a campaign against the tyranids in his youth.

'I understand, Lord Sylvester,' Wester grated into the vox, 'but events have moved faster than we could–'

Wester winced as a wrathful sound blared from his headset. He wrenched it from his ear, visibly angry as he took a moment to master himself.

'Lord Sylvester, I suggest you take it up with Colonel Wassenby at your earliest convenience, but I surmise that you are currently otherwise engaged. Wester out.' Wester spoke with a cold efficiency, throwing down the headset and passing the handset to the vox-operator.

'Major Wester,' Eridan said, saluting. Wester returned the gesture, but his expression remained sour.

'We finally get a working vox to the front, and the first thing Lord Sylvester does is to ask why he hasn't been placed in command of the entire Miracil theatre,' Wester said, spitting the words as he stepped out of the Chimera. 'Tell me you have better news, lieutenant.'

'I do, sir,' Eridan said.

'Good.' Wester looked Eridan up and down. 'You look like refried shit, Markas. Let's get a drink.'

Eridan followed Wester into another of the Chimeras and accepted the stamped tin mug that Wester offered. The major took out a battered metal flask and poured a measure into the mug, before taking a deep swig of it himself. The amasec was cheap but strong, just what Eridan needed after the last few hours.

He reported everything that he had seen on his ride through the front, and what he had discussed with Captain Kohl on the eastern bank of Trackway Span. Wester remained silent throughout, nodding at the salient points as Eridan spoke.

'Good work. I knew I could rely on you, Markas,' Wester said. 'But we can't reinforce them without the colonel's say-so, and he won't commit any forces to the river without direct vox contact. What of the Kintair? Do we have any confirmation on their position?'

'None yet, but Kohl has sent some of his pathfinders back to find them and pull them into position,' Eridan said, downing the last of his amasec. It burned its way down his throat, warming his stomach as it settled. 'A pair of snipers. Sergeant Nevic and a Corporal Ullaeus.'

Wester nodded. 'A good call. Makes more sense to send a smaller team, they'll move faster and create less noise. Plus, Nevic is a smart operator.'

'So I hear,' Eridan said. The brass lighter in his pocket weighed heavily on his mind for a moment. He considered Sergeant Nevic's objectives – she had a rough road ahead of her, and he didn't envy her that.

'All we can do now is wait and pray that they get the Kintair into position quickly. We're going to need Trackway Span for the next stage of the offensive, and God-Emperor knows it's the only part of this operation that's gone to plan so far.' Wester's eyes roved around the command post as he spoke, scanning for commissars or prying ears.

Eridan nodded his agreement, and looked around the command post for any sign of their new commanding officer.

'Major... Where is the colonel?' Eridan asked as he realised that Wassenby was nowhere to be seen.

'Up there.' Wester pointed at the night sky.

'He's returned to the fleet?' Eridan said incredulously. 'Why?'

'Safer for the commanding officer to be out of the line of fire,' Wester said, as if repeating a message he himself couldn't believe. 'He's going to coordinate from the cruiser *Foehammer*.'

Eridan looked about and knew that was impossible. There were no secure or stable vox-links to any of the ships in orbit, and even if there were, Wassenby wouldn't be able to coordinate the entire Miracil front from there.

'Major Wester!' shouted a vox-operator from a Chimera opposite. 'We've got a link to Seventh Company!'

Wester nodded acknowledgement, his shoulders relaxing as if a measure of tension was leaving his body as he let out a long, slow breath. He placed a hand on the wall of the Chimera, as though steadying himself.

He was caught, Eridan realised, between an absent commanding officer demanding results and an offensive that had spiralled out of control.

'It could be worse, sir. Lord Sylvester could be in charge.'

'I'd take a battle-hungry bumpkin over an over-promoted baggage-brat. Hells, I'd even take a transplant at this point,' Wester said with a shake of his head. It was a rare break in protocol from the old veteran, but it finally gave voice to what the rest of the command squad had been muttering privately since Wassenby had taken command.

'Get yourself seen to by a medicae and get a hot meal,' Wester said, a flicker of that steadfast resolve returning as he seemed to master himself. 'I'm going to need you at full strength. This is going to be a long one.'

Darya's hands searched for a solid hold on the manufactorum's slime-encrusted roof, the countless years of polluted rain having coated the smooth metal with acid-resistant mosses and stagnant rainwater.

'Anything?' Ullaeus said.

She was standing on his shoulders, reaching up for a handhold to drag herself onto the roof, whilst he braced his feet on the highest guardrails of the walkway.

'I think…' Darya said, squeezing her eyes shut as she searched. 'I think… Yes!'

Her fingers pushed through a patch of corrosion beneath a moss bloom, creating a handhold just big enough for her fingers to grasp. She used it to pull herself up, her muscles straining as she pushed off Ullaeus and swung one foot onto the roof. She could then use the leverage to pull the rest of her body up, a technique she'd long perfected in her years as a sniper searching for the best ambush positions and shooting nests.

She didn't stand once she was on the roof, but instead rolled over and extended a hand down to Ullaeus. He jumped up and grabbed her hand, but then used brute strength to pull himself up rather than the efficient technique that Darya preferred.

They'd already checked that the roof was clear of xenos before attempting the climb, using a small mirror tacked to the end of a long-las barrel. It was an ancient trick, but one that still worked, allowing the snipers to check for enemies before placing themselves in harm's way.

For the first time since they'd left the landing fields, Darya felt as if she were standing beneath the open sky. She wasn't hemmed in, deep in the red-brick and rockcrete canyons of the city streets.

'Throne, this is high,' Ullaeus whispered, leaning over the hole in the roof to look down into the manufactorum below.

'We should be able to get an idea of where the Kintair are from up here,' Darya said, looking for a reference point to triangulate their position. The high buttresses of Trackway Span were just visible over the rooftops behind her, occasionally backlit by the heavy-weapons fire whose thunder reached her position a few moments after each flash.

'Trackway Span is slightly north-east of us, which means we're definitely heading west.'

The low city stretched out in front of her, a carpet of ruins and soon-to-be ruins that undulated softly beneath the blunt foundations of human industry. Everything was drawn in shades of black and orange, the light of distant battles creating silhouettes of jagged walls and the detritus of war.

'It's a big sector to search,' Ullaeus said, sighting through his rifle's scope as he scanned the vista before them.

'Look for any sign of fighting,' Darya said, mirroring his action and flicking off the night-vision filter on her own scope. 'Or the lack of fighting, I suppose.'

Tense minutes rolled past as they searched, their low breaths the only sound from the immediate vicinity. The Imperial artillery had stopped several hours before; it made sense to Darya. Artillery was only useful when it was accurate, and when the front line was as snarled up as Captain Kohl had said it was, the big guns were as much danger to Imperial forces as the enemy. It made little difference to Darya's mission, but the comparative quiet was welcome.

'I see a force barricade, due west,' Darya said finally, spotting the cool corona of constant light behind a distant chimney. If nothing else, it was a marker for where the Kintair had yet to reach.

'I see it,' Ullaeus murmured, sighting his own rifle on the barricade's location. 'And next to it, maybe two hundred yards north – another one.'

Darya tracked her sight right, the hair-thin crosshairs of her weapon gliding over fallen habs and bare roofing struts until they settled on a halo of cool light that illuminated a flash of white alloy.

Another xenos barricade.

'I'd put money on the Kintair being the other side of that barricade,' Darya said, lowering her rifle. 'It looks like a fairly consistent line of defences running north to south – could be that the Kintair just haven't been able to breach it.'

'Or they've not even reached it yet.'

'Either way, that's our next search area,' Darya said. She stood carefully on the slick roof and made her way back to the sundered chasm that had split the metal surface almost in two.

She lowered herself back down onto the suspended gantry,

dropping the last few feet to land softly on the welded spars of the footplate. A noise like a moaning grox filled the manufactorum and she froze; the sound echoed back, the groaning of corroded metal slapping back from the hard surfaces within the cavernous room.

'Ullaeus,' she hissed. 'Don't–'

But it was too late. Ullaeus dropped down from the roof to the gantry in one continuous motion, his feet rattling the gantry as his weight slammed into the metal. His eyes widened as he saw Darya's face and outstretched arms balancing herself, and he understood.

'Throne.'

With a resounding crunch, the two snipers were hurled sideways as the suspension cables popped free of their roof mountings along one side, pitching the gantry forty-five degrees downward along half its length.

Darya did not scream. She turned, sliding down the gantry, and jumped, hands reached out. She caught one of the remaining suspension cables and swung, her momentum carrying her on a long parabola that scratched her hands bloody on the rusting cables, until she was left dangling over the inky blackness below.

Ullaeus was less fortunate.

He clung to the lower guardrail as the motion of the gantry slowly subsided and, for a heart-stopping moment, Darya was sure that he had fallen. But he had managed to wrap his wiry forearms around the welded tubing of the guardrail in a rictus grip.

'Good?' Darya asked as she came to a stop.

'Good,' Ullaeus replied, but his heavy breathing was clearly audible through Darya's vox-bead. She twisted to look about.

It was only a short section of the gantry that had collapsed;

the walkway a few yards behind her was still intact, its suspension points being much further from the corroded edge of the broken roof.

'I'm going to try and get to the stable part,' Darya said. 'Less weight on it might make us less likely to fall again.'

'You trying to say I'm fat?' Ullaeus said between deep, calming breaths.

'It is the second time you've broken what you were standing on tonight,' Darya said, carefully edging forwards and transferring her weight to the next supporting cable. The gantry groaned again, but still held.

It took long seconds for her to reach the stable section of the gantry, and she pulled herself onto the metal floor plating with a silent prayer of thanks to the God-Emperor. She pulled off her rifle, cloak and satchel, and retrieved a length of rope from the latter.

'I'm going to throw you a line – at least if it gives I can pull you to safety,' Darya said, unspooling the tightly wrapped cord.

'Sure I'm not too heavy for that?' Ullaeus said. She could almost hear his smile in his voice.

'I'll put you on half-rations later,' Darya said, feeding out some of the slack into a long loop. She swung the loose length, building up momentum, and flung it towards Ullaeus.

The rope clattered against the gantry with a dull clang and slithered within a couple of feet of Ullaeus. It took him a moment to loosen his grip on the railings, fighting the primal urge to hold on as tightly as possible.

'Do you have it?' Darya asked as he reached for the rope.

'Got it,' he said finally, and Darya felt the slack pull taut as he tied the rope about his waist. 'I'm going to try your route – along the suspension cables.'

'Go carefully,' Darya said, wrapping her end of the rope around one of the suspension cables as an improvised belay. 'Once you get close enough, throw me the fail-safe and your gear.'

Ullaeus pushed himself up slowly, his eyes fixed on the long drop to the manufactorum floor hundreds of feet below.

'Eyes up, Iago,' Darya urged.

He pushed himself up to his hands, then inched his way to lean against the deck plate. The gantry swayed softly as he reached up for the opposite guardrail, which turned into a groaning lurch as he pulled his weight up from the lower edge.

Darya could hear him swearing under his breath as he moved, a constant stream of curses in Low Gothic, High Gothic and a swathe of other dialects that she wasn't familiar with. He didn't stop to throw her his gear, but pulled himself to safety hand over hand, until he finally came to rest on the deck plate next to Darya.

'Stupid mistake,' he cursed, rubbing his hands over his face. 'I shouldn't have jumped down. That was damned stupid.'

'You're tired. That's what happens when we're stretched so thin we can't grab an hour's rest,' Darya said, untying the loop from around Ullaeus' waist and reeling the rope into a tight bundle once more.

'You're tired. You didn't jump,' Ullaeus said.

'How does that saying go? Any one you walk away from?' Darya said. She pulled her gear back on quickly, checking the bindings on her rifle stock before clipping the strap back on over one shoulder.

'That's about crash landings, not falling gantries.' Ullaeus smiled, pushing himself to his feet.

'Same difference,' Darya said. 'Come on, the sooner we're out of this place the better.'

9

The sniper's art was known by a number of names within the battle group, and a thousand more in the unnumbered myriad regiments of the Astra Militarum.

Pathfinding. Overwatch. Stealth work.

In the 217th, it was fieldcraft.

The term covered everything that allowed snipers to move unseen through enemy positions, gathering information and creating ambush opportunities. The best could go as far as to strike at the enemy's command structure, killing commanders and generals in order to sow chaos and discord in the enemy ranks.

Not all regiments fielded snipers in teams like Darya's – most sharpshooters were embedded in line units to provide sniper support, but Captain Kohl saw the advantage a skilled team could be to the Cadian 217th.

As Darya and Ullaeus moved west towards the rear of the t'au positions, their skills were tested to their very limit.

They moved like spectres through the xenos' prepared positions, stretching back hundreds of yards from the forward barricades the Cadian snipers had spotted from the rooftops. The t'au patrolled the gridded streets with drone flights, swooping Devilfish transports and squads of fire warriors, their hard horned feet clattering off the stone streets. Almost every route was covered by organic or inorganic eyes.

Almost every route.

Darya and Ullaeus had a few advantages as they worked through the rear of the enemy lines. The first was their cloaks, treasured garments that were rare amongst the under-equipped Cadian regiments after the fall of their home world. They were woven through with cameleoline fibres that helped to veil the wearer from anything but the most attentive eyes, taking on the colours and tones of their surroundings and masking them from view.

The other main advantage was that the t'au would expect a full assault from the Imperial forces that had bludgeoned their way through the city, not a pair of trained infiltrators. The few fire warriors who watched the northern and eastern approaches were easily dealt with by knife and garrotte, the snipers' long-range rifles relegated to reserve weapons only to be used in the event they were discovered.

Darya and Ullaeus stopped using verbal communication in close proximity to the xenos. Instead of vox-beads, they employed hand signals and body language to communicate, something that was second nature to Darya's squad after so many years fighting at each other's sides.

When they came within sight of the glowing barricades, the heavy enemy presence made moving via the streets all but impossible. Drones hovered at roof level, their underslung weapons pointing away towards the west and the last known position of the Kintair Rifles. A Devilfish transport drifted overhead, its spotlights stabbing down through the gloom to scour the dark corners and shadowed nooks as fire warriors patrolled below.

Darya and Ullaeus knelt in the arched doorway of a ruined building, watching the armoured t'au warriors for a gap in their lines, for something that would catch the enemy's attention long enough for them to slip by. An artillery barrage or air strike would be perfect cover, and would allow her and Ullaeus to cross the terrain at far greater speed.

Ullaeus pointed over the street to the open doorway of the Administratum building opposite, its door hanging from the frame by a single hinge. The void-black scorch marks above each window lintel and the shattered glass on the street told of the long-dead inferno that had claimed the building, but the carved stone above the door still read *Honest Labour is its Own Reward*.

Darya nodded at Ullaeus' suggestion. She pointed for him to go first, bringing up her rifle to cover him as he broke cover and bracing it against the carved stonework of the doorway.

In the grainy green light of the scope, she could see even more t'au on the street than she had initially thought. There must have been twenty between her and the barricade, which itself supported a massive energy weapon above a white alloy rotunda. The name came to her from the rushed briefings aboard the drop-ship – a Tidewall gunrig. From the reports, that energy weapon was capable of catastrophic destruction, which she had no desire to see first-hand. They had to be cautious.

Once Ullaeus had made the other side, Darya pointed to herself and then the doorway beneath *Honest Labour*, and waited for Ullaeus to nod his understanding. She would cross to scout the building first whilst he provided cover, then he was to follow when she sounded the all clear.

She held up three fingers, then two, then one, and darted out of cover as a patrolling t'au fire warrior turned away towards the west. She ran doubled over, silent but for the whisper of her cloak as it trailed over the cobbled street, and stepped into the building.

The interior within the fire-blackened structure was still, with a lingering taste of burned plastek on the air. Charred desks dominated the room, the once neat lines ruined by the flames that had ripped through the building a long time before.

But Darya's attention was drawn to a window on the wall opposite, and the lone figure who looked out of it onto the square beyond. She dropped low and drew her *kvis*, the short, curved dagger she carried in a sheath on her shoulder. Once she was certain they were the only two people in the room, she inched forwards through the desks and remains of chairs that had been melted almost beyond recognition.

It was a true t'au, this one: armoured and helmeted, short and broad in stature, its thick arms holding tight to the boxy rifle in its grasp. Darya inched closer and closer, each footstep carefully placed in the ash that carpeted the plascrete floor.

Then the xenos was finally within reach, and it was time to strike.

She stepped in close, wrapped her free hand beneath the t'au's chin and dragged it up, baring its neck for the kvis to strike – but the helmet came loose in her grip. Instead of slicing the xenos' throat, her knife slashed a deep gouge into its cheek as the helmet came away in her hand.

It turned with a snarl of pain, brandishing its weapon in an attempt to push the Cadian away. Darya couldn't allow it to cry out, not so close to so many of its own kind. On pure reflex, she smashed the helmet into the side of the t'au's skull with enough force to knock it off balance, but lost her grip on the helmet in the process.

It gasped in pain and dropped its weapon, which was all

the opening Darya needed; she tackled the t'au to the floor in a clatter of armour on plascrete and rammed her kvis into its exposed throat whilst her free hand clamped its mouth shut.

It tried to scream then, as blood spurted out over Darya's hands, punching ineffectually at her arms but failing to loosen her grip. She worked the knife through gristle and bone, her stomach clenching with each fresh sensation felt through the knife, but it was working. The blows grew weaker and weaker as the pool of blood inched over the ashen floor, until its eyes finally unfocused and the body went still.

'Filthy xenos,' Darya swore and pushed herself off the dead fire warrior. She clicked her vox twice to indicate the all clear, then wiped the blood from her hands and knife on the t'au's fatigues.

Ullaeus appeared in the doorway almost a minute later, by which time Darya had dragged the body into a shadowy corner and taken up a position overlooking the square on the other side of the building.

'All good?' he subvocalised.

'Messy.' Darya inclined her head to the pool of cooling blood. Two parallel trails led from it to the feet of the dead fire warrior, and Ullaeus nodded his acknowledgement before taking up a position next to her at the window.

The square beyond had once served as a storage yard for the buildings that enclosed it, with a single access road visible on the western edge. In it stood nine t'au Devilfish troop transports set out in neat rows, the smooth contours of their forward armour indescribably alien against the backdrop of the blocky, square Imperial buildings. The vehicles were at rest, their anti-gravitic fields idle as stubby alloy feet extended from below to hold them clear of the muddy ground. Their rear hatches were open and waiting for the God-Emperor alone knew what, watched over by several fire warriors, who scanned their surroundings diligently.

It was clear that the t'au in the vicinity had more than enough transport to get themselves clear of the low city and across the Spatka, but Darya could only think of one reason that they'd be holding position here whilst Imperial forces cut deeper into Miracil around them.

'Extraction team,' she subvocalised as they ducked back down. 'The t'au are waiting to extract something – or someone.'

If her mission to find the Kintair weren't so important, Darya would have found a good position with clear lines of sight to take out the high-value asset that these t'au were preparing to extract. But those weren't her orders.

She could only hope that the Kintair were alive, and that she could use them to take out the asset in a less clandestine assault.

The ceiling in one corner of the room had given way, providing an access point to the floor above. Darya pointed up at it and Ullaeus nodded, crouching down and cupping his hands to give her a boost. Using this to reach the upper floor, she quickly scouted the room beyond before heading back to the hole in the floor. She took the fail-safe charge off Ullaeus first, stashing it in the room behind her before leaning down to grab Ullaeus' wrist.

Darya crept towards a window that overlooked the main street they had left earlier. Several t'au had moved down it in a patrol pattern, accompanied by a pair of gun-wielding drones. The lenses of the t'au's helmets glimmered red in the dim light as they continued on their patrol, leaving a sizeable stretch of the street clear of any xenos.

It was the perfect time to move.

She led Ullaeus through the dark rooms of the burned-out Administratum block, keeping to the shadowed corners where the floors would be strongest and therefore least likely to creak or give way. They passed through the long clerical rooms that appeared to run the entire length of the square's northern edge, until Darya and Ullaeus were directly overlooking the glowing barricades at the end of the street. The corner wall was gone, broken down into a slope of debris and broken bricks that covered a short section of the t'au barricade. On the far side of the breached wall stood a tall heavy-weapon emplacement that commanded a fearsome view of the vista beyond.

'I can see why the Kintair haven't reached their position,' Darya whispered.

The city beyond the barricade was utterly sundered for half a mile to the west, as if an unseen giant had swept their hand through the myriad structures and knocked them flat to the polluted earth. Nothing had escaped the punishment rained down upon the ruptured earth, the deep craters left by artillery and the chasms of muddy earth created by orbital lance strikes the only cover left between the t'au barricades and the distant silhouetted buildings. Subterranean water pipes, cracked and uncovered by the bombardment, sprayed their contents high into the air at several points.

A trio of Leman Russ chassis burned in the middle distance, still in their attack formation, flames licking from their empty turret rings. Heavy-bolter rounds burned off in dramatic intervals, sending sprays of sparks from the warped sponsons. The legs of a Sentinel stood atop a shadowed slope to the right of the burning tanks, the cab and body section missing but for sharp spurs of armour plating that had been little defence against the t'au's combined firepower. Darya didn't need her night-vision scope to know there were hundreds of bodies hidden in the dark on that field. She could smell them on the air, the cloying sourness of early decomposition beneath the stink of burned flesh.

It was a stark reminder of what the t'au could do to a force that fought on their terms, facing them head-on in an attritional battle. Their barricades, prepared positions and heavy-weapon emplacements were an anvil, and the Imperial hammer had been found wanting in this sector.

'The Kintair?' Ullaeus asked.

'I don't know. Maybe,' Darya replied and lifted her scope. 'No regimental markings that I can see. The light's too low and there's not much left… But no sign of a vox-transmitter either.'

She turned the scope to the far end of the killing field, to the low ruins of buildings that had escaped intact, at least in part. The dial clicked softly beneath her fingers as she increased the zoom through to its highest setting and scanned the distant landscape in enough detail to make out individual soldiers looking back, hunkered down in the thin cover offered by the broken masonry.

'Imperial forces, far side,' Darya whispered, resetting her scope and pulling away from the doorframe.

'I see them,' Ullaeus confirmed, his own scope pressed to his eye.

'I can't see a path through though,' Darya said, looking for a gap in the enemy line that they could exploit. Now they were up close, it was clear that no such gap existed. The t'au had created a near-impenetrable wall on one edge of the killing field, with multiple positions providing overlapping arcs of fire that would catch them in moments if they were seen. Yet another Devilfish appeared from their right, trailing a flight of drones in its wake, minnows following behind an ocean predator that scoured the empty field for prey.

'Where there's water coming in, there's a pipe to take it back out again,' Ullaeus said, pointing towards the jets of pressurised water fountaining up on the battlefield.

'Sewer access,' Darya said. Sewers were a good way for small teams to travel through cities unseen, but carried their own set of risks. Cave-ins and blockages weren't uncommon, and there was little chance of finding an exit exactly where you wanted to be, but Darya couldn't see a better option to cross the battlefield unseen – not without a lengthy detour in any case.

Sure enough, a plate stood at the base of the enemy barricade, its corroded surface a sickly orange beneath the pristine white alloy of the t'au fortifications. It wasn't one they could use, but showed that there were accessible sewers in the area. Darya could only hope that they extended beneath the killing field and hadn't been utterly destroyed by the bombardment.

'I've got one here,' Ullaeus said.

They had ended up on the upper floor of a small manufactorum, overlooking the square where the enemy transports waited under guard.

Darya approached and looked down to where Ullaeus was pointing. A rusting metal disc was set into the cobbled stones of the corner of the square, half hidden between two thick buttresses and a layer of collected debris.

Angry shouts echoed from the Administratum building, followed by a burst of activity from the troops in the square below. A screeching, teeth-rattling alarm resounded from the sky, which Darya realised must have been coming from the drones circling above.

'They've found the body,' Ullaeus cursed, looping the strap of his long-las over his head.

'Get it open, I'll cover us. Go!' Darya barked.

Ullaeus slipped out of the window and dropped to the floor a storey below in a graceful squat, turning his back to the square as he set about trying to silently move the debris and rubble off the sewer access cover.

Darya crouched in the window, her heart hammering as she

watched over the square for any movement towards Ullaeus. A lone fire warrior darted from between the waiting Devilfish transports, but didn't spot Ullaeus in the dark corner.

A scrape of metal on plascrete told her that Ullaeus had managed to move the plate. She looked down just in time to see him dropping into the circular void, his cloak flowing behind him as he jumped down to check the way was clear.

'*Clear,*' he voxed a few moments later.

Darya mounted the window ledge and lowered herself out of the window. She dropped the last six feet to the ground in a low crouch and surveyed the square.

The Devilfish transports were even more intimidating from the ground. She could see their rotary burst cannons jutting from beneath their forward armour, and a pair of gun-wielding drones either side of that.

God-Emperor help anyone who finds themselves on the wrong side of those, she thought.

There wasn't time to linger; the longer she was visible the greater the risk of discovery, and they would have enough difficulty navigating the sewers without a small army of t'au chasing them down. She slipped into the sewer access, dragged the cover plate back into place over her head, and began her descent into the darkness.

10

'God-Emperor above, this is foul.'

Darya had to agree.

They were twenty feet below street level, in a smooth-walled tunnel caked in hundreds of years of flaking refuse from the city above, just high enough that Ullaeus could walk without scraping his head against the roof.

Tide marks lined the grime on the sloping walls, showing how high the scummy waters could rise when they were in use. The stream of sewage at the bottom of the tunnel was only a couple of inches deep as Darya and Ullaeus sloshed through, moving quickly away from the square.

Where above ground there had been at least a little light given off by guttering fires and the bruised haze of the Great Rift, the sewer tunnels were blacker than the void itself. They were forced to use the night-vision filters of their rifle scopes to traverse the cramped, stinking space.

Ullaeus led the way, his confident, broad steps eating up the yards as Darya followed behind with the fail-safe charge weighing her down. She kept each breath of the foul air as shallow as she could, fighting the urge to retch each time she inhaled.

Ullaeus stopped to vomit as they reached a three-way junction. Darya waited as he spat bile into the stream of sewage at his feet, trying to focus on gauging their location. Without points of reference, it would be easy to drift off course.

'It's fragging grim,' Ullaeus grunted, spitting the taste out of his mouth. Darya passed him her water canteen and he washed the taste from his mouth with a nod of thanks.

'I'll take point,' Darya said, taking back her canteen and stowing it on her belt.

She squeezed past him and took the left tunnel, which by her reckoning would take them directly beneath the killing ground beyond the t'au barricade, and set off again into the stinking dark.

They continued at pace until a muted rumble grew to a shuddering roar in the confines of the tunnel. The stream of sewer water leaped up in fingers of filthy liquid, whilst chunks of rotting effluvia slipped down the walls in trails of foul sludge.

'Throne,' Darya hissed as she lost her footing and slammed heavily against the slimy wall, off-balanced by the heavy fail-safe charge on her back.

'You good, boss?' Ullaeus' voice echoed in the dark as the aftershocks died away.

'All good. You?' Darya said.

'I'd be happier back above ground rather than down here with the rats,' Ullaeus replied.

Darya smiled, but something about what he'd said nagged at her as she started forwards again. As she scanned the tunnel ahead, she realised what it was that was bothering her.

'There aren't any rats,' she said.

'There must be.'

'I've not seen any, have you?'

'Rats live anywhere,' Ullaeus said. She could tell by his voice that he had turned back to check the tunnels behind. 'How dead does a planet have to be for the rats to abandon it?'

'Maybe they can't survive Attruso's winters. They're meant to be damned cold.'

Darya's scope alighted on a sliver of light, burning shockingly bright in the grey-green of the scope's filter. Without her scope it was a barely visible streak of grey against the boundless dark.

'Light up ahead,' she said.

She tensed as she approached the shard of light, her breathing shallow and her finger resting on the trigger guard in anticipation.

It was the leading edge of a long, sweeping curve in the tunnel which ended in a sudden opening. The dim light of the sky bled down into the tunnel, illuminating the edges of hanging sewage tendrils that dangled from the sundered ceiling.

The opening led out into a deep crater, the bottom filled by dripping raw sewage from the broken tunnel and the fractured edges of a water pipe that jutted from high up on the crater's walls. Wafts of cold, crisp air barely reached the crater floor, but they were a welcome change from the foetid atmosphere they emerged from.

'Scope high,' Darya ordered. She stepped out of the tunnel onto the loose ground of the sloping pit, scanning the rim of the crater as Ullaeus followed her and did the same.

'Clear to the rear.'

'Front clear.'

Darya took the lead up the loose soil of the crater walls as Ullaeus covered her with his long-las. Falling soil had banked up at the very top to create a raised lip around the crater's mouth;

Darya slowly edged her eyes over the rim to check they wouldn't be seen before waving for Ullaeus to follow.

They were at least a quarter of a mile from the t'au barricades, which gave off a haze of bluish light that reflected off the thick clouds above. The emplaced railguns loomed high over the surrounding buildings, grim sentinels of unbelievable power that watched over the battleground before them. Thankfully, they were still at that moment.

'I don't envy the Kintair on that attack,' Ullaeus said.

'Only a fool would attack that head-on,' Darya replied. 'No splash damage behind the t'au barricade means they had no artillery or orbital support. The xenos were ready for them.'

Ullaeus swore under his breath.

'The attack in this sector has been a complete mess,' Darya said, pulling back from the crater's edge. Bodies were visible across the battlefield, even in the dim light cast by the t'au barricades. A carpet of the dead lay face down in the shell-churned mud or looking out over their fallen comrades with unseeing eyes, the tell-tale sign of at least one failed frontal assault.

'Let's hope that there are enough Kintair still standing to take that barricade.'

Darya nodded her agreement. First Company's slog through the low city to Trackway Span was still fresh in her tired mind, and even though she and her team had been ahead of the main push for the most part, she knew from the other sergeants that the advance had been hard going. Pulling back and giving up the gains at Trackway Span was nigh on unthinkable – the stealth assault she and her team had carried out might have worked once, but the second assault would undoubtedly cost hundreds more lives.

Those lives weighed the heaviest on her mind.

'Let's find out,' Darya said, pushing herself away from the

eastern lip of the crater. She half crawled, half scrambled her way around the crater's lip to the western edge, before rolling over the banked dirt to the muddy ground of the killing field.

Together, she and Ullaeus dragged themselves across the dirt until they were hidden from any t'au eyes behind a Leman Russ that was lying on its side, the charred bodies of the unlucky crew dangling limply from the open hatches.

The dead were cast in sharp relief as the patrolling Devilfish passed overhead, its spotlight lancing down as it swept the earth below for targets. Darya and Ullaeus crouched low, huddling beneath their cloaks and trusting to the light-bending fibres woven through the cloth to keep them hidden from view.

If the t'au transport spotted them it made no sign, its engines thrumming as it continued on its patrol route, its school of drones following in its wake.

From there they ran, bent double, until they came into shouting distance of the buildings on the western edge of the field.

Darya and Ullaeus dropped into a shallow crater and sighed with relief. Safety, and other Imperial soldiers, lay within a short sprint. After so long sneaking through enemy-held territory, the knot of tension at Darya's core felt almost unbearable as she realised it was there, held at bay for so long by experience and an iron will.

'Psst!' Darya hissed loudly. 'Kintair!'

A whistle blast sounded, followed by a sudden flare of blinding light as multiple high lumens burst into life. Las-beams rent the air, buzzing over Darya's head as she dived back down behind the scant cover of the crater's shallow edge.

'What the frag are they doing?' Ullaeus shouted over the roaring gunfire. 'Hold your fire, damn you!'

Dirt sprayed the snipers as they huddled down further into

the crater, mud bursting into the air as a withering volley of lasgun fire peppered the ground either side of them and behind.

Darya scrambled desperately for her short-range vox-bead, pressing it hard into her ear with a squeal of feedback.

'Kintair! Cease fire, Kintair, we're friendly!' she said quickly, but the gunfire continued. 'Throne's sake, Kintair, *we are friendlies!*'

The whistle blast sounded again followed by more shouts to cease firing. Darya and Ullaeus kept their heads down as the last lumps of las-beam-cooked dirt clattered back to earth, both breathing heavily.

'*Okay, friendlies. Stand up, nice and slow,*' a heavily accented voice crackled back over the vox.

Darya clipped the vox-handset strap to her neck so she had her hands free, and made to push herself to her feet.

'These bastards better not shoot me,' Ullaeus growled. 'I'm not going out to friendly fire.'

'We're getting up,' Darya said into the vox, extending her arm so her rifle was held over her head. Ullaeus did the same a moment later, and they broke cover together to come face to face with a forest of primed lasgun barrels.

'*Move forwards slowly, friendlies,*' the voice said.

Darya obeyed and motioned for Ullaeus to follow, which he did with a string of muttered curses.

The walls ahead were lined with silhouetted soldiers wearing the standard Cadian-pattern tripoint helmets and flak armour. Darya couldn't help but feel a sharp sense of tension as she stepped forwards into clear view of so many weapons.

'*Doorway, a few yards to your right,*' the voice said. Darya could see it despite the near-blinding light of the lumen lamps high above, and made for it at the same slow, careful pace. One of the figures high above put up its weapon and disappeared from view whilst the rest kept their weapons trained on the two Cadians.

Darya stepped through the doorway first and was met by two nervous-looking troopers in unfamiliar fatigues. Both were aiming standard-pattern lasguns at Darya and Ullaeus.

A tall, thin man emerged from an empty doorway behind the kneeling troopers, his face hidden in shadow. Darya could see the lasgun in his hands clearly enough though, and noted that it too was pointed at her.

'Who in the hells are you?' the thin man said. It was the same man who had been speaking to her on the vox.

'We're looking for the Kintair Rifles,' Darya said, her hands still in the air.

'You've found them. Now who the frag are you?' the man pressed, stepping in closer.

'Sergeant Darya Nevic, First Company, Cadian Two-Hundred-and-Seventeenth. I need to speak to your commanding officer at once,' Darya said.

The man let out a barking laugh that was devoid of any humour.

'I guess that'd be me, eh?' he said. 'Put up your guns, lads.'

The two kneeling troopers lowered their weapons and got to their feet. Darya relaxed with a sigh and let her arms fall, as the thin man stepped into the lumen's light.

'Now, to what do we owe the pleasure, Sergeant Nevic of the Cadian Two-Hundred-and-Seventeenth?'

11

The officer had close-cropped auburn hair and a strong jaw, his stubble peppered with patches of white. His skin was weather-beaten from a lifetime spent under a harsh sun, with deep wrinkles around his eyes from long-faded smiles. His expression was cold as he led them to a makeshift tent behind the line of defences, a look that was foreign on his kind features but that had become familiar through long use.

'Lieutenant Bol Ceres,' he introduced himself, taking a seat on an upturned ammunition crate. Darya and Ullaeus saluted stiffly, but Ceres only made a half-hearted attempt to return the gesture. He pulled a battered leather pouch from inside his jacket, produced a pair of thin lho-papers and tobac and started rolling.

'Which regiment, sir?' Darya asked as he collected any stray fibres of tobac and tucked them back into the pouch.

'There's only one regiment of Kintair Rifles in this battle group, sergeant,' Ceres said. 'And before you ask, there's only one company left after the last round of consolidations. Last count put us at about four hundred souls.'

Darya looked about the position at the sorry state of the Kintair Rifles. They had taken a battering, that much was clear; there must have been twenty wounded troopers lying in various states of semi-consciousness behind Ceres, whilst the soldiers manning the forward defences appeared to be in little better condition. She could make out the stained gauze of hastily applied dressings on most of them; one even rested the grip of his lasgun on the wall in front of him, his left arm strapped to his chest in an improvised sling.

'I'm glad we've found you, sir,' Darya said, turning back to Ceres.

'You look like it,' Ceres said with another mirthless laugh. 'Though, I'm interested to hear why the famed Ghost of Cocleratum has come halfway across the sector searching for us, looking like hammered shit and smelling twice as bad.'

'God-Emperor forbid the blessed Cadians ever take a backward step,' Ceres said dryly as Darya finished explaining her mission. He pulled out a box of thin card matches and lit both lho-sticks, passing one to a nearby trooper whose face was half-covered in browning bandages. Darya's mind flicked back to Yanna, her stomach clenching as she thought of her and the rest of the squad several miles away.

'With respect, sir, to our knowledge it's the only beachhead we've got on the other side of the Spatka. If we have to fall back, we're going to pay dearly to retake it.'

'You're asking me to spend Kintair lives now so you don't have to spend Cadian lives later,' Ceres said.

'No, sir. We're here to help you achieve your objectives and get your vox-relay into position,' Darya said calmly, keeping her voice as even as she could.

'It amounts to the same thing,' Ceres said. He sighed, blowing out a plume of bluish smoke. 'I've heard the stories about you, Nevic. Your antics are famous across the battle group – but even if they're true, stories don't stop plasma bolts or hypersonic rounds.'

'People talk. I prefer action,' Darya replied.

'Ha! I like it,' Ceres said, letting out the first genuine laugh Darya had heard from him. It suited him far more than the cold exterior he'd been wearing so far, she thought. But his tone darkened as he continued.

'You sound like a character right from the propaganda reels, talking like that. But we've attacked that line twice and we couldn't get close. Those damned railguns picked off our armour like a lasgun takes out a rodent, whilst their drones and flyers took care of my men.'

'You attacked head-on?' Ullaeus said.

'Of course we fragging did,' Ceres spat, rounding on Ullaeus. 'Our captain had all the tactical nous of a sack of corpse starch, Emperor keep him. Then our commissar demands we go again, and gets a one-way ticket to the Throne a few minutes in, along with half of our bloody men.'

'Sir, we–'

'No,' Ceres cut across her. 'I'll not walk my men into that again. We can't even get close enough to see the bastards, so we're going to wait for air support or artillery or the next wave.'

Ceres turned away, one hand over his face as he breathed deeply. Darya glanced at Ullaeus, who looked shocked. Both knew that such an outburst would have seen Ceres shot as a coward by a commissar, had one been present.

It left Darya with few options, but she made her decision quickly.

'What if we can help, sir?'

'Help how?' Ceres asked, turning back to face the two Cadians.

'Corporal Ullaeus and I just came through enemy lines to within spitting distance of you without being spotted,' Darya explained. 'If we can get some of your men back behind their lines we might be able to–'

'Are you saying that you can get four hundred of my men behind their gunline without being seen? I find that hard to believe,' Ceres said. 'We all heard that alarm half an hour ago. Wouldn't say you made it the whole way without being spotted.'

'They found a body, they didn't find us,' Darya said, raising her hands to try to calm Ceres. 'We're not saying we can get you all behind their lines, but we can get some of you through.'

Ullaeus nodded. 'A couple of squads, maybe.'

'And what would that achieve?' Ceres asked, rounding on Ullaeus.

'A great deal,' Darya said, stepping closer to Ceres. 'If we can get a strike force behind their lines, we can take out their heavy weapons and sow enough destruction to allow your main force to breach their lines from the front.'

Ceres exhaled a forked plume of tobac smoke from his nostrils, narrowing his eyes at Darya whilst he considered her words.

'That could work,' he admitted. 'How many men would you need?'

'As many as you have who can hold their nerve,' Ullaeus replied, resting his arms over his long-las. 'Jumpy troopers don't tend to last long on stealth missions.'

'Do you have anyone who's trained in fieldcraft?' Darya asked.

'I'm not sure what that is,' Ceres said, his expression blank.

'Wet work, sniping, pathfinding. The Catachan Devils call it bushcraft.'

'I have a few troopers who have bushcraft experience,' Ceres said, nodding.

'What about armour? Tanks, Sentinels or anything?' Darya asked.

'A couple of pieces – a squadron of Wyverns and a couple of Chimeras,' Ceres replied. 'The adept is working on a couple of the others, but there's enough to get the job done if we get in close.'

'The adept?'

Ceres led Darya and Ullaeus further back from the killing field to a fallen hab-block, its innards bared and cast down in a heaped slope at its base. Thin mattresses were half-buried beneath cooking implements, timeworn chairs and splintered masonry, tangles of wiry insulation sheeting fluttering like wisps of smoke from a candle.

At the foot of the slope stood a red-robed figure, short but almost inhumanly stout, a cog-toothed axe strapped across their back. They were working on the sponson of a Leman Russ battle tank, white-blue sparks spraying freely as fresh metal was welded over a jagged hole in the tank's armour.

A tanker knelt on top of the sponson, covering his eyes as the adept worked. Once the sparks ceased he thanked the robed machine priest with a deferential bow before slipping into the tank through a battered hatch.

'Adept Lambda-Mu,' Ceres called out as they approached.

The adept turned in sections, their shoulders first, then their midriff, then their thick metallic legs, servos whirring audibly as the red fabric of their robes unfurled from their twisted form.

'Lieutenant Ceres,' a mechanical voice purred, the intonation entirely inhuman. The adept's hood twitched in her direction, and Darya had the uncomfortable feeling that she was being scanned or studied. 'These soldiers appear to be Cadian. You have been reinforced?'

'Not quite,' Ceres said, stopping just short of the adept and indicating the two Cadians. 'Sergeant Nevic and Corporal Ullaeus, Cadian Two-Hundred-and-Seventeenth.'

'Greetings,' said the adept, the robotic voice emanating from their lower torso rather than their hood. An articulated limb reached out to Darya, unfurling and extending telescopically until a three-fingered claw gently grazed the fringe of her cloak. She made no effort to move away, as doing so might offend the emissary of the Adeptus Mechanicus.

'You are equipped with cameleoline cloaks and long-las. Is it safe to assume you are sniper specialists?'

'That is correct, honoured adept,' Darya said, making the sign of the aquila and inclining her head in the formal greeting. The adept's articulated arm withdrew, folding back in on itself as it slipped back beneath the red folds of their robes.

'They're here to help us take the barricade,' Ceres explained. The adept made a whirring sound as they turned to the lieutenant, a gap in their robes showing a flash of polished silver armour plating beneath.

'You lack the necessary forces to assault the xenos position without significant reinforcement. Your chances of failure are ninety-seven point three per cent.'

'We have a way behind their emplacements,' Darya said as the adept began to move, their segmented body turning from the shoulders to face the Leman Russ once more.

'Explain,' the adept said flatly.

'We passed through the enemy positions to reach you, and we can take the same path back with a strike team. Destroy their heavy weapons and disrupt their lines, allowing a frontal assault to get within range from the west.' Darya looked about at the waiting tanks.

'It looks like you have all the armour you need to get your forces close, lieutenant.'

'How many have you got in working condition?' Ceres asked the adept.

'*Heaven's Hammer* – inoperable. *Might of Fire* – operating at seventy-three–'

'Just the numbers please, adept. Troop carriers, battle tanks and Sentinels,' Ceres interrupted. The adept's mechanical voice blurted a short blast of harsh binharic which made Darya's teeth itch.

'Operational assets consist of two Leman Russ battle tanks, standard pattern. Two Wyvern support tanks, Metallica pattern. Three Chimera troop transports, Mars pattern. One Sentinel, Mars pattern,' the adept reeled off in their robotic voice.

'That's good. We–'

'This does not include my charge,' the adept interjected, cutting Ceres off mid-sentence.

Darya had to fight the urge to smile at the adept's petty interruption.

'Is the vox-relay still in full working condition?' Darya asked as Ceres stared wryly at the adept.

'It is in full working order,' the adept replied, their hood turning to face Darya.

'I'm glad to hear it,' Darya said, reaching behind herself and shrugging out of the fail-safe charge's straps. 'But my orders are that if the relay can't be securely positioned by dawn, it must not fall into enemy hands.'

She set down the charge on the ground in front of the adept and stepped back. The adept looked at it as if deep in thought, before two small arms emerged from within the robes and pulled the fail-safe charge beneath their shadowed folds.

'The blessed machinery of the Omnissiah will not fall into the hands of the enemy,' the adept said in their strange tone. They moved suddenly and without warning, turning on their axis and stomping to the rear of the Leman Russ. They raised an arm from within their robes, the flesh withered and grey in the dim light, pocked with liver spots and injection ports embedded into the clammy flesh.

Darya shuddered, but followed the line of their gnarled finger to a Chimera parked beneath a corrugated iron shelter less than twenty feet away. It had been painted in Mechanicus red, and an unfamiliar energy weapon jutted from the front armour where a heavy bolter or flamer would usually have been mounted. The rear of the transport had been stripped away, the cargo compartment, turret and driver's compartment gutted to make space for a collapsed frame of iron and shining copper, topped with a semicircular transmission dish.

'I calculate that your operation has a forty-two point one per cent chance of success,' the adept said in a low burr, just loud enough for the Cadians to hear.

'Better odds than two minutes ago,' Ullaeus said with a forced smile. The adept ignored him, and Ceres simply shook his head.

'What are we looking at on the other side?' Ceres asked, turning to Darya.

'Other than their main defensive line? Scattered teams of scouts mostly,' Darya said.

'There are those flyers in the square,' Ullaeus added.

Ceres gave a dismissive shake of his head. 'We've seen them. Looks like a couple of support vehicles.'

'They have nine,' Ullaeus corrected him, 'parked up in the square on the other side of the barricade.'

'Nine? What in the hells do they need nine for?' Ceres said in surprise.

'Observation – the xenotype t'au have exhibited a proclivity for rapid redeployment in multiple theatres. Hypothesis – their current deployment could be abandoned with sufficient pressure.'

Darya, Ullaeus and Ceres turned in surprise to the adept, who responded to their stares with stoic silence.

'There's another possibility,' Darya said after a few moments. 'We thought it might be an extraction team. Think about it – First Company have reached the river to the north and it's only a matter of time before our forces to the south do the same. They're risking being encircled the longer they stay. It'd be pointless for them to make a stand here, in an area that holds no tactical advantage, unless they were waiting for something.'

Ceres nodded in agreement, his eyes dark in the dim light.

'Okay. Let's say you do get a team to the other side. How will you signal the rest of the attack?' Ceres asked.

'You need at least two of their heavy-weapon emplacements to be down to create a corridor for your armour to move up and cover your troops,' Darya said, thinking as she spoke. 'Once we take out the second railgun, your men advance. That could work?'

Ceres folded his arms over his chest and studied Darya for a moment, before closing his eyes and pinching the bridge of his nose between a callused thumb and forefinger.

'Okay, sergeant. We're with you.'

12

Lieutenant Ceres had declined to be part of the strike team, saying that his place was with his men on the frontal assault. Darya respected his decision to lead the main attack, but she couldn't push away the suspicion that his motivations might not have been completely altruistic.

Instead, Ceres had insisted that his second-in-command, Sergeant Dal Feon, join the infiltration team.

The man had the small, deep-set eyes of a rodent and the demeanour to match. His unkempt beard grew in uneven clumps around a number of burns that created a patchwork of scars over his face and scalp, which he failed to hide beneath long locks of greasy hair.

'Yer both mad, I swear,' he slurred, the words choked by his thick accent as the team crawled through the churned mud of the killing field.

'Shut up,' Darya hissed for what felt like the hundredth time.

She wished Ullaeus was by her side, but her corporal was

bringing up the rear to ensure their strike team made it back to the sewer in one piece. Shepherding eight of Lieutenant Ceres' hand-picked troopers across the battlefield would have been all but impossible alone, and Darya thanked He on the Throne that she had Ullaeus with her to help. She knew that if he were closer, he would have already asked for permission to kill Feon for a few minutes of peace.

'If I die on my belly in the stinking dirt–'

'It'll be because you wouldn't shut up and gave us away. Keep quiet or it won't just be the t'au trying to kill you.'

She turned back, careful to keep her rifle out of the mud as she glared back at Feon's ravaged face. He was smiling, the bastard.

God-Emperor, grant me strength, she prayed silently, then pressed on through the stinking mud. She scanned the pitch-black landscape ahead for a reference point to orient herself, but the half-buried Leman Russ was nowhere to be seen.

'You lost?' Feon said from behind her.

She didn't have the strength to respond. Instead, she pulled her scope to her eye once more and scanned the battlefield around her, noting that the trio of burning Leman Russ battle tanks were far off to the right. They were on the right heading, but the t'au barricade seemed far closer than it had when they'd been on their way to the Kintair lines.

Then, finally, her scope caught the straight edge of a tank sponson, standing out against the rugged, irregular terrain of the battlefield.

'This way,' she whispered, turning to the left and wriggling over the lip of a shallow crater. A lone figure lay prone at the bottom, their long black coat bunched up to cover their torso and head.

'So that's where he got to,' Feon said softly, as if he'd just found a trinket that he'd misplaced, rather than a commissar.

Darya ignored him and pressed on, cresting the lip of the crater and pushing on until she was in the shadow of the Leman Russ. The crater with the sewer access pipe lay within sight, its depths hidden by all-consuming darkness.

She heard the enemy Devilfish before she saw it, a throaty thrum that shook the cold metal of the Leman Russ as it drew closer.

'Down!' she hissed back along the line, and pushed herself flat against the armour plating as the flyer's lumen beam played across the ground nearby. Behind her, eight figures dropped to the earth and became one with the darkness.

All but Feon.

She watched in disbelief as he shuffled forwards on his knees and reached up to one of the corpses hanging out of the Leman Russ. He licked his lips and worked at the clasp of a blackened wrist-chron, his eyes wide as he struggled with the warped metal.

Darya slid backwards and kicked out at him, knocking him to the ground with a wet slap as the spotlight danced across the top of the Leman Russ and moved on. Darya moved to pin him down as the drones moved past, but stopped as she saw a flash of steel in the dark.

'What in the hells do you think you're doing?' she hissed angrily.

'Why the frag do you care? You didn't know them,' Feon spat back.

'I care that you nearly got us caught, you damned idiot!'

She waited until the Devilfish and the drones were further away before speaking again, letting her anger at the Kintair cool.

'Complete silence once we're in the tunnel. When we get to the other end, four of you follow me, the others follow Corporal Ullaeus. If you frag this up it's your friends who die, so do as you're told.'

Darya rounded on Feon, whose expression was unreadable in the dark.

'You're with me,' Darya said coldly.

She led the squad over to the crater, wishing that it was her team at her back and not just Ullaeus and a pack of conscripted amateurs. With her team, she could almost guarantee success and minimal casualties; with this rag-tag crew, it was almost certain that some would die.

If Feon wasn't one of those who made it out unscathed, she doubted that it would weigh on her.

She reached the lip of the crater and knew she'd found the right place just by the smell. The pungent, salty stink of sewage wafted up from the dark, turning her empty stomach.

'Frag me, that's rank,' Feon whispered, covering his mouth with one hand.

Darya rolled over the crater's lip and slid down, her rifle raised at the pitch-black hole at the crater's floor where the sewer pipe was exposed to the open air. She carefully worked her way around the growing pool of water and sewage in the crater's basin and moved to the threshold of the sewer pipe before turning back to the Kintair.

'Stay close to me – it'd be too easy to get lost in there. And keep quiet.'

She moved down the pipe as quickly as she could without her footsteps slapping against the wet stone, her scope tight to her eye, searching for any sign of life in the rot-encrusted conduit.

Soon, the footfalls of her impromptu squad behind her became so loud that she was forced to drop the pace so as to prevent their premature discovery. It was yet another reason that she wished she were leading her own squad, who would have known to place their feet more carefully.

Where it had taken less than half an hour for Darya and Ullaeus to navigate the sewers, it took almost twice that for the squad to reach the corroded metal ladder spokes deep within the underground tunnels.

'I'll go up first,' Darya breathed. Within the tight confines of the pipe, her voice would carry a long way, so she kept it as quiet and low-pitched as possible. 'Once the way is clear, Ullaeus will come next. There is a building directly near the ladder, once you're clear of the pipe you get in there and into cover.'

She didn't wait for a response, but said her own prayer to the God-Emperor as she pulled herself onto the first rung of the ladder and up towards the light above, slim points punched through the cover's surface.

God-Emperor, may your blessings shine on me this night.

Another step, two more rungs passed beneath her hands as she left the sewer tunnel and entered the access pipe.

May your grace shine on the team I lead in your name.

Flaking rust crackled beneath her fingers as she climbed still further, the metallic tang growing stronger.

Guide Iago Ullaeus to his goal. Please, protect my friend.

Finally, she came to rest directly below the pitted underside of the manhole cover.

Throne protect us all.

Her hands didn't tremble as they met the cold, thick metal of the cover plate. She pushed against them, bracing herself through her legs on the rungs below, as the cover slid clear of the pipe. Her tired muscles burned and her joints ached, but still she pushed, until there was enough space for her to crawl free.

She emerged onto the square slowly, her rifle at the ready, expecting a bolt of white-hot plasma at any moment.

But no shot came.

She scanned the windows that looked down on the square in tense anticipation, waiting for the shout of alarm or the muzzle flash of an incoming shot. She tensed as her eyes roved over the sleek Devilfish transports waiting in formation nearby, but still no shot came.

Ullaeus emerged from the pipe next, tapping Darya's shoulder as he vaulted the low window to her left and cleared the room beyond.

Darya waited a few moments before gesturing for the next person to follow, then the next after that. One by one the team emerged from the pipe, each following their orders and crawling over the windowsill into the Administratum building.

The last to emerge was Feon, who hawked and spat loudly the moment his head was clear of the pipe. Darya's heart froze as she saw a sudden movement between the Devilfish transports.

'Freeze,' she hissed.

To his credit, Feon stopped stock still, halfway out of the pipe, his hand resting on the cobbled floor of the square.

A t'au warrior emerged from between two of the transports, gesticulating animatedly as if arguing with someone that Darya couldn't see.

She waited until he turned momentarily, then grabbed Feon by the scruff of the neck, pulled him bodily from the pipe and pushed him through the open Administratum window.

There was no time to pull the sewer cover back into place. In any case, the noise would almost certainly raise the alarm, so she dived into the darkness of the building behind Feon.

Inside, the squad had taken up positions around the room, their weapons raised and ready.

'You four,' Darya whispered, pointing to the soldiers closest to Ullaeus. 'You're with Corporal Ullaeus on the northern emplacement. The rest of you are with me. God-Emperor be with us.'

They nodded, all wide-eyed with fear except for Feon, who was looking out of the window into the square. He seemed different in that moment, more focused now that he could see his enemy.

Ullaeus nodded at Darya, then moved through a door that led to the northern edge of the square. Darya gestured for her group to follow her until she reached the room where she had killed the t'au guard a couple of hours before.

The body had been removed, with only a pool of clotted blood showing that it had ever even been there. The rest of the room was unchanged, but for the cloven footsteps of t'au feet that marked the soot-encrusted floor.

Darya had Feon help her up onto the floor above through the hole in the ceiling, then pulled him up without a sound.

Footsteps cracked across floor plating deeper within the building, and both Darya and Feon froze. She edged closer to the doorway that led into the offices, and saw two t'au fire warriors at the window, watching the street below.

Clearly the t'au had increased security since she and Ullaeus had passed through earlier. It wasn't a surprise given that they'd raised the alarm, but it made things more complicated.

Darya looked over to Feon and pulled out her kvis. He mirrored her, pulling a thin, short-bladed knife from his belt.

Darya pointed to herself and held up a single finger.

I'll take the first one.

Feon nodded and slipped the strap of his lasgun off over his head, then laid the weapon carefully on the floor.

They moved into the room together, their feet whispering over the plascrete floor as they moved in close behind the t'au.

Darya's kvis opened her fire warrior's throat at the same moment that Feon's knife opened his, both dragging the soldiers back from the window and pinning them to the floor. Darya pulled her t'au's rifle from its frantic, spasming hands and pushed it across the floor out of reach, then slammed the knife into the gap between armpit and chestplate. Dark blood splashed over her hand, hot and wet, slicking the wooden handle of her kvis as she twisted the blade deeper.

To her right, Feon had forced his knife up under the chin of the t'au warrior's helmet, driving the blade into the xenos' brain. Its feet twitched beneath him, and he smiled.

'Neatly done. I thought Kintair was an agri world,' Darya whispered as Feon pulled the knife free and wiped it on the cloth of the dead t'au's sleeve. Darya did the same with the blade of her kvis, before sheathing it on her shoulder once more.

'I'm sure there are Cadians who aren't soldiers,' Feon said with a toothy grin.

'I wouldn't know,' Darya replied, 'I wasn't always Cadian.' She crawled back to the first room and held out a hand to pull up the next member of the team.

Once all five were on the upper floor, they worked their way through the building to the western edge, where the outer walls had collapsed.

Below, t'au fire warriors knelt in the cover provided by their energy barriers, overseen by the looming shape of the railgun high above. Their asymmetrical shoulder pads were emblazoned with a symbol Darya didn't recognise, standing out in sharp red against the cool grey of their armour.

'Pick your targets, controlled bursts,' Darya whispered as her team took up positions in the windows overlooking the rear of the t'au barricade.

'There must be fifteen of them down there,' one of the troopers breathed.

'Harut-eels in a barrel,' Feon said in a low voice. 'Don't show the lieutenant up in front of the Cadians.'

'We go on three. One... Two...'

A single lasgun report whip-cracked through the heavy silence. *Shit.*

There was no taking back the shot, which sparked off the frame of the railgun as it missed the nearest target by several feet. Darya focused on a fire warrior with a red streak down his helmet and fired, the long-las shot punching him off his feet and into the energy barrier in a blaze of blue light. Another shot, then another, each pull of the trigger sending a fire warrior sprawling to the floor.

The whine of lasguns was joined by the hissing crack of plasma weapons as the t'au warriors returned fire, smashing chunks of glowing stone from the window frames and sending a couple of Darya's team back into cover. The t'au alarm was blaring its teeth-grinding screech again, though it struggled to be heard beneath the fusillades of gunfire lancing across the street.

Then the railgun started to move, whirring into life as it pivoted on the circular stanchion at its base, seemingly directed by the bare-headed t'au manipulating a projection of glowing hexes at its base.

'Target the operator!' Darya shouted to her team. The Kintair peppered the rotunda with las-fire, taking the bare-headed operator and two of his comrades crouching in cover behind it, but the railgun kept moving, even as Darya fired shot after shot into a glowing panel at the stanchion's base.

The square barrel came to rest pointing directly at Darya's team.

'Move!' Darya yelled, springing to her feet and grabbing the collar of the first Kintair trooper she passed.

The railgun fired, blasting the room apart in a hurricane of light and debris, before the sound caught up with the hypersonic round. It was the crashing of an impossible wave, the passing of a heavy maglev train and the end of the world all in one moment.

It punched her off her feet, the collar of the Kintair trooper still clenched in her fist as she landed heavily, rolling away to put more space between herself and the weapon's impossible power. Air rushed past her back into the room, dragging on her cloak as the wave of pressure equalised in the round's wake.

'Fragging hell!' Feon screamed from beside her; she realised that she was still holding the scruff of his neck, and let him drop.

'Keep moving!' she roared, chancing a look out of the nearest window.

There were only a few t'au fire warriors still standing, but it apparently only took one to man the controls of the railgun. Darya took aim and fired in one movement, and the t'au nearest the gunrig's rotunda collapsed in a heap, a neat hole blasted through the centre of its helmet.

Plasma fire peppered the window frame either side of her, spraying her with shards of stone that stung her face as they cut into her flesh. She threw herself back, just as a resounding boom shook the building and a high plume of flame and smoke appeared in the north-facing windows.

One emplacement down, Darya thought.

She pushed herself to her feet and darted back through into the room that had been blasted by the railgun, ignoring the bloody ruins of the three troopers who hadn't got out in time. She flicked her scope's filter to the heat-sensitive setting and took aim, using the cloud of settling dust as cover to take out the first of the remaining two t'au warriors on the barricade. The last was in cover on the far side of the railgun, and had previously been hidden by its bulk – it wore a headset not unlike the drone controllers she'd seen across Miracil over the last three days.

She shot that t'au through the head, destroying the controller and ending the xenos' life with one squeeze of the trigger. It left the railgun with no living t'au nearby to guide it, which would buy her a little time to take it out for good.

'Feon, are you with me?' she shouted, spinning back into more solid cover as plasma shots hissed through the air over her head.

'Here, somehow,' Feon shouted back from the next room, between bursts from his lasgun.

Darya moved back into the other room and knelt beneath an open window next to Feon's position.

'I need you to cover me. Shoot and move, make them think there's more of us than there are,' Darya explained quickly. She pulled her grenades from her belt along with a length of med-tape. She gave the frag grenades to Feon, then lashed the krak grenades together with the tape. 'I'm going for the gun.'

Feon said nothing, but took the offered grenades with a nod.

God-Emperor, protect me.

Darya dashed back through to the railgun-shattered room and out into the open air, emerging from the clouds of choking smog onto a loose slope of rubble and debris. She slid down, first on her feet then her knees, until she reached solid ground at the foot of the rise.

The t'au who had been manning the barricade were all dead, smoking holes burned through their fractured armour. Darya sprinted past their prone forms to the relative safety of the gunrig's rotunda, where fewer of the t'au along the street had a clear shot at her.

Feon's lasgun crackled down the street, followed by the familiar *crump* of frag grenades. Darya was happy for him to draw their fire until the railgun was dealt with, but knew that it was only a matter of time before his luck ran out.

But, as she looked around the rotunda, she couldn't see anywhere to pack the explosives that was guaranteed to take out the railgun. The xenos position was seamless, with less than a hair's breadth of space between the interlocking panels.

She swore as she cast about, looking for any kind of gap or nook that might work, until her eyes settled on the weapon itself and the wide channels cut into the barrel's length.

Perfect.

Darya slipped her long-las' strap over her back and started

to climb, using the exposed innards of the support column as handholds and footholds to scramble up.

Plasma scorched the grey metal housing as the t'au spotted her, redirecting their fire away from Feon to protect their main defensive asset. Her heart hammered all the harder as she climbed, thumping so hard she was sure her entire body must have been shaking with the rhythm.

With one hand holding her steady, she pulled a pin from the bundled krak grenades and shoved them into the gap in the railgun's barrel, hissing with sudden pain as the residual heat scorched her fingers. T'au voices cried out in alarm as she dropped from the railgun in a hail of plasma fire, landing heavily in the scant cover of the rotunda.

Then the grenades exploded with a thunderclap of light and sound, the charges cooked off prematurely by the heat of the railgun's barrel. The blast knocked the air from her lungs as it slammed her hard into the alloy plating at her feet, peppering her with searing slivers of shrapnel and debris. Spots of white-hot pain prickled across her back and arms as the explosion reverberated down the street.

With leaden limbs, Darya dragged herself up the incline, trying to blink away the mental fog as a voice in her head told her to keep moving. She glanced back to see the railgun's smoking barrel peeled back like the skin of a tropical fruit, utterly useless. A distant whistle sounded, but she didn't have time to consider what it meant.

'Fragging crazy Cadians!' Feon shouted, appearing in front of her and dragging her up into cover behind a toppled desk.

'You good?' Darya shouted back, shaking her head to loosen the last of the sense of dislocation from her mind.

'Me? Ha!' Feon laughed, snapping off a few shots down the length of the building. 'You just shoved a bundle of grenades down a railgun barrel and you're asking if *I'm* okay?'

Enemy fire flashed through the air overhead, coming from deeper within the building and in through the windows.

Darya chanced a look over the rim of the desk. Several t'au fire warriors were shooting from cover a few rooms away, the red lights of their helm lenses visible even in the dark.

'We have to move!'

Darya drew her autopistol and loosed a few rounds at the advancing t'au. A long-las was a good weapon in the right hands, but it wasn't made for suppressing fire.

'We just need to hold on until Lieutenant Ceres gets here,' Feon said, slapping a fresh charge pack into his weapon as he spoke.

'No, we need to move on those Devilfish transports before they get them into the air!'

Darya holstered the autopistol and rolled out from behind the desk to a window that overlooked the square, readying her long-las as she moved. Lances of red light were peppering the transports from the northern perimeter, whilst blue-white plasma rounds were spat back from the buildings opposite. It was pandemonium.

Where the hell are the Kintair? Darya thought.

'Ullaeus? Are you there?' Darya spoke into her vox-bead, just as an unarmoured t'au made a run for the nearest transport. She put him down, lifting her rifle and squeezing the trigger with one smooth motion.

'Still here, trying to keep them from the transports but ammo's running low,' Ullaeus replied, his voice barely audible despite him only being a few dozen yards away.

The t'au alarm was suddenly joined by the amplified chatter of xenos speech, the words unintelligible but their urgency clear.

'What the frag is going on?' Feon yelled from behind Darya.

'No idea, but be ready for a counter-attack!'

At that moment, a flurry of drones swooped from the transports, disgorging themselves like a cloud of flies from a rotting corpse. They moved in perfect unison, their robotic grace somehow just as jarring as their sudden appearance. Most were the standard pattern that Darya and Ullaeus had encountered before on Attruso, but mingled in the flocks were larger, weightier patterns that carried rotary cannons and other heavy xenos weapons. The drones came to a sudden stop in the air over the square, and the rotary cannons began to spin.

'Take cover!'

Then the drones opened fire.

It was a storm unlike anything that Darya had ever experienced. Searing-hot flares of white flame raked the upper storeys, splintering stone and shattering the heavy plasteel lintels. Feon was screaming, his hands over his head and his rifle forgotten at his feet.

Part of the window caved in next to Darya, forcing her back as the brickwork disintegrated under the unending rain of fire.

Through the crack, she saw three enemy soldiers emerge from the sewer tunnels her own team had used earlier – the first was a human in t'au garb, but the two that followed had the stouter build and reverse-jointed knees that marked them out as xenos. All three bore long rifles with complex scopes, and their armour was a black so deep that it seemed darker than the void itself.

Snipers.

They darted out of her field of view towards the transports. The human sniper looked at first glance to be wearing a ragged cloak, but Darya realised they were strips of white fabric tied to his armour, which trailed behind him to blur his silhouette.

Masonry was falling in chunks from the walls and ceiling, eating away at the little cover they had left. There was no time left to watch.

'Feon, come on!' Darya shouted, lying prone and crawling on her belly towards the doorway.

His eyes were wide as he looked back, with fear or anger she couldn't tell. But he did as he was ordered, getting into a prone position and following as Darya crawled hand over hand into the next room under a shower of plasma, rockcrete shards and stone dust.

'Where did they go?' Darya shouted over the barrage, pointing in the direction of the t'au that had been deeper in the building, but Feon didn't appear to hear her. He pushed on ahead, keeping his head down as he moved into the next room.

The boom of Imperial artillery joined the cacophony outside as airburst shells detonated in the midst of the drones, cutting their rate of fire as they fought to stay aloft in air filled with shrapnel and sudden changes in pressure.

The Kintair are here.

But the drones didn't let up their fire, even as more Imperial shells burst in the air around them and knocked them from the sky. Shrapnel, both Imperial and t'au, began to shower through the open windows in bursts of razor-sharp metal, as the Kintair bombardment intensified.

Darya waited for the next barrage before moving from cover to take aim at the blasphemous xenos constructs, shooting as many as she could between explosions and their raking salvoes of plasma fire.

She shouted her defiance as her long-las shots joined in the maelstrom, letting out days of pent-up aggression, tension and rage that had been compartmentalised and stashed away in the deepest recesses of her mind as she fought. She'd used up every last ounce of her will, strength and tactical ability to save her team, her company and herself. And at that moment, under incredible enemy fire and beneath the killing rain of an Imperial

Wyvern mortar barrage, there was nothing else. It was just her against her enemy.

Then the Kintair poured into the square, pitching wild bursts of las-fire into the dark sky. Most missed the drones, but the weight of fire brought down the t'au constructs by the handful.

The t'au themselves were in full retreat, allowing the drones to soak up the Imperial fire as they ran to their transports from every direction to try to escape. Darya picked them off until the trigger of her long-las went loose in her hand, whilst still more were caught by Kintair troopers or falling drones, left to bleed out on the cobbles of the square as the Devilfish transports took to the air and skimmed away to the east.

13

Lieutenant Ceres was front and centre of the Kintair assault, breaching the barricades that had claimed so many lives from his regiment.

Despite the long-overdue victory, he was quiet as he met Darya, Ullaeus and the survivors of their team in the centre of the square.

Of the ten that had set out from the Kintair positions on the other side of the field, only six remained: one of Ullaeus' team had been caught in the drones' fire, and Dal Feon and Darya were the only survivors from her team.

'Damned good work, all of you. Feon, log the casualties with Kulloch. The rest of you, get back to your squads,' Ceres ordered, his laspistol and chainsword still in hand. Members of his command squad surrounded him in a protective circle, whilst teams swept the buildings that ringed the square for any stragglers. Dal Feon led the others away.

Ceres stopped over the body of a t'au that lay face down on

the cobbles, turning it over with the toe of his boot so its dead eyes faced the lightening sky.

'It was an extraction force,' Darya said hoarsely. She took another deep swig from her canteen, but it did little to alleviate the raw, metallic taste in her throat.

'Team of three snipers used the same infiltration point we did to get inside the square, only a few minutes after we did. Could even have been behind us in the tunnels, I don't know... Either way, once they arrived the t'au seemed in a hurry to leave.'

She didn't mention the human in a t'au uniform who had been leading them.

Lieutenant Ceres nodded as he looked around the square, until his eyes settled on the sewer-access tunnel in the corner.

'Boros, get a krak charge down that sewer access so it can't be used again.'

A trooper snapped off a quick salute and darted off in the direction of the sewer, readying a brace of grenades as he moved.

'I suppose thanks are in order,' Ceres said, holstering his laspistol and extending a hand to Darya. The barest hint of a smile crossed his features, and she took his hand and shook it.

'No thanks needed, sir. But if you can get that comms unit up double time–' Darya began.

'Already on it,' Ceres cut in, just as the dark-red hull of the converted Chimera entered the square behind him, led by Tech-Adept Lambda-Mu. They carried a massive cog-toothed axe in their mechanical grip, whilst their flesh hands made the sign of the cog over their heart as they walked.

'We'll be setting it up here. The venerable tech-adept has assured me that if your regiment are where you say they are, then they are in range, and it's a defensible position that we can use. We may even be able to push on towards the river.'

'Thank you, sir,' Darya replied. She drew her flare gun and

loaded it with the green flare that Captain Kohl had given her. She fired it into the slate-grey sky, where it flashed white for a moment before turning a lurid green and beginning its lazy descent. Dawn was less than an hour away, and Darya's thoughts were already back with her company.

'That looks painful,' Ceres said, pointing to Darya's scorched hand.

'It's nothing.' Darya shook her head. It wasn't nothing, it was throbbing like a bastard, but for some unknown reason she didn't want to let on to the Kintair lieutenant.

'Kulloch, take a look at her hand,' Ceres said, and one of his command squad stepped forward with a med-kit in hand.

'No, sir, honestly it's fine, we need to be getting back to–'

'Your company will manage for a few minutes whilst you're looked at and take on some water.'

Darya looked to Ullaeus, who simply shrugged and pulled his long-las over his head and unclasped his cameleoline cloak.

It was an odd feeling, to be at the centre of a bustling hive of activity but to be so still, Darya thought. Kulloch dressed her burned fingers with a cooling salve and a spray of counterseptics, before giving her the usual speech about keeping the wounds clean and dry. She nodded along, conscious of not only the time but also that the longer she stayed still, the more tired she seemed to feel.

The other Chimeras pulled into the square as Kulloch moved to look at Ullaeus, and Darya took the opportunity to take a seat with her back against the Mechanicus Chimera. Lambda-Mu had two bulk-lifting servitors that they were directing with bursts of harsh binharic.

The next thing she knew Ceres was standing over her, silhouetted against the slate-grey sky. He offered her his canteen, which she accepted with a nod of thanks.

The night had given way to the grey light of pre-dawn, and the Kintair had made the square their own. Heavy-weapon emplacements were visible through holes blasted in the walls of the Administratum buildings, whilst cables were spooled out from the Mechanicus Chimera into the open hatches of the Kintair Chimeras.

The wounded had also been moved up to their new forward operating base, and Darya could see Kulloch walking amongst them. Those who were upright were all staring at her and Ullaeus.

Darya was uncomfortable beneath their gaze, and noticed that it wasn't just the wounded who were watching her. Troopers all around the yard were staring at the two Cadians, their expressions a mix of awe and… anger?

'You'll have to forgive them,' Ceres said, taking a seat on the cobbles next to Darya. 'It's the first time we've served alongside Cadians and… well, you've lived up to your reputation.'

Darya took a long swig from the canteen as Ceres spoke, grateful for the drink despite the chemical-laced tang of the reprocessed water.

'We weren't always Cadian, sir, but I remember what it was like when I saw the Two-Hundred-and-Seventeenth in action for the first time,' Darya said after a moment, passing the canteen back to Ceres. He looked at her in confusion as he took it, a question forming on his lips.

'I'm Coclerati. Corporal Ullaeus is from Verspator, one of the five hundred worlds of Ultramar. We were transplanted from our home regiments to bolster the Cadian regiments after the Fall.'

Ceres looked from Darya to Ullaeus, who was having his arm wound wrapped by another medicae whilst Kulloch tended to the more seriously wounded.

'I had no idea, I thought that Cadians were… well, you know.'

'Cadian?' Darya said with a wan smile. 'We are and we aren't, depending on who you ask. It's a little complicated to be honest, sir.'

'I can see that,' Ceres said, returning the smile. It warmed his cold features for a moment, before a cold shadow drew across them once more.

'The Rifles are far less interesting. Kintair is an agri world, a forgotten ball of green and blue in the arse end of nowhere, an arrangement that suited us until some bright spark from the Administratum remembered that we had more to give than just our tithe of crops.'

'You were conscripted?' Darya asked, but she already knew the answer. It was apparent from their lack of basic equipment and specialist troops amongst their ranks, clear signs of a regiment that didn't receive the support it needed. No matter how brave or capable the Kintair proved themselves to be they would only ever be regarded as cannon fodder by command, and command didn't waste good resources on cannon fodder.

'We were farmers,' Ceres said, a distant look in his eye. He blinked it away, as if remembering himself. 'And now we are something else.'

Ullaeus approached and offered Ceres a quick salute before turning to Darya.

'Sir. I'm all patched up and ready to go, boss – we should be able to get back just after dawn, with the Emperor on our side.'

Darya nodded and pushed herself to her feet, using the immovable Mechanicus Chimera to lever herself up. Her legs were almost numb from sitting on the hard ground, and her muscles had developed a deep and painful ache that competed for attention with the bruises and scrapes across her body.

'We'll be on our way, sir, with your leave,' Darya said to Ceres as he too pushed himself back to standing.

'Query. What are your orders regarding the cypher keys?'

Lambda-Mu appeared from the rear of the Chimera, telescopic limbs retreating back within the shadowy interior of their rust-red robes with a whir of gears and servos.

'I'm sorry, adept, I'm not sure what you mean,' Darya said. Her mind was dulled with fatigue, but something in what the tech-priest had said woke a sudden knot of anxiety in her stomach.

Lambda-Mu extended an arm from one sleeve, a withered grey limb of pallid flesh and knotted joints that held a finger-sized stick of dull metal out to Darya.

'The data-relay is now fully operational. The cypher keys contained within this data-spike will allow access to the encrypted frequencies – please take them, sergeant.'

Their mission wasn't complete, not yet, and the thought set Darya's heart racing. Ullaeus let out a string of expletives that would make an Imperial Navy rating blush.

'Captain Kohl can't use the vox-relay without the right codes?' Darya asked, breathlessly. The relief she had felt at the sight of the Kintair reaching the square had disappeared, replaced by a rising panic that twisted the bile from her stomach up into her throat.

'Indeed,' Lambda-Mu said, and proffered the data-spike once more.

'We have to move. Now,' Darya said quickly, grabbing the data-spike and stashing it in her satchel. 'How long until dawn?'

'An hour, no more than that,' Ullaeus said as he looked to the eastern sky.

'Lieutenant Ceres, adept.' Darya nodded at both and made the sign of the aquila as she backed away, nervous energy already buzzing in her limbs.

She didn't stop to see if they returned the gesture or wished her and Ullaeus good luck – she was already running with

Ullaeus close behind, both praying that they would reach Track-way Span in time.

Lieutenant Eridan paced up and down within the tight confines of his command Chimera, his arms folded, one hand tugging nervously at the short growth of stubble on his chin. The vox-operators were hard at work transmitting orders to the newly contactable front lines, but Eridan's attention was on one operator and one operator alone.

'Anything?'

'Nothing yet, sir.'

'Try them again,' Eridan ordered, and the operator unplugged an input cord and began to intone the canticles of appeasement. As he finished the prayer, he reinserted the metal plug and began the hail again.

'Captain Kohl of First Company – this is regimental command, please acknowledge. Captain Kohl of First Company...'

Major Wester strode into the Chimera wearing a thunderous expression, a stress tic beneath his left eye flexing the scarred skin of his cheek. He held out a handwritten missive on thin parchment, stamped with the Imperial aquila.

'Colonel Wassenby wants a full report by vox on the disposition of our forces in one hour.' Wester shook his head. There was clearly more that he wanted to say, but he restrained himself in front of the troopers, and gestured for Eridan to follow him.

Eridan paused to tell the vox-operator to notify him immediately should he make contact with First Company at Trackway Span, then followed Wester outside the Chimera.

'He's staying up with the fleet then?'

'Apparently so. Any word from Captain Kohl?' Wester asked.

'None yet, sir, but we're still trying.'

'Damn it all.' Wester looked to have aged twenty years in

the last few hours as reports of blown bridges had been confirmed across the entire Miracil front, and embattled troops had begged for reinforcement and resupply as the comms network had been re-established.

Between them they'd managed to shore up almost the entire advance, save for the salient around Trackway Span. Wester had even managed to scrounge up air assets from the Imperial Navy to run a supply drop to an encircled detachment from the Cadian 401st.

But that was the extent of what they could achieve without support from the higher ranks, and Colonel Wassenby had been nigh on unreachable since his withdrawal to the fleet. Both Eridan and Wester knew that the next few hours would be crucial to the next stage of the Miracil campaign, one way or another.

'Sir! I've got a signal!' the vox-operator shouted.

Both Eridan and Wester leaped back into the Chimera and huddled close to the vox-station, as the operator switched the output from headset to an audio speaker.

'Captain Kohl, are you receiving?' Eridan said into the operator's vox handset.

'This is Lieutenant Ceres of the Kintair Rifles,' the voice crackled through, barely audible over the buzz of static. *'To whom am I speaking?'*

'Clean up the signal,' Eridan said to the vox-operator, before continuing. 'Lieutenant Ceres, this is Lieutenant Eridan at Command Post Alpha. It's good to hear you're still alive out there, Kintair!'

'Thank you, lieutenant, but we're in dire need of–'

'Lieutenant Ceres, this is Major Wester. Have you had any contact with Captain Kohl of the Cadian Two-Hundred-and-Seventeenth?' Wester cut in.

'No, sir,' Ceres said, and both Eridan and Wester swore silently.

'But we had assistance from a Sergeant Nevic from his company. She is in transit to Captain Kohl's position with the necessary assets to re-establish communications.'

Both Eridan and the vox-operator let out sighs of relief, whilst Wester shook his fist in triumph.

'What's their estimated time of arrival, lieutenant?' Wester asked.

'They've only just left, sir, and there are enemy elements still active in the field. We have a high number of wounded and are dangerously low on–'

'Hold fast, lieutenant, help is on the way,' Wester interrupted, then turned to the vox-operator. 'Get Lieutenant Ceres a medicae and a resupply as soon as you can. Eridan, with me.'

Wester led Eridan out of the Chimera again, away from any prying ears. Eridan paused to check the glowing chron read-out above the vox-stations, and calculated that there was less than an hour left before dawn.

'Nevic will be moving quickly, she knows what's at stake, sir,' Eridan said in a low voice.

'Do you trust her to get back to First Company before Wassenby orders their withdrawal?'

'She's the Ghost of Cocleratum, sir.'

'Then let's hope she's more than just a story. Either way, there might be a way I can buy her some time.'

'What's your plan, sir?' Eridan asked, looking over his shoulder for anyone who might overhear.

'Are you sure you want to be a part of this? If this goes wrong, it's going to be a very short court martial,' Wester said. He fixed Eridan with a stern look beneath his furrowed brows, his violet eyes almost glowing in the pre-dawn light.

'I'm with you, sir. For Cadia,' Eridan said.

'Good man,' Wester replied with a nod. 'First off, I need you to find Captain Bechmann from the Three-Hundred-and-Thirty-Eighth. We're going to need her tanks in range for this to work...'

Everything hurt.

Pain lanced through her feet with every footfall on the fractured plascrete, her hard-soled boots doing little to cushion the impact of each hurried step. Her shins ached from the punishing pace and the bruises that she knew would create a patchwork across her entire body. Her arms throbbed from the weight of her long-las, and she could feel the thunder of her heartbeat in her burned and bandaged fingers.

But the worst pain by far was in her shoulders, from so many hours of tension and compartmentalised fear – not of being discovered or killed, but that she might fail her regiment and her friends.

And that fear was damnably close to becoming reality.

Darya and Ullaeus threw away any pretence of caution as they ran through the streets of Miracil, fuelled by desperation as much as duty as they raced towards Trackway Span. They left the Kintair in their wake, flying past the squads of conscripts trying to secure the streets and into territory that held all manner of dangers.

Deep in the recesses of her mind, a familiar voice told her that it was all pointless, weaving tendrils of doubt that threatened to shatter her resolve. She pushed the voice away, ignoring the cackle of mocking laughter as she tried to persuade herself that it was the fatigue talking.

'Boss,' Ullaeus gasped from behind her.

She half turned, and took in Ullaeus' ruddy, sweat-drenched face and his limping gait, and knew that the voice was right. She slowed the pace until they were barely walking, dragging in lungfuls of ash-laden air as a cold breeze moaned down the street.

'We're not going to make it by brute-forcing it.' Ullaeus dropped to one knee as he tried to catch his breath.

They were in a narrow street which curved through the ruptured heart of Miracil's lower city, hemmed in on both sides by the high walls of industrial buildings and warehouses, watched over by the scarred, empty eyes of the skull of the Mechanicus.

'I'm open to suggestions,' Darya replied, wiping the stinging sweat from around her eyes.

'Vehicle?' Ullaeus suggested, but Darya shook her head.

'I've not seen anything we could commandeer, have you?'

'Can't say I have,' Ullaeus said. He looked up to the sky, careful not to look at the source of the violet light that discoloured the pre-dawn. Looking directly at the Great Rift invited the Arch-enemy's attention, and could send a man mad within moments.

'We could try the short-range vox, see if there's anyone nearby that could give us a lift?'

'No, it's too risky. We don't know if the xenos might be listening,' Darya said after a few moments' consideration. She had no desire to bring a t'au ambush down on their heads, exposed and unsupported as they were.

'The t'au can hear us on the vox, I'm sure of it. We could do more harm than good, broadcasting our position over the vox without any clear target,' Darya explained, just as the street reverberated with the shuddering bark of a nearby autocannon being fired, no more than a hundred yards away. Ullaeus and Darya both dived into the lee of the nearest wall, hunkering down to make themselves the smallest targets possible until the gunfire ceased.

'Or we could ask whoever's on the right end of that auto-cannon?' Darya said to Ullaeus, with a broad smile.

Darya led as they looked for a way towards the point the gunfire was coming from, picking their way through a derelict warehouse until they found themselves emerging at the centre of an escalating battle between an advancing Cadian force and an airborne enemy that Darya couldn't see.

At the centre of the street, a Cadian soldier manned a fixed autocannon from the shallow slope of a crater, the weapon's elevation as high as its tripod would allow. Behind and around him, Cadians took cover below the crater's lip and in doorways and behind fractured buttresses, their own weapons trained skywards.

'Drones?' Ullaeus asked from behind Darya.

Darya dragged Ullaeus back as the sound of hissing jets grew from a whisper to a piercing scream. Plasma fire raked the Cadians on the street, lancing down from the sky followed by a gout of smoking black flame, just as the autocannon roared back into life.

'Cover!' Darya shouted.

She let go of Ullaeus as they both darted deeper into the building. The flyer landed outside, and Darya caught a glimpse of a boxy robotic head nestled atop broad shoulders – a Crisis suit, with two weaponless drones hovering at its back.

Its shoulder-mounted weapons opened up on the Cadian position, whilst an arm-mounted flamer sprayed liquid fire in a wide arc. Even from within the building, Darya could feel the heat prickling at her sweat-drenched skin.

But the Cadians didn't take the fire lightly; the autocannon rattled back into life along with a handful of lasguns, their volleys splashing off an azure-coloured dome of energy that sparked into life in front of the Crisis suit, faint hexagons burning white-hot beneath the blue light.

'What do we do?' Ullaeus hissed.

Ullaeus was one of the best snipers in the regiment, if not the battle group; Darya knew he wasn't asking for instructions.

He was asking if they should continue their mission and leave the Cadians outside to their fate, or do whatever they could to help them.

'They're Cadian.'

'Understood.'

'Take out the shield drones first,' Darya ordered over the reverberating gunfire, pointing out the two unarmed drones that hovered in the Crisis suit's shadow.

She and Ullaeus sprang forwards, taking up firing positions behind the reassuringly thick reinforced doorframe.

'I've got left!' Ullaeus barked.

'I've got right – fire!' Darya shouted back, and two hissing beams of white light lanced from their long-lasrifles across the short space into the shield drones.

Darya's shot thumped into her drone's exposed underside, but it did nothing but spray a short burst of sparks. Ullaeus' shot was blocked by a haze of azure light that sprang up milliseconds before it could hit home.

Neither shot had taken down its target.

'What the–' Ullaeus cursed, but Darya was already dragging him into a new position. Plasma fire ripped through the reinforced stonework of the warehouse's doorway, showering them both with brick dust and vaporised mortar.

'We got its attention, at least!' Darya spat as she led Ullaeus deeper into the warehouse towards a set of rusting metal stairs that led to the floor above. They raced up, their boots making the metal ring as they passed, their fatigue forgotten beneath a surge of combat adrenaline. They were able to take up new positions overlooking the street from the first floor, just as the Crisis suit used its flamer to immolate the ground floor.

The Cadians were pulling back now that the snipers had diverted the Crisis suit's attention, using the momentary break in fire to drag the autocannon back from the crater into a new firing position further down the street. Darya was glad; shielded as it was, the Crisis suit was more than a match for the Imperial soldiers.

'Left drone on my mark,' Darya ordered as they took cover below the empty upper window frames. 'Fire!'

Darya and Ullaeus fired in unison, and this time both their shots smacked home into the shield drone's upper armour plating. They burned through into the blasphemous machine's innards, shorting its workings with a sudden plume of blue flame, and it dropped from the air to smash on the street below.

The Crisis suit's head jerked up, and Darya found herself eye to lens with the xenos mech. There was something about the way it held itself in that moment, in its posture or bearing, that communicated the battlesuit's anger at her actions.

It was then that Darya understood it wasn't the mech that was angry – that was an organic emotion. What she was seeing was the anger of the battlesuit's pilot, which meant that somewhere deep in the guts of that machine was a xenos warrior, one that she was looking into the eyes of through the lens in the helmet assembly.

If it had a pilot, then that meant the pilot could be killed.

'Time to move, boss!' Ullaeus shouted and ran from the room. Darya hesitated, just for a moment. It was long enough for the Crisis suit's shoulder-mounted weapons to swivel and take aim.

An autocannon shell smashed through the Crisis suit's head, spraying sparks and mangled components across its armoured shoulders as the Cadian las-fire resumed from the street below.

The shoulder-mounted weapons fired anyway, spraying the upper floor of the warehouse as Darya dived back from the window. She made a mental note to thank whoever was manning the autocannon and scrambled from the room.

Ullaeus was already firing in the next room, so Darya passed it by and dived into the last room on the landing. It was bare but for a little metal desk and the long-dead corpse of its last occupant. The body was slumped in the corroded frame of a chair behind the desk, the flesh seared from its bones and left to rot to thin leather in Miracil's air.

She stepped past it without a second look, and took in the scene through the thin window beyond.

In the street below, the Crisis suit lurched around as if drunk, firing blindly into the building opposite as it tried, and failed, to fight off the Cadians who poured gunfire at it and its lone remaining shield drone. The jets mounted to its rear hissed and spluttered, but were apparently too damaged to lift the xenos mech out of danger.

A throaty roar filled the street alongside the squeal of metal caterpillar tracks churning across stone, and a Chimera transport ground into view behind the Cadians fighting on the street. Its multi-laser screeched into life, spitting bolts of white light against the Crisis suit's shield as it drove towards the xenos at full speed.

Darya stood back and watched eagerly as the Chimera smashed into the Crisis suit, blunt human dogma crushing xenos blasphemy beneath its titanic weight before the damaged jets could carry the mech clear. The Chimera driver slewed the transport around, dragging the t'au with it, trapped beneath the vehicle's thick front armour plating.

With a sudden twist of comprehension, Darya called out.

'Ullaeus, get back from the–'

The Chimera's engine gunned, its exhausts spewing black promethium fumes as it lurched forwards and crashed through the warehouse wall directly beneath Ullaeus. The entire building shuddered with the impact and seemed to sag, groaning beneath its own weight as years of dust were shaken from the bare rafters.

The corpse at the desk fell limply to the floor and shattered, scattering mouldering bones across the bare plascrete as the building lurched again. Darya kept her footing by holding tight to the window frame, just as the Cadians finished off the remaining shield drone.

Ullaeus appeared in the doorway, covered in plascrete dust and bleeding from a fresh cut over his left ear that had already plastered his hair to the side of his head. He slumped against the doorframe and blinked a few times.

'We really need to move,' he said as the building shifted again, and had to grab the doorframe to keep his feet.

'You good there, Iago?'

'I'll be fine. We don't have time.'

'Agreed,' Darya said, and followed Ullaeus out of the room towards the stairs they had used to get to the first floor. The fight still raged on outside the shattered windows.

The suit was pinned beneath the transport, one arm ripped off at the shoulder, whilst the other held the weight of the Chimera's bulkhead from crushing its torso.

But whatever source of power the suit had, it was failing fast.

The elbow joint began to tremble first, its servos whining as it fought against the mass that pinned it to the floor, fractures appearing in the armour plating to reveal the straining xenos tech beneath.

The Chimera's treads moved in a metallic blur, churning up the plascrete floor of the warehouse as it scrambled for grip, until it inevitably found purchase. The vehicle slewed sideways once more and its right treads tore chunks from the Crisis suit's torso, and with a crunching, grating sound, the transport crushed the suit beneath its weight like a mess tin beneath an ogryn's boot.

The suit stropped thrashing in the dirt and dust, and showed no further signs of life as the Chimera backed out of the building. Lumps of dislodged brick fell on its armoured back with thudding impacts. Darya and Ullaeus followed it out of the cavernous hole it had made in the warehouse wall, ignoring the dark fluids leaking from the Crisis suit's crushed torso.

Outside, the surviving Cadians made to secure the street against further threats, jogging past the transport in good order under the eyes of a sergeant that Darya recognised.

Her suspicions were confirmed when the turret hatch of the Chimera opened and Lieutenant Munro did his best to clamber out, hampered by a number of wounds that were patched in browning gauze. He held himself stiffly as he swung his legs clear of the hatch, the stump of his left forearm held tight to his chest.

'You damn near ruined a well-prepared ambush, Sergeant Nevic,' he said as he slid down the Chimera's slanted front armour, which had been stripped back to shining metal in the fight against the Crisis suit. 'We've been tracking that bastard for over an hour. Last survivor of a cadre that were holding an intersection due west of here.'

'I'm sorry, sir. We were only trying to–' Darya began, but Munro rounded on her before she could explain.

'Don't waste your time and mine on excuses, sergeant. I want to know why we still can't raise Captain Kohl on the vox. I saw your flare almost an hour ago.'

Munro swayed once he'd finished speaking, as if the effort it had taken to get the words out had drained his dwindling reserves of strength. Darya could see the grey pallor of his skin beneath the dirt and grime, the lack of focus in Munro's eyes. The man was clearly running on stimms and sheer force of will, as if to spite the injuries that should have laid him low. She resisted the urge to hold out an arm to try to steady the officer;

she knew he would resent it, and she didn't know if she would have the strength to spare.

'The Kintair are in position, sir, but the new channels are encoded. We need to get the cypher to Captain Kohl as soon as we can, but it'd take hours on foot.'

'Afraid of hoofing it for a while, sergeant?' Munro half sneered, before wincing with pain.

'No, sir. Just afraid of letting the captain down,' Ullaeus spoke up from behind Darya.

Munro's gaze wavered.

'You need our Chimera.'

'Yes, sir,' Darya said.

Munro sighed and looked up the street at his remaining men. There were less than ten of them still standing, with half a dozen casualties being tended to by their comrades or lying dead on the plascrete.

'Take it.'

'Thank you, sir. We'll send help back–'

'You're wasting precious time, sergeant. Get going.'

Darya bit back her anger and forced herself to salute the superior officer, then ran to the Chimera. Munro was already shouting orders to the driver as Darya and Ullaeus piled into the troop compartment, and the transport leaped forwards before the rear hatch had even begun to close. Darya gave up a quiet prayer to the Emperor to look after Lieutenant Munro and his soldiers as they flashed past in the closing hatch and then disappeared from sight completely.

'Fragging trueborn Cadians,' Ullaeus swore.

The journey to Trackway Span was faster by Chimera, but no easier.

Every few minutes the driver shouted for them to get low

or to brace as t'au air assets tore by overhead, most seemingly passing within inches of the transport judging by how badly they vibrated the occupants within.

'What's going on out there?' Darya shouted into the vox after the third close flyover in as many minutes. Of all the ways to die, being burned alive in an exploding troop carrier wasn't one she'd necessarily choose.

'Looks like the some of the t'au are pulling out, back towards the Spatka,' the driver's voice crackled back, distorted by the hum of yet another flyer overhead. *'Vox coverage is still patchy, but I'll see if I can find out more.'*

'Pulling out or regrouping?' Ullaeus said as Darya took her seat opposite him.

'They'll be regrouping. The rest of the Two-Hundred-and-Seventeenth will be rolling up pockets of resistance across the low city. Why make a final stand here, right at the start of the war?'

'Makes sense. If I were them, I'd be pulling back over the Spatka to use it as a natural barrier,' Ullaeus mused. 'But if we were the only ones to capture our bridge...'

'Then Trackway Span is about to get hit hard,' Darya said. 'Do you think we've got enough of the God-Emperor's grace to see us through it?'

'Don't let Commissar Tsutso hear you saying that.' Ullaeus flashed a thin smile. 'The might of the righteous will always prevail and all that.'

Darya shook her head. Nothing about the last two days had felt right to her, fighting over a city that had long since lost any value to either side.

'They'd burned the lower city long before we turned up,' Darya said, hoping that by speaking her thoughts aloud they might coalesce into a coherent view of the situation. 'No rats or rodents, not even in the sewers. They're withdrawing from the lower city...'

'Way above our pay grade,' Ullaeus said. He pulled a water canteen from his satchel and offered it to Darya, who accepted it with a nod. She didn't comment on the Kintair markings etched into the shoulder of the canteen; she'd long since learned not to ask where Iago Ullaeus managed to scrounge useful things. 'I'd put money on it being linked to that team you saw back at the square, though.'

'Probably,' Darya agreed, and passed the canteen back. 'But what were the team in black doing behind our lines?'

'If they were snipers like you say, it could be anything. If it were us, it'd be any of the big three.'

'Assassination, sabotage or area denial. I'd rule out the last one given they were withdrawing...'

'Which leaves assassination or sabotage... and I'm not sure we'd notice a sabotage in our advance,' Ullaeus said with a grim smile.

The Chimera lurched sideways and came to a grinding halt before Darya could respond, the hull ringing with sudden impacts from plasma weapons.

'*We're here, but we're a damned big target,*' the driver's voice called out.

'We'll make the rest of the journey on foot,' Darya called back, and Ullaeus made towards the rear hatch.

'*I think you might have to, sergeant,*' the driver replied.

Once they were outside the transport, Darya could see what he meant.

'God-Emperor on His throne,' she swore.

Trackway Span still stood, but the t'au energy weapons had taken their toll on the once proud structure. Stanchions had finally been brought down, whilst the bridge's surface was pitted and cracked like the iron relics recovered from the salt sea on Cocleratum.

As they watched, a lance of blue-white light flashed across the river into the bridge's side, reducing the carved cherubim to atoms in a spray of stone and discharged lightning. Cadians manning the barricades on the near bank scattered as debris showered from the sky, each fragment of shattered ferrocrete the size of a man's torso.

'Thone!' Ullaeus swore. 'It's taken a beating.'

'It's made of stern stuff,' Darya said as she led Ullaeus towards the forward Cadian positions at a run. 'At least I hope it is. We'll need it again if the xenos push back the beachhead.'

'True enough – I don't fancy swimming the Spatka.'

'I don't think we'd get a chance to swim back, Iago.'

The improvised fortifications they'd come through earlier in the night had been reinforced with sandbags and prefabricated barricades, backed up by moulded plascrete fortifications that bore the tell-tale mark of the Adeptus Mechanicus.

'They've not forgotten about us, at least,' Ullaeus said as they were waved through the rear defences and into a shelled-out building that overlooked the bridge. There, they found a haggard-looking sergeant broadcasting over the vox. He looked up as the snipers entered.

'Sergeant Nevic,' he said by way of greeting.

'Sergeant Dorran,' Darya replied with a nod. 'We need to speak to Captain Kohl – any chance you've been able to raise him on vox?'

'Not yet. There's a signal, God-Emperor be praised, but we're locked out of the active channels,' Dorran explained, leading Darya and Ullaeus to a window that overlooked Trackway Span. 'We've had some limited supplies from the rear, but there's no way a tank is getting over that – not while we're under fire like this.'

Darya could see that he was right. From the window's vantage point, she could see patches of the bridge had been blown away entirely, either by fire from the opposite bank or aerial assault. There were even spots where the bridge's surface had given way entirely, and the rushing waters of the Spatka were visible beneath the contorted reinforcement bars.

'That's a long way to walk in the open,' Ullaeus murmured.

'Who said anything about walking?' Dorran said with a yellow-toothed grin.

He led them through to a room in the rear of the building. It was empty but for the loose rubble banked up against the walls, rolls of bloodied bandages and a dirtcycle.

'An officer came through a few hours back and left this behind. He hasn't come back to collect it yet,' Dorran explained. He rapped a knuckle against the fuel tank, and the dull ring told them that there was still a good amount of promethium left inside. 'I guessed that the God-Emperor had some other plan in mind for it.'

'This could work. It's exposed, sure, but if we're fast enough...' Ullaeus said.

Darya looked over the bike. It looked battered yet serviceable, but there was another problem.

'I've never ridden one of these,' Darya said, looking from Dorran to Ullaeus.

'I have,' Ullaeus said, 'in a past life anyway.'

'We'll set up the covering fire from our side, keep the xenos' heads down long enough for you to get to the other side,' Dorran offered.

'Get your men ready, we need to be quick,' Darya said. Dorran jogged from the room and started shouting orders, whilst Darya and Ullaeus unclasped their cloaks and stowed them in their packs. Loose clothing was a bad idea around exposed machinery, and the cloaks were too valuable to get damaged.

Ullaeus passed his long-las to Darya and rolled the dirtcycle outside, into the cover of a nearby barricade. A couple of troopers raised their eyebrows as Ullaeus began reciting the litany of activation and pumped the starter. Their expressions turned to laughter as he tried a second time, a third, a fourth, until the engine clattered into life on the fifth attempt. The dirtcycle was clearly in need of a tech-priest's attention.

'Come on, boss,' Ullaeus said as he swung his leg over the saddle and shifted the bike's weight into a standing position. Darya stepped onto the rear of the seat and took a firm grip on the reinforced material covering Ullaeus' shoulders.

'Go.'

Ullaeus gunned the engine and the dirtcycle lurched forwards out of cover towards the pocked surface of Trackway Span. The movement sparked a redoubling in the rate of fire from the t'au positions on the eastern bank, and Darya could just hear Sergeant Dorran bellowing at his men over the sound of lasguns, autocannons and heavy bolters spitting white-hot rounds across the river at the distant t'au positions.

Ullaeus clearly had some skill with a bike, Darya had to admit. He urged the dirtcycle to uncomfortable speeds, grazing the rims of craters and weaving between piles of fallen masonry as they made the bridge. The covering fire only kept the t'au's heads down for a short period however, and soon the air was filled with return fire that not only targeted the Cadian positions on the western bank, but also the two snipers trying to pass over the bridge.

'End in sight!' Ullaeus shouted as they crested the side of a particularly deep crater, ducking low as plasma rounds flashed past close enough for Darya to smell the ozone they left in their wake. She followed their dissipating trails back to their source: a black-armoured figure on a rooftop only a couple of hundred feet away, their silhouette flickering against the dawn sky as they aimed a long rifle down at Darya and Ullaeus.

The figure fired again.

'Ullaeus!'

Darya's arms were wrenched from Ullaeus as the dirtcycle was ripped from beneath her, launching her into the air in a breathless moment of weightlessness. It ended in a painful, bone-jarring thud that became a skin-scouring slide across the rough plascrete and debris of the bridge's surface.

It took her a few seconds of looking directly down into the stinking brown waters of the Spatka to realise that she'd finally come to a stop, and several more to urge her battered body into movement.

Heavy-bolter shells tore ragged chunks from the rooftop where the t'au had been, but Darya knew that any sniper who could make that shot would know to relocate before their enemy could retaliate.

It didn't mean that there weren't other sharpshooters waiting for their chance to strike. She moved as fast as her scoured and bruised body would allow, crawling on her belly into the relative cover of the bridge's surviving stanchions. The dirtcycle had come to rest less than twenty feet away, the crash leaving it a smoking ruin of twisted metal and smoking rubber.

'Ullaeus? Iago? Where are you?' she croaked, but the words were swallowed by the flickers of brilliant las-fire and streaks of white-hot plasma that stitched the air above her.

'We have him,' a voice said, as strong hands grabbed her upper arms and pulled her to her feet. Numbly, she let herself be dragged off the surface of Trackway Span, over the twisted rails and into cover on the far side, chased every step of the way by incoming fire.

She'd regained most of her senses by the time they passed over the ruins of the old t'au defences, their once pristine white metal scorched, gouged and muddied by Imperial traffic.

'Captain Kohl,' Darya managed to say, looking up into the face of someone she recognised but couldn't name.

'He's at forward command,' the trooper said and pushed Darya back as she tried to rise. She waved him off angrily and rose unsteadily to her feet. Ullaeus was on an improvised stretcher nearby, being tended to by a medicae in the same spot where Darya had shot the final t'au defender when her team had taken the position the day before. It felt like weeks ago.

'Get me to Captain Kohl, now,' Darya said.

Lieutenant Eridan watched the ships of the Adeptus Mechanicus descend from the sky, fat-bellied portable manufactoria that would add to the prefabricated complex that was taking shape on the landing grounds beyond Miracil.

A cup of recaff had gone cold in his grip as he watched the ships weave their way through the pre-dawn sky. He took a sip and sighed, his breath forming a fug in the morning chill.

Eridan was standing on the rear hatch of his command Chimera, listening to his vox-operators trying to raise Captain Kohl on the vox. In the transport opposite, he could just make out the silhouette of Major Wester in the sickly green glow of the holo-table, the miniaturised figures of the rest of the command staff moving animatedly as they discussed the current state of the Miracil campaign.

'Sir,' a voice said excitedly from inside his Chimera. 'Sir! I have a connection!'

Eridan tossed the cup aside, and darted back into the transport to snatch the proffered vox headset.

'Captain Kohl, please respond,' he said into the vox handset.

'*Eridan…*' a voice crackled, then cut out. The vox-operator retuned the set, adjusting dials until the signal came through clearer than before.

'*Eridan, is that you?*' the voice said. The hammering of gunfire could be heard beneath the voice, loud and close.

'Confirmed,' Eridan said.

'*Sergeant Nevic has just arrived. I'm officially requesting reinforcements, artillery support, air cover – whatever you can give us!*'

'Already on it, captain,' Eridan said breathlessly, chancing a nervous look over to Major Wester's transport. 'Can you confirm your coordinates?'

Kohl rattled off his positions and the dire state of his ammunition reserves. First Company still held Trackway Span's eastern bank, but their position was perilously tenuous.

'Thank you, captain – tell your men to keep their heads down,' Eridan said. He dropped the vox-set and ordered the operator to start coordinating the resupply of Trackway Span.

It was time to put Major Wester's plan into action.

Eridan moved to the next Chimera, where a vox-operator waited with an open line to Captain Bechmann from the 338th. Eridan took the offered set from the operator, and spoke into the vox handset.

'Captain Bechmann, we are go. Coordinates to follow,' Eridan said, then read out the coordinates that Captain Kohl had given him.

'*Understood,*' Captain Bechmann replied in her trademark drawl. '*Thunder is incoming.*'

Almost a mile away at the forward artillery positions, Eridan knew that a forest of Basilisk-mounted Earthshaker cannons would be traversing to take aim at the coordinates. It would be an incredible sight to see, but Eridan had more pressing concerns as he made his way to Major Wester's transport as fast as protocol allowed.

He approached the major from his right, and passed him a pre-prepared note as a holo-projection of a logistarum official droned on about equipment shortages and the lack of reliable supply routes.

'First in contact. Bechmann supporting,' the note said.

The major read the note and smiled, crushing the thin parchment slip in his fist.

'Is there something you'd care to share, Major Wester?' a voice sneered from the holo-table, silencing the nasal monotone of the logistarum official who had been speaking.

Colonel Wassenby's taut, severe features were cast in glowing green, giving him the look of a vengeful wraith straight from the children's rhymes back on Cadia. There were others around the table, other high-ranking officers and advisors, most clearly far from the front lines.

'We have an update from First Company at Trackway Span. We have redeployed assets to support, and–'

'Ah yes, Captain Kohl's company,' Wassenby said with a shake of his head. Eridan couldn't say whether the interruption was due to the momentary lag common to surface-to-fleet communications or sheer rudeness, but he knew which he'd bet his money on.

'I have given their situation some thought, and given the isolated nature of their position it would be best if they–'

'Isolated? Isolated how?' a heavily bearded man drawled, the pale cast of his skin down to more than the holo-table's less-than-flattering hue. It was said that Lord Sylvester of House Gyrrant rarely left the throne of his Knight these days, and it showed in the wisps of thinning hair scraped across his liver-spotted scalp and the loose skin of his face and neck: tell-tale signs of weight lost to sudden illness.

'First Company have taken the eastern bank at Trackway Span,' Wester explained. 'We have diverted some support elements to reinforce their position, including artillery.'

As if to punctuate his words, the ground shook as the barrage began. The lumens in the Chimera flickered as the waves of subterranean thunder rolled over them and through the transport's suspension.

'*I will divert a lance to their position,*' Lord Sylvester said, but Colonel Wassenby countermanded him.

'*You will not, Lord Sylvester. You will consolidate your forces as previously agreed. Major Wester, you will order Captain Kohl to withdraw from Trackway Span with all haste, so that we might–*'

'*Withdraw?*'

Lord Sylvester's voice shook with barely restrained contempt.

'*Why would we withdraw? They have taken the only intact bridge for five miles in either direction! Without the foothold at Trackway Span the Miracil assault becomes a drawn-out siege. You'll lose as many men to the bitter winter as the enemy guns.*'

Eridan had known Wester for long enough to know when the man was trying to suppress a smile, and the curl at the corner of his lips was growing.

'*Their position is isolated and we do not have the reserves required to both hold that position and prepare for the next stage of the assault,*' Wassenby seethed, speaking as if to a child.

'*There will be no next stage without bridges across the Spatka. My Knights cannot walk that river, nor can we fly over it,*' Lord Sylvester said.

'That's not to mention the effect a withdrawal would have on morale,' Wester added.

Colonel Wassenby ran his tongue over his teeth as he moved to clasp his hands behind his back, his expression cold even through the limited resolution of the holo-projector.

'If you dare to order a withdrawal, Colonel Wassenby,' said Lord Sylvester, his hololithic representation lethally still, *'I will march my Knights into the breach myself and we will hold it until my house's blood is all but spent.'*

All present, both in the flesh and by holo-table, knew that it would be a waste of House Gyrrant's Knights. They were line-breakers, attacking assets who were most effective on the charge. If they were used isolated in static defence it would only be a matter of time before the t'au picked them off.

'Very well,' Colonel Wassenby said finally, looking to the advisors on either side of him. *'Reinforce First Company with reserves from the Four-Hundred-and-First and the Three-Hundred-and-Thirty-Eighth. Major Wester, prepare for my arrival. I will be taking more direct control of the Miracil front.'*

The light of the holo-table cut out with a flash of static, and the semicircle of figures disappeared.

'What now, sir?' Eridan asked. He felt as if they had won a significant victory that morning, but one which all but guaranteed that the battle ahead would be both gruelling and brutal. Their only hope was to force their advantage and keep up their momentum.

'My part's been played,' Major Wester said, placing his fists on the holo-table as he hunched forwards. 'You have work to do, with the Four-Hundred-and-First and the Three-Hundred-and-Thirty-Eighth.'

Darya watched the first shells fall from the barricades, where she'd taken up a position overlooking the streets approaching the Cadian line. She had run out of ammunition for her long-las and had taken up a standard lasrifle from the hands of a fallen Cadian. She was putting it to good use on the waves of human and t'au soldiers, drones and flying mech suits that tried desperately to find the gap in the Cadian defences and land a killing blow.

They scattered as the trickle of artillery fire became a stream, then a flood.

Darya felt like Miracil itself must crack beneath the destructive power of the Imperial guns, hammering buildings flat and raising plumes of blasted earth hundreds of yards into the air. The t'au turned and fled, scattering towards their own lines to the east, chased all the way by Imperial shells and gunfire. Commissar Tsutso was roaring a litany of hatred against the xenos as they ran, standing heroically over a barricade and brandishing his chainsword.

Darya wanted to play her part in it, to revel in the victory hard won, but with each shot her focus drained away and her aim became less sure. Her shots missed, first by inches and then by yards, her hands shaking as she tried in vain to rub the gritty sensation from her eyes.

There was nothing more she could accomplish here, nothing more she could add. She had done her part, and she was spent.

She handed over her lasrifle to the first soldier she passed, and made for the medicae station to the rear of the Cadian positions. Corporal Ullaeus had been placed on a makeshift pallet bed near where Yanna rested fitfully, her face half-hidden beneath a thick pad of bandages. Ullaeus was little better, his face purple with fresh bruises, runnels of dried blood crusting in the contours of his ears. His breathing was shallow and uneven, as if each breath were painful even to his unconscious mind.

Darya took a seat between them and closed her eyes, rocked to sleep by the drumming thunder outside, telling herself that she was in her father's sprawling manse by the great salt sea. The clamour outside was the crashing of waves on the rocky shore, and the screaming of shells was nothing more than the call of avians roosting in the high towers of her home world.

14

Inhale.

Hold the breath. Allow the frigid air to warm in your lungs. It is the breath of the world, and only by accepting it may you become part of it.

Exhale.

Trust in your helmet's rebreather functions to dissipate the hot steam of your breath. It is an advantage that our enemy does not possess. Look how it hangs over their positions, how it stirs as their leaders walk their lines. It is the will of the world made manifest. Trust in it, as we have placed our trust in you.

Trust in the strength of your weapon, in the strength of your body, but know it is your conviction that is your truest weapon, and it is never stronger than when it is guided by the greater will.

You see the soft plumes of their breath on the air. Do you feel the will of this world guiding your aim? It calls to you, as prey must call to the predator. It is the natural order of things – the harmony of the universe manifest.

Do you see them? The one with authority? They are the head of the serpent. Without them, the body will wither and die.

They are fools, these gue'la, to believe that a distant god could contend with the Greater Good.

Show them the error of their ways.

Land the killing blow.

'SNIPER!'

The cry echoed through the foundry, carried on a wave of primal fear that no amount of discipline, drills or training could stamp out.

Darya ran towards the shout as the soldiers around her dived into cover, running in a low crouch to present the smallest possible target as she darted between piles of debris and fallen roof panels. She slowed as the shouts grew quieter, replaced by cries of anguish and barked orders.

Almost there.

She stepped through an improvised doorway blown through the side of a frozen furnace and into the hall beyond.

Darya no longer felt any awe when she entered the impossibly large manufactoria – though their scale was something beyond her imagining even in their dilapidated and ruined state – but the foundry still stirred something in her stomach.

Plascrete buttresses held back walls of blackened metal, each higher than a hab-block and ten times as ornate. The two-tone skull of the Adeptus Mechanicus stared blindly down over thick baths of solidified ore, whilst crucibles the size of Leman Russ battle tanks were suspended from overhead cranes, left to rust in the dark.

Darya noted the ample cover provided by the extinguished furnaces along the right wall and the gantries hidden in the shadowed ceiling almost a hundred yards above. The enemy sniper could be hidden anywhere.

Cadian troopers knelt in cover behind buttresses and baths of slag-encrusted metals, reaching no more than a third of the way into the hall.

'Do you have eyes on the shooter?' Darya called out.

'No!' a corporal shouted back.

'It's Sergeant Rast!' a man shouted from far deeper into the room. 'I can get to him if I just–'

'Stay where you are, all of you,' Darya yelled back, pressing herself deeper into cover. 'Everyone stay down until I say otherwise.'

They obeyed. Darya may only have been a sergeant, but in that moment she had the highest authority, no matter the stripes that anyone else in the room wore.

'Team, I'm in the foundry room south of assembly room kappa,' Darya muttered into the vox. 'Is anyone nearby to assist?'

'Negative, myself and Yanna are tied up to the north,' Arfit voxed back.

'I'm with Bellis a room away, give me a minute,' Ullaeus' voice crackled a moment later.

Gunfire, both Imperial lasgun and t'au pulse rifle, echoed through the halls of the industrial complex in an arhythmic background staccato. Orders were bellowed in Low Gothic and foul xenos cant, the t'au words unintelligible but their meaning clear.

'At least one shooter, most likely at height, no clear position as yet,' Darya explained over the vox, preparing him for what he would be walking into.

'Understood. I'll keep my head down.'

'Psst!' Darya hissed at a nearby Cadian, sheltering behind a nearby ore bath. 'Throw me your helmet.'

The Cadian, a young woman, looked confused but complied. Steam rose from the woollen hat she'd been wearing beneath her helmet as she threw it to where Darya knelt. Darya would have used her own, but she'd not worn a helmet for years; they were too bulky and noisy for stealth work.

'What are you–' the trooper began, but Darya pressed a finger to her lips to silence her. With practised balance, she secured the helmet to the butt of her rifle and slowly raised it over her head, as if she were a trooper inching their way out of cover to get a good look at the ground ahead.

She forced herself to breathe as the heartbeats ticked by, ready for the buzz-smack of the plasma round that had to be coming.

Inhale. Exhale.

The squad watched intently as she moved the helmet still further, just short of revealing that it wasn't being worn.

Inhale. Exhale.

Any second now. The sniper would take the bait any second…

Darya pulled the helmet back with a muttered curse.

'Friendly incoming,' Ullaeus said, close by. He picked his way over a low scattering of furnace fuel that had escaped a ruptured containment tower, and made his way to Darya.

He had his cameleoline cloak wrapped tight about his shoulders and his hood up, which seemed to blur the edges of his silhouette in the poor light as the cloak took on the colours and hues of the environment.

'Good to see you,' Darya said as he dropped into cover next to her.

'And you, boss.' Ullaeus gave her a tense nod.

'No takers,' Darya said, before plucking the helmet from the butt of her rifle and tossing it back to the trooper. 'My thanks.'

'They could have relocated?' Ullaeus offered.

'No. They're still there.'

She knew the sniper hadn't moved because she wouldn't have either; they'd killed an officer without being seen, so they were safe for at least one more shot.

Unless there were counter-snipers hunting in the area.

Holding tightly to her rifle, Darya dropped to her stomach and slowly edged around the contoured side of the ore bath and crawled deeper into the hall, Ullaeus following in her wake. They kept to the shadows, using the pillars and dangling crucibles to block the line of sight to the most likely positions of the sniper nests, until they came within sight of the fallen sergeant.

A clearly shaken corporal knelt behind a ruined crucible, its foot-thick alloy skin flaking with corrosion. The corporal was agitated, as if fighting the urge to run to his officer's side.

'What's your name, corporal?' Darya asked as she took a knee in front of him.

'Corporal Lenz, ma'am,' the man replied.

'Oh, best not to call her that, makes her feel old,' Ullaeus said with a smile.

Darya took an offered strip of mirrorglass from Ullaeus and carefully extended it under the domed base of the crucible; Sergeant Rast lay prone only a few yards short of a red-robed corpse.

Bait.

'Okay, Corporal Lenz, I'm going to need your helmet and your lasgun,' Darya said and began to pull her cloak off over her head.

'Woah, I really think that I should be the one wearing the get-up,' Ullaeus argued.

'I really think you should get ready to shoot the bastard,' Darya said with a grin.

'I'm serious. I'd rather not have to explain to Captain Kohl why I'm still here if you're not. Besides, it's definitely my turn.'

'Damn it,' Darya muttered. She knew her corporal was talking sense, but it didn't make the decision any easier.

'Give me your helmet, Lenz,' Ullaeus said, and held out his hand for the other corporal's gear. He dropped everything that might weigh him down – his laspistol joined his satchel and cloak in an unkempt pile, but he took the time to hand Lenz his long-las as he took the other man's lasgun.

'You look after that until I'm back,' Ullaeus said with a nod, then slipped on the borrowed helmet, the corporal's stripes emblazoned across the front. It was odd to see Ullaeus wearing any symbol of his rank, since snipers never wore any.

'Remember, cover to cover. Don't stay in the open any longer–'

'I've got it, boss,' Ullaeus said, cutting across Darya as he readied the unfamiliar weight of the lasgun in his hand. Darya gave him a reassuring nod and slipped to the other end of the crucible, edging out as far as she dared without exposing herself completely.

'I don't understand,' Corporal Lenz said. 'What are you–'

'Go,' Darya hissed.

Ullaeus burst out of cover and sprinted across Darya's eyeline, but her job wasn't to watch him. Her eyes were fixed on the high rafters and the inky shadows in the deepest recesses of the roof, watching for any sign of movement that would give their target away.

She forced herself to remain still even as her heart hammered, waiting for the muzzle flash that could end her corporal's life.

Darya had been shot at with many weapons in her twenty-five standard years, and each made a different sound. Las-bolts barely made a noise as they passed by, more a whooshing of displaced air than an identifiable signature. Solid-shot rounds sounded like the flapping of insects sped up to incredible speed, the larger the round the deeper the thrum of wings.

As the enemy sniper fired from the deepest recesses of the shadowed roof, she knew that the plasma round that skimmed past Ullaeus' head was the hissing of water on a white-hot blade, angry and carnivorous as it burned through the chill air.

Her reaction was almost pure instinct; the stock of her long-las hit her shoulder in the same instant that her eye settled into the scope, already zeroed into the point where the shot had come from. Then she squeezed the trigger.

A figure dropped from the rafters at the far end of the room, falling bonelessly through the air like a child's doll to land on the edge of a distant ore bath. It bounced from the rim with a wet slap, and came to rest on the ground beyond.

'I say we let Corporal Lenz confirm that one,' Ullaeus said over the vox, his tone saturated with mock disgust.

'Agreed. I think we're clear.'

Cadians broke cover as news of the all clear filtered through the ranks, and worked their way forwards through the ample cover in the room. Darya was more cautious, and continued to watch the high reaches of the room until she was sure that the sniper had been working alone. Only then did she advance towards the pair of prone forms on the ground ahead.

Darya moved over to the sergeant's body and turned him carefully onto his back. As she had surmised, he was dead: a blackened hole had been scored through the centre of his flak armour, destroying his heart and lungs in a blast of superheated viscera. The wound still smoked, letting off a stink of burned carbon and scorched meat.

'Sergeant Nevic,' a voice said from next to her, and she straightened up. It was Corporal Lenz.

'Your squad showed good discipline today,' Darya said. The corporal slipped his gear back on and took back his rifle when Ullaeus emerged.

Lenz looked down at Sergeant Rast, a tic pulling on the skin below his right eye as his mouth tightened into a severe line.

'Corporal?' Ullaeus said as Darya pulled on her gear. 'You okay there, Lenz?'

'We're being killed by inches,' Lenz said, his throat tight. 'One by fragging one.'

Darya looked from Lenz's violet eyes to Sergeant Rast's and let out a sigh.

'He's with the God-Emperor now,' Darya said. The words felt like a hollow consolation, but Lenz nodded as if he appreciated them. 'Do you know your orders?'

'Yes, sergeant,' Lenz said. 'We were to secure this hall and the infrastructure and link up with Lieutenant Munro.'

'Best hop to it then, corporal,' Darya said, making an attempt at a reassuring smile. 'Looks like you're the acting sergeant now.'

Lenz thanked the snipers, then assembled his men for the push into the next section. They moved forwards carefully towards a twenty-yard-high hole blown in the far wall, some thanking Darya and Ullaeus whilst others reverently made the sign of the aquila and offered short prayers as they passed by.

'Squad, another sniper down in the field. Keep your eyes open and your weapons ready,' Darya said into her vox-bead, and listened for the chorus of acknowledgements.

'Obvious bait,' Ullaeus sighed as he looked from Sergeant Rast's prone form to the bundle of red robes and augmetics a few yards away.

'Obvious to us,' Darya said. 'Less so to a group of sleep-deprived troopers rushing to make their rendezvous.'

She walked over to the robes and checked for traps or trip-wires as Ullaeus closed Rast's eyes and said a short benediction to the God-Emperor. She found no obvious traps, so slowly peeled back the red robes from the body beneath.

It had been a tech-adept or tech-priest, that much was clear from the collection of complex augmetics that made up almost half of the body. The flesh elements had long since rotted away, leaving little more than a patina of organic residue on the brass and dark steel structures. The lenses that replaced its organic eyes had been shattered, and the mechanical limbs bent and twisted as if they had been beaten by heavy weights. Here and there, tool marks were visible on strengthening struts and alloyed bones.

Not as if, Darya thought. *This creature literally was beaten to death.*

A slim claw-like appendage grasped a slip of parchment no longer than Darya's finger, its surface marred by punched chits that formed a coded message that Darya couldn't read. She teased it from the adept's cold steel fingers, being careful not to tear the thin material as she held it up to the light.

'What's that?' Ullaeus asked.

'No idea,' Darya replied, then slipped the parchment into her satchel. 'Whatever it is, it doesn't seem right to leave it around for the xenos to find.'

Ullaeus grumbled a noise of agreement.

'Boss?' Yanna's voice crackled suddenly.

'Receiving, Yanna,' Darya said, pressing the vox-bead deeper into her ear. It was an unnecessary habit from her days in the Coclerati Janissaries, when the equipment had been far inferior to what she had been issued in the Cadian 217th, but old habits died hard.

'I've received an update from Captain Kohl, he's asking for you.'

'Okay, patch him through,' Darya said.

'No, boss, he's asking for you to come back,' Yanna's voice crackled. *'Said it's too sensitive for vox.'*

Darya swore inwardly and released the vox-bead.

'Tell him I'm on my way,' Darya replied, 'I want you all teamed up whilst I'm away – move in pairs and watch each other's backs. All clear?'

The squad voxed their agreement.

'You reckon this is the big push?' Ullaeus asked, raising an eyebrow.

'God-Emperor knows,' Darya replied. 'Do you think we have enough left for an attack like that?'

Ullaeus looked down at Sergeant Rast, whose skin was turning the sickly grey of bloodless flesh. He didn't offer an answer.

15

Why do we strike at their leaders?

That is a complex question, with no simple answer in your tongue.

To the T'au'va it is por'sral – the battlefield of the mind. Honoured Mui'el is an expert in such things, but we fire caste have our own ways.

The ta'lissera, *our sacred bond binding warrior-spirits together, is not unique to the t'au. The humans forge their own bonds, in blood, on the battlefield. To break such a bond can be fatal, unleashing a despair that can break the enemy as surely as the most perfect* Mont'ka.

We wound so they might watch their bond-mates bleed. We strike at their leaders so they have nowhere to look for guidance, but to us.

We kill their idols, so they have nothing left to believe in.

Darya's route back through the foundry complex took her through cleared halls of manufactorum lines, blasted refectories that stank of mould and long-spoiled food, and courtyards dominated by statues dedicated to Adeptus Mechanicus luminaries and effigies that Darya didn't recognise. All bore the scars of hard fighting, from scorched and pitted walls to bloodstained floors.

She passed heavy weapon squads relocating to support the forward positions, medicae auxiliaries stretchering the wounded and the dead to the relative safety of the rear, and troopers making ammunition runs.

It had been three weeks since the Cadian 217th had taken Trackway Span – three weeks of fighting the xenos to a stand-still across what had been dubbed the Cadian Salient. It was the only Imperial foothold on the eastern bank of the Spatka, a bulge in the front line that stretched deep into t'au territory.

Every yard of that territory had been won through hard fighting and the blood of the 217th, secured in part by the artillery bombardment that had caught a swathe of t'au forces in the field as they tried to push the 217th back over the Spatka. For almost a week, Darya had watched the Imperial Navy and Cadian artillery batter a mile-deep buffer zone between the 217th's defences and the t'au front lines. Nothing moved on that wasteland now, lest either side begin the bombardment anew – the Cadians with their shells or the t'au with their endless barrage of rockets.

Only one covered route remained to link the two sides: the industrial complex that stood on the southern quarter of the salient. It was an imposing black mass that clung to the edge of the Cadian line like a barnacle to the hull of a ship, so large that the 217th had named it Iron Hill. It had become the focus of the battle for Miracil as the Adeptus Mechanicus had forbade its destruction through wanton artillery bombardment, though, in Darya's mind, the troops that fought in its manufactoria and smelting halls were only a fraction less destructive.

Heavy-calibre rounds chuntered deep within the complex as she passed through the western approach and into the trenches of the Cadian Salient. They were a warren of switchbacked plascrete alleys, installed by the Adeptus Mechanicus under the cover of the week-long bombardment. Pre-cast sections of trench were dropped into servitor-dug excavations, and often on top of the waiting automata. Firing steps lined the eastern wall, facing the devastation of no-man's-land, whilst occasional gaps were left in the western wall for connecting trenches that led back to the Cadian command centre. The Cadians had dubbed it Creed's Row.

Darya waded through resting Cadians who lay on the firing steps or even the rough textured floor, wrapped in blankets and improvised sleeping sacks as they awaited their turn in the push-and-pull fighting in the industrial complex.

'Clear a path!' someone shouted from behind her, and Darya squeezed herself between two soldiers who sat with their backs against the trench wall, heads lolled in sleep despite the nearby gunfire. A stretcher team jogged past carrying a prone figure who was missing one of his arms, half of his face hidden beneath browning medi-dressings.

Darya used the gap the stretcher team left in their wake to reach the next communications trench, leaving Creed's Row for Sniper's Alley, which was far less ordered. The walls were scavenged plates of frost-rimed corrugated alloy and the occasional Aegis defence panel, all holed and scored by enemy plasma weapons, whilst the floor was little more than bricks and patches of plascrete that had been sunk into the mud floor.

The Cadians manning the trench all moved to let her pass with a muttered 'Sergeant Nevic' or a gestured aquila, which were returned with a nod or a friendly word to those she knew. She ignored those who whispered 'Ghost' reverently under their breath.

'Good hunting out there, sarge?' one trooper called from an improvised dugout cut into the trench wall, complete with a scavenged tarpaulin roof and a small fire. The call was taken up by others along the trench, but they took care to keep their heads below the trench lip; Sniper's Alley had earned its name in the two weeks since its construction.

'Some!' Darya called back, which brought fresh cheers from the troopers huddled together against the cold.

She passed through the trench to the western entrance, which began in the foundations of an abandoned manufactorum, then up through the basement and into the Cadian headquarters at Trackway Span.

The Cadian 217th had not been idle in their three weeks occupying the salient; Hydra anti-aircraft platforms were stationed outside the building and on the approach to the bridge, their long twin-linked cannons scouring the skies for enemy rocket strikes, drones and other flyers. The building itself had been cleared of the machinery and assembly lines that had snaked across its floor, replaced by medicae tents, portable generatoria and the sprawling headquarters centred around Captain Kohl's command Chimera.

Darya headed for the latter, resisting the urge to join the line of troopers queuing for heated rations, some talking in small groups whilst others watched the repeating roll of propaganda vids projected on the wall above them.

How long has it been since I last had a hot meal? Darya thought. *This is the first time I've left Iron Hill in three days, so it's at least that long.*

Static warfare had been the domain of the sniper since humanity had fired the first gunpowder weapons, and her team were stretched thin despite occasional support from the sharpshooters embedded in other units. What little rest they could get had been taken in the field, which invariably meant cold rations and little sleep.

'Sergeant Nevic,' a gruff voice said.

Captain Kohl limped out of his Chimera, leaning heavily on a crutch that clanked on the access-hatch ramp.

'Captain,' Darya said, giving Kohl a deferential nod as he weaved his way between the tables of vox-operators and snaking power cables. 'How's the leg, sir?'

'Damned painful,' Kohl grumbled, flexing a bandaged hand as he fought the reflexive urge to salute.

They were wounds earned during the defence of Trackway Span, and Darya had heard several increasingly far-fetched stories about how they had been sustained. In truth, she knew that he had been on the extreme edge of the Imperial front as the shells began to fall, and had been caught in an explosion that cost him several fingers and inflicted shrapnel damage to his leg. He had been lucky to escape with his life – many more had not, including two of Darya's own team. Frantt and Kadden had died in the defence of Trackway Span, as inseparable in death as they had been in life, robbing Darya of her two best saboteurs.

And two of her friends.

'I'm sorry to hear that, sir,' Darya said.

'So am I,' Kohl said. 'A priest once told me that pain was good for the soul, that it's the God-Emperor's way of telling us that we're still alive. Still damned hurts though.'

He continued past Darya and gestured for her to follow, which she did. It felt odd to be moving at such a slow pace, but she didn't comment. After a few days of darting into cover, or waiting patiently for the perfect shots on advancing xenos, she was just glad to be stretching her legs.

'Lieutenant Munro reported the death of Sergeant Rast a short while ago,' Kohl said as they walked. 'Acting-Sergeant Lenz has given a good account of your response.'

'He seems like a good man. Will the promotion stick, sir?' Darya asked, ignoring the compliment.

'It may have to, at the rate we're losing officers,' Kohl said, and called out to a trooper waiting in line for food. 'You! Have two cups of recaff brought to Relief Station Zero.'

The trooper saluted and left the line, heading for the front of the queue at a slow jog.

'Relief Station Zero, sir?' Darya asked.

'That's right, sergeant,' Kohl said. 'Come on, Commissar Tsutso is meeting us there.'

The meat locker was the last place that any Cadian on Attruso wanted to end up.

Relief Station Zero – the meat locker – was the husk of a building on the eastern bank of the Spatka, overlooking the patched remains of Trackway Span itself. Darya couldn't tell if it had been a hab-block or an Administratum building, as it had been cut almost in half by the fighting and its inner floors destroyed, leaving a hollow tower whose interior was open to the elements above. The exterior was plastered with thin paper posters that depicted Cadian troopers in a range of heroic poses, from bayoneting xenos to feeding starving refugees. Each was emblazoned with a slogan: *For Cadia! For the God-Emperor!*

Darya pushed aside the tarpaulin flap that served as Relief Station Zero's door, and Kohl nodded his thanks as he limped through into the sour air within.

The Cadian dead lined the walls in neat rows, some covered by waterproof sheets but most lying in the open. Their boots had been removed, as had their flak armour, helmets or any reusable materiel; that was piled up outside, ready for collection by the Munitorum priests who would clean, repair and re-sanctify it, then recirculate it for use once more.

'Today's offering to the God-Emperor,' Kohl said solemnly. 'Thirty-eight souls at the latest count.'

Darya said nothing. As a sniper she was familiar with death, both framed by the scope of her long-las and in the tense heart-pounding chaos of the battlefield, but the industrialised and ordered nature of Relief Station Zero still jarred her.

Kohl started moving again, through the main chamber into a smaller room in the back of the building.

The bodies in the smaller room were all raised from the floor on mismatched tables, each in their own corpse sack lined with black plastek to protect it from the elements and any local scavengers until burial or recycling. It was a luxury only afforded to officers in Miracil.

Commissar Tsutso didn't greet Darya or Captain Kohl as they entered, but continued intoning a prayer over the dead. They waited for him to finish before announcing themselves.

'Commissar Tsutso,' Kohl said.

'Captain Kohl, Sergeant Nevic,' the commissar said, and both made the sign of the aquila over their hearts. Commissar Tsutso's returned aquila was flawlessly delivered, the black leather of his gloves creaking.

'We need to leverage your expertise,' Captain Kohl said to Darya, and gestured for her to approach the corpse sacks on the table.

'Someone is targeting our command ranks,' Commissar Tsutso explained as he unzipped the sacks one by one, until the bodies of six officers were revealed.

Darya gritted her teeth but couldn't stop her hand from reaching up to cover her nose; the smell was foul, a mix of spoiled meat, sweat and stale bodily fluids that made her eyes water. Kohl was affected too.

'Throne,' he swore, covering his own nose with his hand.

There were four men and two women, all very much dead, though in various states of early decomposition. All had been dead less than two days, their skin bloodlessly pale, with dark circles under their eyes. Darya suspected that were she to turn them over, they would appear badly bruised from where their blood had settled beneath them.

'Is there a possibility that these officers were all killed by the same person?' Kohl asked.

Darya set down her rifle in the corner of the room and approached the bodies, noting the wound patterns and range indicators on their clothing.

There was a clear observable pattern to the way they had been killed, that much was obvious. All but one had been shot through their upper chest, directly over their heart, the blackened edges of the wounds and the size of the entry point consistent with the focused plasma weapons of the t'au. She explained as much to Captain Kohl and Commissar Tsutso.

'That much we had gathered for ourselves, sergeant,' Commissar Tsutso said. 'As Captain Kohl noted, we are more concerned that there is a possibility they were all killed by the same sniper.'

'It's possible. If not, then the shooters certainly received the same training,' Darya said, looking over the bodies once more. 'The wound placement is almost identical on these five – all shot from the front at range, all centre mass to hit a vital organ. Their deaths would have been quick.'

'A small mercy,' Kohl said quietly.

'And this one?' Tsutso said over the last corpse, one that had no visible wounds on its front except a scrape on the face, as if the dead man had fallen without trying to raise his hands.

Darya shook her head and pushed the body over onto its front. It wasn't easy, and Commissar Tsutso didn't move to help.

'Shot in the back,' Darya said, looking over the spread of

wounds stitched haphazardly across the corpse's back. 'See here, the even scorching around the wounds? These shots were taken on the same level, whereas the others were shot from above. You can tell by the ovoid wound patterns.'

'Unlikely to be the same shooter?' Tsutso asked. Darya looked to Captain Kohl, who narrowed his eyes.

'Go on, sergeant,' Kohl sighed.

'These are from a lasgun, commissar. The others have all the hallmarks of a plasma weapon, and the angle of a sniper facing them at an elevated position. These are from a lasgun burst on the same level, most likely in much closer proximity.'

'You misheard me, sergeant.' Commissar Tsutso's expression relaxed into an impassive glare. 'This man was killed by an enemy sniper, the same one who killed these other unfortunate souls.'

'Of course, sir. Six victims of an enemy sniper,' Darya said, rolling the corpse onto his back and making to close the corpse sack, but Tsutso's gloved hand grabbed hers. She winced at the strength of his grip, but shook her hand free.

Tsutso loomed over her, his expression cold as he twisted the dead officer's tunic so he could read the name patch attached to the man's chest.

'I will need to interview Second Lieutenant Collister's platoon at the earliest opportunity,' he said to Captain Kohl, whose expression was equally cold.

Darya stepped back from the table and picked up her rifle and satchel. The sooner she was out of that room the better.

'You haven't been dismissed yet, sergeant,' Commissar Tsutso said.

'Sorry, sir. Just making myself combat ready.'

She'd heard talk of deteriorating morale over the last few weeks, especially amongst the detachments from the 401st and

338th, but Cadians shooting their own officers... That was unthinkable, even to Darya as a transplant.

'It would appear that intelligence is correct,' Kohl said. Commissar Tsutso's eyes finally left Darya as he turned to face the captain.

'Captain...' he said in a warning tone, but Kohl shook his head.

'She should know, since she's going to be hunting this bastard.' The captain limped forwards to lean on the nearest table.

'I wasn't called back just to look at some bodies for you, was I, sir?' Darya asked.

'Indeed not, sergeant,' Kohl sighed. 'We've been monitoring enemy communications these last weeks, what little we can intercept in any case. We identified a repeated code word amongst the nonsense and xenos jargon – "Longshot".'

'An operation name? Shorthand for something?' Darya asked. Kohl and Commissar Tsutso shared a look.

'We don't believe so. Context clues indicate that it's a name, or an honorific in their language.'

'Foul xenos barbarism,' Commissar Tsutso muttered.

'Is this new intel, sir?' Darya asked, keen to move the conversation on from honorifics.

'No. We've tracked Longshot back through the last three weeks of intercepted communications – the first record is from the day of the bombardment, alongside their word for Trackway Span,' Kohl explained.

It took a few moments for the pieces to fall into place in Darya's mind, but her understanding landed like a shell.

'The sniper in black – the one who shot the bike on the bridge when we were on our way back,' Darya thought aloud. 'Maybe even the one we saw being extracted during the Kintair assault?'

'Perhaps,' Kohl said with a nod.

At least we finally have a name for you, you bastard, Darya thought.

'And these are his latest victims,' Darya said.

'We believe so. Their wounds are too uniform, their deaths too well timed to be opportunistic,' Kohl said. 'But most importantly, no snipers were found in the vicinity of any of the victims.'

'So he's not nesting in a single ambush position,' Darya said. 'He's shooting and moving, just like we do.'

Kohl nodded. 'It would appear you have a mirror in the field, sergeant. But that's not all. When the environs were cleared, there have been reports of white cloth being tied to likely sniping positions. A marker, of sorts.'

'A taunt,' Darya said.

'Most likely,' Kohl agreed.

'This information is likely to be extremely damaging to morale, sergeant. I'm afraid that we must ask you to keep the details of this conversation within your team,' Commissar Tsutso said. 'With no mention of Lieutenant Collister.'

'Yes, sir. Of course, sir,' Darya said.

Tsutso's shoulders seemed to relax at that, and the remaining tension drained from the room like a passing breeze. Darya understood why.

To give an enemy sniper a name gave them power; it marked them out as an enemy to be feared, which was detrimental to morale at best. Usually they were treated only with contempt and derision, which robbed them of their most powerful weapon: fear. Lieutenant Collister was an example of what disruption to morale could do to even highly trained soldiers.

'The t'au have been known to rally behind figureheads before, but an unseen threat to our officers... It's a direct attack on our command chain and our resolve. We may need to leverage our own assets to counteract the impact on our morale,' the commissar mused. Whatever he meant, his words clearly weren't for Darya so she swallowed her questions as Kohl nodded.

'We can discuss any ideas of yours later, commissar. For now, come with me, sergeant. I think we need to refresh your standing orders.' Kohl limped from the room without a backward glance at the commissar or the bodies. Darya didn't have the protection of his rank, and made the sign of the aquila before she followed the captain.

They were met outside by a trooper holding two cups of cooling recaff. Darya accepted hers with muttered thanks, despite having no appetite for food or drink after what she had seen in the meat locker.

'You'll have to forgive the commissar, he's under a lot of strain,' Kohl said quietly as they made their way back to the command centre, moving as fast as his injuries would allow.

'Of course, sir. He's a member of the Officio Prefectus, it's not my place to–'

'Cut the groxshit,' Kohl said. He made a show of taking a large pull from his recaff cup as a squad marched past, heading for the front lines. 'You and I both know what the rank and file think of the crows, and most of the time it's not unwarranted.'

Darya stared in shock at Kohl's scarred features, at the faded bruising along his jaw and up to his augmetic eye. She knew from experience that he could be unorthodox at times – his support of Darya's all-sniper squad was evidence enough of that – but this level of candour was still a surprise.

'Smile, sergeant. Smile and wave to them,' Kohl grunted, still grinning himself as he nodded at the passing troops. Darya did as she was ordered, but still felt numbed by his unguarded words.

'Sir, I–' Darya began, but Kohl waved his hand to silence her.

'The Commissariat are an essential part of the Imperium's

military machine. Without them, we would fall apart. You saw as clearly as I did what happens when discipline breaks down.'

Darya nodded. It would take a while for what she'd seen in Relief Station Zero to fade from her mind's eye, especially the scattered burst of las-fire that had taken the lieutenant's life. She frowned, aware that she couldn't remember the dead man's name.

Just another face amongst hundreds of others.

'I want you to find and kill this Longshot, if he exists,' Kohl continued, resuming their slow walk back to the command centre. 'Morale isn't an unknowable mystery, it is a malleable, mouldable resource. Discipline makes it rigid and resilient, and discipline comes from the top down. Whoever is killing our officers knows this.'

'It's a tried and tested tactic, sir,' Darya agreed.

'We know it works, and it's working,' Kohl sighed. 'We should have recognised their plan after General Matliss.'

'I… We were told she died of natural causes, sir.'

The news of the general's death had been circulated through official channels in the days following the bombardment, stating that her advanced years had caught up to her as she directed the invasion of Miracil. Commissar Tsutso had said so as he addressed the troops, and that her last words were to invoke the wrath of Cadia itself upon the interloping xenos, exhorting her regiment to even greater feats of bravery.

Captain Kohl frowned at her, his brow furrowing over his augmetic eye.

'Of course she did,' he said. 'But this doesn't solve our current problem.'

'Understood, sir,' Darya said. 'If I can put my entire squad onto the task it would be much faster.'

'Agreed. Pull them back for a rest and get them briefed, this needs to be your top priority,' Kohl said, his crutch clacking on the hard plascrete floor of the command centre as they passed back into the relative quiet of the cleared manufactorum. The patched roof above allowed columns of light to leak down through the air, illuminating the motes of dust disturbed by the activity below. Kohl slowed still further to watch the drifting particles for a moment.

'They were all trueborn Cadian. Did you notice that?' Kohl asked quietly.

'The officers?' Darya asked.

'Yes.'

Darya had noticed; it was an unconscious reflex for a transplant to check the eye colour of other people within the regiment, which apparently even extended to the dead. All of their eyes had been violet beneath the rheumy grey pallor, marking them as having grown up in the shadow of the Eye of Terror, before it had split the skies to become the Great Rift.

'I noticed, sir.'

'Dying by inches.'

'There's some fight left in us yet, sir,' Darya said.

Kohl looked at her in a way that told her that she'd misunderstood, but he didn't elaborate.

'How many are left in your squad now, Nevic?'

'Five, sir. Corporal Ullaeus, Troopers Yanna, Arfit and Bellis, and myself. We lost Frantt and Kadden in the bombardment.'

'Damn shame that. You operate in pairs, don't you?'

'As often as we can, but we've been operating alone in Iron Hill. It's a lot of ground to cover, sir.'

'Waste of resources to see you picked off,' Kohl said in a low voice. 'We're expecting some replacements from off-world in the next few hours–'

'Are we pushing forwards, sir?' Darya cut in.

'Not quite,' Kohl said with a shake of his head. 'We're to give all the indications of a push later today, hopefully pull some of the enemy forces from our flanks to give Third and Seventh Companies breathing room to get across the Spatka. God-Emperor willing, we'll be able to get a foothold in the assembly plant in Iron Hill's northern quadrant whilst we're at it.'

'It'll be good to get inside that monolith, but it'd be even better to have some friends on this side of the river,' Darya said.

'It'd be damned good,' Kohl agreed. 'But one thing at a time. I'll have the reinforcement rosters checked for potential marksmen, see if I can't rustle up some replacements.'

They'd reached the command centre, where several vox-operators were clearly awaiting the captain's presence.

'I'd be happy for any support you can give, sir,' Darya said quickly, before the captain's attention was dragged away. 'Anyone with scouting experience would be ideal.'

'I'll see what I can do,' Kohl said as he passed her his empty cup. 'Dismissed.'

Darya backed away and watched as Captain Kohl was mobbed by the vox-operators jostling to be the first to speak to him. She turned to leave, but remembered the parchment strip she had recovered from the foundry.

She weighed up the impulse in her mind, then made her way into the command centre to where a lone vox-operator sat scrawling a message onto a paper slip, his fingers blackened and spotted with ink.

'Busy, Kroller?' Darya asked as she sat down on the desk next to him.

'Always busy, Sergeant Nevic,' Kroller said without looking up. He dabbed a stamp onto an ink pad and jabbed it down onto the paper slip with enough force to rattle the table. He held the slip up over his shoulder for it to be snatched away a moment later by a waiting trooper.

'Too busy for a favour?' she pressed on, reaching into her satchel and pulling out the parchment slip.

'Depends on the favour,' Kroller said. He still hadn't looked up, but slipped back one earpiece of his headset as he started scribbling out another note.

'You're a code-breaker. Figured you're the one to speak to about breaking a code.'

Kroller smacked two stamps onto the next paper slip and held it up to have it snatched away yet again.

'That depends on what you have to offer,' Kroller said, flipping a switch on his vox-set and removing his headset completely.

'How about a week's lho ration,' Darya offered.

'Two. Plus whatever's left in your recaff mug, I'm gasping,' Kroller countered.

'Done,' Darya said happily, and passed her untouched mug of recaff to the code-breaker. It was cold by then, but he didn't seem to mind as he gulped it down and held his hand out for the parchment slip. Darya handed it to him, and he held it up to the light.

'It's an Imperial cypher, looks like binharic to me...' he muttered, then pointed to the ragged bottom edge of the slip and passed it back. 'Deal's off. That's Adeptus Mechanicus property, I'm not going near it.'

Darya looked at the slip in the light and there, right at the ragged bottom where it had been torn off, was the slightest impression of a bisected skull within a cog ring.

'Huh. So it is,' Darya said. She drew her kvis and sliced off the Mechanicus symbol, leaving only the punch-patterned section, then passed it back to Kroller. He looked from the parchment to the curved dagger in Darya's hand, then reluctantly accepted the parchment slip.

'Three weeks' lho ration,' Kroller said.

'Deal. Let me know when you know what it says.' Darya secured her kvis back into the sheath on her shoulder.

'Could be a while,' Kroller said. 'Next time send Ullaeus. He's much easier to negotiate with.'

'Just let me know,' Darya said, then activated her vox-bead. 'Squad, pull back to headquarters for refit – we're going hunting.'

16

Less than an hour later, Darya had assembled her squad in one of the corners of the manufactorum where the last remaining conveyor belts had been piled. The wall behind them was plastered with the same thin posters that had been affixed to every standing wall behind the Cadian lines, but here they were obscured with soot and plascrete dust.

Her team were all in the same uniforms they had worn for the past week, stained with sweat, grime and dust, their faces tired beneath their grease-paint camouflage.

'Counter-sniping,' Ullaeus said from where he was sitting atop a motor unit. He blew on his steaming mess tin, which contained his second serving of hot rations since he'd returned.

'Feels like more of the same to me,' Arfit said. He was lying on the rubber belt of a conveyor with an arm over his eyes, in a position that couldn't have been comfortable.

'Less reactive, more proactive,' Darya said between mouthfuls of hot, thin stew. Rehydrated vegetables and freeze-dried meat never tasted better than after a few days on cold protein blocks and ration sachets.

'It'll be good to go back on the offensive,' Yanna said. She chewed tentatively; the scar on her face wasn't fully healed yet, the skin still raw and puckered from where the medicae had sewn it back together. Her facial tattoos no longer lined up, but the Episcan seemed almost happy to have earned such a prominent scar, especially one that was so similar to Darya's.

Bellis said nothing; he looked like he was actually asleep, his empty mess tin in his lap as he sat slumped against the base of Ullaeus' motor unit.

She'd briefed her team as soon as they'd had a chance to grab some hot food and some chem-treated water, filling them in on what she could from her meeting with Captain Kohl and Commissar Tsutso. She'd left off that one of the dead had been killed by his own men, and Captain Kohl's inference that General Matliss' death had been anything but natural.

They had been as excited as Darya at the prospect of the incoming push, even if it was just a feint to ease the way of other elements of the 217th. It was progress, a sense of building momentum that served to stoke their morale better than any sermon or propaganda vid.

'I'm just happy we're finally pushing on the assembly plant,' Arfit said, and Darya had to agree. The monolithic building was one of the largest in Iron Hill, and all attempts to breach its walls had been unsuccessful so far.

'So long as our target isn't hiding inside,' Darya said.

'Could be we've got the sniper already,' Ullaeus suggested, scraping his spoon noisily on the inside of his mess tin to collect every last morsel of food. 'We got that one this morning, the one who took out Sergeant Rast.'

'Could be you're going to scratch through the bottom of that tin if you're not careful, Iago,' Bellis said without opening his eyes. Arfit snorted with laughter.

'Enough,' Darya warned as Ullaeus drew back his arm to throw his spoon at Bellis. He lowered it as he caught Darya's eye, and shrugged. 'Captain Kohl seems to think that his Longshot theory holds water, so until further notice we are going to hunt this bastard down. Having looked at the reports myself, this looks like the work of an expert and not the prepared positions we've come across so far. Intel shows that the officers were killed all over Iron Hill, which also means that our target is moving.'

'There are rat-runs all over the upper levels,' Yanna said. 'That's most likely how they're getting around.'

'That's my thinking, but with the high ceilings and blown roof panels we can't rule out sniper drones,' Darya said. 'I can't imagine it'd be too difficult to pilot a drone through there.'

'Cowards,' Arfit muttered.

'Let the xenos use their heretical tech, it's no substitute for this,' Bellis said, tapping the side of his head.

'Not if we're careful and watch our corners,' Darya agreed. 'Our man is targeting officers, which means we'll be shadowing the highest rankers in the offensives across Iron Hill. Arfit and Bellis, you're on one team – Yanna and Ullaeus are the second.'

'What about you, boss?' Ullaeus asked.

'I'll take the new recruits that Captain Kohl assigns to us,' Darya replied with a shrug. 'God-Emperor willing, he'll find us a few who can shoot straight.'

'If not, they can at least be distractions,' Arfit said.

'I've heard you make good target practice, Iago – maybe you should be teaching them?' Bellis laughed, and the rest of the squad joined him in light-heartedly jeering their corporal.

'I'll go anywhere with the Ghost of Cocleratum watching my

back,' Ullaeus said, and the squad turned to Darya in anticipation of her response.

'Not that bloody name again,' Darya sighed.

'You want to hear what they're saying about you on the front,'
Yanna said. 'Word is that you can move through a fully lit room
unseen, appearing to take your shot before disappearing as fast
as you arrived. Like a ghost.'

'Throne save me,' Darya muttered to herself. 'Okay, from now
on I want you all to put down that kind of talk. We're meant
to be a stealth unit, not celebrities.'

'Enjoy the fame, boss,' Ullaeus said. 'Speaking of...'

Darya followed where Ullaeus was looking, over to a crowd
of waiting Cadian troopers. They were all looking over at the
snipers and Darya, turning away as soon as she looked back.
Her own squad failed to suppress their laughter.

'Shut up, the lot of you,' she growled. 'We're heading out in
an hour. Rearm and rest up, I'm going to see the captain about
these new recruits.'

She left the squad to their jokes and friendly ribbing, inwardly
happy that some semblance of normality had returned.

Frantt and Kadden's deaths during the bombardment had
been a heavy blow for the surviving squad, more so for Bellis
and Arfit as they had been left as the only remaining pureblood Cadians in the team. Darya supposed that her squad was
a microcosm of the troubles facing the wider regiment – pureblood Cadians were becoming a minority within their own units
as the crusade wore on, which had the potential to increase the
friction between the pureblood and transplanted troops.

It was good to hear them laughing again.

The crowd of waiting troopers parted respectfully as Darya
strode towards the command Chimera, where Captain Kohl
was speaking animatedly into a vox-set.

'I have forty per cent of my troops committed in Iron Hill, sir... Yes, I understand, but with our current casualty rate...' Kohl's voice trailed off.

'Can we help you, sergeant?' a waiting adjutant asked as Captain Kohl slipped off his headset and pushed himself awkwardly to his feet.

'I need to speak to the captain,' Darya said, nodding towards Kohl. 'About those reinforcements, sir?'

'Ah yes, Nevic,' Kohl said distractedly as he passed the vox handset back to the operator. 'I've found you someone – Trooper Mas Keen. A Whiteshield until very recently, but he has above-average marksmanship scores. He's all I can spare.'

'I appreciate the help, sir,' Darya said, but Kohl had already turned away to shout across the room.

'Sergeant Gosht! Get Trooper Keen over here now!' he bellowed, his voice cutting over the burble of conversation and the ever-present hum of the portable generatoria.

'A Whiteshield, sir?' Darya asked.

The lack of consistent replacements from the famous Cadian training regiments after the fall of Cadia had led to the 217th starting the transplant initiative. If the flow of trueborn Cadians was resuming, Darya wondered what would that mean for the transplants.

'The resettlement colonies are finally bearing fruit. Time will tell if they make the kind of Cadians we're all used to,' Kohl said as Sergeant Gosht arrived with a tall and remarkably clean trooper in tow.

'The Three-Hundred-and-Thirty-Eighth's loss is our gain I'd say, sir,' Gosht said with a grin. 'Nevic, still clinging on are you?'

'Gosht,' Darya said and shook the other sergeant's extended hand. 'You know me, just keeping the trueborn Cadians like you out of a job.'

'Ha! I'll let you take a bullet for me any day,' Gosht laughed.

Kohl dismissed the two sergeants with a nod and returned to the vox-banks, and Gosht led Darya and Keen a short distance from the command centre.

'This lanky streak of piss is Trooper Mas Keen, fresh off the landing barge and learning not to salute on the front lines. Isn't that right, Keen?'

'Yes, sergeant,' Keen said curtly as he stood to stiff attention, his chin high and shoulders back.

'Keen, this is Sergeant Nevic. Pay attention to her and you'll learn something. Who knows, you might even live long enough to earn a medal or two,' Gosht said with a sly wink to Darya. 'Good luck with him, Nevic. I'm heading back to Lieutenant Munro with the new blood.'

'How many replacements did you get?' Darya asked.

Gosht looked knowingly at her and nodded away from the command centre. Darya followed as he put a little more distance between them and the vox-operators.

'You wait over there,' Gosht said to Keen, who backed away a few paces.

'Did you hear about the Three-Hundred-and-Thirty-Eighth?'

'No, I've been in the field the last few days. What's happened?' Darya asked.

This was how most news travelled amongst the troops – not through official channels and Commissariat-approved briefings, but through the troops themselves and through gossiping non-commissioned officers like Sergeant Gosht. The news had to be taken with a pinch of salt, but there would be grains of truth beneath the exaggeration.

'Half the regiment was deployed on one of the penal worlds in-system, a rock called Horticus. They got the corpse starch kicked out of them,' Gosht said conspiratorially. 'Word is that these reinforcements were sent for the Three-Hundred-and-Thirty-Eighth, but the powers that be divided them up amongst the other Cadian regiments instead. We got about two hundred, and the Four-Hundred-and-First got twice that. The Three-Hundred-and-Thirty-Eighth might be heading for a complete re-founding.'

'Throne,' Darya whispered. That was big news, especially mid-campaign when the fleet arm's forces were all engaged across the system. 'Where's that from? Official communiqués?'

'Not official, but I know a guy who's friendly with the fly boys. One of them knows an officer who's a bit loose with the confidential info. Apparently he saw the original fleet manifests first-hand,' Gosht said, as if that were definitive proof.

'Interesting,' Darya said, rather less confident that the information was one hundred per cent accurate.

'I know, right?' Gosht said, raising his eyebrows. 'Anyway, I've got places to be. Good luck with that one.'

'Why's that?'

'He's made it pretty clear that he's not happy with his assignment. I've only known him half an hour and he's already getting on my nerves,' Gosht explained. 'Supposed to be a decent shot, but God-Emperor knows how since his head's buried up his–'

'Sergeant Gosht! Why are you still here?' Captain Kohl bellowed from the command centre.

'Just handing over, sir!' Gosht shouted back, then jogged away towards a crowd of troopers standing to attention near the exit to Trackway Span.

'Come on, you're with me now, Keen,' Darya said, and gestured for Keen to follow.

His gear was brand new, untouched by dust or grime, and his boots still bore a parade-ground sheen as they squeaked across the plascrete floor. He was also tall, which was a disadvantage for a sniper as it made him a larger target and he would find it more difficult to take up positions in cramped spaces. His eyes were a vibrant violet, which marked him out as having been born on Cadia, but his face was set into a natural sneer, as if he were looking down his nose at his surroundings figuratively as well as literally.

'You passed through the Whiteshield programme?' Darya asked as they walked.

'Yes,' he replied curtly. 'I'm a Cadian.'

'It's sergeant, sarge or sir.'

'Yes, sergeant.'

'You're unhappy with your assignment, Keen?'

'No, sergeant...'

'It feels like there's a "but" at the end of that sentence,' Darya said, stopping just out of earshot of the snipers. Keen rolled his eyes as he stopped next to her.

'I'm a little disappointed, sergeant. We were expecting to join the Three-Hundred-and-Thirty-Eighth, which is a reputable Cadian regiment,' Keen explained.

'The Two-Hundred-and-Seventeenth is a damned fine regiment, trooper.'

'To you, maybe,' Keen said.

'And what's that supposed to mean?'

'Permission to speak candidly, sergeant?'

'As if you haven't already?' Darya said. When Keen didn't elaborate, she motioned for him to continue.

'Do you know what the Two-Hundred-and-Seventeenth are called? Outside the regiment, I mean?' Keen asked.

'Sure. The Gauntlet Runners,' Darya said, searching her memory for any other name that they might have earned.

'The *Missing* Two-Hundred-and-Seventeenth,' Keen said coldly. 'Because when Cadia fell, the Two-Hundred-and-Seventeenth were nowhere to be found.'

'Yes, they were engaged on Mesaphys at the time,' Darya said, nonplussed. 'Plenty of regiments weren't there to fight at the Fall. But what's that got to do with–'

'They defied orders and didn't go to the defence of *our* home world,' Keen said angrily, baring his teeth as he spoke. Darya couldn't help but notice the emphasis he put on the word 'our'.

'They didn't defy orders, boy. They fulfilled their oaths,' said Darya, stepping in close. 'I've read the reports on the war for Mesaphys. The Two-Hundred-and-Seventeenth still have their honour. They didn't abandon their post and leave their allies to die, they fought until the war was won before going to Cadia's defence. How old were you when Cadia fell? Five years Terran standard? Six?'

'I am a Cadian,' he said defiantly.

'Yeah? So am I. So's that Episcan over there with the tattoos. That one sat on the machine? He's from Verspator, one of the five hundred worlds of Ultramar, and he's still Cadian.' Darya pointed to Yanna and Ullaeus in turn, which drew their attention.

'I know where you're from and who you are,' Keen said in a low voice. 'Everyone knows about the famous Sergeant Nevic, the Ghost of–'

'Never say those words again,' Darya muttered, silencing Keen with a grim look. 'Or they'll be the last words you ever speak.'

She turned and stalked away back to her team, the thought of her home world twisting her stomach.

Ullaeus met Darya's eye as she approached and nudged Bellis awake with the toe of his boot.

'This the new recruit, boss?' Ullaeus asked.

'Trooper Mas Keen, meet the rest of your squad,' Darya said, aware that some of her anger had bled into her voice as she gestured towards the relaxing snipers. Keen seemed to steel himself, and made towards the squad.

'Corporal Iago Ullaeus,' Ullaeus said, jumping down off the machine and over Bellis, coming to a soft landing in front of Keen. He offered the new recruit his hand, which Keen shook briefly.

'I'm Yanna,' Yanna said without rising, but also offered Keen her hand. Again, he shook it briefly before moving on down the line.

'Arnout Bellis,' Bellis said as Keen shook his hand with more enthusiasm.

'Mahnet Arfit,' Arfit said from the conveyor, and arched an eyebrow as Keen gripped his hand.

'So, Trooper Mas Keen,' Ullaeus said, 'what do you know about sniping that warrants your admission into our merry little company?'

'I had the highest marksmanship scores in my Whiteshield unit.'

'Oh good, he can shoot straight,' Bellis said.

'He has the wrong rifle though,' Yanna said, nodding at Keen's standard-issue lasgun.

'Trooper Keen has to earn his long-las,' Darya said, putting an end to the joking at Keen's expense. Whether she liked him or not, he was part of her squad now and that made him her responsibility, and she would still have to mould him into a deadly servant of the Imperium.

'Between us, we're going to teach him everything he needs to know to be a full member of this team.'

'Might take a while with this one,' Ullaeus added.

'It'll take as long as it takes,' Darya said, speaking half to the team and half to Keen, who turned to face her.

'I'm a fast learner, sergeant,' he said defiantly.

'I hope so, because you're going to be on the front lines in half an hour,' Darya said. 'That means I want you back here in a cameleoline cloak and a used pair of boots before then.'

'A used pair of... Where am I supposed to get a used pair of boots? Is there something wrong with the ones I'm wearing?' Keen asked.

'They're too new, they squeak like a stuck grox-calf. Consider this your first lesson – sniping is about more than shooting straight. It's about using what's between your ears,' Darya said.

'Or what isn't, in some cases,' Ullaeus muttered. Darya ignored him.

'Use your head, Keen. I want you back here in thirty minutes wearing that cloak and those boots. No stealing or borrowing them either.'

Keen seemed like he was about to argue, but thought better of it as he looked about the squad, who were all looking back at him expectantly.

'Drop your gear here,' Ullaeus said, 'but take your rifle. Can't have a commissar catching you without a weapon on your first day, can we?'

Keen looked exasperated, but did as he was told. He shrugged off his pack and left it on the conveyor belt at Bellis' feet, then jogged towards the exit back to Trackway Span.

'Harsh lesson, that one,' Ullaeus observed as he watched Keen go.

'It is. But it's an important one,' Darya replied. 'We mess up, people will die. He needs to learn that as soon as possible.'

'I know,' Ullaeus said. 'Do you think he'll know where to look?'

'I don't know,' Darya admitted. 'Follow him, make sure he finds the meat locker. Get him his cloak too.'

'On it, boss,' Ullaeus said.

As Ullaeus walked after their new recruit, Darya thought back to her first day with the snipers in the Coclerati Janissaries and the baptism by fire that she'd received.

She'd worn a dead man's boots for almost two years, and could still remember her first glimpse of the corpses over a decade later.

It was almost midday when Ullaeus returned with Keen in tow, and the rest of the squad were performing the last of their gear checks before heading out. Ullaeus ran some last-minute checks on his own gear, testing his scope and rifle charge, before declaring himself good to go.

'You're looking the part,' Darya said to Keen, who gave her a slight nod of acknowledgement.

His shining parade-ready boots had been replaced with a worn pair which barely made a sound on the plascrete floor as he moved. The cloak was a rough offcut of cameleoline fabric that draped to his mid-calf, but had enough loose folds at the neck to give him a hood.

'That's all I could scrounge up,' Ullaeus said as he noticed where Darya was looking.

Keen's rifle looked fresh off the production line, a standard-pattern lasrifle with iron sights and no scope. Darya made a note to put in a request for a long-las when they returned – it would take days to be fulfilled anyway, which was time enough for Keen to earn the right to carry one.

'Keen, you're with me. The rest of you, keep your eyes open and the vox clear unless absolutely necessary. We keep our heads down until we find this bastard or his hiding spot. Clear?'

The squad let out a short, sharp grunt of affirmation.

'Keen, you're going to need one of these,' Darya said as she led the squad towards the trenches. She handed him a vox-bead, the same as the ones worn by everyone else in the squad. It consisted of an earpiece that sat in the ear, attached by a hair-thin wire to a strap that fastened around the wearer's throat.

'Range is good to about half a mile, less in densely packed urban environments,' Darya said as Keen slipped the bead into his ear and fastened the strap.

'Like an industrial complex,' Ullaeus said.

Keen nodded. 'Okay. How do I get it to pick up my voice?'

'Like this,' Darya explained, holding a finger to the throat strap. Her voice was picked up by the vox-strap, and amplified by the earpiece a millisecond later.

'We use clicks for shorthand,' Ullaeus said. 'You can either click with your tongue, or by tapping the vox-strap if you're in earshot of a target.'

'One for yes or acknowledgement, two for no, three for assistance required,' Darya said.

They made their way down the stairs into the manufactorum's basement, then out through the blasted hole and into the cold, damp air of Sniper's Alley. A dirt-rimmed Cadian trooper shouted for Keen to keep his head down and the young trooper stooped, the top of his helmet still level with the trench lip.

'How come you're not wearing helmets?' Keen asked as they passed onto Creed's Row and turned south.

'Too bulky and too noisy,' Darya said, 'and they make for an easily recognisable silhouette.'

At least he's started asking the right questions, she thought.

'We can move quieter and faster without them. And what's the best defence against being shot?'

'Not being seen,' the squad chorused back.

'Should I take mine off or...?' Keen's voice trailed off as a wounded soldier was carried past on a stretcher, leaving a trail of blood drops in his wake.

'You keep it on until you learn the basics,' Darya said.

If he lives long enough. The dark thought wove through her mind. She didn't feel that it would be helpful telling him that the standard-issue Cadian helmet was little to no defence against a pulse-rifle shot.

A voice began to speak, the sound carried clearly across the blasted landscape beyond the trench lines, clearer than any vox-emitter that Darya had ever heard. There was none of the thin reediness or muffled consonants that were common to Imperial vox-casters. It was as if the speaker were just out of sight somewhere in no-man's-land.

'In the name of the Throne,' Keen cursed from behind Darya, 'what is that?'

'Better get used to it, it's not going anywhere,' Darya said as they passed from Sniper's Alley onto Creed's Row, and the voice's pitch grew to an impassioned cry.

'You do not know why you fight, or whom you fight for!' the voice said, its accent strange but unmistakably human. *'You do not fight for yourselves or your families. Why fight for a distant Emperor? Why die for generals who will not mourn your passing? Lay down your arms and be welcomed into the T'au'va! Fight alongside your brothers and sisters for the betterment of all humanity – for the Greater Good!'*

Trooper Keen looked both shocked and angry as the voice delivered its blasphemous sermon, rising to a dramatic crescendo as it came to the end of its first loop and started again. It was met by groans from the Cadians stationed in the trench, who had to shout over the voice to continue their conversations.

'What–'

'Propaganda. False promises of the xenos designed to wear us down,' Ullaeus shouted.

'Why don't we…?' Keen said, just as the message ended and the last echoes of the voice bled away through the chill air. 'Why don't we do anything about them?'

'We did,' Darya explained, pressing herself against the trench wall to allow a young trooper to pass, a case of bolter shells stowed on his shoulder. 'It's drones, up in the sky. We shoot them down, they send more up. Don't worry, ours will start up soon.'

As if on cue, the distant strains of 'Flower of Cadia' drifted over no-man's-land from hidden loudhailers across the Cadian trenches, announcing the start of the day's roll of victories and inspirational speeches.

Darya thought it was a blunt but effective move, for the Commissariat to drown out the xenos propaganda with the Cadians' own.

'Imperial forces continue to cut a bloody swathe through the foul xenos lines…'

The propaganda talked about strategic gains across Attruso, but no mention was made of Miracil. There never was, as far as Darya knew. The entire Miracil front was just as stagnant as it was in the Cadian Salient, so there would be little to draw inspiration from.

Hopefully that changes today, she thought.

They passed through the trenches towards Iron Hill with the voice as their companion, telling them about victories in far-off systems that none of them had ever heard of, interspersed with audio statements supposedly from the warriors who had won them.

'The God-Emperor watched over us and guided our hand to victory!'

'Together we will crush the traitor, the heretic and the xenos! For the God-Emperor!'

Darya kept her eyes on the trench ahead, at the Cadians running lit matches along the seams of their uniforms to burn out the lice that had settled there, at the troopers who stood watch over the line wrapped in blankets against the early winter chill. This didn't feel like victory. She recognised the propaganda for what it was, and allowed it to wash over her.

They reached the final corner as a hoarse Munitorum priest began his sermon, his voice underpinned by a low buzz over the loudhailers. Darya indicated for her squad to drop low, and led them towards the looming structures of Iron Hill.

'Though the road may be hard and fraught with terrors, take solace in Him, for you do His work!'

'Eyes ahead and stay sharp once we get inside.'

Darya led the squad through the chain of craters that marked the end of the trench system, motioning for them to keep low as they darted up the debris-strewn steps and into the complex itself.

The entrance had once served as an overbearing expression of the Adeptus Mechanicus' power over the lowly efforts of the planetary corporate elite. There was little artistry in the pillars of rockcrete wound with frayed cables and topped with turrets of arcane design, their energy weapons long since cooled and left to rust. Likewise, there was nothing inviting about the slumped automata that corroded silently in the shadow of the marble pillars, or the high weapon emplacements manned by long-dead servitors. No, the entrance was designed to intimidate, not impress.

Darya's team joined the swell of troops passing into the vaulted avenue beyond, lined with statues cast in the images of forgotten Fabricator Generals, as the last echoes of the loudhailer died away.

The air within reverberated with gunfire, stinking of sweat and stale ozone from the warren of rooms deeper inside the complex.

'I'll find the forward command centre, see who we can shadow,' Darya said.

Ullaeus led the squad out of the main thoroughfare into the shadowed corners of the avenue, making room for the ammo-carriers and reinforcements rushing towards the fighting.

Darya followed the tangle of thick cables to an alcove recessed into the plasteel wall of the avenue, behind the towering pedestal of a robed statue.

'Lieutenant Munro,' she said.

'Nevic,' Munro grunted by way of greeting.

He manned a vox-station with a lone adjutant. His wounds had healed to the sickly yellow of old bruising, the worst patched with synth-skin. His left hand had been replaced by a rudimentary three-fingered augmetic of dull grey steel, leaving him to favour his right as he directed the battle for the complex.

'Captain Kohl messaged ahead,' Munro said, moving over to a portable holo-table set back in the depths of the alcove. It flared into gentle, flickering light as a translucent tri-dimensional wireframe sketched itself in the air over the holo-prisms. 'What's your plan?'

'Three teams of two, each shadowing officers in the three main assaults to the north, east and south. Our man should be present at one of them – if he turns up, we'll take him out,' Darya explained as the image rotated gently in the air.

'Your plan is to use my officers as bait?'

'More like bodyguards, sir. Our target is hunting officers – we could watch for this bastard for days in hides and prepared nests without crossing paths.'

The way that Munro bit back a response told Darya that he knew that, but that it didn't make the idea any more palatable.

'Are we even sure it's one operator? They've seeded snipers throughout this damned complex,' Munro asked.

He's clutching at straws, Darya thought.

'Intelligence suggests that we're after one operator on the move, as well as the pre-prepared sniper positions,' Darya said.

As Lieutenant Munro sighed, Darya felt a degree of sympathy for the contrary Cadian officer. Despite their losses and the constant fighting through the manufactoria and foundry halls, the Imperial forces had made precious little progress. They were hamstrung by their own limitations, unable to bring their formidable artillery and air assets to bear, which left them fighting on the t'au's terms.

'Fine,' Munro said eventually. 'Second Lieutenant Carr is leading the attack on the assembly complex to the north. To the south, Lieutenant Boredin is reinforcing a position in the foundry sector.'

Each direction was punctuated with a jabbing augmetic finger that blurred the tri-dimensional image.

'And to the east, sir?'

'That would be me, sergeant,' Munro said. 'I'm leading a relief force to our positions in the generatoria complex just north of the foundries.'

'I'll be watching over you then, sir,' Darya said with an encouraging nod.

Munro ran his tongue over his teeth, considering his words, and for a moment Darya thought he was preparing a cutting remark.

'My objectives are likely to meet the least resistance,' Munro said in a low voice. 'Would it not be a better use of your expertise to shadow Lieutenant Boredin or Second Lieutenant Carr?'

Darya blinked. It was the closest that Lieutenant Munro had come to paying her a direct compliment.

'With respect, sir, you are the ranking officer,' Darya said as carefully as she could, given that she was informing him that he was a likely target. 'My team are expert counter-snipers. Your men will be as safe under their care as under mine.'

'As you say, sergeant,' Munro said, and checked his wristchrono. 'I'll be setting out in the next five minutes.'

'Understood, sir. We'll be ready,' Darya replied.

Her squad looked up expectantly as she returned, almost invisible in the shadowed corners of the avenue.

'We have our orders. Arfit, since you're so excited about the assembly plant, you and Bellis will be looking after Second Lieutenant Carr during the attack.'

'Thanks for that, Arfit,' Bellis said.

'Ullaeus, Yanna – you're going south into the foundry sector with Lieutenant Boredin. Keen, you're with me, watching over Lieutenant Munro.'

'We're on it, boss,' Ullaeus said with a confident smile.

'I know I don't have to tell you all to be careful out there, but I'm going to do it anyway. This Longshot isn't an amateur – we're hunting someone who's almost as good as us. This t'au bastard thinks he can kill our people with impunity – I say that's xenos arrogance. We are the hammer of humanity, the wrath of the God-Emperor made manifest, and we're going to show him how wrong he is. For Cadia.'

'For Cadia,' her team chorused, their expressions resolute.

She looked at each of her team in turn, as if committing their faces to memory. A sour feeling was growing in her gut, the way she always felt before a battle, only somehow stronger, strengthened by a sense of foreboding.

'Good. God-Emperor guide your aim out there,' Darya said.

The squad broke apart, the pairs splitting off towards their objectives as Darya watched and prayed under her breath.

'God-Emperor, if you can hear me, please watch over your faithful servants. Protect them as they implement your holy will and take the fight to the enemies of mankind.'

17

Of course they will send out hunters. They are afraid.
  Afraid that they fight an enemy who knows their minds.
  Afraid that their resolve will fail before they can break ours.
  Afraid that for all of their bravery, in us they have met their match.
  We will show them that their fears are justified.

Munro's route to the generatoria complex led through claustrophobic corridors of blackened plasteel, over floors of heat-distorted
grating that allowed a glimpse of the cable-strewn sub-floor
beneath. Lumen bulbs hung dead in rusting wire enclosures every
few yards, discoloured by dust and rimed with grimy fluids.

Darya scouted ahead of Munro's platoon with Keen at her
back, half to ensure their path was clear and half to gauge how
Keen advanced through the scant cover available in the empty
corridors. He was capable if a little eager, which Darya judged
to be more a symptom of his age than a desire to impress.

The thick metal walls did little to blunt the noise of distant gunfire, or the t'au loudhailer that continued its pleas for the Cadians to lay down their arms and join the enemy.

'Does that voice ever stop?'

'You learn to block it out,' Darya said. 'Keep your voice down and speak softly with less sibilance. Your voice won't carry as far.'

Keen nodded his acknowledgement and advanced towards a dark void in the wall ahead, where an unlit doorway gave way to the room beyond. Darya took up position behind him as he activated the lumen pack on his lasgun, then followed as he burst into the room.

The lumen's beam danced across empty tables, broken phials and battered instruments of unknown purpose. Satisfied that there was no danger, Darya signalled the all clear and led Keen back onto their path.

'What in the name of Terra happened here?' said Keen.

'Who knows what the Mechanicus do in their halls?'

'No, I mean in this city.'

'Inhabitants took up with xenos. That's all we need to know.'

Despite what the Commissariat liked to believe, soldiers of the Astra Militarum didn't spend all of their short time out of combat in solemn prayer. They talked and joked with one another, built up friendships and established close-knit ties with their squadmates and other peers within the regiment.

But they never openly questioned the official word of the Commissariat – such discussions would be private conversations with their closest comrades. Darya had been comfortable speculating about Attruso's recent history with Ullaeus, a man she'd served with for several years, but wasn't foolish enough to do so with a man she'd only known a few hours.

Keen, however, appeared far less guarded.

'There's no evidence of energy weapons or anything like that.

It's as if the Attrusans rose up with hand tools and improvised weapons.'

'Keep your mind on the job,' Darya said as they came to a pair of sliding double doors, both hanging crooked from their overhead rails.

Darya slipped through carefully, finding herself in a familiar thoroughfare that ran between her building and the next, connected high above with walkways. Tall buttressed walls stretched into the distance, a black metal canyon that separated the generatoria complex from the other buildings within Iron Hill.

She watched for movement for a few seconds before indicating for Keen to follow through the doors.

He made to run towards a doorway set into the building opposite, but Darya managed to grab him by the cloak before he broke cover.

'Use your head,' she said. He looked down at her with an indignant look and failed to pull himself free from her grip.

'We cover the angles by widening the position,' he hissed back.

'When you're in a squad. We don't have the luxury of numbers so we use our heads,' Darya said, keeping her voice low and soft. 'Always assume there's a sniper waiting for you to break cover. Look up there – I can see at least five positions that have a clear line of sight onto the gap and the cover you were running for. Until they are cleared, you don't move.'

Keen let out a tense breath then looked where Darya was pointing, at the underside of the walkways and the lines of trailing cables and crenellated roofs above. Darya pulled him back into the shadow of the doorway then raised her rifle to scour the way ahead for snipers, hidden or otherwise.

'Look through there,' she said finally, pushing her rifle into Keen's hands. He took it carefully, leaning his own rifle against the crooked door behind him. 'Right side, second walkway.'

Keen raised the rifle to his shoulder and pressed his eye to the scope's perished rubber eyepiece. His breath caught in his throat.

'Xenos,' he whispered. 'They're not moving.'

'One of Corporal Ullaeus' kills a few days ago,' Darya said.

Darya took the rifle back from Keen, whose eyes lingered on the weapon as Darya reset the scope and tightened the cloth wrappings on the forestock.

'That bastard killed three troopers before Ullaeus was called in.'

'I understand,' Keen said with a half-smile. 'They tell stories about your weapon, you know. I heard it's a blessed weapon, that it never misses.'

'A weapon is only as capable as the hands that– Shh,' Darya whispered and dropped to one knee, movement from further up the avenue catching her eye.

'Xenos?' Keen mouthed, making to grab his own weapon. Darya held up a hand to stop him, and passed back her long-las with a nod.

'*You do not know why you fight!*' The voice echoed down the thoroughfare as the drone descended between the walkways, its vox-speakers blaring.

'Did you fire a long-las in training?' Darya whispered, motioning for Keen to line up his shot.

'Yes, sergeant,' Keen muttered back.

'Good, same principle. Only now the target is moving – brace it tightly and slow your breathing. Put one shot through the underside of the drone, centre mass, on my mark.'

Keen took several short, shallow breaths and pulled the long-las in tightly. Darya wanted to say more, to tell him to lead the target, but held back.

'Okay, on my mark. Three, two, one… Shoot.'

He pulled the trigger, but his aim was slightly off and the

las-bolt slammed into the drone's armoured dome. The impact knocked the drone sideways through the air until it was able to compensate, spinning round to bring its underslung pulse weapon to bear.

'You have time for another shot. Slow your breathing and adjust your aim,' Darya said, but picked up and readied Keen's rifle just in case. It wouldn't hurt to have a backup.

Keen let out one long breath and pulled the trigger; this time the shot missed completely.

Darya raised Keen's lasgun and took aim down the sights, lining up the three metal prongs on the advancing drone, then squeezed the trigger.

A burst of las-fire spat from the muzzle at the distant drone. All three shots smacked into the dull metal underside, spraying sparks and garbling the vox-speaker's message into an unintelligible whine as it fell from the air, shattering against the plascrete below in a spray of alloy components and a short burst of flame.

She turned to face Keen, who was gritting his teeth as he glared at the smouldering drone.

'You almost had it,' Darya said, passing Keen his rifle as he offered her long-las to her.

'The sights–'

'There's nothing wrong with the sights. You pulled the trigger too quickly, which knocked your aim off. Next time take a moment to settle, and squeeze.'

Keen fought to swallow the angry retort that curled his lip, and nodded.

'We heard a few shots back there,' Munro said as he arrived alongside his platoon a few minutes later. 'Have you made contact with the enemy?'

'Just a drone, sir,' Darya said.

Munro's platoon wrenched the crooked doors apart and scattered into the thoroughfare, some running to clear the doors on the opposite building whilst others knelt behind buttresses and trained their weapons on the walkways above.

'I've had no word from Boredin or Carr,' Munro said quietly as his soldiers burst into the generatoria building.

'No news is good news, sir,' Darya said.

'Hmm,' Munro grunted non-committally.

A trooper shouted the all clear, and Darya waited until Lieutenant Munro was out of the thoroughfare before leaving it herself.

The generatoria building had once been one of the beating hearts of Iron Hill, its promethium generators running day and night to provide power for the myriad facilities that spread tumour-like around the complex.

But as Darya took her first steps inside, the building shook not with the thrum of generators, but the pounding rhythms of battle.

Munro's platoon moved through the antechamber at speed, eager to reach their comrades in the generatoria hall beyond, but finding their path blocked by an inches-thick blast shutter of articulated plasteel panels. The percussive blasts of gunfire were barely muted through the door, punctuated with regular thumps of high-calibre rounds impacting nearby.

'Unless you've got some well-disguised ogryns or a meltagun with you, we're not getting through there,' Darya said as she weaved her way through to the front, where Munro was barking orders into a vox-receiver carried by one of his men.

'Sergeant Lenz, respond,' Munro said. 'We are at the eastern ingress. Get this damned door open!'

'Keen, with me,' Darya shouted as Munro nodded at Sergeant Lenz's garbled response. 'Listen close. It's going to be a mess in there. Stay on my shoulder until we get into a good vantage point, understood?'

'But, sergeant–' he said, but Darya cut him off.

'Do not get bogged down, Keen. Stay with me,' Darya said, raising her voice as the lumens set into the wall above the door burst into life, splashing the room with crimson light.

The shutter screeched, dust rattling from the frame as it began to collapse upwards into the wall around it.

The noise went from muted pops to a thunderous roar as the foot of the shutter left the ground, then gave way to the cavernous generatoria beyond.

Row upon row of promethium engines dominated the vast floor, their squat forms a promise of power that had long since idled into dormancy; some were aflame, belching plumes of black smoke as generations of blessing oils burned alongside the last dregs of fuel in their innards. Tangled nests of belts, driveshafts and thick cabling sprouted from the intact units, creating reaching tendrils that extended beneath the panelled floor and up past maintenance gantries above. The roof allowed lances of thin winter light through its pocked surface, giving way to glimpses of pale grey sky between knots of connective cabling.

Darya ran into the rows of generatoria, carried by the press of bodies as Lieutenant Munro led his teams into the maelstrom of battle. She couldn't even see the far side of the room through the forest of engines and the rolling smoke, but knew that it was several hundred feet away; all of the generatoria halls around Iron Hill were built from the same template.

There must have been fifty Cadians already in the room, fighting against a force that easily equalled them in numbers – at least until Munro's reinforcements arrived.

A handful were cut down as they ran to join their comrades

at the defensive line directly in front of the doors, rushing to cover behind boxy power units and hastily assembled Aegis panels. Plasma rounds created vortices of swirling smoke as they lanced out of the false darkness deeper within the generatoria hall, both from ground level and the raised gantries as the t'au pushed deeper through the polluted haze.

Munro ran towards a waving soldier, who Darya recognised as Sergeant Lenz, kneeling behind a barricade.

'Keen, with me!' Darya cried over the crack of las-fire, heading towards a stairway up to the first gantry level. 'Keen!'

Trooper Keen was fighting a battle in his own mind; his training had conditioned him to support his fellow soldiers and fight shoulder to shoulder until the bitter end. Darya was asking him to forget hard-learned lessons whilst retaining others so he could fight as a deadly individual as well as part of the stronger whole.

It took him several heartbeats to make his decision, gritting his teeth as he ducked low and ran to Darya through the volleys of pulse fire.

'Good man, Keen. Come on!' Darya shouted, taking the stairs two at a time up to the first level, where Cadians and t'au traded gunfire from behind their barricades: the humans behind sandbags and solid-alloy shields, the xenos behind glowing force fields that flared with azure light.

Darya turned back on herself as she made the landing and headed for the next stairway.

Pulse-rounds scorched the air all around her. Keeping low, she moved fast and without pause.

'Throne above!' Keen shouted as he followed behind.

'Keep moving!' Darya yelled without looking back.

She only stopped when they reached the safety of the next barricade, just short of the stairs up to the second level.

Down on the floor below, both sides traded volleys of suppressing fire as Munro's reinforcements got into position. It would be a matter of minutes before the Cadian numbers would begin to tell and their momentum ended the stalemate.

Darya's eyes were drawn to a drone armed with a single long rifle, two-thirds of the way up the hall, that moved erratically through the smoke.

Sniper drone.

She took aim with her long-las, tracking the drone's sharp movements until it came to a stop with its weapon pointing in her direction.

Her weapon hummed in her grip as she squeezed the trigger, adding her long-las' note to the chorus of whining lasweapons that split the air with their fury. The drone twisted as it fell, tumbling away as it dropped out of sight.

'Good shot!' a nearby trooper cheered between controlled bursts from his own weapon.

Darya didn't reply, leading Keen towards the next stairway just as plasma rounds hammered into the thick metal wall behind them.

The black iron stairs were warped and bent, several steps missing completely where they had been blown clear some time before. Darya didn't slow, and motioned for Keen to follow as she used her momentum to jump the missing steps and storm up to the second floor.

Darya coughed in the hot, smoky air of the upper level, the heat from the superheated plasma and las-fire exchanges below raising the temperature ever further the higher they climbed. The chasing pulse fire lessened as they made the upper gantry, giving Darya the time to finally scour the upper level with her scope.

'Watch my back,' she shouted to Keen as she swept her scope through the haze of oily smoke. The heat-sensitive filters were all but useless because of the background temperature, so she had to rely on magnification alone.

She couldn't see a sniper on the upper level or the level below, black armoured or otherwise. She saw plenty of the t'au troopers with short, boxy weapons that put her in mind of lascarbines, and even a couple of humans dressed in xenos uniforms, but none that stood out as snipers.

Logic told her that it didn't mean their target wasn't there, only that they hadn't found him yet. But her years of hard-won intuition told her something different: Longshot wasn't here. The sniper whose handiwork she had seen would have already taken down Sergeant Lenz and Lieutenant Munro, and quite possibly Darya too.

She scanned the gantries again, searching for any sign in defiance of what her gut was telling her.

Damn.

'Squad, this is Nevic. Our target isn't in the generatoria complex. He's likely at one of your positions. Acknowledge,' Darya said quickly, moving back from the edge of the walkway and into the shadows that clung to the greasy walls.

A succession of clicks and muttered affirmatives set her mind at ease. Her squad were still alive out there, but that didn't mean her job was done.

'It's time you start earning your keep, Keen,' Darya said to the young recruit. His knuckles were white as he gripped his lasgun tightly, and he shook slightly as he nodded.

'You shoot and you move – no heroics. You're a sniper now, which means you have to be clinical. Do you understand? Prioritise the squad leaders, the ones with designs on their heads or shoulder pads.'

Keen nodded again and shuffled forwards, out of the shadows towards the handrail. Darya got up into a crouch and moved away, putting some distance between herself and Keen to divide any return fire.

A whistle screeched out from below, echoing from the high metal walls as the Cadians let out a furious war cry.

'FOR CADIA!' they bellowed, and their rate of fire doubled. Cadians vaulted the barriers in tight fire-teams, darting into cover under the sudden hail of suppressing fire, Lieutenant Munro at the head of the charge.

For a cold bastard, he's a damned good officer, Darya admitted to herself, and raised her rifle.

A t'au fire warrior gesticulated towards the advancing Cadians, the short, sharp movements of his arm and the red linear designs on his helm drawing Darya's eye. He went down in a boneless sprawl as her first shot took him through the neck, just above the armour seal.

Keen's rifle whined twice, his shots lancing down into the t'au lines.

'Shoot and move!' Darya shouted as she repositioned herself, running twenty feet before dropping to her knees to line up her next shot.

A figure coalesced through the drifting smoke, kneeling on the level below. He'd hidden behind a control panel that jutted from the wall before Darya moved, but she had the angle from her new position. Through the magnification of her scope, she recognised the headset and projected hexagons of light before him: a drone controller. His head snapped to one side as her shot scattered brain matter and skull fragments over the walkway plating.

A white barrel-like object caught her eye on the ground level, but she was forced to move again as pulse-rounds hammered into the railings inches from where she knelt.

'Keen! Target the white cylinder on the ground!' Darya shouted into her vox as she ran, trusting her cloak to shield her from view.

Munro was taking ground with brutal efficiency. He used his augmetic fist as a bludgeon, hammering the xenos aside with vicious blows that were followed up with surgical shots from his laspistol. Darya could see him charging forwards through the plasma fire as Cadians fell around him, urging his troops onwards by sheer force of will.

Keen cried out as the t'au targeted his position, white-hot pulse fire turning the metal around him to dripping slag.

'Move! Keen, you have to move!' Darya shouted. She followed the path of the fire aimed at her recruit, snapping off two shots into the xenos targeting him. The first fell back in a dead heap, but the second shrugged off her shot on his oversized left pauldron. He repositioned almost immediately to put an engine unit between himself and Darya before she could fire again.

The top of the cylinder snapped up in Darya's peripheral vision, the glinting lenses dragging her attention away from the t'au warrior and back to her main target. Keen cowered where he was, his weapon clutched to his chest as the gantry around him continued to smoke as it cooled.

Darya took aim, and fired.

The cylinder was much like a drone – a piece of xenos tech that could move and shoot autonomously, equipped with a pod of missiles that were only armed when the drone activated. Darya knew exactly where to hit.

The missiles exploded in a blast of heat and shrapnel, tearing through the back of the t'au lines with destructive force. Fire warriors were incinerated or thrown from their feet, some crushed against their glowing barricades and the generatoria housings by the force of the explosion.

Munro leaped at the opportunity and led his men forwards, screaming encouragement over the last echoes of the blast. Those fire warriors that could escape did, falling back through wide doorways into the halls beyond. The rest put up a valiant defence, but did not last long as the Cadians surged forwards in a tide of las-fire, bayonets and righteous anger.

'I told you to move,' Darya said as she dragged Keen to his feet a minute later. His clear skin was marked with small burns from where he'd been splattered with molten metal, his new flak armour blackened and scorched. 'You shoot and you move – that's what the cloaks are for. Next time, you will listen.'

They met Lieutenant Munro on the floor of the generatoria hall as he was marshalling his forces, pulling forwards the Cadian defensive positions as gunfire rattled in the next chamber.

'Are you pushing on, sir?' Darya asked as the Cadians moved amongst the xenos, bayonetting each corpse to ensure it was truly dead before dragging them towards a growing pile by the northern wall.

'No, sergeant,' Munro said. 'We're the anvil, not the hammer. We have a flanking force sweeping in from the north. We will break the alien between us.'

Munro had a look of grim resolve in his violet eyes as he spoke, his face splattered with blood so dark it was almost purple in the shifting light. 'That was your doing?'

Darya followed Munro's eyeline to where the missile turret had stood, replaced by a scorched black crater littered with smouldering alloy fragments.

Darya nodded. 'Yes, sir.'

'Damned good shooting,' Munro muttered.

A tremor shook the generatoria hall, followed a few seconds later by the rumble of a distant explosion. The sound rolled through the building like a wave, and the Cadian troopers looked to each other in alarm.

'Letho, find out what the hell that was,' Munro shouted and strode off towards a trooper carrying a bulky vox-pack.

'*Boss,*' a voice said on Darya's vox. She recognised it as Arfit's, but he sounded strained and breathless.

'Arfit? What's going on?'

'*Bellis is down,*' Arfit said, a burst of plasma fire just audible behind his words. '*I can't get to him, I–*'

The vox cut off, just as a second distant explosion rocked the generatoria and set the walkways rattling on their mounts. Fear gripped Darya's chest, cold and twisting.

'Arfit, are you there? Arfit?'

'*I'm alive, boss. We're… We're pulling back. The assembly complex. It's… It's gone.*'

'I'm on my way.'

The assembly complex had been a maze of conveyors and tracked assembly lines, overhead cranes and multilevel gantries that the tech-priests would use to bless the sacred machines through every stage of their construction. When Darya had last been there, the stale air still tasted of a thousand years' accumulation of sacred incense and blessed unguents.

But as Darya approached, all of that history was lost beneath the black cloud of billowing smoke that choked the air, rising high into the atmosphere like ink through water. The main building of the assembly complex had been as large as any that Darya had ever seen, but now it burned in hues of red and orange so bright they sucked all other colours from the world below.

The heat was oppressive, even from hundreds of feet away, where Darya and Keen found Arfit slumped against the hull of an immobilised Leman Russ.

His copper skin was scorched and blackened with soot, half of his cloak burned away into wisps of glinting fabric that resembled a tangle of fishing wire. He stared straight ahead at the flaming building, hollow-eyed, as if blind to the destruction raging before him.

'Arfit,' Darya called out as she approached.

'Boss,' he said. He was barely audible over the roar of flames and the crash of collapsing structures.

Second Lieutenant Carr was nearby, a severe-looking woman with a shaven head and bright violet eyes, who shouted orders to her men as they assembled a defensive line. Troopers dragged their wounded back from the flames, their screams mingling with the whine of lasguns. A soldier shivered at Carr's feet, his flesh melted like candle wax.

'Bellis?' Darya asked as she knelt beside Arfit. He shook his head slowly, without meeting her eyes.

'He... He was dead before they blew the building.'

It was then that Darya noticed that Arfit's right arm was hidden beneath the remaining fabric of his cloak. She pulled it aside carefully, and Arfit made no move to stop her.

His hand was clamped over a seeping wound the size of her fist, a handful of blood-soaked bandages just visible beneath his fingers.

'Keen, go and fetch a medicae,' Darya said.

Trooper Keen tore his eyes away from the flames that were reaching hundreds of feet into the air, and ran in search of help.

'I saw him,' Arfit said, strength returning to his voice, his eyes focusing on Darya's. 'I saw the bastard that got Bellis. The one in black armour, the sniper.'

'Did you get him?' Darya asked, fearing she already knew the answer. Arfit shook his head and nodded down at the wound in his side.

'He got me first, the bastard... I didn't even see him until he was already sighted on me. It's the white strips on his armour, I don't think it's just for show. It breaks up his silhouette, makes him damned hard to see, like camouflage...' Arfit said between pained breaths.

Arfit's words rattled through Darya's memory, the cold weight of responsibility settling in her stomach. Her mind flew back to the figure in black running from the sewer weeks before, and when he'd shot the dirtcycle from beneath her and Ullaeus. She couldn't shake the feeling that if she'd been faster, she could have dealt with Longshot long ago.

'Good man – we know what we're looking for,' Darya said, swallowing the sour taste of guilt as she pulled another bandage from her own medi-pack and moved Arfit's hand away. The blood welled immediately, and she pressed the fresh bandages into the wound. Arfit hissed in pain.

'He went for us, boss. He didn't take a single shot at Carr. He went straight for us,' Arfit murmured, his eyes glazing.

'Not yet, Arfit. We still have a job to do,' Darya pushed harder on the bloody bandages, and was glad to see her man's eyes refocus as he gasped with pain.

Darya saw Commissar Tsutso long before he saw her.

He strode purposefully across the 217th's command centre towards where Darya sat outside the medicae tent, where the chemical stink of counterseptics was less nauseating.

It was only as his eyes met hers that she realised he had been looking for her.

Darya got to her feet and made the sign of the aquila as the commissar came to a halt.

'Nevic,' Tsutso said. 'Follow me.'

He led her back to the headquarters tent, where Captain Kohl was waiting. He wore his flak armour and his cap was tucked under his free arm, the other holding his crutch.

'Sergeant,' he said by way of greeting.

'Your first attempt at Longshot did not go to plan,' Commissar Tsutso said.

Darya bit back the bitter response before it passed her lips, and shook her head.

'Your man?' Kohl asked.

'If he survives he will be out of action for several weeks. Bellis... didn't make it out, sir.'

'His loss has been counted amongst the sixty who didn't make it out of the plant alive,' Tsutso said to Kohl.

'Throne,' Darya whispered. She had no idea that the losses were so high – her only concern had been Arfit's survival.

'Added to the sixteen lost in Munro's action, and another twelve in Lieutenant Boredin's,' Kohl said, 'today's losses are the highest since we took Trackway Span.'

'What about Third and Seventh Companies? Did they make it across the river?' Darya asked.

Kohl and Commissar Tsutso shared a look, and the captain shook his head.

'Both attacks failed, with heavy losses by all accounts. We're still on our own.'

'Only through the harshest trials may the faithful succeed,' Commissar Tsutso quoted. 'But as I have disclosed to the captain, word of today's losses are already spreading across the line. This blow to our morale cannot go unanswered.'

'Which is where you come in, sergeant,' Kohl said. He looked almost apologetic in that moment.

'I'll get back out to hunt down this Longshot, sir. We even have a description, so we know who we're looking for,' Darya said, but Commissar Tsutso shook his head.

'This goes beyond damaging the will of our enemies, sergeant. We need your help fortifying our own,' Tsutso said.

'Sigma, privacy filter,' Kohl grunted, and his servo-skull rose from its position on the table to wait by the tent flap. The bustle from outside grew suddenly dim.

'My thanks, captain. Sergeant, my role, like any member of the Commissariat, is to enforce discipline. Most often that takes the form of the threat of punitive measures for breaking discipline, but it also includes identifying opportunities to bolster morale,' Tsutso explained. 'I have identified you as one such opportunity. Your name carries weight within the battle group, and Colonel Wassenby has agreed that action must be taken in light of today's events.'

'I'm not sure I understand,' Darya said.

'You are a figure that Cadians across the Miracil front will rally behind,' the commissar said. 'A figurehead, a physical embodiment of the God-Emperor's will to inspire our troops to redouble their efforts. The Ghost of Cocleratum.'

'Sir, I'm a sniper not a figurehead. I just need more time, to find this Longshot and–'

'This isn't an offer, Nevic,' Kohl said. 'This order comes from far above me. The transport is already on its way.'

18

The next few hours passed in a blur of rubble-choked streets and ruined habs as the cargo-8 raced through the low city towards the landing zone.

Darya barely noticed any of it. She sat staring at her hands, still stained with Arfit's blood, brooding over the events of the last twelve hours. Bellis' death weighed heaviest on her mind, and she knew that the loss would badly affect the team. They wouldn't just miss his skills as a sniper, but also his relentless ability to lift the spirits of the squad with a well-timed joke, even in the darkest moments.

Captain Kohl sat opposite Darya in near silence, the only sound coming from the clicking of his data-slate as he read through reports of the day's actions. Judging by the grim expression on his face they didn't make for pleasant reading.

Then the transport rumbled to a juddering halt, and the rear hatch was jerked open to reveal the interior of a hangar, large enough to hold squadron upon squadron of Leman Russ battle tanks, all emblazoned with the winged lightning insignia of the Cadian 401st. A regiment's worth of Chimeras were neatly assembled towards the far end of the long room, every transport's paintwork unmarked by weapons fire, dirt or dust.

'Damned bracing, isn't it,' Kohl said. He led the way from the transport, stowing his data-slate in an interior pocket as he navigated the steps back down to ground level.

The captain was right – the temperature had dropped several degrees since they'd left the city. She could see the heavy snowfall outside through the hangar doors, which were closing against the building blizzard with a whine of motors.

'Where the hell are that lot going?' he muttered to himself, looking out over the tankers as they busied themselves with their charges, stowing ration crates and kitbags through hatches and under waterproof covers on the exteriors of the tanks.

'Captain Kohl, Sergeant Nevic?' an adjutant called out as he approached. He stopped just short of Kohl and snapped off a salute, the first that Darya had seen in weeks. 'If you'll follow me please, the colonel is expecting you.'

The adjutant led them through reinforced halls and corridors that Darya recognised from every prefabricated headquarters building she'd had cause to enter during the crusade's protracted campaigns. It was ruthlessly simplistic: rockcrete panels were shuttled down from orbit and assembled, plumbed and powered until the headquarters became a defensible position complete with running water, electricity and a dedicated comms suite. The height of luxury, compared to the conditions at the front.

The adjutant didn't lead Darya through to any of the sections she'd visited before, but to the officers' quarters in the upper levels.

'Captain Kohl and Sergeant Nevic, sir,' the adjutant said as he opened a pair of panelled doors. They swung into a well-lit room complete with a large holo-table, cogitator station and a wall lined with plush crimson curtains that hung in graceful pleats.

A group of men stood waiting in the room, their conversation cut short as Darya and Kohl entered.

The first Darya didn't recognise. He was a bear of a man, with broad shoulders and long dreadlocks of russet hair peppered with silver. He wore the orange-and-gold heraldry of House Gyrrant on his tight-fitting tunic, but his fair skin had the pallor of someone who did not spend much time in the sun.

The next was a commissar, a man who barely looked old enough to shave, never mind wield the bolt pistol holstered at his hip. He puffed his chest out proudly, the golden brocade across his uniform glinting in the room's warm lumen light. A servo-skull hovered near his shoulder, its eye sockets replaced by wide, void-dark lenses.

Two officers of the 217th stood with their arms clasped behind their backs, their uniforms worn and patched, looking as tired and battle weary as Kohl and Darya. Darya knew them both by name. One was Lieutenant Eridan, whom she'd briefly met at the start of the Miracil campaign. The other was Major Wester, the highest-ranking officer of the 217th who still lived.

The last wore the pristine dress uniform of the Cadian 401st, complete with epaulettes and an ornamental cord of braided gold that looped beneath his left armpit. His features were stern and severe, which put Darya in mind of a particularly sour schola-master from her childhood.

The infamous Colonel Wassenby, whom she recognised from the refectory vids. He was a regular feature above the line for hot food, where he'd be shown pinning medals on beaming troopers or touring the front lines and shaking hands with everyone he passed. Ullaeus had once commented, 'I don't know where the hell he's touring, but it isn't Trackway Span.'

'Captain, sergeant,' he said, his voice unexpectedly deep and resonant. 'Welcome to Command Post Alpha.'

Both Kohl and Darya saluted the colonel and his companions and waited to be introduced.

'I don't believe that you've met Lord Sylvester, Prince Consort of House Gyrrant,' Wassenby said, gesturing his hand to the large man clad in House Gyrrant colours. 'And this is Commissar Bowness, of the Officio Prefectus.'

The commissar clicked his heels together and inclined his head, but Lord Sylvester was far more animated. He threw his arms wide and approached Darya with a broad, yellow-toothed smile.

'You are smaller and fiercer than I expected,' he said, his voice hoarse with lack of use and his accent strange to Darya's ears. To her surprise, he clasped her shoulders and planted a kiss on each of her cheeks. 'Though from my Knight, most appear small to me.'

Darya could see the data cables and articulated cords that snaked in amongst Lord Sylvester's dreadlocks, disappearing into a cluster of ports across his scalp.

'It's an honour, my lord,' Darya said, stepping back into a short bow that began at her waist, just as she had learned as a child.

'You have the old manners,' Lord Sylvester said, his smile widening still further. He mirrored her, stepping back into a graceful bow of his own.

'Quite,' Colonel Wassenby said, clearly bored by the larger man. 'I believe you already know Lieutenant Eridan and Major Wester?'

Kohl stepped forwards and shook the other men's hands warmly, whilst Darya inclined her head politely.

'Wester, you old dog,' Kohl said, a genuine smile parting his lips. 'How's life in the north?'

'Cold,' Wester said with a tired grin.

If the rumours were true, Major Wester had been sent to the far north of the Miracil front with the 217th's Ninth Company in punishment for supporting Captain Kohl's First Company without Colonel Wassenby's approval.

Colonel Wassenby approached Darya and extended a hand.

'Sergeant Nevic, it's good to finally meet you. I've heard a great deal about your exploits,' he said warmly, and Darya grasped his hand.

A sudden clicking erupted from Commissar Bowness, or more accurately, from the servo-skull at his shoulder. He'd repositioned himself further away while Darya's attention had been on Wassenby, so he had an unobstructed view of the pair's first meeting.

'Eyes on me, sergeant – it's just a pict-capture device,' Wassenby said without breaking eye contact, his pleased expression becoming fixed until the clicking stopped.

'Shall I set up the medal pict next, colonel?' Commissar Bowness asked, his voice strangely familiar to Darya.

'By all means,' Wassenby said, turning back towards the waiting officers. 'Gentlemen, to the table if you would?'

Darya allowed herself to be steered towards the wall covered by the curtains as Commissar Bowness was joined by a pair of commissar cadets.

'Were you not told to wash before coming?' he asked, taking in her soot-stained, grimy uniform.

'No, sir,' Darya said evenly. 'I've just come back from an active operation.'

The commissar clicked his tongue and dispatched one of the cadets to fetch a list of items that Darya didn't catch. The servo-skull watched her with strange intensity, its darkened lenses making her skin crawl, but she was far more interested in the conversation taking place around the holo-table, where Lord Sylvester had produced a bowl of fresh fruit that he offered to Captain Kohl.

'I hear supplies are thin on the front,' Lord Sylvester rumbled, his baritone voice clearly audible from across the room.

'We are surviving, my lord,' Kohl replied, but took a pair of long orange fruits anyway. 'Though I am sad to say we aren't quite as comfortable as the rear.'

Darya lost Colonel Wassenby's response beneath the fussing of Commissar Bowness, who demanded that Darya remove the grease paint that she and her team used to camouflage their faces. She did as she was asked, accepting the offered alcohol-soaked cloth and rubbing it against her cheek.

'Your pistol,' Bowness said, holding out a gloved hand for the gun. 'We'll give it back, but we need to give you a standard-issue weapon for the picts.'

His cadets returned with a clean combat jacket, which she shrugged into beneath her cameleoline cloak. The commissars stepped back to admire their work, which gave Darya a moment to listen to what was being said at the holo-table.

'The operation was a failure. Your distraction failed to win any kind of meaningful objectives, which leaves us with limited options,' Wassenby said, his arms folded across his chest.

'If you were to commit but a fraction of the Four-Hundred-and-First to the battle for Iron Hill, we could force the enemy–'

'As I have already explained ad nauseam, *captain*,' Wassenby said, spitting the last word with venom, 'the Four-Hundred-and-First's objectives are to hold the landing zone and the supply routes into Miracil, not to–'

'Our objective is to take Miracil,' Lord Sylvester cut in, speaking through a mouthful of fruit. 'Unless that has changed?'

Wassenby's reply was lost as Commissar Bowness' cadets stepped in close to scrub away the last smears of grease paint that Darya had missed.

'We have just a few short questions for you, sergeant. Answer as enthusiastically as you can,' Bowness said as one of his cadets held out a portable vox-thief to Darya, the long wire connected to a recorder unit tended to by the other cadet.

'We are joined by Sergeant Darya Nevic of the Cadian Two-Hundred-and-Seventeenth – the famous Ghost of Cocleratum,' Bowness said, and Darya suddenly realised where she had heard his voice before: he was the voice of the loudhailers that over-powered the t'au propaganda broadcasts. 'Sergeant, tell us what it's like on the front lines?'

Darya looked from Commissar Bowness to his cadets.

'What should I say, sir?' she asked.

'The truth – that it's a pleasure to fight in the God-Emperor's service and all hardships are worthy in His name,' Bowness said.

'It's a pleasure to fight in the God-Emperor's name, and all hard-ships are worthy in His service,' Darya said. She looked down at her hands, at the dry blood that had collected beneath her fingernails.

'Close enough,' Bowness said as he turned to the cadet man-ning the recorder unit. 'Ortan, is that coming through?'

The cycle repeated over and over, as Bowness asked Darya questions and supplied the answers, making clear whenever her tone did not meet his standards.

Eventually the commissars had what they needed, and Bowness stepped away to try to catch Colonel Wassenby's attention.

'Sir, we need the support here and now. I'm not sure how opening up yet another front–' Major Wester was saying.

'You don't need to understand, you just need to follow your orders,' Wassenby interrupted, before noticing the young com-missar at his elbow.

'We're ready for you, sir,' Bowness said. He handed Colonel Wassenby a small, dull metal box from a pocket in his long coat.

'Into position in front of the banner, sergeant,' one of the cadets said, and steered Darya to where a white box had been painted onto the floor in front of the curtains. 'Both feet in the box and stand to attention, please.'

Darya did as she was told, a puppet made to dance.

'Chin up, shoulders back,' Bowness said as he positioned the lens-eyed servo-skull.

Wassenby smoothed the front of his tunic as he crossed the room, and pulled a black medal from the box by its red ribbon. He was well rehearsed, and played his part with ease.

'Sergeant Nevic, for your bravery and dedication I hereby present you with the Award for Conspicuous Gallantry,' Wassenby said in a loud, clear voice as he pinned the medal to her chest, stepped back and saluted. She returned the salute in shock. 'Good hunting out there, sergeant.'

It felt wrong to her, every part of it. Kohl had explained what was going to happen before they'd left Trackway Span, but it still felt wrong. She was no figurehead and had no desire to be, but it wasn't in her control. Perhaps it never had been.

'Excellent, sir. Now perhaps one with the sergeant holding her weapon?' Bowness asked.

'Good thinking, commissar.' Wassenby plucked the medal from Darya's chest, then motioned for her to unsling her long-las and hold it to the ready.

'Sergeant Nevic, for your bravery and dedication...' Wassenby repeated, going through the motions once more, but Darya was looking over the colonel's shoulder to Kohl, Wester and Lord Sylvester, who were watching the pantomime with obvious unease.

'Good hunting out there, sergeant,' Wassenby finished, and Darya realised that she was supposed to speak.

'Thank you, sir.'

'Very good,' Wassenby said, and turned back to Bowness. 'You have everything you need, commissar?'

'I believe so, sir.'

'Excellent. Thank you, sergeant.' Wassenby offered Darya his hand. She shook it again, and watched as the commissars gathered their equipment and made to leave. One of the cadets returned her autopistol and collected the borrowed laspistol, then the crows were gone.

'We are not your guard dogs,' Lord Sylvester was saying in a low, dangerous voice. 'House Gyrrant is a proud–'

'This is what the God-Emperor needs from your house. The Two-Hundred-and-Seventeenth will be stretched thin, and we will need your support. House Gyrrant cannot win this war alone, unless you plan to press forwards against the t'au without the Astra Militarum at your back?' Wassenby argued.

'With respect, sir, I must voice my reservations about this plan. The supply lines to the north are already strained, and we cannot reinforce them with our current manpower or materiel,' Major Wester said.

'I cannot leave without voicing my own concerns too, sir,' Kohl said carefully.

Colonel Wassenby shook his head.

'The plan is already in motion. The Four-Hundred-and-First will redeploy to the south of the city and begin a second front there. You have your orders.'

Kohl gritted his teeth, but saluted the colonel alongside Wester and Eridan.

'Sergeant, with me,' Kohl said, and made for the door alongside Wester, Eridan and Lord Sylvester. They were almost clear of the room when Wassenby called out to Kohl.

'Oh, about this Longshot business,' Wassenby said, almost

casually. 'Leave it alone. We're investing a lot of trust in Sergeant Nevic, and I'd like to see a return on that. Am I understood?'

'Yes, sir,' Kohl said, gesturing for Darya to follow before turning on his heel and striding off down the corridor.

'The damned fool will see us all dead whilst he chases glory to the south,' Lord Sylvester said in a voice so low it was barely more than a growl.

Darya stood a respectful distance away from Kohl, Wester and Eridan as they formed a semicircle around the bear-like Lord Sylvester in the hangar at the base of the command building.

The tankers still worked to prepare their vehicles along each wall, whilst more Chimeras were being loaded with large crates near the entrance. The great double doors stood closed against the night, but a long puddle was forming where the snow had melted under the entrance.

'He wants to score a decisive victory in a single strike, but that's not how the t'au operate,' Major Wester said, keeping his voice quiet.

'All this will do is tie up our reserves on a second static front,' Sylvester agreed.

Eridan frowned. 'I hope not. It will be a great waste of lives if his gambit fails.'

'What are you thinking, Kohl?' Wester asked.

'I'm thinking that my place is at the front where I can do some good,' Kohl said. 'Gentlemen, if you'll excuse me.'

'May our next meeting be in victory,' Lord Sylvester said, and inclined his head to both Kohl and Darya.

Neither Kohl nor Darya spoke until the cargo-8 had passed out of the landing zone and back into the low city, when the shadows of the ruined buildings chased the meagre light of dawn through the observation slits cut into the transport's hull.

'I'm sorry, Nevic. I know that wasn't… pleasant,' Kohl said. His augmetic eye gave off a dim red glow in the unlit cabin, but not enough for Darya to see him clearly.

'I understand that it was necessary, sir.'

'Perhaps. It doesn't mean it was easy.'

'No, sir.'

Darya unclipped the medal from her chest and ran a thumb over the embossed metal in the dark. She could feel the symbol of the Cadian Gate, two thick pillars either side of a stylised skull, all topped by an angular keystone. She'd met Cadians who'd inked the symbol into their own flesh, but she knew the feel of the symbol because it was one of the sigils that had been engraved onto her long-las by its previous owner. He was a man she had respected, even if they hadn't quite seen eye to eye on everything.

'Where will they use them, sir? The propaganda picts and the vids?'

'Here,' Kohl sighed. 'At least, that's what Commissar Tsutso told me. We're hoping that support from the Ghost of Cocleratum will help fortify morale, especially in light of recent events.'

Darya let out a slow, calming breath.

'You're still not comfortable with the name, are you,' Kohl said. It wasn't a question, but more of a statement of fact.

'No, sir.'

'Why is that?'

'It's complicated, sir.'

'Try me, sergeant.'

'Because I didn't die on Cocleratum, sir. I survived when better men didn't and it's hard to be reminded of it, like I'm supposed to wear it like a badge of honour,' Darya said, her hands instinctively moving to her long-las.

'And yet you still carry Mir's rifle,' Kohl observed. Darya flinched.

'That's... That's me doing my duty. And remembering them as they were. It's complicated, sir.'

The silence stretched out between them for a moment, broken only by the jostling of the cargo-8's suspension.

'It is, but I think I understand. However, there's something you need to understand too, Nevic,' Kohl said and leaned forwards in his seat. 'I knew what we were risking when I sent you, Ilya and Mir into Elborescum. Any guilt that you feel for their deaths belongs to me.'

'The way people have looked at me ever since that day... I never wanted to be a figurehead, sir.'

'We all serve in our own way, Nevic. Sometimes others are forced to choose that way for us, which brings me to the subject of Longshot.' Kohl's tone was resigned. 'You're not to hunt Longshot again. As much as I hate to... That is to say, we can't risk losing you against him.'

'You're standing me down from operations, sir?' Darya said incredulously.

'No. But I am forbidding you from hunting Longshot – your team are perfectly capable of hunting him on their own, but you are not to go after him yourself. Is that understood?'

Darya's fist clenched painfully tight around the medal.

'Perfectly, sir.'

19

Do you see it, my student? The thin veneer of bravado that masks the rot beneath.

They clutch at reeds in their desperation, but they are already drowning.

Their will is almost broken, and now is our time to strike.

We will seek out this scarred one. They have hung their hopes on her, and we will hang her from the highest tower of this blighted world.

Arfit's breathing was slow and steady as he slept, his skin less pallid than when Darya had left his side several hours before.

The medicae tents were filled with wounded Cadians and the stink of counterseptics. The least injured were seated outside on improvised chairs, conveyor belts and even the floor in some cases, their wounds patched with browning gauze and discoloured bandages. Most sported burns from the destruction of the assembly complex, and it was clear that several would never fight again.

It was there that Ullaeus found her, with Yanna in tow.

'You all right there, boss?' Ullaeus asked, cradling his long-las in his arms.

Darya looked up from watching Arfit's chest rise and fall, fearful that it could stop at any moment.

'I am now,' she said. It was true; there had been a knot of tension in the pit of her stomach since she'd returned to the command centre to find that members of her squad were still in the field.

Yanna walked past Darya, pausing to lay a reassuring hand on her shoulder on her way to check on Arfit.

'They're showing your medal ceremony on the vid reel,' Yanna said. 'Congratulations, boss. It's well deserved.'

'They've also been plastering these up on the walls alongside all the others,' Ullaeus said, holding up a poster. It showed her standing against the broken silhouette of a burning city, long-las held over her chest, with the words *Cadia Stands!* in bold lettering beneath her.

Darya shook her head angrily.

'Didn't waste a damned moment did they.'

'The Hero of Miracil,' Ullaeus laughed.

'Don't,' Darya said, her anger subsiding as she caught the sincerity in his eye. It felt wrong to break the solemn quiet of the medicae tent, so she led her team outside away from the wounded.

The propaganda vids still played over the queue for hot food, showing human troopers charging down a lander ramp, the caption beneath declaring: *Brave Cadian troopers launch a daring attack on the xenos-held moon of Orialchium!* Members of the 217th watched the reels in weary silence, gathered around barrels of burning promethium in an attempt to keep warm.

'Listen, both of you,' Darya said, pulling them in close. 'The Four-Hundred-and-First are moving south to open up a second front, so things are about to get very busy around here.'

'Damn,' Ullaeus said, surprised. Yanna spat on the ground.

'It gets worse. I've been ordered not to hunt Longshot.'

That drew a far more visceral response from them both, and she pulled them further away from the medicae tent as they protested.

'Please tell me this wasn't your idea,' Ullaeus said.

'What do you think? That bastard killed Bellis and put Arfit out of action. I want his head.'

'So what will you do?' Yanna asked.

'I'll follow my orders, for now,' Darya said. 'I'm not being stood down. If I meet him in the field then he's fair game, but I don't want either of you hunting him either.'

'You don't think we can take him?'

'I think you could, but there are three of us covering the entire Cadian Salient now. It's too big of a risk.'

'Four if you include Keen,' Ullaeus said, and nodded over to where the fourth member of their squad was standing with several other trueborn Cadians, watching the vid projection over the queue for food.

It was showing Colonel Wassenby as he pinned the medal onto Darya's chest, his rehearsed speech supplied as Low Gothic runes superimposed over the image.

'Four, of course,' Darya said with a sigh. 'We'll take it in alternating twelve-hour shifts. Minimises risk to us and will help to keep focus high.'

'Feels like a step back, boss,' Yanna said.

'It's not a step back. We're just fighting smarter.'

Ullaeus and Darya shared a look, before he steered Yanna away towards the food queue.

Darya stalked away, casting the medal into a barrel of burning promethium as she passed.

* * *

When news filtered through that the 401st were leaving for another battlefront, even the famed discipline of the Cadians suffered.

As the days rolled by there were scant few symptoms of bruised morale; those that were present were fuelled as much by the falling temperatures as the news of the failed river crossings and the absence of the 401st.

News trickled in of scuffles over fuel rations in the trenches and squad leaders being forced to adjudicate disagreements over blankets and winter gear, but the Commissariat only became involved two weeks after Darya's trip to the landing zone.

As Attruso's distant sun rose over Trackway Span, Darya stood to attention outside Relief Station Zero alongside several other sergeants who had been called to bear witness.

'You stand here convicted of murdering a fellow Cadian,' Commissar Tsutso said, his resonant voice echoing over the loudhailers set up across the Cadian trench lines.

Darya shivered, and not just from the cold. On the opposite side of the street, a young pureblood Cadian named Farrow had been tied to a lumen-post, stripped of his arms and armour so that he stood shivering in only his undergarments. Darya kept her eyes on him and not the posters on the wall behind him, several of which bore her image.

Everyone in First Company knew the story that had led Farrow to this point. An argument over a stolen winter coat had escalated to a brawl between almost twenty soldiers, Farrow amongst them. It had ended with Farrow's bayonet buried in the neck of a transplant soldier named Leodis.

Everyone knew that the fight hadn't been about the coat, not really. It was the culmination of two principle factors: nine years of fighting a crusade that seemed without end, and a proud regiment's bitter disappointment at being left to guard a forgotten front whilst another regiment was given the chance at glory.

Darya had expected far worse in the last two weeks than a single execution; it seemed that the increased propaganda was smoothing over the cracks in the Cadian morale.

Commissar Tsutso drew his bolt pistol, its freshly oiled black casing glinting in the grey light of the Miracil morning.

'The sentence is death,' Tsutso said, his breath steaming in the cold morning air as he took aim at Farrow's chest.

'Cadia stands!' Farrow shouted.

The shot rang out, echoing across the Cadian Salient so all heard it.

A flash of the iron fist in the velvet glove, Darya thought.

'What a fragging waste,' Sergeant Gosht said from Darya's right where he stood rigidly to attention.

'Take that away,' Kohl grunted to two waiting troopers from Farrow's unit, who moved forwards to cut down his corpse. The bolt pistol had almost split the body in two, splattering blood and viscera over the wall behind the post. They dragged what remained away, one arm dangling to the floor on strings of bloody gristle.

Commissar Tsutso watched, flexing his grip on his bolt pistol, until the dead man's boots slipped out of sight beneath the tarpaulin-covered doorway of Relief Station Zero.

'Dismissed,' Kohl barked, and limped forwards to speak to Commissar Tsutso.

So endeth the lesson.

Darya set off back to the command centre with the other sergeants, their conversations muted by what they had just been forced to witness. It was a warning of what awaited any further loss of discipline, and they all knew it.

'Are you back out on patrol or is it Ullaeus' turn?' Gosht asked as they trudged through the murky grey snow.

'Ullaeus and Yanna should be back by now, so Keen and I will be heading out,' Darya said. 'Why, do you need something?'

'I was just thinking that it'd be good for you to show your face around Farrow's unit if you find yourself up towards Myrak Park,' Gosht said as he glanced back at the empty lumen-post and the blood spattered on the wall behind it.

'I don't think–'

'It'd bolster them after what's just happened, Nevic. Give them something else to think about.'

Darya sighed. It was yet another unwelcome effect of her new profile, and not the first time she'd been asked to make herself visible amongst the other troops since she'd appeared in the vid reels.

'I'll try to find a reason to get over to Myrak Park on the way back from this patrol,' Darya said with a nod. The trench was on the northern edge of the Cadian Salient, far from Darya's patrol route in Iron Hill, but she knew that Gosht was right.

The other sergeant said his goodbyes as they passed into the command centre and kicked the snow from their boots, and made off for the trenches and his unit.

Kroller shouted her over as she returned to the main floor of the command centre, ignoring the lingering gazes of the troopers passing through towards the trenches.

'What is it, Kroller?' she asked as she reached his desk, stained with ink and scattered with torn message slips. Kroller was unkempt, and while his spare frame was wrapped in a blanket to keep off the worst of the cold, he shivered regardless.

'Took a while, but I got it done,' he said, holding out a slip of parchment covered in annotations and scrawled corrections.

'I'd completely forgotten about this,' Darya said in surprise. 'You decoded it?'

'Took some doing. That's why you pay me the big money,' Kroller said with a hoarse laugh. 'Well, the mediocre bribes anyway.'

'Thanks, Kroller, I appreciate it,' Darya said. 'I'll get you those rations when the next supply run comes in.'

'Anything for the Ghost of Cocleratum,' Kroller laughed.

'Screw you, Kroller.'

'Remember, we said three weeks' worth!' he shouted as she walked away, struggling to decipher Kroller's scrawled handwriting in the morning light.

Sol 5141 Cycle Umbra
354 solar cycles since the death of the astropathic choir
The sky still bleeds
Deep-space auguries have detected a flotilla of ships entering the system. Classification: Xenos. Species: T'au. Estimated time to planet-fall: Nineteen days.
Low city is in full revolt. They are coming.

The xenos didn't conquer the system, Darya realised. *It had already fallen.*

She looked around for any sign of Ullaeus or Yanna, and pushed the fall of Attruso to the back of her mind. It was an interesting fragment of the planet's history, but not one that she could use to her advantage.

Her feet grew uncomfortably cold as she waited for her corporal to appear, and she started to pace in order to stamp some feeling back into them. Her movement led her to the medicae tent, where Arfit was still recuperating.

He was awake and sitting up by then, which had set the rest of the team at ease. There didn't seem to be much they could do to lift his mood, however.

'How're you feeling, trooper?' Darya asked as she weaved between the cots of prone soldiers, most still recovering from the burns they had sustained in the assembly plant.

'Oh, you know,' Arfit said with a wince as he tried to shift his weight into a more comfortable position. He was propped up on a bundle of his own gear – Munitorum-issue pillows were little better than plascrete slabs in washable covers, but they were still hard to come by on the front. 'It'd be nice to get a full night's sleep. We're all in pain, we get it, no need to keep moaning about it. You listening, Tolver?'

The heavily bandaged trooper on the next cot held up his hand, the remaining fingers making a rude gesture at Arfit.

'Making friends?' Darya asked.

'Something like that,' Arfit said. 'Won this in a card game last night, so it's not all wasted time.' He held out a small brass lighter, its tarnished surface etched with words that Darya couldn't read.

'Didn't know you were a smoker,' Darya said.

'I'm not, and we're not allowed to smoke in here anyway,' Arfit said with a thin smile. 'One of Tankada's lads won it from a supply runner a few weeks back. Everyone in here has won it at some point.'

Darya just listened; she'd been injured before, and knew that the hardest thing to deal with wasn't the pain or the moans of your comrades, but the endless monotony as you waited to heal. It was why she made a point of visiting Arfit – it gave him someone different to talk to, which would help.

'It's good to see you're not taking it too easy,' she said finally. 'I'm taking over from Ullaeus in a little while, so I need to go. Take care until he comes back, you hear?'

'Will do, boss. You haven't… Has anyone got the bastard yet?' Arfit asked without looking up from the lighter.

'Nothing yet. We'll get him,' Darya said.

As she strode through the command centre, she hoped that was true. Aside from a few possible sightings they'd seen little of their elusive target since Bellis' death, despite the fearsome toll of Cadian officers who fell to sniper fire as the battle for Iron Hill ground on.

'Keen, get over here,' Darya shouted to the young Cadian, who was sitting with several other Cadians in his usual position watching the vids over the refectory queue. He got to his feet and jogged over, his new long-las clutched to his chest.

His skills were improving with every patrol, but Darya still wasn't sure that he had the mentality or self-discipline to become a sniper rather than a sharpshooter. He was too quick on the trigger, too eager to score low-level kills without calculating if a more valuable target might become available.

Until she was sure about his skills and the limit of his abilities, she couldn't allow him to shadow anyone else within the team. That was why he had continued to shadow her, so if he made a bad call then she would be the one to mitigate the damage.

'Boss,' he said by way of greeting.

'Have you seen Yanna or Ullaeus come back yet?'

'Not yet. Have you tried the vox?'

'They'll be out of range if they're still in Iron Hill. Come on, we'll probably meet them on their way back.'

Darya spoke out of hope more than anything else, and tried to ignore the sense of foreboding in her stomach.

Darya led the way through the support trenches to Creed's Row, occasionally trying the short-range vox but gaining no response. Cadian troopers parted to let her pass, muttering her epithet like an intoned blessing as they inclined their heads respectfully.

'Ghost.'

'The damned fools realise that you're still human, don't they?' Keen muttered, once they were out of earshot of the nearest troopers. 'Unless you've been sainted too and no one's told me?'

'Believe me, it's not something I exactly enjoy.'

She'd almost learned to tune out the sound of her own voice on the loudhailers, giving answers that weren't hers to questions that command didn't really want the answers to. It was the same with the endless t'au broadcasts. It was just background noise to her.

But as she moved past a squad of troopers who looked at her in genuine shock, she realised that the t'au had changed their message.

'The Ghost of Cocleratum is no more! Why do you continue your fight when your idols lie dead at our feet? Who will you turn to now that you are abandoned by your kin and forsaken by those who would pretend to watch over you? Abandon all hope in the Imperium as it has abandoned you. Join the T'au'va and choose your own fate, before that choice is taken from you!'

The squad of Cadians looked to Darya in confusion as her heart hammered with fear.

'The Ghost of Cocleratum is no more! Why do you continue your fight when your idols lie dead at our feet?'

'Keen, double time!' Darya shouted, and shouldered her way past the troopers. She broke into a run the moment she had the space, pressing the vox-bead into her ear as she raced towards Iron Hill. 'Ullaeus? Yanna? If you can hear me, please respond.'

'Nevic, where are you?' Kohl's voice crackled over the vox.

'On our way into Iron Hill, sir,' Darya replied, darting between soldiers who looked at her in shock.

'Negative. You are to return to–'

'I'm still alive, sir. Ullaeus and Yanna are out there and I need to find them.'

'Sergeant Nevic–'

Darya yanked the vox-bead from her ear and turned to Keen.

'Keep broadcasting for Ullaeus and Yanna. We're going to find them.'

Iron Hill's entry hall stank of damp clothing and standing water, the imposing metal walls glistening with the last of the night's frost as Darya ran in with Keen in tow, trailing loose snow in their wake.

Their arrival went unnoticed in the clamour of other troopers running back and forth between vox-stations and a bank of cogitators.

'Increased activity reported in the refinery complex, sir,' one called out.

'We have enemy contact in sectors eleven through twenty,' another added.

Lieutenant Munro stood at the centre of the maelstrom, his features etched with a fatigue that he appeared to be holding back by sheer force of will as he orchestrated runners and returned messages with clinical efficiency.

'Wait here,' Darya said, and jogged over to Munro. 'Sir, I need–'

'Pull a squad back from the foundry to reinforce the refinery, and tell Sergeant Tannant to hold his ground. And someone get me Captain Kohl on the damned vox!' Munro barked, before turning to Darya. 'What is it, sergeant?'

'I need to know my team's last known position, sir,' Darya said quickly, competing against more updates for Munro's attention.

'You,' Munro said, pointing an augmetic finger at a flustered-looking vox-operator. 'Get the sergeant what she needs.'

'Yes, sir,' the junior officer replied, and started to sort through a sheaf of printed communiqués. 'Last position update was from the assembly complex, two hours ago.'

'Thank you,' Darya said.

'Sir, an urgent update from Captain Kohl,' another vox-operator shouted.

Darya thought she could guess at the content of that message, and ran back over to Keen before anyone could call her back.

'Assembly complex. Come on, we need to move.'

The assembly complex stood beyond the furthest reaches of Cadian-held territory in Iron Hill, and still cast a long shadow despite the damage it had sustained.

It had once stood as a towering edifice, filled with a warren of rooms within its crenellated metal shell. Chambers the size of Astra Militarum troop landers were stacked one atop the other, each packed with cranes, tracked conveyors and heavy lifting machinery manned by grotesque servitors. A nest of high gantries had provided a path for the overseers to supervise every room and every stage of the assembly line, quite literally lifting the planet's former masters above their workers.

But as Darya and Keen picked their way through the thick snows that blanketed Iron Hill's exterior, there was little left of the complex's once imposing shape. Almost two-thirds of the building had been razed to rubble and tangled scrap by the t'au's wrathful bombardment, leaving only the western face of the complex standing sentinel over its gutted innards.

Bellis' body was lost somewhere deep in that ruin, and Darya could only pray that Yanna and Ullaeus hadn't joined him in death.

She slipped the vox-bead back in her ear now they were out of range of command and wouldn't be distracted by Captain Kohl's orders to pull back. 'Yanna, Ullaeus, please respond,' Darya subvocalised. There was no response.

'I'm not sure that this is a good idea, sarge. Maybe we should turn back?' Keen said.

Gunfire echoed through Iron Hill from the east, occasion-ally punctuated with the boom of heavy ordnance. It only grew more intense as the minutes ticked by, but didn't seem to be getting any closer.

'We're finding our people,' Darya said without looking back at Keen.

They stood on the fringes of the open ground before the assembly complex. A Cadian barricade stood far away to their left, complete with three heavy-bolter emplacements, a forward position that marked the extreme edge of the Imperial lines. To Darya's right lay the path to the complex.

Darya had purposely chosen her path through Iron Hill, skirting around Cadian positions to avoid detection on the way to the assembly complex, as much to save time as to avoid being called back.

'This is as far as we go on foot. Follow me and stay low.'

She dropped to her stomach and began the long crawl through knee-deep snow towards the complex.

It was a long, cold path across the open ground, past the ice-encrusted form of a burned-out Leman Russ, then onwards into the complex itself. They emerged into the ruin through a small hole blown through the exterior wall by some long-forgotten explosion, the once ragged edge melted smooth by the heat of the blaze.

That same fire had burned all colour from the building's interior, leaving only blackened metal and the mottled grey of Miracil's polluted snow beneath the open sky. The air still tasted of bitter ash and scorched metal, despite the weeks since the explosion and fire that had consumed the building.

'Look for any sign they were here,' Darya subvocalised, and Keen nodded his acknowledgement.

She edged forwards through what little clear ground there

was between piles of sagging floor plates and the twisted crane components. Boom arms and gigantic girders created an undulating landscape beneath the heavy snowfall allowed in by the sundered roof, breaking through the glistening blanket to create blackened voids amidst the grey.

Darya was forced to crawl beneath a fallen lifting frame, which pressed the sodden layers of her uniform against her skin. She fought the urge to shiver despite the freezing cold and the extra weight, and forced herself on.

'I can't see anything,' Keen said from somewhere else in the complex. 'There's too much rubble.'

Darya reached the northern corner of the complex and found a plascrete stairway that had survived the blaze almost unscathed, despite the thick soot encrusting the steps themselves.

There were footsteps in the soot.

'Keen, on me, northern corner stairwell,' Darya subvocalised.

She dropped to one knee and cleared the stairway above; the handrails had been warped and bent as far up as she could see, but the stairs themselves stretched up at least three storeys. There was no sign of anyone in the stairwell besides her.

'What do you think, Militarum-issue?' Darya asked as Keen arrived, pointing down at the boot prints that led up the stairs.

'Could be,' Keen said non-committally.

'Well it's not t'au, since they don't wear boots,' Darya said. 'I'll take point.'

She led the way up the stairs with her long-las at the ready, being careful to place each of her steps in the existing treads. The walls were oppressively dark, and more than once she thought she caught a flicker of something in the corner of her eye. Each time it turned out to be nothing more than an indistinct ripple in the scorch marks, but it was enough to put her on edge as she reached the first landing.

Light poured in through the empty doorway, and Darya quickly moved into cover behind the solid plascrete to the left of the opening.

The gantry beyond stretched a few yards out into the empty air then disappeared, the ragged edge the only sign of where the remainder of the deck plating had fallen away.

'It's not high enough to get a decent view over the complex,' Keen noted as he took up a position on the other side of the doorway.

'No. Plus, the footsteps don't end here,' Darya said.

She followed the prints up the next flight of stairs to the landing above, where they led out of the stairwell and onto the gantry over the main floor. The walkway sagged in places but appeared complete, and was covered in an inches-thick layer of snow that had melted into grey water at various points.

But Darya's eyes were drawn down the walkway to the prone figure that looked out over the complex below, their weapon shouldered and aimed, their body covered by a thin layer of snow.

'Yanna, Ullaeus, are you there?' Darya subvocalised.

If the figure heard Darya it gave no sign, but continued to watch over the black-and-grey landscape below.

'I'm going out there,' Darya said to Keen. She expected him to resist or to try to argue – Ullaeus or Yanna would have – but he said nothing. He simply nodded and took to one knee to give himself a more stable shooting platform.

'I'll keep an eye out,' he said.

Darya left her satchel with Keen and took to her stomach once more, crawling out towards the prone figure, using the height of the gantry and the layer of snow to conceal her movement.

She was less than five yards away when she realised that whoever the person was, they were dead.

The air around the corpse smelled faintly of burnt meat over the complex's metallic sear, and it gave no sign of the rise-and-fall of breath. Darya inched closer; she had to see it with her own eyes, despite every instinct telling her what she already knew.

It was Yanna.

Darya pulled back the cameleoline hood to reveal the young Episcan's tattooed features, which stood out even more starkly against the blood-drained pallor of her skin. Her sharpened teeth were still bared as if in challenge, though both of her eyes had been consumed by the blackened crater that was all that remained of her upper face.

'It's Yanna. Plasma shot to the head,' Darya subvocalised to Keen.

'*Shit.*'

'I know,' Darya said softly. She let the hood fall back over Yanna's features, covering the ruinous wound and the barely healed scar that had been so much like Darya's own. 'I'm sorry, my friend.'

She reached out to squeeze Yanna's hand in one final gesture of friendship, when she felt something in the Episcan's gloved grip. It was a strip of white cloth, reflective and smooth like satin in the cold winter light, and it set Darya's heart to racing.

If the xenos sniper had been close enough to leave a token on Yanna's body, he'd been close enough to leave a trap, or worse.

Darya pulled slowly back on Yanna's hood and cursed.

Yanna's vox-bead was gone, alongside the vox-band around her throat. Longshot was there, and he was listening.

She had to protect Keen; it was the only thought in her head in that moment. She had already lost Yanna and likely Ullaeus too, and she couldn't lose yet another squad. Only when he was safe would she be able to hunt Longshot.

But how?

She was trapped on the gantry, her only escape to her rear and in a position that her enemy was doubtless watching through his scope.

One thing at a time.

'Keen, I need you to listen to me very carefully,' Darya said, aware that she was likely speaking to more than just him. 'I've got eyes on me. I need you to get back to command and tell them that I need Captain Bechmann. Do you understand?'

'*Captain Bechmann? But–*'

'Yes or no, Keen. Do you understand?'

'*Yes, boss,*' Keen said.

The language had to be clear enough for Keen but too oblique for Longshot; she had to ensure that Longshot stayed on her and didn't figure out what she was saying and make his escape.

After all, everyone on the Cadian Salient knew about Captain Bechmann. She had been in one of the first reels shown in the command building, being awarded a medal by Colonel Wassenby for her role in directing her artillery company in their week-long barrage around Trackway Span.

Through Keen, Darya had just asked for an artillery barrage on the assembly complex.

The minutes ticked by at a torturously slow pace.

The chill leeched into her bones through the snow-sodden material of her uniform, and after the first hour it was all she could do not to shiver.

She distracted herself at first with prayers to the God-Emperor. She asked Him to forgive her pride, to watch over Keen as he carried his vital message, and that He might take Yanna into His embrace with warmth. Darya prayed for Frantt, Kadden and Bellis, and finally for Ullaeus.

Her gut told her that Longshot was still there, still waiting. All snipers knew the patience that their work required, the hours waiting for their target to give themselves up. It was only a matter of waiting for the other's nerve to break, or for them to make a mistake. Then it was just a case of squeezing the trigger.

But as Attruso's distant sun reached its zenith and began its short journey towards the horizon, Darya's thoughts turned to a bleaker outcome than the one she had planned. What if Keen didn't make it back to camp? Or worse, what if he did but hadn't understood, or her request for an artillery strike was denied?

As the sky began to darken, Darya began to consider the real possibility that the order for the strike might not be given. She could lose Longshot in the darkness, missing her chance at revenge on the man who had killed Yanna, Bellis and Ullaeus. Their deaths would be for nothing, and after her defiance in leaving camp she doubted she'd be allowed out of Commissar Tsutso's sight ever again, if he didn't shoot her for disobeying orders. At best she would become a true figurehead, with no control over her own fate.

She couldn't let that happen.

Her options were few, but she still had a few routes off the gantry. Some were riskier and would be more painful than others, but as she clutched the strip of white material in her hand, she knew that they would work.

'Okay, you bastard, let's see what you've got,' Darya said into the vox, the chattering of her teeth giving away how truly cold she was.

She pushed her hands into the snow either side of her, wincing at the pain in her joints as she pushed herself above it and into a low crouch.

Stay low. Present a smaller target.

Yanna was heavy, despite her slight build. The snow had

melted beneath her from her body heat, soaking her uniform through just as it had Darya's. It didn't matter; all that Darya cared about was getting her friend off the floor.

'I'm sorry, Yanna,' Darya said as she finally got the other woman's body over her shoulders and began the long trudge back towards the doorway behind her.

Something bright and hot slammed into Darya's shoulder hard enough to throw her off her feet, and all she knew was falling.

Consciousness returned, and with it came pain.

It seemed that there were few parts of her that didn't burn with the angry buzz of broken bones and torn ligaments, even deadened as they were by the icy chill of the snow bank she had fallen into. Her left shoulder, legs, hips, ribs and the right side of her face all burned despite the cold, leaving her with only her right arm trapped beneath her chest against the metal floor.

Her long-las was gone and she was face down in the drifting snow, but the plan had worked... in a way.

Yanna's body had taken the worst of the plasma shot, but Darya hadn't expected the force of the impact to be so strong. From her limited view, half submerged in the snowdrift, she was back on the floor far below the gantries, and there was no sign of Yanna's body. It had been the only way she could think to shield herself from the shot, and she prayed that Yanna's spirit would forgive her.

She fought to stay still, both to help with the plan and to limit the pain that each tremor had on her injures. Hiding her breathing was the easiest part, since each breath had to be shallow so as not to stoke the white hot flames that erupted in her ribs with each inhalation.

There was no way to track the passage of time as she lay face down on the floor of the assembly complex. It could have been minutes or hours later when she finally heard a sound that set her heart racing once more.

Snow crunched beneath heavy feet as someone moved nearby, each step bringing them closer to Darya. Adrenaline surged through her, each nerve crying out for her to crawl away, to scramble to safety with what little strength she had left.

She fought the urge down and waited, the stiff fingers of her right hand closing about the handle of her kvis.

The footsteps came to a stop only a few feet away, approaching Darya from behind.

Come on, you bastard. Leave your token so they know it was you.

The figure moved again, planting a foot either side of Darya. He gripped her collar and pulled, and it was all she could do not to cry out as she was turned onto her back.

The kvis slid silently free of its sheath and licked out across Longshot's throat.

Blood sprayed from the grievous wound as he let out a strangled snarl and fell back, putting one hand to his throat as the other pawed at a sidearm at his hip.

She had relied on his arrogance to bring him close, and it had worked.

He quickly gave up on the pistol. He used both hands as he desperately tried to staunch the rhythmic spasms that shot blood across the snow-covered floor, falling onto his back as his strength gave out. Longshot was a human dressed in t'au garb, the black armour tailored to his larger proportions and combined with what could have once been Imperial equipment. The few white strips tied to the panels of his armour were turning red as they were caught in the spray of his blood.

Darya watched with grim satisfaction as Longshot thrashed against the floor, his booted feet scraping furrows into the crimson snow. The kvis was a solid, reassuring weight in her hand as Longshot's erratic movements slowed and grew weaker and weaker, until finally they stopped completely.

'I got you, you fragging traitor,' Darya managed to say.

She tried to focus her eyes on the still figure of Longshot, only to realise that her left eye was swollen shut. The right was watering, the sensation so cold that it hurt to look down on her enemy.

She stared as long as she could, before the shadows at the corners of her vision grew to envelop her in a dreamless sleep.

20

Rough hands pushed Darya onto her back, tearing her from peaceful nothingness and back into a world of cold and pain. She gasped in a long-overdue breath, the burning of oxygen-deprived lungs adding to the stabbing heat radiating from her ribs.

Keen's face loomed over her in the evening gloom, his expression tense as he checked her over. Explosions echoed from somewhere far away, underscored by the rattle and snap of small-arms fire.

'I... told...' Darya managed to gasp.

'Don't try to speak,' Keen said. He reached up and loosened the strap of her vox-bead and pulled it clear, then plucked her kvis from her hand and stowed it in his belt.

Then Darya noticed her long-las in his hand, and understood. He followed her gaze to it, then back down at her with a shrug.

'I don't think you'll be needing it any more, sarge.'

Darya spat a gobbet of bloody phlegm that slapped onto the worn synth-leather of his boots.

'The feeling was mutual, sergeant.'

Keen raised her long-las over her head and brought it crashing down.

The world lurched.

Snow crunched and creaked.

Pain, angry and unyielding, flared across her back and ribs as the world lurched again.

She opened her right eye – the left was swollen shut or blinded, she couldn't tell – onto a world of inverted colour. The sky was black as pitch, the purple bruise of the Great Rift spreading from behind a jagged ruin off to her right, whilst the ground had been blanketed in pearlescent ivory. The snow was all but unbroken but for a churned track that wound a long path between unfamiliar buildings, terminating at Darya's feet.

She was being dragged through the rat-runs by a strong hand that gripped the collar of her fatigues, winding a jagged path through the various buildings of Iron Hill.

'Stop,' she croaked, but the person pulling her didn't hear over their gulping breaths. 'Stop, please.'

'You're awake, boss?'

Ullaeus lowered her slowly to the ground and worked his way around her side, appearing above her in silhouette at first. It was only as he knelt beside her that she realised that he was in little better condition than she.

His left arm was bound in an improvised sling, the hand covered in a misshapen bundle of bloodstained bandages that were black in the dim light, but his face bore the worst of his wounds.

The right side of his head was a mass of puckered burns and blackened, raw skin, as if his head had been held over a fire until the flesh had melted. His right eye was sunken in its socket, his blond hair burned away and the corner of his mouth curled into a taut grimace.

'It doesn't hurt,' he lied, his relief clear on the unscarred half of his face. 'I caught a plasma ricochet. I had to use the last of my stimms to keep it at bay...'

'I got him,' Darya said through the relief flooding her chest, lending her strength at the thought that even one of her friends was still alive. Her mouth tasted of old blood, and she could feel it caked over her lip and chin beneath the searing heat of her broken nose.

'I saw, boss. I came to and found his body next to yours. I couldn't leave you there.'

Where are we? she tried to ask, but all that came out was 'Where...?'

'We're still in Iron Hill, boss. The t'au are on the offensive and our guys have been pushed back. I'm trying to find us a way back to our lines, wherever they are,' Ullaeus explained in a soft voice that wouldn't carry far.

Darya could hear the sounds of battle in the background, far closer and more intense than they had been at the assembly plant. The whip-crack of lasguns could have been less than fifty yards away, and she could almost make out the orders being shouted at gunlines nearby.

'I'll get us back, boss. I promise,' Ullaeus said, and waded through the snow behind her. She felt him grab her collar and begin dragging her again, each step he took tugging painfully on her injuries.

She must have lapsed into unconsciousness during the long walk through Iron Hill, but came to as Ullaeus started speaking excitedly.

'Boss, do you hear that? That's a Chimera engine!'

Ullaeus was right. The throaty grumble of a promethium engine was getting louder, closing in on them from the direction Ullaeus was heading.

'I'll be back, boss, I swear,' Ullaeus said quickly, and lowered Darya back to the snow again. She was shivering uncontrollably by then, each spasm reminding her how injured and helpless she was as Ullaeus scrambled away through the snow. He called out to the Chimera again and again, his voice almost lost beneath the grinding engines.

Then they roared once and went idle.

'She's over here. Careful, she's wounded. We need to get to an aid station,' Ullaeus was saying, though Darya couldn't see to whom.

'Throne, you're not wrong. You two, grab the sergeant and get her back into the Chimera,' a familiar voice said, and Lieutenant Ceres of the Kintair Rifles appeared in her sightline. Strong hands gripped her shoulders and feet, lifting her from the floor and making their way unsteadily back through the snow to a Chimera.

Heat and light spilled out of the open rear compartment, where a rifleman was hurriedly assembling a collapsible stretcher. They placed Darya on it as Ceres looked over Ullaeus' wounds in the red light of the Chimera's lumen.

'That looks damned painful,' Ceres said.

'I'll live, we just need to–'

A flash of light illuminated Ullaeus' face in the darkness as a laspistol shot rang out.

Darya let out a wordless cry as Ullaeus stumbled back from Ceres, clutching at his chest as he fell to the ground. Ceres fired twice more at Ullaeus' prone form and turned to face his men.

'Get her into the transport and sedate her,' he ordered.

Darya tried to rise, fighting impotently against her broken

body, but between the cold and her injuries she barely had the strength to raise her head from the stretcher.

The Kintair ignored her strangled cries and lifted the stretcher into the Chimera and roughly set it down between the benches. A cold-eyed trooper slammed a syrette into her thigh as a figure appeared in the hatchway beside Ceres.

'We should be getting underway, my lord,' Ceres said to the newcomer.

The t'au's helm lenses glowed blood-red in the centre of his helmet as he looked down at Darya. His armour was a shade of black so deep that he would have been indistinguishable from the shadows behind him if it weren't for the strips of white cloth bound to his armour.

Longshot's outline blurred as the sedatives took hold, and the red light of his helm lenses chased her into unconsciousness.

21

So passes another acolyte, his fire extinguished in service of the Greater Good.

Of course, I mourn him in my own way. I mourn the many tau'cyr *spent teaching him our art, the many* decs *spent contemplating the greater mysteries with him. I mourn the future he will not fulfil, the service to the Greater Good that will have to be shouldered by others.*

Only through teaching the way do we come to understand our place within the T'au'va. I will honour his memory by continuing my own study of the Rip'yka *and how it may serve por'sral.*

Darya swam in an ocean of memory, drifting on the surface of the great salt sea.

She was with her mother in the Garden of Fountains, watching the rainbows of light that shimmered over the cold spray. Avians sang as they played in the sky, fluttering between the high towers of pale stone.

She knelt on a high platform scattered with decayed auto-cherubs, looking down on a monster that wore her uncle's face.

She stared dumfounded at the slip of parchment in her hands. The words on it made no sense, but had been marked with General Agha's signature regardless.

'I'm sorry, Nevic. I truly am. The regiment will be poorer for the loss of your bloodline.'

'I don't understand, captain. I'm Coclerati, not Cadian.'

She could hear the pain and confusion in her own voice, despite the void-black half-mask she wore. It was part of her identity as a wayfinder, just like the intricate long-las she carried and the layered robes of dark material that made up her uniform, and it was all being taken away.

'It is the will of the God-Emperor, glory be upon Him.'

'Glory be upon Him,' Darya echoed numbly.

Grief and fear washed through Darya's mind, flooding through her consciousness in a wave of sickening loss.

I can't lose everything again, she thought. *I can't...*

Darya spasmed as life returned to her body, her thrashing movements sluggish and heavy. The lack of pain terrified her. Everything should hurt – her face, shoulder, arm and leg – but there was nothing. Not the blissful absence of pain or the numbness of anaesthetic, just... nothing.

Am I dead?

She forced her eyes open, and flinched back from the blinding light.

Her left eye was blurry and dotted with black spots, but her right eye told her an unbelievable truth.

She was suspended in mid-air above a pristine white floor, in a small circular room that was devoid of furniture or decoration, filled instead with light from an unseen source. Darya tried to look up but found the movement blocked by an invisible force that held her steady.

Then she realised that she wasn't breathing.

The thought set her heart racing, which triggered a shrill alarm that warbled as she thrashed and tried to drag in an impossible breath. Her body would not respond. The breath would not come. She would drown in this strange prison of light.

A door sliced itself into existence in the wall opposite and a lone figure dressed in white strode in, each step clacking as the toe-hoof struck the white tiles.

It was a t'au.

It has come to watch you drown.

It approached her without fear or concern and reached below her with its thick-fingered hand. The alarm cut off abruptly, to be replaced by a calm voice.

'Calm yourself,' the t'au said in flawless Gothic. 'The gel is breathing for you. Please, you must remain calm.'

It didn't make sense. None of it made sense. Why was she still alive? Why did it not try to kill her, as she would try to kill it if their roles were reversed?

'If you do not calm yourself I will be forced to sedate you,' the t'au said, the chasm in the centre of its face flaring as it drew in a breath.

Her heartbeat began to slow as the darkness did not come for her. She felt none of the signs of being choked or drowned. There was no fire growing in her lungs as they were starved of oxygen, or the burning adrenaline to give her the strength to escape.

'Thank you,' the t'au said, looking past Darya to a point she could not see. It nodded as if satisfied and stepped back.

'Wait!' Darya said, and to her surprise her voice echoed from the hard white walls, despite her lack of breath.

The t'au did not stop, stepping through the door without a backward glance. The door slid closed and became indistinguishable from the surrounding wall again, as if it had never been there at all.

She did not know how long she waited, hanging immobile in the air as thoughts raced through her mind. Was this a t'au prison? A form of torture? Where was she?

There were no answers to any of the questions she had, and each possible answer only led to yet more questions that ran roughshod through her mind. It could have been minutes, hours, or even days, she couldn't tell as all concept of time melted away.

There she drifted, between waking and sleeping. She thought she recalled a t'au in black armour watching her from the doorway, but when she had focused on the flashes of white on his arms and torso she had realised that the door was closed.

The most pain she felt was when she thought of Ullaeus, of Yanna and Bellis, of her friends that she had left behind. They could not be dead, could they? They were so very vital, filled with life and memories and dreams, too alive to have died the way they did. Then came anger, as she fought for each fraction of movement, each flexed muscle a victory in her mind.

She begged the God-Emperor to save her from the torment of un-being, to let her die so she could be with the family she had carved for herself from a regiment that hadn't wanted her. He did not answer.

There was only one path left to her, one course that made sense in her mind. She would have her revenge.

'Darya Nevic?'

Words were spoken in a language that Darya didn't understand. The second voice was subservient to the one who had spoken her name, that much was clear.

'Do you dream, Darya Nevic?'

Darya opened her eyes, the black spots in her vision completely gone and her sight sharper than it ever had been.

Two t'au stood before her, one in long flowing robes of thick ivory fabric chased with bronze silk, the other the t'au that had spoken to her before.

'How do you know my name?' Darya asked.

She had spoken to herself a lot during her solitary confinement, marvelling at the loss of her need to breathe. She had sung, screamed and cried to test the limit of the gel prison that both held and sustained her. It felt odd to finally speak to another living creature.

'Very good,' the robed t'au said, its dark eyes narrowing in what Darya took to be a smile.

Its skin was darker than the one in white, the blue so deep that it seemed almost purple in hue, its hands held before it with fingertips entwined.

'How do you know my name?' Darya repeated.

'We know much of you, Darya Nevic,' the robed t'au said. 'Your home world, your many feats and accomplishments. Your dreams, such as they are.'

'Why?'

'There is time for that,' the t'au said. 'Tell me, Darya Nevic, do you know where you are?'

'I...' Darya fought the urge to answer, to continue a conversation that went against every teaching she had ever learned. Xenos were perfidious scum, an evil blight that wanted nothing more than to destroy humanity. They existed to be purged in the righteous fire of the Imperium... but she had been alone for so very long.

'I am Sergeant Darya Nevic, Two-Hundred-and-Seventeenth Cadian Regiment.'

'Hmm,' the t'au said, pursing its lips. It turned and swept from the room with the white-clothed t'au before Darya could shout for it to return, to continue to speak to her, to remind her that she still lived.

The cycle began there and continued in relentless repetition. The robed t'au would return and ask Darya a simple question: did she know where she was? She would respond with her name, rank and regiment, and the t'au would leave her alone until she couldn't bear it. It would return only after the screaming had stopped, when Darya was sure that her mind would break and she would lose herself to the emptiness she felt.

'Do you know where you are, Darya Nevic?'

'Do you know where you are, Darya Nevic?'

'Do you know where you are, Darya Nevic?'

Darya's tears wouldn't flow. They stuck to her eyes, held fast by the gel that enclosed her, clouding her sight as the gel slowly absorbed the water away.

'I… I don't know where I am,' she whispered.

'Very good, Darya Nevic. Allow me to tell you.'

The t'au introduced himself as honoured Mui'el, a humble servant of the T'au'va. When Darya asked who T'au'va was, Mui'el simply raised his arms and told her that it was everything. It made no sense to Darya, but she didn't press him for fear of beginning the cycle of abandonment once more.

She learned that she was not imprisoned, but in a device called a healsphere. It was healing her many terrible wounds, Mui'el explained at length, even going so far as to summon Fio'vre Non. He was the white-garbed t'au who had first spoken to Darya, and had been the one to alter the healsphere technology for human physiology.

'Your sub-frame was badly damaged when you arrived,' Fio'vre

Non explained, projecting a tri-dimensional image onto the wall opposite Darya using a handheld device. Darya marvelled at the technology, having rarely seen such an image cast by anything smaller than table-sized.

The image horrified her in its detail. So much of her body had been utterly broken – her eye socket, nose and jaw had shattered, and several vertebrae had been fractured alongside her shoulder, arm, leg and a number of ribs.

How am I alive?

'My skeleton,' Darya corrected the medic, who considered the word then nodded his thanks.

'Skeleton. Thank you,' Fio'vre Non said. He backed out of the room with a deep bow to honoured Mui'el, always facing him until after the door closed.

'I thought you said you were a servant?' Darya asked Mui'el.

'I am,' he replied, still smiling warmly.

The silence stretched between them, and Darya searched for something to speak about with the t'au. She dreaded his absence. She couldn't imagine anything worse than to spend another minute alone in that room, and would do almost anything to continue the conversation.

'Why are you keeping me alive?' she asked. It was the question she most wanted to ask, but she also feared the answer.

'Why would we wish you dead?'

'You sent men to kill me.'

Mui'el's smile became fixed, the warmth leaving his eyes as his lips drew back from his teeth like a growling canid.

'I did not send the *shas* to kill you,' honoured Mui'el said, his palms meeting and parting in a flowing gesture whose meaning Darya couldn't decipher.

'Okay,' Darya said. She believed him. 'And it doesn't bother you that... I...'

'That you killed them? No,' honoured Mui'el finished for her. 'They served the T'au'va just as I do. Had they not given their lives, do you think you would be here now?'

'I suppose not,' Darya admitted. 'But you haven't really told me where "here" is.'

Mui'el narrowed his eyes, as if weighing up a decision in his mind.

'I will show you.'

Darya feared removal from the healsphere, worried that her body had forgotten how to breathe and that she would suffocate in the open air, or her injuries would leave her vulnerable.

Fio'vre and his assistant removed her from it regardless, lowering the healsphere to the floor, where it disgorged her in a flood of odourless gel. Strong t'au hands caught her before she hit the floor, wrapped her in clean white robes and held her steady as the retching began, only releasing her when all of the gel was gone from her stomach and lungs.

Her limbs were sore but strong, and she was soon able to stand on her own without help. Fio'vre Non and his assistant left her with several soft towels to scrub the remaining gel from her skin, alongside a fresh set of clean robes made from a comfortable, thick material.

It was only when honoured Mui'el appeared in the opening doorway that she realised the thought of escape hadn't even crossed her mind.

'Would you walk with me, Darya Nevic?' he asked.

The corridor outside her room was brightly lit by unseen lumens that cast everything in clear, crisp white. The walls seemingly stretched away for miles in either direction, unmarked by doors or any sign that they were anything but one solid piece of unspoiled material.

'What is this place?' Darya asked.

'It is a place of healing,' he said, and lifted slightly into the air before her. She realised that he was standing on a thin platform much like a drone, its workings and armour not dissimilar to the many that Darya had destroyed in Miracil.

He swept forwards on the platform, holding his hands together so the palms met and the fingertips of two fingers were touching. Through their conversations, Darya had come to understand that the t'au language must rely on gestures far more than Gothic, but had yet to learn what they meant.

Darya followed behind him, her bare feet slapping on the cool tiles. She followed through a door that appeared from the wall, much as the one in her room seemingly appeared and disappeared, and into a room that was lit with warm organic light.

'You are in Miracil, Darya Nevic, as the T'au'va would see it be.'

The wall to Darya's right disappeared into transparency and Darya started in surprise as the vista beyond revealed itself.

Proud buildings of crisp white and ivory stretched out from the near distance, devoid of the blunt brutalism and gothic ornamentation of Imperial architecture. Each line was smooth and flowing, graceful curves shaping every structure for the sake of their own artistry.

But it was the greenery that stole Darya's breath.

Manicured grass lawns carpeted the ground, divided by elegant pools and gravel pathways that glimmered in the sunlight, tall trees swaying in a breeze that Darya's skin ached to feel.

'I don't understand,' Darya whispered. 'Miracil is dead, it's… I don't understand.'

'This is the T'au'va, Darya Nevic,' honoured Mui'el said, laying a hand softly on her shoulder as she gazed at the figures in the gardens far below. They sat on benches and on the lawns, human and t'au alike, as if entirely unaware of the war that scarred Attruso's surface.

'I need you to explain that again, honoured Mui'el,' Darya said, her hands trembling on the cool glass. 'What is the T'au'va?'

'The T'au'va is more than a belief or a simplistic creed. It is the will to unite all sentient life behind a single impulse, to create the greatest good for the greatest number,' Mui'el explained.

Darya sat on the floor of her room, her legs crossed beneath her as if she were back in the schola, the floor cleared of the gel and the empty healsphere.

At least, she thought it was the same room. It was certainly as featureless and unremarkable as the room she had been held in.

Honoured Mui'el sat on his platform in front of her, his legs crossed beneath his robe as his hands flowed lithely through a series of beautiful gestures. A pair of fire warriors watched from positions near where the door had appeared, both helmeted and bearing pulse weapons, though Mui'el spoke as if they weren't there at all.

'In your tongue it is "the Greater Good" – the balance of scales between action and outcome. On one side is the work of our people, on the other the benefit of all. Do you see?'

'I believe so,' Darya said, massaging a pulsing tension headache that had begun as she looked out over the landscape that honoured Mui'el had called Miracil. 'But I don't see how the T'au'va is different to the Imperium. I've been fighting all my adult life to protect my people. How is that not the same as what you do?'

'The difference is that we do not simply fight to protect, Darya Nevic. We fight to unite and overcome adversity as one cohesive whole, not to subjugate all within our petty fiefdoms.' Mui'el spoke passionately, bringing his hands together and interlacing his fingers to create a solid whole. 'Is that the way within your Imperium?'

Darya wanted to deny mankind's flaws, but the lie died in her throat before she could give it voice. She knew it wasn't true; she'd seen the evidence for herself a hundred times over on every world she'd ever set foot upon. Miracil alone was a gallery of scars that humanity had inflicted upon itself, from the chains that had once held workers in the manufactoria to the wanton pollution that rendered the waters so poisonous that even the rodents couldn't survive.

'The Imperium isn't perfect,' Darya said, knowing that those words would have seen her shot as a traitor or heretic if she'd spoken them to a fellow Imperial citizen.

'Nothing truly is,' Mui'el said in a conciliatory tone, 'but it does not mean that we should not continuously strive for it. Does your Imperium seek to improve, to achieve some small sliver of perfection? Or does it hide behind dogma and tradition?'

'I… We fight…' Darya stuttered, the headache growing to a thudding pain behind her eyes. She got to her feet and the two fire warriors tensed, ready to strike if she made any move towards Mui'el, but he held them back with a gesture as Darya paced back and forth.

'If the fight is all there is, what happens when the fight is done?' Mui'el asked.

'There is the God-Emperor,' Darya said reflexively.

'Ah yes, the God-Emperor. I have heard much of He on Terra.' Darya stopped pacing and looked at the seated t'au.

'What have you heard?'

'That all mankind fights in His name, that He is everywhere

and sees all. I find that second part hard to believe, but I am the first to admit that I do not know all of the universe's many mysteries.'

'It is not for us to question His nature, only to fight and die in His name,' Darya said, as if by rote.

'What of those who interpret the God-Emperor's will? Do they explain His plan or simply demand that you comply with their orders?'

'To question the Ecclesiarchy is to question the God-Emperor Himself,' Darya said.

'And there is the main difference between the Imperium and the T'au'va. We know we are imperfect, but strive to reach our zenith together. The Imperium believes itself to be perfect and seeks to remain exactly as it is.'

Darya stopped pacing as the headache began to recede, but noticed that the two fire warriors were still tensed and ready to strike.

'How would things be different under the T'au'va?'

'But who leads it? Who decides what needs to be done?' Darya asked.

Several hours had passed as Mui'el had explained the T'au'va's ways to Darya, providing answers and explanations for each of her many questions. The fire warriors had remained stoically still throughout, but Darya knew that their eyes were on her and her alone.

'There are no leaders,' Mui'el said, his hands settling into still-ness on his knees. 'There are guides, who counsel the will of the whole towards the best outcome. I am one such guide.'

'Like a politician, then?'

'I am familiar with that word,' he said with a shake of the head. 'But no, we are not like your politicians. We do not lie for our own gain, or for individual advancement. Such things are counteractive to the T'au'va.'

'How do your people divide the labour? How do you decide who must fight and who must farm?'

'We have the castes, where people are given to the work that best fits their abilities. For example, those suited to war are the fire caste, those with affinity for technology or engineering are the earth caste. The water caste are adept at the ebb and flow of debate and thought-play, and those with a need for travel are the air caste.'

Darya nodded at the explanation of the castes, understanding how each could contribute to a greater whole.

'So… you are water caste?' Darya asked.

'Not quite, Darya Nevic,' Mui'el said with an indulgent smile. 'I belong to the fifth caste – the ethereal. We are the spirit that binds all other castes together, moving amongst them and yet through them for the betterment of all.' He moved his hands through a series of shapes, until finally they settled with forefinger against thumb.

'You are the leaders, then.'

Honoured Mui'el narrowed his eyes and dropped his hands to his knees again.

'We have no leaders, only the Greater Good.'

Darya sat and considered the ethereal's words, and the possibilities there might be in such a world.

She didn't think that the t'au would chain their earth caste to their workstations as the Imperium did in the dark mills of industry, building weapons to wage war against enemies that had no wish but to live in peace. They would not build the Iron Hill and lobotomise their workers into little more than flesh automata, all the better to wring more hours of backbreaking labour from their bodies before they broke.

'I know that you came to this world after they had risen up,' Darya said. Honoured Mui'el tilted his head slightly, but did not speak. 'Did your people conquer them after they were already divided?'

'No,' he said, his hands moving once more. 'We came in peace and were received with peace. We arrived into a system bereft of direction and in the grip of famine, cut off from your home world by the Devourer of Hope. We offered our help, without limit or condition, and they accepted without hesitation. Over time they came to understand the T'au'va, and were drawn into the greater whole.'

That made sense from what Darya had seen in her time on Attruso. Warehouses and manufactoria had been burned whilst habs had been left untouched, at least until the Imperial forces had arrived. The combat had been hand-to-hand, the rising of an angry mob and not the organised rebellion of an armed force. Even Keen had noticed that much.

She grimaced at the thought of Trooper Mas Keen, who had left her to die in Iron Hill. And for what? The crime of being born on another world, to another people?

'You are angry, Darya Nevic,' honoured Mui'el observed.

'One of my men, he…' Darya swallowed. 'He left me to die.'

'I am sorry,' the t'au replied, and Darya believed that he meant the words.

'Is this the point you offer to put a gun in my hand and give me the chance to go after him?'

'No, Darya Nevic, it is not,' the t'au said. 'The *rotaa* grows short, and you are not yet recovered. Tomorrow we will walk the gardens, if that pleases you.'

Darya got to her feet as the ethereal's platform rose higher into the air and swept towards the doorway that appeared in the white wall. She found herself bowing to him, but could not explain why.

22

The grass was cool and sharp under her bare feet, the soil beneath rich and thick with life. Darya could barely believe that anything could grow in the polluted soil of Miracil, but the greenery wasn't just growing – it was thriving. She walked through dappled shade thrown by tall trees that honoured Mui'el explained had been brought from a distant world as seedlings, and had grown to maturity under the care and protection of the T'au'va.

It was beautiful in a way that Darya couldn't explain. She'd never stood in a place where the dominance of stone and plascrete hadn't been asserted with squat buildings or the artless spires of the hive worlds. Even on her home world, nature was only tolerated within strictly enforced limits; the t'au used it synergistically, working with the organic forms to create archways of fragrant blooms and wildflower beds that teemed with insect life.

'The gori-hornets gather nectar from the flowers and collect it within their hives, where it ferments to become a sweet paste that can be harvested and eaten,' honoured Mui'el explained as Darya studied the shimmering metallic insects, their translucent wings humming as they moved from flower to flower.

'That must take a while,' Darya said, not entirely sure that the t'au wasn't making a jest at her expense. Each gori-hornet was no bigger than the tip of her finger, and surely couldn't carry much of the flowers' nectar.

'You would be surprised. They work together as a hive, hundreds of individuals labouring as one,' he said. Darya snorted, and the t'au raised an eyebrow. 'Was I too unsubtle, Darya Nevic?'

'A little,' Darya said. 'And please, call me Darya.'

They moved on, Darya enjoying the temperature change in the grass as she walked from the shade to a stretch that was bathed in warm light.

Almost as soon as they had left the medicae facility, Darya had realised that the sky above was not the same as the one she had fought beneath in Miracil. They were beneath a protective dome of energy that must have been miles across, and stretched so high at its apex that it was barely visible at all.

'You haven't asked me any questions,' Darya observed after a few minutes' silence that was only disturbed by the buzzing wings of the insects and the rustle of wind through the nearby greenery. She had expected honoured Mui'el to ask her about troop disposition and deployment, or possible attack routes and cypher codes.

'I have asked you many questions during our time together,' honoured Mui'el countered.

'Not relevant ones,' Darya said.

'All of my questions have been relevant, Darya,' he replied, making a gesture that resembled a wagging finger.

'You've asked about my understanding of your people, your culture. Nothing about the war, about my regiment.'

'Do you wish to talk about these things?' he replied with a welcoming wave of his hand.

'No, but I...' Darya began, unsure of where her mind was leading her.

'Feel free to speak your mind, Darya. You are not in the Imperium now, we do not punish honest thought here,' honoured Mui'el said, his hands settling in his lap.

'We are taught never to be captured, to fight to the death. To be captured means torture and interrogation, where we are forced to betray our comrades,' Darya said.

'We have not tortured you,' the t'au said, which Darya couldn't agree with. The days of isolation in the white room, denied any sensory feeling by the healsphere, and the absence of any visual stimuli had felt like torture to her. What other word could there be for it?

Manipulation.

'You healed me. I did not expect that,' Darya hedged, unwilling to openly disagree with her host.

'You were wounded.'

'We do not do the same for your soldiers,' Darya said softly.

'Our fire warriors do not expect mercy from the Imperium. You show none for your own people, never mind those you perceive as your enemies.'

Darya was surprised at the bluntness of that response. She watched as the ethereal held his hand out and allowed a gori-hornet to alight on his finger, then blew softly on it to encourage it on its way.

'What do you know of the Imperium? Of my people?' Darya asked.

'Everything I need and more. M'yen Shoh is not the first world on which we have encountered your species,' he said. 'My apologies. M'yen Shoh is the name of this planet in our tongue.'

'How did the people of Attruso feel about you renaming their planet?'

'They did not care. It is a name, a breath given meaning. Nothing more,' honoured Mui'el said, his hands forming a symbol over his chest.

'It is their identity,' Darya argued. 'It is the place of their birth, of their ancestors' before them!'

'And those who survived the lifetime of backbreaking labour, the uprising and the ensuing famine felt little connection with it. They wished to be reborn anew, alongside their world,' the t'au said.

Darya looked away, afraid that she had overstepped herself in arguing with the ethereal. She waited for him to summon the guards who lingered just out of view, as they had from the moment she'd been escorted from her room to walk alongside Mui'el, but they did not approach.

Darya noticed that there were far fewer people out in the gardens than she had seen the day before, which she assumed was because she was there.

'I'm sorry that I… That is to say, if I–'

'I am not offended, Darya. You bear the weight of a lifetime's repetition of Imperial rote. It is tattooed onto every facet of your mind.'

'You speak as if you know me,' Darya said.

'I have met many of your kind, and each of you are the same in that regard,' Mui'el said, his platform drifting forwards so that Darya was forced to follow him.

'And yet you're here talking to me,' Darya said. 'What is it that makes me so special? Is this a test, or an evaluation of some sort?'

The t'au sighed, but continued leading Darya through a winding path bounded by neatly trimmed hedges and flower bushes.

'I know your history, Darya. I seek to know the person that history has created.'

'My history?' Darya asked, a little taken aback.

'Yes. Would you like to hear what I have learned?' he asked, but continued before she could respond. 'You were born on a planet named Cocleratum, and served in their janissary regiments until the Cadians took you. Since you were transplanted, you have fought on many worlds and earned just as many honours, but have never sought fame. You simply gave your all to your mission and endeavoured for the best outcomes, even when your service took you back to your home world.'

'Stop,' Darya said quietly. 'Please.'

'You were damaged on Cocleratum,' the t'au said, his head tilting slightly as he looked intently at her.

'I received this scar there,' she replied, her thumb tracing the line from her eye to her lip.

'No, I speak of a different kind of damage, one that lingers within the mind. And I do not believe it was all from when you returned as a Cadian,' he said.

Darya's heart hammered as he spoke of her history with greater detail than anyone she had ever met.

'Are you a witch?' she asked. 'Can you see within my mind?'

'No, Darya. We t'au have no dreamers within our castes. I have learned all I have through conversation.'

'Conversation with…' Darya began, but the words evaporated as they stepped into a grove of trees planted into a perfect circle, a shallow fountain set into the grass in the centre. A man knelt by the pool, drawing his fingertips through the clean, clear water.

Bol Ceres.

Two fire warriors appeared in the periphery of her vision, the warning clear.

Rage burned at her core as she looked upon her friend's

murderer, setting her nerves ablaze with the need to attack, to beat him to a pulp and drown him in the shallow pool at the base of the fountain.

'He came to us seeking a new life, not only for himself but for his people,' honoured Mui'el said.

'He murdered my friend,' Darya said, unable to keep the fury from her voice as her fists clenched until it became painful.

'He did what was necessary to create the maximum good for the most people,' honoured Mui'el explained. 'I ask that you speak to him, as I have.'

'Why?' Darya asked. 'I want to kill him.'

'And yet you will stay your hand,' honoured Mui'el said. 'His life belongs to the T'au'va now, to the Greater Good, just as yours will.'

It was a test, then. To see if she could be of use to the t'au.

Ceres watched her with wary eyes as she stepped forwards, away from the ethereal and into the sheltered glade. A child laughed nearby, the noise making the Kintair flinch, but he didn't look away from Darya.

He wore robes much like hers, loose-fitting and comfortable, woven from a fabric the colour of dried blood.

She stopped on the opposite side of the fountain, the low stream of burbling water the only barrier between her and the need to kill him. It took all of her focus and restraint, exercised through her years fighting as a sniper, not to launch herself at Ceres.

'Nevic,' he said eventually, inclining his head in greeting.

'Murderer,' she replied coldly.

'I was given an order,' he said. 'I couldn't allow us to be discovered. The attack on Iron Hill was only meant to be a short distraction and our window was closing.'

'He was wounded, like I was! You could have saved him, brought him with you!' Darya said, her voice rising.

'You know I couldn't. Do you think he would have come with us willingly? At best he would have raised the alarm, at worst he would have raised the alarm *and* injured or killed several of my people. I couldn't allow that.'

'Your people are on the other side of the barricades,' Darya said.

'Don't you dare come at me with that,' Ceres growled. 'You're either Cadian or you're nothing to the Imperium. A number on a cogitator, a tally on a record sheet. We are forgotten, given second-hand gear and third-hand food, and God-Emperor forbid you don't thank them for the piss in your canteen.'

'That's a fragging lie and you know it.'

'Don't you dare!' Ceres shouted, scaring nesting avians from the surrounding trees. The child's laughter abruptly ended, replaced by the sound of a parent ushering them away.

'You spend a few hours with us and you think you know our lives? We've been left to die on the banks of a fragging river. One in three supply runs makes it to us, and even then they only provide a quarter of what we need, the rest going to the "brave Cadians" fighting the good fight up the line.'

'You see a little hardship and you jump over, is that it?'

'I don't see you fighting your way out of here like an honest Imperial citizen,' Ceres laughed. 'You're wandering the gardens chit-chatting with a xenos, so you can get off your high horse and back into the shit with the rest of us.'

The trickling water was the only sound in the glade as the two glared at each other across the fountain.

Two steps, that's all it would take and my hands would be around his throat, she thought.

'Why are you here?' Darya forced herself to ask, pushing the thought away and breathing through the anger.

'To save my people.'

* * *

Ceres scratched at the stubble on his chin as they sat at either end of a bench, set back from the fountain beneath the shade of the trees.

'We listened to the broadcasts for so long, as supplies dried up and nothing useful was ever sent, despite our pleas. I even went back to the landing zone to petition Colonel Wassenby myself, but he wouldn't see me. I saw their stockpiles, though. Promethium, food, water, winter clothing, ammunition. You name it, they had it rotting in storage. Then I lost two men to the river.'

'Your men drowned?' Darya asked. In truth she didn't care, but she knew Ceres wouldn't continue unless she asked.

'They drank water from the Spatka. It ate at them like acid. They took days to die,' Ceres said with a shake of his head.

'Then the t'au approached you and offered you a way out.'

'No. They'd already made contact with us by then. They offered us aid, whatever we needed. We declined at first, threatened to kill them if they tried to turn us again, but after my men died for something so simple as clean water...'

Darya leaned in close and laid a hand on his shoulder, which made the fire warriors behind her tense. She could hear the creak of their armour as they shifted their weight, ready to intervene.

They need him alive, she thought.

'Lieutenant, you're full of groxshit,' Darya said in a warm voice.

Ceres turned to face Darya, anger twisting his features.

'What the–'

'This isn't about saving your men. You want to poke the Imperium in the eye, and for what? Because they didn't send you your Sanguinala gifts?'

Ceres shot to his feet and Darya did the same, ready to react if he swung for her. He was thinking about it, she could see that – his knuckles were white and bloodless as his fists clenched.

'Look at them,' Darya said as the t'au drew close. 'They're ready to save your life, to save you from me. You've not just come over, there's more to it than that and I want to know why.' She stepped away and settled back into her seat.

Ceres blinked in surprise as Darya became passive. He waved a hand to his bodyguards, who backed off.

'You're more than a trigger finger,' Ceres muttered and carefully took his seat, ready to react if Darya leaped at him. He became more relaxed the longer they sat, a tic spasming under one eye.

'Tell me why Bol Ceres hates the Imperium enough to turn his back on it. Tell me why you want to start a new life in the T'au'va,' Darya asked.

'You first,' Ceres said, looking away.

'What are you talking about?'

'You've been here ten days, and you've not even tried to escape. You're walking the gardens talking with a xenos, when every oath and doctrine demands you kill everyone here. I'm not the only one who's angry with the Imperium.'

It can't have only been ten days, can it?

'I am angry,' Darya admitted, giving voice to thoughts that carried a death sentence behind Imperial lines. 'I'm angry that they wanted to turn me into something I'm not. They took my name and hung a legend on it like a cloak, gave me victories that never happened and buried the actions of people I cared about. It was lie upon lie upon lie... And I have to ask what else they've lied to us about. To all of us.'

'Go on,' Ceres urged.

'I have seen things, Ceres. Nightmares that had no right to exist in the waking world. I still see them when I sleep, at the corners of my eye... If the God-Emperor were all-powerful like the Ecclesiarchy say, they would not exist.'

Darya squeezed her eyes shut and tried to push away the

memories of Cocleratum, of the mission that had made her name but cursed her with horrors that still plagued her dreams. It had taken weeks for her to recover from the physical wounds, but she would never forget the mental ones.

'Darya, I–'

'Is He too weak to hear our prayers? Does He even care?'

Ceres nodded, his eyes widening at the haunted look that had crossed her face.

'So you're questioning the core tenet of the Imperium. I'm sure every commissar within a thousand light years just got an itchy trigger finger,' Ceres said, forcing a smile.

'If we don't fight for Him, then who do we fight for? Each other? I'm in a regiment where half hate me for not being Cadian enough, and the rest hate me for looking like I want to be,' Darya said.

'I saw the propaganda reels and the posters,' Ceres said with a nod. 'It was the straw that broke the servitor's back for some hold-outs amongst my men. Another reminder that we are also-rans, if we're remembered at all.'

'I'm not asking why your holdouts wanted out,' Darya reminded him. 'I told you my story, Ceres. I want to hear yours.'

Ceres sighed. 'You know that Kintair is an agri world? Before I was Lieutenant Ceres I was Shift-Foreman Ceres, looking after five hundred workers on our agri-collective. My wife...'

'What is it?' Darya pressed.

'We wanted a child. For years we petitioned for a reproduction credit, until finally our name was drawn and we were given the chance to start a family of our own. We had a son,' Ceres said with a sad smile. 'Tarit, we named him. He was six months old when the call came down – Primarch Roboute Guilliman had announced his glorious crusade. There was to be a conscription from the able-bodied men and women of Kintair, to found the First Kintair Rifles.'

Darya's heart sank as she listened to the painful truth within his words. She'd heard horror stories about the conscription of entire hive cities, where weapons were pressed into hands no matter if they were able or not, to be used as chaff before the trained regiments were committed to battle. Ceres' story was no different than any of the millions who faced such a fate.

'I was selected. I was taken from everything I had ever wanted, everything I had ever worked for. I had a wife and a son, and they were taken from me.'

'Had?' Darya asked, unsure if she wanted to hear the answer.

'They could still be alive, I don't know. The whole galaxy is at war, it's not like they're going to give a conscripted officer any space in the communications packet.'

'Throne,' Darya swore.

'The Imperium took everything from me,' Ceres said, emotion trembling through his voice. Tears welled in his eyes and he made no move to wipe them away as they fell. 'They took everything. I owe it nothing. My men owe it nothing.'

'Bol, I… I'm so sorry,' Darya said.

In spite of what he had done, of the fact he had murdered her friend in cold blood, she felt desperately sorry for him in that moment. Darya looked away, giving him a modicum of privacy as the tears continued to flow unabated, and glanced over to where honoured Mui'el sat in conversation with a figure in black armour tied with strips of white cloth.

'Longshot,' Darya muttered.

'What?'

'The t'au speaking to honoured Mui'el. It's Longshot,' she said.

'Longshot? No, that's Shas'el Tan, the head of their fire warriors,' Ceres said, collecting himself and breathing through the last of his tears. 'Longshot is what they call *you*.'

* * *

'I told you that I did not order your death, Darya. That is because I recognised that you could be of far greater value to both of our peoples if you were to live.'

Darya sat in the centre of the bench, facing Mui'el on his platform and Shas'el Tan, who knelt on the grass.

'And yet your warriors killed my men and almost killed me,' Darya said.

'Which is natural in the course of war, even if it was against my wishes. Shas'el Tan has been censured for his zeal,' Mui'el said.

The black-clad warrior placed his hands on the ground and bowed low, until his helmet was brushed by the taller blades of grass. He held the pose for a count of five, then returned to his kneeling position.

Darya looked the black-clad warrior up and down. From her understanding of the t'au rank system gleaned from her conversations with Mui'el, he was either a hero or a commander of the fire warriors. His armour was finely crafted and darker than the night sky, and he would have been all but invisible in the shadows if it weren't for the cloth strips attached to the plates on his shoulders, arms and thighs.

'You killed many students of our art, and several of my acolytes. I sought your death in service of the Greater Good, but if you would join that service as an ally I would set aside the enmity that exists between us,' Shas'el Tan said in a deep voice that was only slightly muffled by his helmet.

Darya offered him a short bow from her seated position, but kept her eyes on him as she would a predator that was coiled and ready to strike. She understood that his words had been for Mui'el, not her.

'You wanted me alive and now you have me,' Darya said to Mui'el, who had watched the exchange in measured silence. 'I can only assume that you have a plan for me – I am not so naïve as to think my treatment has been entirely altruistic.'

'You are correct. There is a place for you within the T'au'va, if you would wish to take it up. In return for your service we would offer that which you most desire,' the ethereal said, forming his hands as if opening a book.

'Which is?' Darya asked.

'We offer you the chance to disappear.'

'You offer me death?'

'Of a kind. We would hone your name into a weapon to be wielded against those who stand against the T'au'va, and then we would put it aside, as all weapons must be in the end. You would take on a new name, and begin your life anew.'

'A new life of my own making?'

'Exactly. If my understanding of you is accurate, you do not enjoy the fame your excellence brings. You do not court notoriety or celebrity, you disdain it. You excel to protect those around you, for the greater glory of a larger whole,' Mui'el explained. 'You already fight for a greater good. Within the T'au'va, it would be for the Greater Good of all.'

Darya's emotions roiled beneath the impassive mask of her face.

To join the ranks of the t'au would be a betrayal of everything she had fought for all her adult life, of the system that had raised her and moulded her into the person she was. It would be to turn her back on forty millennia of human endeavour across the stars, of everything her ancestors had striven for since the dawn of humanity.

But what of those she would have to leave behind? She thought of Arfit, her last surviving squadmate, who could be dead for all she knew. Captain Kohl, a man she deeply respected, would have thrown her into the face of the Archenemy itself if

he thought it might secure a victory. There were passing famil-
iarities and acquaintances within the Cadian 217th too, but
none that weighed so heavy as the choice before her. What was
there to hold her back?

But the deepest part of her knew that such concerns weren't
the reason she hesitated. It was because, for the first time in
her life, she was being given a choice. To take the path that she
wanted rather than be restricted to the one that had been laid
out before her. She could decide her own individual future, a
freedom that was intoxicating even if refusal would likely lead
to her immediate execution.

'What would I do for the T'au'va?' Darya asked. 'What is it
that I can offer?'

'You would be given to that which would provide the greatest
good,' honoured Mui'el said, his fingers steepled in a gesture
of contemplation.

'War?'

'For now. We have need of skilled soldiers, officers and commanders such as yourself, and, as I have said, there are more ways to fight
than to bear a weapon.'

'You will strike the *Kauyon* of the mind,' Shas'el Tan said.

'Shas'el Tan speaks truly. You could save a great many lives in
the coming battle, both on our side and yours. You would not
have to abandon the few friends you have remaining in your
regiment – you could save them,' honoured Mui'el said.

'What would you have me do?'

23

Darya allowed herself to be led from the gardens and into one of the sweeping architectural marvels that lined the gardens, through immaculate corridors with arched ceilings and gently curving walls, and into a wide room overlooking the greenery outside.

Mui'el's bodyguards took up positions outside the door, leaving Shas'el Tan as the ethereal's only t'au protector in the room, but Darya reckoned that he was more than enough.

Darya expected the black-armoured fire warrior to explain what would happen next, but was surprised when Ceres stood beside the window and manipulated a control hex to darken the glass. Hidden lights provided a soft glow around the room's edge, until Ceres pressed a final hex.

A panel of cold blue light bloomed over the darkened window, the crisp lines coalescing into what Darya recognised as an aerial map of the Miracil front. She saw Trackway Span and the Cadian Salient, which looked terrifyingly exposed when rendered in its true proportions. Iron Hill was clearly depicted in its dilapidated state, right down to the destroyed half of the assembly complex. The only details missing were the t'au positions: their territory was blurry, and positioned at the very edge of the light panel.

They don't want to give too much away, Darya thought.

'Imperial surveillance has increased tenfold since the diversionary attack on Iron Hill,' Ceres explained.

'The one you used to slip over the river,' Darya said.

Ceres nodded. 'Yes. I need to get back to the vox-relay to prepare my men and to ensure that the next stage of the plan is successful. To do that, I need to make it back to our lines undetected.'

To punctuate his point, Ceres indicated an area of the map far from the Spatka.

'Plan? What is the plan?' Darya asked.

Shas'el Tan's helmet turned from Darya to Ceres, and he shook his head once.

He is someone who expects to be obeyed, Darya thought.

'Tell her,' honoured Mui'el said, without looking at the black-armoured warrior.

Shas'el Tan began to speak in the t'au tongue, the syllables blending together into a dance of consonants and rhythmic emphasis, his hands clasped together as if praying, but the ethereal silenced him with a glance.

'Tell. Her.'

'They know that the Four-Hundred-and-First have pulled back from the landing fields,' Ceres said without meeting Darya's eyes. She didn't have to ask who had given them that information. 'Without the landing fields, orbital supply drops become impossible, and the Three-Hundred-and-Thirty-Eighth have left a skeleton force there at best.'

'The Two-Hundred-and-Seventeenth hold the main route to the landing zone,' Darya said.

'Only if the attacking force comes by road,' Ceres said. 'T'au transports don't need roads. They will cross the river opposite the Kintair positions, we will join up with them and take the landing fields. This will leave the Two-Hundred-and-Seventeenth encircled and without orbital supplies.'

Ceres drew a line on the map, sweeping through the Kintair positions to the edge of the city, then back round towards the Spatka to the north. It encompassed almost the entire area held by the 217th, fifty times larger than the Cadian Salient.

'And House Gyrrant? And the other elements of the Two-Hundred-and-Seventeenth to the north?' Darya asked.

'We will deal with them,' Shas'el Tan said coldly, his voice mechanical from within his helm.

'By the time the forces to the north can reinforce Trackway Span, the Cadians there will either be dead or with the t'au,' Ceres finished.

'And you want me to turn the Cadians at Trackway Span?' Darya asked.

'We would ask you to try,' Mui'el replied.

'I think I understand,' Darya said with a nod. 'You need me to get you back to the square, where the comms link is set up.'

'Without being detected, yes. I will disable the relay, knocking out comms across the sector and ensuring that the ships in orbit are unable to support Imperial ground forces.'

'Why not just fly back?' Darya asked. 'It'd be the fastest route.'

'Too many eyes in the sky,' Ceres said. 'Air defences make the risk too great.'

'Can't fly, can't risk crossing in your Chimera,' Darya reasoned. 'You need a guide.'

'Will you do it?' Shas'el Tan asked.

Another test, then.

'I can get you back,' Darya said after a moment's pause.

'Not alone. With a team,' Shas'el Tan ordered.

'It would be easier with just two,' Darya said, but honoured Mui'el shook his head.

'We cannot send you alone,' he said.

'I could get a few through… The smaller the group the better,' Darya said.

'Could you get, say, five of us back?' Ceres asked.

Darya nodded. 'I can work with that.'

Mui'el clasped his hands together and smiled.

'Prepare yourselves. You leave at nightfall.'

'Long time no see, sarge,' Dal Feon said, ducking through the circular hatch and into the troop compartment of the Devilfish transport.

'Feon,' Darya said. 'How the hell did you live this long?'

'Born survivor,' Feon said, offering her a forced smile.

He joined the three Kintair on the bench opposite Darya, sinking into the seat's padding with an appreciative sigh.

'Beats a Chimera, doesn't it,' Darya said.

'It does that,' Feon agreed. 'Ceiling is a little low for me, but I'm not one to complain.'

The other Kintair in the transport laughed, and Darya smiled along with them. They all looked half-starved and sickly, sporting a greasy grey pallor that their time with the t'au didn't seem to have cleared.

Perhaps they've had it as bad as Ceres said, Darya thought.

They were all dressed in their Astra Militarum fatigues, even Darya, who had been surprised when she was given a fresh Cadian uniform alongside her cameleoline cloak.

Ceres was the only one entrusted with any sign that they had defected to the t'au. He wore one of their armoured wrist-guards under his tunic sleeve, equipped with a projection device and the t'au equivalent of a vox.

He was studying the device as Feon took his seat and accepted the offered lasgun from another trooper. When he realised that Darya was watching him, he jerked his sleeve down to cover it.

'You'll need to keep that hidden as we move,' Darya said.

'I know,' Ceres said. He had regained some of the resolute composure she had seen when she had first encountered him all those weeks before, back when he was a lieutenant in the Kintair Rifles and not a traitor to his own people.

'That makes six. Are we getting underway?' Darya asked.

The light outside the transport was fading beneath the false sky of the shield dome, indicating the end of another rotaa for the t'au.

'Soon,' Ceres said. He checked his laspistol's charge and clicked his teeth, fidgeting as he waited for some unknown sign.

Shas'el Tan appeared in the rear hatch and rested a gloved hand on the lintel.

'What you do is for the Greater Good. You are T'au'va now, all of you,' he said, his helmet turning towards Darya as he stressed the last three words.

'For the Greater Good,' Darya chorused with the Kintair. It was a cry she had heard a hundred times in the battle for Miracil, both in Gothic and – she now knew – the t'au's strange language. It was disconcerting to understand what the words meant.

The rear hatch slid closed with a hiss of hidden hydraulic motors, blocking Darya's view of the outside but for a small circular porthole of armoured glass. She stood up to catch one last look at what they were leaving behind, before they headed back into the ruined city.

'I never thought I'd see somewhere like that,' she said as the transport hummed into life, raising them smoothly from the ground. External jets fired, their sound muted by the layers of armoured alloy that separated her from the superheated air.

The paradise of lush green shrank away, growing smaller and smaller until it disappeared entirely behind the foundations of a new tower being constructed by humans in green robes. They did not look up as the transport flew past, speeding through half-built streets and avenues that became gradually more human in their appearance, the elegant, sweeping lines of t'au architecture lost behind blunt grey structures and the grime of a city past its prime.

Then they passed from the dome entirely, and out into a Miracil that Darya didn't recognise.

Winter had taken hold during her convalescence with the t'au, and it appeared that the promise that Attruso's winters were mild had been yet another Imperial lie. Snow blanketed the gridded streets of the upper city, piling inches deep on every surface strong enough to hold it whilst still more fell from the sky in fat lumps.

But as they sped through a world rendered monochrome in grey snow and muddy black, Darya's eyes were drawn to the city's occupants.

Snow-covered tent cities dominated the packed streets, where refugees from the low city had claimed what little space was made available to them. Thin figures in ragged clothes held out hands that were swollen and purple from the cold, begging for scraps that it seemed no one had to give. They were all human, every single one of them. From the melancholic wanderers who stared blankly at the grey sky above, to the winding queues of blanket-clad people who waited in line, presumably for a daily allocation of rations.

It was a different world to the one within the t'au dome that Darya had left behind.

'Who are these people?' Darya asked. 'Are they not in the T'au'va?'

'They're the sick, the ill and those too weak to fight,' Ceres said, standing to join Darya at the porthole. He leaned to look out, his lip curling in distaste.

'And those strong enough–'

'Have been armed and taken to the front,' Ceres said quietly.

'Conscripted,' Darya argued.

'No, not conscripted. Sent where they will be able to do the greatest good, defending their home from invaders,' Ceres said with a scowl.

'Sounds like conscription to me,' Darya muttered as Ceres turned away and took his seat again.

Loose snow whirled in the Devilfish's wake as it hurtled through the streets, and Darya found that she had seen enough of the high city too.

'I take it I'm not being given a weapon?' Darya asked. Everyone else within the transport had their lasgun and other weapons, which made the lack of Darya's all the more conspicuous.

'Shas'el Tan's orders,' Ceres said. 'You shouldn't need one to get us past the Cadians unseen.'

Darya didn't argue. The t'au's caution made sense, even if she would have felt more comfortable with a weapon in her hands.

'It'll be another hour before we get near the front lines,' Feon said. 'May as well take a seat, Nevic.'

Darya cast one last glance out of the porthole, but the blustering snow had settled on the outside of the armoured glass and hidden the world from view. She crossed back to the padded bench and took her seat beside Ceres, who had his eyes closed.

'Anyone have any cards?' Darya asked. The Kintair looked at one another and shrugged.

'Useless, the lot of you,' Feon grunted and pulled off his

helmet, producing a pack of worn playing cards from inside the padded cradle. 'Do you know any games?'

'Good job we weren't gambling,' Darya said as the transport slowed a short while later, throwing down her hand into Feon's upturned helmet.

'No commissars to stop us any more,' Feon said, gathering the cards and slipping them back into their battered cardboard sleeve.

'We'll still have discipline,' Ceres said. He hadn't taken part in the game, seemingly trying to keep some semblance of their structure intact as he led them into their new lives.

'Nothing wrong with a friendly wager, Bol,' Feon said with a wicked smile. Ceres glowered at the sergeant's use of his given name as the rear hatch hissed open onto a frozen street bathed in orange light.

The frozen wind outside was biting after the warmth of the t'au dome, stinging her cheeks and setting off a deep ache within her recently healed bones. She pulled her cameleoline cloak tighter about her but it was little help; whilst it was a fantastic camouflage tool it offered almost no defence against the cold.

'Form up,' Ceres barked at his squad as he disembarked, his breath forming a plume of steam that rose lazily through the air.

He led them west towards the setting sun and the defensive positions that the t'au had fortified in their long standoff against the Cadian 217th. Heavy-weapon emplacements had been hidden in hollowed-out buildings and below false roofs, hiding them from orbital augurs as they covered the ground with enfilading fields of fire. Much like the Cadians, the t'au had also been digging trenches, though their systems were more complex and ran far deeper than those on the Cadian Salient. And, as Darya followed Ceres down into the maze of sunken paths, she realised that they were also far better equipped. Dugout-access doors, sleeping bunks and even cooking stations were set into the trench walls at regular intervals, where the Astra Militarum barely had adequate firing steps.

If we'd tried to attack this it would have been a massacre, Darya thought.

Ceres led his men and Darya through several checkpoints unchallenged by the t'au manning them, if they were noticed at all. The grey-armoured xenos seemed content to allow the humans to pass amongst them in a way that their human auxiliaries did not.

The humans who had thrown in their lot with the t'au were more densely packed into the forward trenches, where the stench of sweat and death hung in the air like a cloud, cutting through the winter chill. Clean white trench walls gave way to boards smeared with mud and other dark substances, then to scavenged plascrete panels and debris that reminded Darya of the Cadian trenches.

The occupants began to shout out to the Kintair and to Darya as they noticed unfamiliar humans amongst them, asking where they'd been and if they had seen so-and-so in the upper city.

'Please, did you see her? My wife, she–' a woman gasped, grabbing Ceres' uniform as he passed through her trench.

The t'au officer watching over the woman's squad barked an order that Darya didn't understand, but the woman evidently complied and allowed Ceres to pass.

He fought to keep his expression neutral but Darya could see that he was shaken by the confrontation in the way he kept looking back over his shoulder at where the woman was being reprimanded by the officer.

Night fell with a shiver of dying light as they passed into the shadow of Iron Hill, the last of the warmth leaching from the world as Miracil entered its long dark cycle.

'What happened?' she asked Ceres as he turned south to skirt the perimeter of the battered Adeptus Mechanicus complex.

'The t'au attacked to provide a distraction for us,' Ceres said. 'I don't think it was a token offensive.'

The high manufactorum halls, refineries and data-vaults had been replaced with drifting smoke, their mighty walls brought low by a battle that had long since ended. The devastation stretched throughout the complex in a path of seemingly wanton destruction, weaving between structures that looked untouched by war and removing others from existence.

'Throne above,' Feon said.

Their path south and then to the south-west took them through a yard of assembled Sentinel scout walkers that stood in neat ranks, unused and idle beneath a thick layer of snow. From there the path led due west to the end of the t'au trench system and the low ruins of riverside habs.

'This is where you take over, Nevic,' Ceres said in a low voice. She looked at each of the Kintair's weapons in turn.

'Still not giving you a weapon,' Feon said with a wolfish smile.

'I'm not looking for a weapon,' Darya retorted. 'I need a scope, or a pair of magnoculars. Do you have any?'

'Afraid not,' Ceres said.

He was right. They all carried basic-pattern lasguns that didn't even have lumen-mounts, never mind scopes.

'Okay, we do this the old way. Follow where I tread,' Darya said, and pulled herself out of the trench and onto the virgin snow.

She followed the line of the ruins, keeping tight to the walls and staying in the shadowy corners as much as she could, despite the pale glow of the snow. Each step was considered, slow, and almost silent as she pushed the snow away with her boots before shifting her weight. The Kintair following her were less stealthy, their feet crunching loudly through the packed snow.

'When I said follow in my tread, I meant it literally. Step in my boot prints,' she hissed back down the line.

The snowfall began again as they came within sight of the river, where the ruined habs ended and a shallow slope led down to the water's edge. The Spatka had frozen, which made Darya feel a dull pang of regret as she recalled that Yanna and Bellis had placed a wager on whether a river that large truly could freeze.

'Was it frozen when you came over in the Chimera?' Darya asked, kneeling in the lee of the last wall atop the slope. Her legs were wet and half-frozen, the melted snow making the chill fabric cling to her skin uncomfortably.

'No, we had help with that,' Ceres replied. 'They set up a pontoon to get us over.'

'That'd be safer than the ice,' Darya muttered.

'It looks solid enough,' Ceres said.

Darya glanced at him. 'You can never tell until you're on it, and even then usually only after it starts to crack.'

'Then we'd best pray that it doesn't crack,' Ceres said, and motioned for Darya to go first.

She exhaled, her breath misting as she moved forwards in a low crouch through the deepening snow to the edge of the riverbank.

The line between shore and river was lost beneath a thick layer of white powder, but further across the frozen surface Darya could see patches of pearlescent, ice-rimed brown where the contaminated water had solidified.

Ceres was still several steps behind her as she eased herself forwards, sliding her boot through the snow until she found solid ground. She pushed down with all her weight, until she was satisfied that it wouldn't crack. Another step followed, then another, and then she was out onto the ice of the Spatka.

They were painfully exposed, Darya knew that, but it was the only way to cross that didn't take them deep into territory held by the Cadians or House Gyrrant.

'Quickly,' Darya hissed back along the line. 'Follow my path.'

She led them across the ice as fast as she dared, strung out behind her like water fowl trailing behind their mother, until she reached the far bank with a sigh of relief. Ceres arrived a minute later, followed by Dal Feon.

The remaining three were far slower across the ice, and the last was barely halfway when they first heard it.

A loud ping echoed across the ice, the same sound a hard-mass round made ricocheting through a large building. It was followed by a flurry of others, each growing deeper and deeper in pitch, and then the deep, stomach-trembling crunch of something incredibly large cracking.

'They need to move,' Darya whispered, looking north to where the distant shadow of Trackway Span was just visible through the river's chill mist.

Darya, Ceres and Feon all waved the others forwards, silently urging them to rush as the river ice cracked and began to splinter, throwing up wisps of settled snow where the fault lines snaked across the surface.

The last man began to run, his feet pounding the ice like a drum as he fought to stay upright. Another made the shore and shouted for the next man to hurry, only to have Darya throw her hand over his mouth with a hissed 'Shut up!'

The second man was only yards from the shore when the ice collapsed beneath him, the surface giving way under his running feet. He fell forwards into the freezing brown torrent and came up spluttering and gasping, splashing close enough for Ceres and Feon to pull him to safety.

'Keep quiet, Garand,' Feon hissed as he pulled him up the shore in a shivering heap.

The last man was not so lucky. Great plates of ice rumbled and shifted, giving him no path to the western shore. He tried to stop but his momentum forced him on, kicking his feet out from beneath him so he slid from the ice and out of sight with a stifled cry.

'Damn! Can we–'

'No – he's done for,' Darya said, more to Ceres than anyone else. 'You go out there, it's suicide.'

'She's right. We can only hope that the current takes him quickly,' Ceres said.

Thick plates of ice shifted on the current, crunching and groaning as they were jostled by the river's flow.

'Come on, we have a long way to go,' Darya said.

'For the Greater Good,' Feon said with a shrug.

She led the remaining group up the riverbank towards the cover of a turbine shed, checking it was unoccupied before kneeling beneath a shuttered window.

'This is the difficult part,' Darya said to the Kintair as they took a knee around her. 'There will be roving patrols of Cadians between here and your positions, so if I say something, you do it. Understood?'

They all nodded. The trooper who had fallen in the river, Garand, nodded a little too vigorously, failing to suppress a shiver that spasmed across his entire body.

He'll be lucky if he makes it, Darya thought.

Darya led the way through the ruins of Miracil, following a similar route to the one she and Ullaeus had used to evade the t'au when they had been sent to find the Kintair.

She led them through abandoned warehouses and around the walled edges of storage yards, waving them across empty streets as they jogged from doorway to doorway in an attempt to minimise the time they spent in the open.

'Where the frag are we?' Feon hissed as they darted from the cover of a high wall into a long warehouse. 'I don't know any of this.'

'It's the best route to where we're going,' Darya said, pausing to catch her breath in the warehouse's shadowed interior.

'Not the fastest route,' Ceres said, his own breaths coming in shallow gasps.

'No, but it's the safest,' Darya said, and indicated that they should follow.

They stayed back from the empty windows, moving between plundered crates and overturned boxes until they reached a patch of rubble where the floor above had fallen through.

'The safest?' Feon said doubtfully.

'What's wrong, Feon? Scared of a little work for once?' Darya said.

He snorted in response, which Darya took to mean that he didn't have a witty retort.

'So what happens to you next?' Darya asked, stooping to pick up a couple of fist-sized lumps of debris with her left hand, the right slipping a sharp chunk of plascrete into her pocket. She dropped the stones in her left hand as Ceres gave her a warning look, but he didn't stop her.

It's not much, but it's something, she thought, the subtle weight of the plascrete swinging in her pocket as she moved.

She led the group over the rubble towards a pair of double doors that hung open, the doorway covered by a spreading patch of snow.

'Next?' Ceres asked with a frown.

'Next, as in when the t'au come through. Will you become fire warriors to serve Shas'el Tan?'

'If that is where we are needed,' Ceres replied.

'And what about after that, when Shas'el Tan has won the war?' Darya asked. She had reached the door and checked that their route wasn't watched from further down the street, drawing back inside the warehouse when the coast was clear.

'It will be a victory for all, not just Shas'el Tan,' Ceres said. 'Anyway, he is no longer in sole control of the fire warriors. Honoured Mui'el has taken a more active role since...'

'Since Shas'el Tan sent his acolytes to kill me.'

'Something like that.'

Darya led them out of the doors, through a pair of gates towards a huge manufactorum with two chimneys, one emblazoned with the Imperial eagle whilst the other stood just high enough for the words *Isso Corp* to be visible.

'Through here?' Ceres asked.

'Yes. It should cut out a good chunk of the journey,' Darya said.

She made to open the doors to the manufactorum, but Ceres held out a hand to stop her.

'Feon, clear it,' Ceres ordered. Feon nodded and ran forwards with the other two troopers. Feon went in through the darkened doorway first, followed by the others immediately after, whilst Darya waited outside with Ceres.

'Something wrong?' Darya asked.

'We're the two most valuable people here. I'd rather not walk us into an ambush,' Ceres explained as Feon called the all clear.

'Everyone's equal under the T'au'va, Ceres,' Darya said, holding the man's gaze for a moment before entering the manufactorum.

It was unchanged since the last time Darya had been there, but for the drifts of thin snow that collected beneath the holes in the ceiling and on the fallen chimney, the highest stairways and the elevated walkways. The hole in the ceiling looked larger than she remembered, and for a moment she feared that her plan might not work.

No turning back now.

'We're going up,' Darya said. She moved towards the stairs before the others could intercede, and began the long climb up the many winding stairways towards the roof. 'See up there? There's a point we can cross over the chimney.'

'Why don't we just climb over the chimney?' Feon asked.

'I wouldn't want to climb that even if it weren't covered in snow,' Darya said, pointing down at the high, craggy mound of snow-covered brick that was all that remained of the fallen chimney.

'We go up,' Ceres said, putting an end to the debate.

'Woah,' Feon said as he looked over the side of the highest walkway, down to the floor far below.

'Yeah, don't do that,' Darya warned him. 'Keep your eyes up and ahead, never down.'

'Nevic, what is that?' Ceres asked.

He pointed out into the centre of the walkway where an entire section hung on its side, half of the supporting struts torn from the rotten metal of the manufactorum roof so that the only route across was to walk on the handrail, using the support lines as handholds.

Darya remembered the heart-stopping moment Ullaeus had dropped down and nearly killed them both, the memory making her smile in spite of the sense of loss.

'It's the way through – it's safe, I've crossed it before.'

'I'm not crossing that,' Feon said with a bark of sardonic laughter.

'It's either crossing here or working our way back down to the floor, and another half an hour on the streets. It's up to you,' Darya said.

'Wait,' Ceres said. He walked to the very edge of the undamaged walkway and looked down, then reached out to the nearest support strut and shook it. It did not move, but rattled the loose section.

'I'll go first if you want,' Darya offered.

Ceres looked from Darya to Feon, who raised an eyebrow.

'You're scared that I'll run?'

'Think of it as caution. I'm sure you understand,' Ceres said, his eyes studying the hanging section. 'I'll go first, then Nevic.'

'Bol, I'm not sure that's a good idea,' Feon said.

'If it falls, shoot Nevic,' Ceres said coldly. 'If it doesn't then she goes next.'

Darya tried to ignore the three gun barrels that lowered in her direction as Ceres took a strong grip on the first hanging strut and swung forwards, his booted feet slipping on the handrail. Darya tensed as they kicked out, then found their grip on the wet metal pole.

He inched his way across, never releasing a handhold until he had a firm grip on the next, until he jumped down to the secure walkway on the other side a few minutes later.

'See?' Darya said. 'No problem.'

Darya was far less cautious, swinging her weight out onto the support strut and landing on the handrail with a thump that rattled the length of the walkway. She made it to the far side in less than half the time it had taken Ceres, her heart hammering with each step, until she came within jumping distance of him.

She leaped with both feet, clattering into Ceres and sending them both staggering as the fallen section bounced off the walkway either side of it with ringing thuds. But it didn't fall.

Damn.

Garand, still shivering from his fall into the Spatka, was chosen to go next and it was clear that he was anything but comfortable with their choice. His hands were still swollen with the cold, the pink flesh discolouring with the strength of his grip as he lurched into mid-air, reaching for the second strut as he clung hard to the first.

'Come on, we have you,' Darya said, stepping back onto the fallen section and holding out a hand, her other gripping the nearest strut.

'Nevic!' Ceres said in a warning voice, but Darya didn't move.

'You can take over if you want, but I'm definitely lighter than you,' she said over her shoulder. Her hand strained on the support in her hand, pulling on it as subtly as she could. It didn't move in her grip, the rotten metal above holding fast.

Darya waited, encouraging Garand onwards as the metal creaked, but it still didn't give.

'Come on, you're almost there, Garand,' Darya said, shifting her weight forwards onto her front foot. She waited until he took his next step and pulled her weight up on the support, then dropped as Garand's foot came down.

Metal shrieked and Darya threw herself back, victorious, as the damaged walkway tore itself free from its housing and fell. Garand's face was a mask of terror as he gripped tight to the unsecured stanchions, falling with them to his death on the collapsed chimney far below.

'No!' Ceres screamed, but Darya was already swinging at him with the debris she had grabbed in the warehouse.

It struck Ceres' rising hand, knocking his drawn laspistol from his grip and turning to powder in her hand. The laspistol bounced from the floor panel and out into the darkness below.

'You damned...' Ceres cried, swinging his fist in a wide,

punishing arc. She was smaller and faster, but he was by far stronger; she dodged aside and ran for the other end of the walkway, keeping Ceres between her and his men.

She heard someone shouting not to shoot for fear of hitting Ceres, then leaped down a flight of stairs with as much speed as she dared.

'Get back to the others, I'll deal with Nevic!' Ceres yelled, and Darya felt his weight rocking the stairs beneath her feet as he thundered after her.

She didn't stop, using the rails to guide her leaps down flight after flight of stairs, trying desperately to remember anything she could use against her pursuer.

'I can't let you escape, Nevic!' Ceres shouted, his footfalls echoing down the staircase.

She turned from the stairs onto a short landing that led to the next set of stairs, ducking as several wild shots flew at her from the other side of the factory.

Feon, she cursed. The shots drew clouds of dust from the brick walls, but with each burst they grew closer. She dived under the handrail next to her and fell heavily down the next flight of stairs with a cry of pain.

The floor of the manufactorum was almost within reach, only a few stairs away, when she heard a cry of anger from above.

Ceres dived at her from the landing, slamming into her and pushing her bodily through the guardrail with a clang of broken tubing to land heavily in a snowdrift banked up against the fallen chimney.

'You will not ruin–' Ceres roared, looming above her, but Darya cut him off with a wide punch that caught him across the mouth. He reeled back, spitting blood and phlegm as she scrambled away, dazed and tangled in her cloak.

She wasn't fast enough. Ceres was back on her before she

could regain her feet, where he pinned her down and wrapped his brutally strong hands around her throat.

'You will not ruin this!' Ceres hissed through a mouthful of blood and spittle, his eyes bulging. 'You will not kill my people!'

Darya thrashed beneath his weight, hands scrambling through the snow to the oily floor beneath, but finding nothing to use against the Kintair.

It's just you against him, one-on-one, her pride screamed. *Brain against brawn.*

She raked her nails over his face as if clawing at his eyes. He threw his head back out of her reach, exposing the lump of cartilage in his throat.

She punched at it savagely, grinning with malice as he leaped back off her, clutching at his neck.

'This is not about your people,' Darya gasped, finally getting enough grip to scramble back away from him. 'This was about you, Ceres. It was always about you, nursing a hurt you never should have felt... But you had no right to take it out on *my* people.'

She spat her words like venom, baring her teeth at the choking Kintair officer in her rage. He was recovering, pushing himself up from the floor, but Darya wouldn't allow that.

She leaped on his back, clamping her legs around his waist and slipping her forearm under his throat, using the other arm to pull it painfully tight. Ceres gagged, trying to force her arm loose, scratching at her flesh as he fought to stand.

'His name was Iago Ullaeus,' Darya hissed as his legs gave way and his struggling became weaker and more sluggish. 'Say his name, you coward. Say it!'

Ceres slumped forwards, his face purple even in the low light, but Darya didn't let go. She held the chokehold until her arms shook with the effort, muscles burning with the exertion as she felt Ceres die.

His head dropped limply to the plascrete as she released him and scrambled to her feet, breathing heavily from the exertion.

'It's better than you deserved, you bastard.'

She left the body face down in the scattered snow and muck on the manufactorum floor and ran for the nearest door.

Once outside, Darya paused and let the cold air cool the sweat on her brow and lower back, enjoying the sensation for a moment.

Then she turned to the north-east, back to the Cadian lines.

24

Darya's path back to the Cadian lines took her perilously close to the Kintair, but she managed to evade their attention through cautious sprints across the snow-laden streets.

The path grew less familiar the further she walked, and she feared that she'd lost herself in the ruins of Miracil until she heard shouted orders in a distinct Cadian accent. A new fear replaced the first as she pushed on towards the source of the voice: what if she had already been declared traitor, or they believed that she had turned on the Imperium?

The knowledge that the t'au attack was only hours away quickened her steps; if they shot her, so be it. She had given her all, and no more could be asked of her than that.

Darya knelt in the shadow of a broken wall and chanced a look around the jagged corner. She had reached the rear defences of Trackway Span, and looked down the intimidating barrel of a heavy bolter emplacement.

'Two-Hundred-and-Seventeenth!' she yelled. 'Friendly coming in!'

'Approach!' a Cadian voice shouted.

With a deep, calming breath, Darya stepped out with her hands raised high, wincing as the heavy bolter was cocked loudly.

'Frag me...' another voice cursed. 'Is that Sergeant Nevic?'

Darya looked up into the impassive face of Commissar Tsutso, who looked down on her with barely concealed contempt.

The troops on the bridge had no sooner let her through than an officer appeared and put her under armed guard. He'd sent a runner back to the command centre for guidance as the vox was apparently acting up, which set Darya's nerves jangling.

From there she'd been led across the bridge to a room near Relief Station Zero, out of sight of the rest of the company, where the commissar waited beside a chair outfitted with thick metal restraints.

He had watched as the other Cadians pushed her into the chair and bound her in place, and only spoke after dismissing them with a wave of his gloved hand.

'Explain yourself, Sergeant Nevic,' he rumbled as he circled her. In the dim light of the room he was a looming spectre hanging over her head, a doom waiting to fall.

'Sir, the xenos are coming,' Darya pleaded. 'The Kintair have turned, they're going for the landing grounds and–'

'What in the name of the God-Emperor... Nevic?' Captain Kohl breathed from somewhere behind Darya. 'You're alive?'

'I am, sir, but please, you must listen–'

'I need to ascertain whether anything you say can be trusted, Nevic,' Commissar Tsutso said coldly. 'A member of your own team reported your death over a week ago, even going so far as to bring back your equipment as proof, and you turn up not only alive but to the rear of our position? Tell me, what would you make of that?'

'I'd say that the trooper is a liar who left me for dead,' Darya said.

'Where have you spent the last ten days?'

Darya closed her eyes and let out a slow breath.

'As a prisoner of the t'au, sir.'

Commissar Tsutso spat, and glared at Darya and Captain Kohl in turn.

'It's not like that, sir. I–'

'You allowed yourself to be captured by the enemy. Who knows what foul poisons they poured into your mind. The rules are clear. You shall be interrogated and executed.'

'You'll do no such thing, Commissar Tsutso,' Kohl said from the door.

'She cannot be trusted.'

'I say we hear what she has to say,' Kohl said. Tsutso shook his head but made no move to stop Kohl as he walked into Darya's eyeline, his expression impassive. She never thought she'd be so glad to see his craggy, scarred features again.

'We don't have time for this. The t'au are going to attack the landing zone. There's no time for this, for any of it!'

'And why is that?' Commissar Tsutso asked.

'Because twenty minutes ago your vox went down,' Darya guessed. It was the best estimate she had for when Dal Feon might have made it back to the Kintair headquarters, and judging by how both Kohl and Tsutso reacted, she wasn't far off the mark.

'And how could you know that?'

'Because it's all part of their plan,' Darya said. 'Please, you have to believe me.'

'We don't have to believe a word you say,' the commissar replied. 'Not until you explain where you have been for the past ten days, and why you still live despite your own squad-mate declaring you dead in the field.'

'Nevic, listen to me,' Kohl said, 'This will go a lot faster if you just explain everything.'

'I left the camp to find Yanna and Ullaeus, I swear...'

'Did anyone see you kill Lieutenant Ceres?' Commissar Tsutso asked.

'No, sir, and I didn't wait for the Kintair to come looking. I got back here as fast as I could.'

'What about the time you spent as their prisoner?' Kohl asked. 'You were only gone for ten days, but what you describe would have taken double that.'

'It is a known technique,' Commissar Tsutso interjected when Darya tried to explain how she had been psychologically manipulated in the white room. 'Deprive the subject of stimulus and drug them, robbing them of their perception of time, and introduce your interrogator as the only route to freedom. It is a method employed by the Inquisition.'

Darya didn't want to know how the commissar had come by that information, but still didn't understand.

'But sir, it felt like I was there for weeks, not a few days,' Darya argued.

'In your mind you were,' the commissar said. 'Continue.'

She then told them everything of her conversations with honoured Mui'el and Bol Ceres, right up to her apparent defection.

'I realised that the ethereal was lying whenever his hands didn't follow his words,' Darya explained. 'From that I was able to understand everything I needed to about them and their kind. It's all lies, sir, every one of their claims about joining up with a caring empire. I saw the slums and the freezing refugees on our way back to the t'au lines – the t'au live in comfort, but humans are little more than convenient labour when they're useful, and an inconvenience when they're not.'

'I am more concerned with the lies that you didn't recognise,' Tsutso said, his expression still cold as he looked down at her. 'The lies they told to turn you against your regiment and your people. The lies that, according to you, turned Ceres and his men against the Imperium.'

'Ceres had a hatred of the Imperium long before he came to Attruso, sir. That seed had been planted when he was taken from his people and conscripted into the Astra Militarum – all the t'au did was feed that anger.'

'And what seed did the xenos cultivate within you, Nevic? You were torn from your people and pressed into the Cadian Two-Hundred-and-Seventeenth. Are you saying that you bear no ill will towards the Imperium for that?'

'I did, once,' Darya said truthfully. 'But that anger died when I understood why it was necessary.'

'And why was it necessary?'

'Because we needed them to keep fighting, and to be seen to keep fighting after everything they'd lost. Just like when you put me into the propaganda reels and the speeches.'

'To inspire greatness in those who see and hear it,' Commissar Tsutso said.

He stepped behind Darya and she heard the scrape of metal on leather, picturing in her mind a bolt pistol being drawn from its holster.

'You have been used roughly by the Imperium, Sergeant Nevic. But there is still work left to be done,' Tsutso said, reaching around her with a long barbed key in his gloved hand. He twisted it into the restraints at her wrist and they snapped open.

'Tell us about the attack,' Captain Kohl said.

'They're going to use the Kintair Rifles to cut off the salient, encircle the entire Miracil front and take out the landing fields.'

She stood with Commissar Tsutso, Captain Kohl and Lieutenant Munro around the stout holo-table in Captain Kohl's command tent. Darya drew her hand through the motes of light depicting the Miracil front, sketching a curved line around the Cadian positions at Trackway Span, through the section held by the Kintair Rifles and on to the low city.

'A sound plan,' Kohl grumbled. He scratched at his chin with a three-fingered hand, the bandages finally removed to reveal puckered scar tissue across his knuckles.

'We have, what, two or three days' supplies at the front?' Munro said. 'We'd be starved out within a week.'

'Morale would give out before then,' Commissar Tsutso sighed.

Kohl leaned on the holo-table with both arms extended, grimacing as he tried to put some weight on his injured leg.

'This is the culmination of all their plans,' Kohl said. 'Weeks of wearing down our morale, waiting for an opportunity to strike when we are at our most vulnerable.'

'No plan can account for all elements,' Commissar Tsutso said, looking through the map of Miracil directly at Darya.

'The Kintair have knocked out our long-distance communications, so we can't coordinate with our allies, contact the fleet…' Munro listed off each disadvantage on his fingers. 'And cannot warn the Three-Hundred-and-Thirty-Eighth.'

'Which makes restoring comms our highest priority,' Captain Kohl said with a final nod. 'Nevic, I need you on that. Munro–'

'Me, sir?' Darya said in surprise.

'Yes, you,' Kohl said matter-of-factly. 'You will lead a strike team to secure the comms link and hold it until you can be reinforced.'

'If I might make a suggestion, sir,' Munro began, and Darya waited for the inevitable suggestion that someone else lead the team, 'Sergeant Gosht's squad are very capable. I'd suggest that they accompany Sergeant Nevic.'

'Good idea. Darya, take Sergeant Gosht and his squad,' Kohl said as Darya tried not to look surprised. 'Munro, you will be leading the attack on the t'au flank as they pass through the Kintair lines. Leave me just enough people to man the defences and mobilise everyone else. Walking wounded, comms teams, even the fragging cooks… Withdraw everyone from Iron Hill and blow the halls.'

'Sir,' Munro said. He saluted and ran from the tent to begin the preparations.

'I will go with Nevic,' Commissar Tsutso said.

'You don't trust me, sir?' Darya asked.

'It is because it is where I am most needed, Sergeant Nevic. The t'au do not have a monopoly on the greater good.'

Kohl nodded. 'Good man. I'll hold Trackway Span. I bled to take this place, and I'm damn well not letting them take it back without a fight, encirclement or not.'

'With respect, sir, if the Kintair cut off–'

'Then I'll die holding this place, and by the God-Emperor I'll make them pay for every inch,' Kohl said. 'It's not Cadia, but it's good enough for me.'

'Good luck, captain,' Commissar Tsutso said, and shook his outstretched hand.

Darya made to leave with the commissar, but Kohl called out to her.

'Don't think I've forgotten about that snake, Mas Keen,' he said. 'We'll deal with him once we're done with the t'au. For now, take this as a statement of our intent.'

He grabbed something from between two vox-consoles and threw it to Darya. She caught it and walked away with a smile on her lips, her kvis' familiar weight reassuring in her hands.

* * *

Less than twenty minutes later Darya was in the back of the Chimera *Hate's Anvil* as it roared over Trackway Span towards the Kintair compound.

Commissar Tsutso sat to her right, closest to the rear hatch, whilst Arfit sat on her left, his long-las laid across his knees.

He had discharged himself from the medicae tents upon hearing that his sergeant had apparently returned from the dead, and had launched himself at Darya and embraced her in a back-slapping hug the moment he saw her.

'It's damned good to see you, boss,' he had said as he released her, his expression caught between pride and pain.

'And you,' Darya had replied, before noticing Arfit's gear stowed on a seat behind him. 'Where do you think you're going?'

'With you, obviously. You need someone you can trust to cover your back.'

Darya checked her borrowed equipment as the Chimera rumbled along. The second pair of combat fatigues helped to keep out the worst of the cold, but the new laspistol and long-las felt odd in her hands after so many years carrying her own.

'Gets a medal, returns from the dead and then saves the Miracil Salient,' Gosht counted down on his fingers on the seat opposite, smiling behind his lho-stick. 'Sounds like you're hogging all the glory to me, Nevic.'

Darya smiled at that and accepted Gosht's offered handshake.

'Good to have you back, Ghost,' he said with a wink.

'You get one and that's it,' Darya said, shaking her head.

Gosht patted down the pockets of his uniform, still smiling as he failed to find whatever he was looking for.

'Anyone have a light?' he asked the squad packed within the Chimera, most of whom shrugged. Arfit reached into his pocket and pulled out the lighter he had shown Darya all those days before; he tossed it to the sergeant.

'Keep it, I don't smoke,' Arfit said.

'Good man,' Gosht said, but his expression changed to one of surprise as he took a closer look at the little brass lighter in the red light of the troop compartment. 'Well isn't that something,' he muttered.

'*Approaching coordinates!*' the driver's vox crackled, and both Darya and Gosht got to their feet.

'I'm sorry, your squad,' Darya said with an apologetic smile. Gosht's features were thrown into sharp relief as he took a drag on the lho-stick. He was smiling again.

'No, you go ahead,' he said, and slipped back into his seat.

'Okay,' Darya said, looking around at the expectant faces who looked back at her. 'Our objective is the vox-relay – everything else is secondary to that. Don't get bogged down, don't do anything stupid – we take the relay and we hold out until reinforcements arrive. Clear?'

'Cadia stands!' Gosht roared.

'Cadia stands!' Darya shouted back alongside everyone within the transport.

'God-Emperor protect this holy company who act in your name,' Commissar Tsutso intoned as *Hate's Anvil*'s heavy bolters opened fire on targets outside the vehicle. Shots crashed into the hull, shaking the Chimera but failing to slow it.

'God-Emperor, give us the strength to smite your enemies,' Tsutso continued, rising to stand at the rear hatch, his bolt pistol in one hand and his chainsword in the other.

'God-Emperor, in your name' – Tsutso's voice rose to a roar – '*we fight!*'

The rear door slammed open as *Hate's Anvil* skidded to a halt on the icy street, and Darya ran out behind Commissar Tsutso, screaming the war cry of the Coclerati Janissaries.

Las-bolts whipped across her vision, missing Commissar Tsutso by a hair's breadth whilst he put down Kintair soldier after Kintair soldier as they charged, bayonets levelled. Blood fountained from torsos blasted apart by bolt-shells, limbs sailing through the air as he hacked and whirled.

Gosht's squad were a testament to Cadia's perfection, forming into tight fire-teams that pumped volley after volley into the charging Kintair until the conscripts broke. Only then did the Cadians sprint into the scant cover offered by the street, pouring accurate suppressing fire at anything that moved.

Darya and Arfit moved at the heart of the maelstrom, popping off aimed kill shots with smooth, practised ease, flowing around each other to cover and call out targets, never once crossing into the others' line of fire. Kintair fell back from windows and high vantage points, dying too quickly to take aim at their attackers.

'Hate's Anvil, move up in support!' Gosht bellowed into his vox headset, running behind his men and pushing them on with roared encouragement.

They drove the Kintair back with sniper, bolt pistol and lasgun, down the street towards a building marked *Tullio and Partners*. Commissar Tsutso bellowed wrathful benedictions with every step, his voice carrying over the clamour of battle.

The Kintair ahead were regrouping, running into cover before the advancing Cadians, and Darya screamed for them to find cover. The troopers complied without hesitation, diving behind raised porches and fallen masonry as the first cohesive defences opened fire from the far end of the street. Commissar Tsutso walked through the withering fusillade with cold fury, stepping into cover as if he were moving out of a light drizzle. Darya marvelled at him between shots, snapping back the heads of Kintair troopers as they took aim.

'*Anvil*, make us a hole!' Gosht shouted.

The Chimera's driver slammed down hard on the accelerator,

tracks churning through ice and stone to launch its titanic weight forwards in a sudden rush of plasteel alloy. The turret-mounted heavy bolter maintained a steady rhythm of fire, swinging back and forth to blast holes in the Kintair defences, whilst the hull-mounted heavy bolter targeted the exposed troops on the street.

Gosht pulled his men up behind the Chimera, using it for mobile cover all the way to the end of the street. Darya and Arfit moved behind it, roving wherever they could find angles on enemies whilst using the vehicle's bulk to shield themselves from the worst of the return fire.

'Battering ram!' Gosht shouted.

The Cadians scattered into the cover cleared by their advance as the transport found another gear, slamming forwards at speed. The turret traversed to face back at the Cadians, protecting the heavy bolter when the Chimera slammed through the wall of Tullio and Partners in an explosion of bricks and snow. It reversed out of the huge hole that it had created, the turret bolter firing shots up the street, as Gosht's team raced into the breach.

'Five with Commissar Tsutso, five with me!' Gosht ordered, splitting his squad to clear the lower floor of the square building whilst Darya and Arfit moved in their wake in search of stairs to clear the upper floor.

'Targets on the square!' Darya called out, dropping her long-las and trusting the strap to hold it tight to her chest. In one smooth movement she drew her kvis and laspistol, taking point as Arfit sniped targets in the square.

A Kintair appeared out of a doorway to Darya's right, screaming a war cry that Darya cut short with a headshot from her laspistol. A woman pushed past the falling body, only to die when the kvis opened her throat.

Where are you, Feon?

'Stairs!' Darya called to Arfit as she found a narrow wooden staircase that led to the upper floor. She advanced upwards, her laspistol covering the doorway at the top.

An explosion rocked the earth, close enough that Darya felt the backwash through the windows as she reached the upper floor. *Hate's Anvil*'s heavy bolters stuttered for a moment, then only one resumed firing.

'We need to hurry this up – *Hate's Anvil* is only going to keep them distracted for so long,' Darya shouted.

'Target is still below and is intact!' Arfit yelled from the windows that looked down over the square. Darya ran over to see for herself, and took in the Kintair defences.

The conscripts might not have been as effective as well-trained troops, but they hadn't been idle in their weeks in Miracil. They had surrounded the converted Chimera in sandbagged heavy-weapon emplacements, fallback positions and ammo caches, turning the bare square into an easily defensible position.

Unless there are snipers above you.

'Shoot and move,' Darya said to Arfit, who offered his hand. She grasped it firmly.

'Don't die out there again,' Arfit said.

'I don't plan on it.'

Arfit moved past her and she let him go, trusting in her man to stay alive.

She moved at pace through the building, clearing each room in turn before stopping to snap off shots at the defenders in the square below. Each shot was a kill that reduced their strength, and gave them the impression they faced more attackers than they did.

Gunfire vibrated up from below as she passed over other battles being waged on the ground floor, until she reached the corner of the building that would grant her the best position for the battle ahead. She refocused on the square below, where Commissar Tsutso was leading the three remaining members of his team in an attack towards the vox-relay.

Darya dropped to one knee, her mouth dry and her heart hammering as she raised her scope to her eye.

Commissar Tsutso moved amongst the Kintair as if blessed by the God-Emperor Himself, and Darya wondered if the awe she felt was close to what others had experienced when she ran through hails of gunfire, only to emerge unscathed.

It was intoxicating, inspiring. The power of the God-Emperor at work.

She cleared a path for him through the defenders, picking off the Kintair on heavy weapons first, then their officers, then...

Feon.

Dal Feon was running towards Commissar Tsutso's squad from their rear, a primed grenade in his hand, his arm drawn back to throw.

Darya squeezed the trigger as her crosshairs danced over the Kintair sergeant's upper torso, then watched in grim satisfaction as he spun to the dirt, crawling towards the fallen grenade...

She heard the distant *crump* of the explosion but didn't see it; she was tracking a Kintair soldier who had broken cover to intercept the Cadians approaching the vox-relay, and shot him down before he'd gone more than a handful of steps.

Commissar Tsutso made it to the Chimera and disappeared into its converted innards, his squad moving into defensive positions around the hull.

Darya jerked back in pain as stone chips sliced across her face, blown free by las-fire from the square below. She cursed her arrogance for staying in one position long enough to be pinpointed.

'Shoot and move, dammit!' she shouted at herself, diving

forwards through the open air to land in the piled snow in the corner of the square.

The Kintair's fire was wilting beneath the Cadian pressure, which gave Darya a short window to get to Commissar Tsutso at the relay.

She took it, vaulting the first sandbagged wall and drawing her kvis and laspistol again. They were better for the close work, even if she missed the familiar weight of her autopistol.

Moving in a crouch, she worked her way through the maze of tight corners and fallen Kintair to the red-hulled transport, where she found Commissar Tsutso trying to work a complex cogitator assembly.

'Sir!' Darya shouted over the din. 'Have we re-established contact?'

'Yes, I'm trying to raise Munro,' Tsutso replied. He adjusted a single dial nestled in a bank of hundreds and picked up the vox handset. 'Munro, are you receiving?'

This is Munro. Message received. Stand by,' Munro's voice said, undercut by a mechanical buzz.

Another explosion shook the earth, and Darya knew that *Hate's Anvil* had been overcome.

A plume of black smoke rose from the direction they had come, and the background chatter of its heavy bolter ceased.

'Friendlies coming in!'

Gosht appeared in the window behind the Chimera, his squad taking up defensive positions around him. Gosht vaulted through the nearest window frame and ran to the transport.

'Good to see you,' Darya said.

'And you,' Gosht replied, with his lho-stick somehow still clamped between his lips. 'Sir, have we achieved our objective?'

'We have, sergeant. Now we hold on for reinforcements,' Commissar Tsutso said.

He turned to face the two sergeants, and for the first time Darya realised that he was wounded.

'Sir!' she gasped, reaching out to support him as he stumbled, blood leaking from several shallow wounds across his chest.

'Shrapnel, nothing more,' Tsutso said impassively, pushing her hand away gently. 'How many men do you have left, Sergeant Gosht?'

'Four, sir,' Gosht replied.

Las-bolts still lanced down into the Kintair cowering in cover across the square, and Darya sighed in relief. Arfit fought on, but he was isolated.

'I need to get back to Arfit,' she said. 'Can you defend this position if we provide overwatch?'

Commissar Tsutso nodded. 'We can try.' He picked up his chainsword and revved the motor, the teeth spitting the remains of shattered bone and gore to the floor.

Darya ran back to join up with Arfit, finding her way through the ruined interior of the building and running towards the tell-tale crack-whizz of his long-las.

'Is the link back up?' he asked as she approached, grinning as he lined up yet another shot.

'Commissar worked a miracle,' Darya said. 'You good?'

'Running low, boss, if you have any cells going spare.'

Darya slid a pair of charge packs from her belt and passed them to Arfit, who immediately ejected his spent cell.

The ground rumbled with approaching thunder, loosing sheets of snow from the tiled roof to scatter on the cobbles below.

'I think things are about to get a lot more interesting,' Darya said.

A roar grew outside the square, one that communicated the pain and anger of a hundred throats. It was enough to shake even Darya's iron nerve, if just for a moment.

'Think they're regrouping, boss?' Arfit asked.

Darya didn't have time to answer. The noise entered the square, taken up by a flood of Kintair that clambered through windows and doorways, scrambling over each other as their fellows trampled them in their haste.

Darya opened fire, but the crowd was so thick she barely needed to aim. Commissar Tsutso had ordered his remaining squad to take up the vacated heavy-weapon positions, and they added their fearsome firepower to the Cadian fusillade.

This isn't a suicidal charge, Darya realised as the ground shook again and again, the source growing closer with each resounding boom.

'They're running from something!' Darya cried, shifting her position to look past the fleeing Kintair.

The dark sky behind the square flared with sudden light, the whoosh of promethium flames illuminating a pair of glowing eyes beneath a pair of hunched orange shoulders.

House Gyrrant had come.

The Knight charged forwards, its flamers blazing with cleansing fire, the heavy stubber mounted on its chest spitting tracer rounds that splashed through the fleeing Kintair below to bounce high into the air.

And the Knight wasn't alone. A pair of Armigers, each armed with flamers and chainglaives the size of a full-grown man, loped past their larger cousin like loosed hunting dogs. They set about the slaughter of the Kintair with brutal efficiency, scattering their defences like children's toys.

Darya could just make out Commissar Tsutso, who had pulled his men back into the safety of the Chimera.

'CADIANS,' an impossibly loud voice blared, amplified beyond all reasonable limits by the Knight's ancient design. *'BATTLE IS JOINED! YOUR BROTHERS ARE ENGAGED TO THE WEST!'*

Thin beams of light lanced down through the night sky ahead, growing from threads to columns the size of hab-blocks as the fleet unleashed their fury on the t'au, caught in the open beyond the safety of their defences.

The noise was the wrath of the Imperium unleashed after weeks of stalemate and piecemeal skirmishes, the Cadians finally loosed to do what they had trained all their lives to do. The transplants fought just as hard, shoulder to shoulder with the children of Cadia, their brothers and sisters in arms, if not in blood.

Darya fought through the centre of the maelstrom of plasma, las-fire, promethium flame and rocket trails, her long-las pinned to her shoulder, her last remaining squadmate at her side.

She knew they were only two warriors in a battle of thousands, insignificant in isolation but for the manner in which they fought.

Where the Cadians crushed their enemies beneath the weight of fire, Darya and Arfit were the surgical blade. They picked out priority targets within the press of t'au bodies, be they human or xenos, and eliminated them with clinical accuracy.

That was their role, and they played it without hesitation.

'Officer, left, beneath the archway!' Darya shouted, sighting her own shot on a fire warrior who was aiming a markerlight at a nearby Leman Russ.

'He's down!' Arfit called back, the barrel of his long-las still smoking as he sought another target.

'Moving, cover me,' Darya called out.

She ran out from beneath the awning and over a pile of settling rubble, scattering snow as she slid in behind the fume-choked air at the rear of the Leman Russ. The new position gave her a better angle on a pair of crouched t'au preparing their own markerlight, and she took advantage of it with two squeezes of the trigger.

'Moving up!' Arfit called and Darya waved him on, sweeping possible firing lines on her squadmate.

'Any sign?' Arfit asked.

'None yet. We keep moving,' Darya said with a shake of her head.

Dawn was fast approaching, a warm orange glow growing to the east which cast the underside of the clouds in shades of pink and blue. Ten hours of battle had left the streets carpeted with the dead, both human and t'au, their blood mixing in the snow to create a slimy black sludge that slid underfoot.

'On me,' Darya said, and rounded the tank to head east past a building that sheltered cowering human warriors in t'au armour.

No sooner were the snipers clear of the building than the Leman Russ fired its battle cannon, reducing the structure to dust and misshapen lumps of stone.

The next street was awash with interlacing lights, crossing back and forth between lines of craters. A damaged t'au transport burned in the depths of a depression on the far end of the street, black smoke billowing from a pair of lascannon holes blasted through its hull.

Darya caught a flash of black armour behind the smoke.

'I see him!' she cried, and leaped into cover behind the base of a shattered statue, plasma hissing past as she checked the charge on her long-las.

She was still learning the peculiarities of the weapon, its foibles and its strengths. It was unerringly accurate, but lacked the power of her old long-las, which could blast through t'au armour at a far greater distance. It also drank charge packs like a Catachan on shore leave.

A titanic Riptide battlesuit thrummed overhead, coming in to land near the burning t'au transport. The Cadians all switched their fire to the massive battlesuit, but their volleys did little more than shimmer against its energy shield. It raised its rotary cannon, the whine of its spin drowning out almost all other sound.

All but the thud, thud, thud of running feet. Darya drew a breath involuntarily as an orange-armoured Knight lumbered past in a dead sprint, giving her just enough time to make out the name *Ignatius* emblazoned across its chest before it barrelled into the Riptide, its reaper chainsword licking out to sever the rotary cannon arm in a screech of adamantine on steel.

'This is our chance!' Darya shouted to Arfit.

They moved up the line as both Cadian and t'au troops lost their focus momentarily, enthralled by the clash of giants only fifty yards distant.

I know you're there. You wouldn't be able to resist this.

Darya ducked as the plasma fire began again, and rockets streaked out of unseen launchers at the back of the Riptide. The backwash of the explosions was scalding in the cold morning air, the warheads detonating harmlessly on the Knight's ion shield. It used the momentum to press forwards, dragging the Riptide away from the burning transport.

'They're moving off!' Arfit called out, following Darya into cover in a crater that had swallowed the corner of a nearby building.

'Keep your eyes out for Longshot!' Darya shouted back.

She was running on anger and wrath after so long in the heat of battle, but her focus was still razor-sharp where Arfit's was beginning to wane.

It's not every day you see two giants duking it out, she admitted to herself.

There, another flash of black armour.

Shas'el Tan stood behind a fire warrior gunline in the scant cover of a crater rim, commanding his troops and manipulating a glowing hex-panel on his wrist.

Where is Mui'el?

Shas'el Tan moved and Darya caught a glimpse of purplish skin and ivory robes standing out against the grime and dirt – honoured Mui'el was there, just as Ceres had said he would be, overseeing the attack for himself.

A Devilfish transport slid into view behind them and turned, its hatch already opening as Shas'el Tan grabbed the ethereal's arm and began to drag him to safety.

She had time for both shots, if she was quick. Darya raised her rifle and fired.

The Knight's ion shield flared, absorbing the shot as it was driven back by the Riptide, before rallying and tackling the t'au battlesuit through a building in an avalanche of stone and breaking glass.

Her rifle whined as the cell recharged; it could already be empty, but she prayed for just one more shot.

'Rocket drones!' Arfit called out, and began blasting the heavy automata from the air.

Just one shot.

Darya pulled the scope close and let out a quick, controlled breath, settling into the stillness required to make the shot she needed.

One shot to kill the man who had masterminded the deaths of most of her squad, ending the family that she had earned amongst the Cadians and personally giving the order to kill her closest friend? Or the spiritual leader of the t'au in Miracil, whose death would break their spirit and destroy their will to fight?

Shas'el Tan pushed honoured Mui'el into the Devilfish transport and turned, his helmet lenses scanning the battlefield as the hatch began to close.

She squeezed the trigger, only inhaling once the shot had hit her target. Honoured Mui'el fell back, his unarmoured head disappearing in a puff of blood and grey viscera.

The Devilfish's hatch closed on Shas'el Tan, and bore him away to safety in a scream of jets that blasted black smoke across the battle-torn street.

EPILOGUE

'You stand here convicted of betraying your regiment.'

Darya stood on the snowy street outside Relief Station Zero in the bitter cold of another Miracil dawn, her eyes glued to Commissar Tsutso as he delivered his verdict.

'The sentence is death.'

Her pulse quickened as the commissar drew his bolt pistol and aimed, her breaths growing shallower as the moment approached.

'Do you have any last words?' Commissar Tsutso asked.

'She's not even Cadian,' Keen whined, before the bolt pistol barked once.

The shot echoed over the stillness of Trackway Span, growing fainter with every repetition until it disappeared into the chill air.

No one stepped forward to move Keen's ruined body from the post. Instead, one of Commissar Tsutso's new cadet commissars nailed a board to the post above where Keen's head had been a few moments before.

Traitor it declared, in bold red writing.

'I hope you rot,' Sergeant Gosht spat.

'His death is no loss,' Corporal Arfit said.

Darya stood between the two trueborn Cadians, who had turned up for Keen's execution without Darya having asked. They both said they were there for their own reasons, but she understood their true motives and was grateful for their presence.

She held her old rifle across her arms, the wrappings re-secured about the previous owner's markings on the weapon, recalibrated and resanctified to cleanse it of any misuse it had seen in Keen's unworthy hands.

Gosht's wounds were healing well, the tight stitches at the corner of his mouth giving him a permanent smirk, whilst Arfit had not only made it out of the Battle of the Low City unscathed, but had been promoted to boot.

'Sergeant Nevic, Captain Kohl is expecting us,' Commissar Tsutso intoned stiffly, his chest puffed out by what Darya assumed was a thick layer of bandages.

'Yes, sir,' she said, making the sign of the aquila. Gosht and Arfit did the same, and Commissar Tsutso mirrored the gesture.

They walked together through the snow back towards the command centre in a warm silence, broken only by the sound of Tsutso's shining leather coat creaking as he walked.

'May I ask you a personal question, Sergeant Nevic?' he said as they crossed out of earshot of the soldiers in the refectory queue, halfway between the medicae tent and Kohl's command centre.

'Of course, sir,' Darya replied.

'Was it an easy decision?' Commissar Tsutso asked, his eyebrow arching as he looked at her askance.

'Yes, sir. Mui'el was the greater danger to us by far. A warrior like Shas'el Tan we can kill. Lasguns and bolters are less useful against ideas,' Darya said.

'That isn't the decision I was referring to,' Commissar Tsutso said, drawing to a stop in front of Captain Kohl's tent.

'As I said, sir. Ideas can be dangerous,' Darya said evenly.

Commissar Tsutso's eyes narrowed but he appeared to accept the answer. He led the way into the tent, where Captain Kohl was waiting.

'Ahh, Nevic,' the captain said, passing her a list of names on a sheet of thin paper. 'The names of your new squad.'

'The merger with the Three-Hundred-and-Thirty-Eighth is going ahead, sir?' Darya asked.

'Major Wester signed it off not half an hour ago,' Kohl said, limping over to a nearby chair and sinking into it with a sigh.

'How's the major settling in, sir? He's got big boots to fill – I saw on the last vid that Colonel Wassenby had demoted himself to spend more time on the front lines.'

'A brave man, Sergeant Wassenby,' Commissar Tsutso mused as he folded his arms across his broad chest and gave Kohl a meaningful look.

'Truly the God-Emperor works in mysterious ways,' Captain Kohl said. 'Nevic, your squad will be arriving later today. Get them up to scratch quickly – I have a job for you.'

ABOUT THE AUTHOR

Rob Young is a writer and graphic designer from Lancashire whose work for Black Library includes the novel *Longshot* and the short stories 'The Roar of the Void' and 'Transplants'.

YOUR
NEXT READ

KASRKIN
by Edoardo Albert

An elite squad of Cadian Kasrkin are tasked with a critical mission behind enemy lines.
They must rescue their general in xenos-held territory before his dangerous knowledge
falls into enemy hands. But not all is as it seems...

An extract from
Kasrkin
by Edoardo Albert

'Looks big.'

'Bigger than you think.'

'Suppose it's hot too?'

'Hot enough to fry a grox steak on the cowling of a Leman Russ.'

'So why not send a squadron of them in then?'

'Heard they tried – didn't get more than a mile before they started sinking.' Sergeant Shaan Malick adjusted his helmet. He wasn't wearing it; he was sitting on it. Beside him, Trooper Torgut Gunsur stared out from the relative cool of the precious shade under the stubby wings of the Valkyrie, his eyes squinting against the glare.

'It's all yellow.'

Sergeant Malick laughed. 'It's the Great Sand Sea. There's a clue in the name.'

Trooper Gunsur unclipped his rebreather and spat, the phlegm arcing out from the precious shade and landing on the sand. It sizzled.

Malick shook his head. 'Keep your spit – you're going to need it.'

'I don't start no mission without spitting on the ground I'll be treading.'

Malick looked at Gunsur. 'Why?'

"Cause it ain't Cadia, and I spit on ground I fight on that ain't home.'

Malick looked away, staring out into the heat haze but not seeing it.

Trooper Gunsur glanced at his sergeant. 'Not so stupid, is it?'

But Sergeant Malick did not look back at him. His fingers strayed to the little plasteel vial hanging from a chain around his neck. The plasteel had been finger-burnished bright by the Cadian rubbing it between thumb and forefinger. The two men were sitting in the jet-blown bowl of sand beneath the wing of a Valkyrie, one of three that had brought the squad of Kasrkin here.

Malick pointed out in front of them. 'It's not all yellow. Some of it is brown and I reckon it goes white in the distance.'

'You mean, where the heat haze hides the horizon?'

Sergeant Malick laughed, then coughed. 'Throne. Wish I hadn't done that. Even the air is hot.'

'Everything's hot on this damned planet.'

Malick turned and stared at Gunsur. 'You saying you don't want to be here, trooper? That's treason.'

Gunsur shook his head, suddenly unsure. 'You playing me, Sergeant Malick?'

Before Malick could answer, another voice spoke.

'Yes, are you playing him, Sergeant Malick?'

The two Cadians scrambled to their feet, the sand beneath their boots crunching.

Sergeant Malick looked at the man standing in front of them.

He was wearing fatigues that gave no indication of rank. He was even barefoot. But everything else about him suggested 'officer'. Malick decided to play it safe.

'Yes, I was playing him. Sir.'

The man nodded. 'Good. I rather hoped you were. It would mean that you might have the wit to lead this team.'

Malick blinked. 'Sir?'

'Assemble the rest of the squad.'

Malick stared at the man. 'Who are you? Sir.'

'Bharath Obeysekera.' The man regarded Malick through sun-slit eyes. 'Captain Bharath Obeysekera. For your sins, you have been given into my command. Now call the troopers.'

'Yes, sir.' With a definite order to carry out, Malick made the aquila and spun off to see it done. 'Fall in!' he roared, in his best sergeant's voice, the sound of it filling the dead, empty desert air.

It was a voice that had Captain Obeysekera putting his hand on Sergeant Malick's shoulder and saying so that only he could hear: 'Use the squad vox-channel. This will be a mission of silence. Best you start getting used to being quiet, Sergeant Malick.'

'Yes…' Malick cut off the second half of his barked reply. 'Sir,' he finished.

'Good man,' said Obeysekera. 'Assemble the squad in the shade – we will all have had enough sun soon. Colonel Aruna will address you first, then I will fill in the details.'

Captain Obeysekera turned away, his bare feet quiet on the sand, and slipped away into the deeper, darker shadows of the interior of the Valkyrie.

Sergeant Malick picked up his helmet and keyed the squad vox-channel, sending alerts to the other seven troopers in the unit. He saw on the auspex integrated into his helmet that they had all acknowledged. Tracer runes showed them all moving to the location he had marked on the auspex, the outlying troops converging from the sentry positions Malick had ordered them to after the Valkyries had landed.

Gunsur leaned over towards Malick. 'The only time I ever saw a captain dressed like that, he'd been stripped and had his ribs opened out by those Gallows Cluster traitors. You sure he is a real captain?'

'Didn't you see?'

'See what?'

'When he went back inside. He's proper 'kin, all right – he's got the eagle on his neck. Besides, I reckon I've heard of him.'

'Yeah? Where?'

'The Sando retreat. He sent his 'kin squad to hold up the 'nids while he marshalled the civvies onto exfiltration vehicles.'

Gunsur looked at his sergeant. 'Yeah? So?'

'None of them got out, but *he* did.'

Gunsur nodded. 'One of those officers.'

Malick shook his head. 'Don't know. But I'm keeping this beauty to hand.' The sergeant picked up the hellgun that was leaning against the ticking plasteel of the Valkyrie. He ran his hand over the use-polished stock of the hellgun, its paluwood the colour of aged honey. 'This beauty will put a hotshot through the eye of any xenos at a mile.'

Gunsur gestured towards the desert. 'You reckon we'll meet any bluies out there, sarge? Don't look like the sort of place they'd be interested in.'

'They're xenos scum,' said Malick. 'Who knows what they're interested in. Besides, from what I hear, there's plenty on this planet to draw the attention of the bluies.'

'Yeah, sand,' said Gunsur. 'Lots and lots of sand.'

Malick cuffed Gunsur on the shoulder. 'There's stuff under the sand's worth more'n most subsectors. That's probably why we're here on…' The sergeant paused and gestured out from the shadow under the wing to the vast dry world that surrounded them.

'It is called Dasht i-Kevar.'

Sergeant Malick and Trooper Gunsur turned around to see Captain Obeysekera, now dressed in the grey and tan of the Kasr-kin, standing at the top of the rear ramp of the Valkyrie holding, of all things, his dress cap in one hand.

'Colonel Aruna will brief you on your deployment here and the strategic objective. I will cover the tactical situation.' Captain Obeysekera pointed over to the next Valkyrie, standing stark and outlined in the sun. 'You don't want to keep the colonel waiting, do you?'

'No, sir,' said Malick. The sergeant glanced at the auspex; the other squad members were drawing in towards the mark.

The three men stepped out of the shade under the Valkyrie's wing. The sun hit them with the weight of lead, pressing down upon their heads.

Captain Obeysekera put his dress cap on his head. 'Only time this has been any use.' He looked at Malick and Gunsur. 'Here, helmets are barely better than bare heads – you want a cap and scarf.'

Malick shook his head. He pointed at various gouges and scratches on his helmet. 'I wouldn't be here without this. Besides, we might need the rebreather.'

'We might need lots of things, but none of them will matter if we can't get to where we need to go.' Obeysekera looked at Malick. 'You're from Kasr Vasan. Hear it had the best logistics on Cadia. You're used to having the right weapon on hand when you need it. I grew up in Kasr Gesh. We were lucky if we had a power pack to go in our lasrifles, let alone a spare. On this mission, we will be on our own. We carry in everything we need, and when we run out we make do with what we've got left over, and when we run out of that we'll use our hands. I expect every man to be able to adapt. If you can't, I'll get someone who can. Understand?'

Malick stared back at the officer. Obeysekera regarded him mildly but steadily.

'I have never failed on a mission.'

'Which is why I asked for you, sergeant. Your record suggests a soldier who is willing to use his brain and think. Is that true?'

Malick paused, staring at Captain Obeysekera, and then, slowly, he began to smile.

'Yes, sir, it is true.' He pointed at Gunsur. 'Not so sure about Gunsur, though.'

'That's all right, sergeant. We can't have troopers thinking, can we?'

Obeysekera set off over the hot sand, his feet, now booted, sinking small pits into the ground as he went, with Malick and Gunsur following, heading towards the command Valkyrie. Reaching the bowl of sand blown out by the Valkyrie's turbofans when it landed, they crested the rim and started down towards the machine squatting in the middle of the wide crater. The sand slid away under their boots, slipping like liquid so that they all but skied down the inside of the bowl. Fifty yards away, the command Valkyrie stood, its lower half hidden by the sand bowl. Other men were centring in on the Valkyrie, some from the third craft that made the other base of the landing triangle, the rest from the perimeter positions that Malick had assigned to them.

The Valkyries themselves were not sitting silently on the sand. Their turbofans rotated gently, pushing air through the vents to placate machine-spirits grinding sand between their plasteel teeth. The pilots sat ready in the cockpits, eyes hidden behind black goggles, while the heavy bolters mounted on the Valkyries continued to track over the landscape, empty though it was. But the heat haze, rising all around them, reduced visibility: anything over half a mile away dissolved into rising columns of heated air, twisting slowly under the sun.

It was a strangely flat landscape, unrelieved by shade, even though the sand rose in static waves to their east as it stretched into the Great Sand Sea. To the west, the land was rock and salt-flat, studded with shallow outcrops and basalt columns.

'There're no shadows,' said Malick. He pointed down at his feet. 'Where has it gone?'

Obeysekera laughed, the harsh sound cut short by the dry heat. He pointed straight overhead. 'Up there.'

Malick squinted up, cricking his neck back and back, the flare guards in his goggles activating. Above him, the sun that squatted over Dasht i-Kevar rode, a white eye sitting on top of the sky arch.

Malick looked back to Captain Obeysekera. 'I don't understand.'

The captain grimaced. 'Don't worry, it won't last.' Obeysekera looked up into the sky too, his eyes becoming slits as he did so. 'Thankfully.' He glanced back to Malick. 'With no shadows it's impossible to judge distance. Speaking of distance, let's not keep the colonel waiting.'

The Kasrkin sergeant saw the sweat pricking through Obeysekera's skin, only for it to evaporate as it appeared.

'This is hotter than Prosan,' he said.

Captain Obeysekera looked back at the sergeant. 'It's about the same in terms of climate. But there are other things…' His voice trailed away as his eyes, squinting against the overwhelming light, took in the Great Sand Sea. 'Let us hope we do not meet them.'

As they neared the command Valkyrie, Malick saw the rest of the squad assembling in the shade under the wings: some squatting, others sitting on their helmets, hands resting upon their treasured weapons, the hotshot lasguns they nicknamed 'hellguns'. The last of the perimeter troopers were walking in, hellguns cradled on forearms. Malick glanced at his auspex: they were all here.

Just as he was about to look away from the display, he saw movement traces and, glancing up, he saw a man in a high-ranking officer's uniform emerge from the Valkyrie.

Aruna. The colonel's reputation had spread sector-wide. He had led the defence of Krack des Chavel against an insurrection of Chaos cultists, woken to frenzy by the great purple bruise that split the night sky. He had planned and led the assault on the ork warband led by Grashbash the Grabbler that had laid waste to three systems. And the word among the Guard was that Colonel Aruna was the brains behind the unusually subtle attempts to retake the Imperial worlds in the subsector that had succumbed to the blandishments, diplomatic and militant, of the T'au Empire.

In Malick's previous experience, whenever the Guard had retaken Imperial worlds that had been lost to the enemy, be that Chaos or xenos, it had been necessary to repopulate the planet after the victory. Aruna had managed to retain a viable population on two of the planets he had wrested back from the t'au.

Colonel Aruna came down the ramp and stood on the sand among the squad of Kasrkin. The 'kin regarded the colonel with battle-hardened eyes, then, slowly, one by one, stood and saluted him. The troops, looking upon the colonel, measuring him, saw him as one of their own: a soldier who had stood in the midst of battle without flinching, a man who had faced death on as many occasions as they had and not let fear prevent him from doing his duty to the Emperor.

As the Kasrkin acknowledged the colonel as their equal, the

colonel returned the salute. Seeing Captain Obeysekera, he nodded to him then turned to the waiting, silent 'kin.

'We have lost a general. You are going to find him and bring him back.'

The Kasrkin greeted the news in silence, but it was a silence that held a wealth of unanswered questions relating to the conduct of the mission and the chance of carrying it out successfully.

'General Mato Itoyesa, commanding officer eastern sector, was returning to headquarters when his Valkyrie was attacked by t'au Barracudas. Attempting to evade the xenos, the general's pilot flew into a sandstorm.'

Colonel Aruna paused as he said that, looking around the watching Kasrkin. They said nothing but Malick saw, from the tightening of muscles, that they all knew what such an action meant: arriving on Dasht i-Kevar, it was drummed into every combatant, be they ordinary soldier, Kasrkin or Imperial Navy, never to deliberately enter one of the planet's sandstorms. Such was the violence of the storms that an unprotected soldier would be flayed in a few minutes. Aircraft such as Valkyries had their engines clogged, their machine-spirits choking on vast quantities of sand, while even the normally indomitable Leman Russ would grind to a stop as the corrosive grains insinuated themselves into gears and bearings.

'Transmissions indicated that the general's aircraft managed to land successfully, but we have only very approximate indications of its location. No further transmissions have been received, despite our efforts to raise General Itoyesa. As the commanding officer of the eastern sector, I do not have to tell you how important it is that the general does not fall into xenos hands.' The colonel paused and looked around the watching, silent Kasrkin. 'It is your job to ensure that he does not. Questions?'

Malick looked at the surrounding troops. There were many questions that could be asked, but they were 'kin: they did the jobs no one else could do. He expected no reply.

But a voice spoke.

'That is what I don't understand. Why did the general's pilot fly into the sandstorm? It was strictly against the orders of the lord militant.'

The questioner stepped forward out of the deep shadows of the loading bay and into the softer shade under the Valkyrie's wings. He was a young man, with all the leanness of youth, but his leanness was sheathed, despite the heat, in the long drapes of the coat of a commissar of the Officio Prefectus.

Colonel Aruna turned towards the young man and shook his head. 'It is a question we shall put to the pilot should he be recovered in a state to answer. I am sure your father will be as keen to learn the answer as you are.'

'I am sure he will. Lord Militant Roshant is... concerned that one of his key generals has disappeared.'

'As are we all, Commissar Roshant,' said Colonel Aruna.

At the name, all the men listening stiffened slightly. Commissar Roshant gave no obvious indication that he was aware of their regard, but Malick saw the halo of self-regard that clung about one of the appointed of the Imperial elite, as invisible and as impenetrable as a refractor field. The Kasrkin sergeant squinted. There was a subtle phase effect around Commissar Roshant that suggested he might actually be employing a refractor field.

'That is also why my father, the lord militant, has ordered me to accompany your men on their mission.' The young commissar paused slightly as he said this. The Kasrkin, no strangers to the ways of Imperial commissars, knew well that he had paused so that he might assess their reaction to this news. What physical reaction they gave was minimal: some tightening of the eyes, quick glances, nothing more.

For his part, Malick looked to Captain Obeysekera, seeking to judge if he had had any warning that the lord militant's son would be accompanying them on their mission. But at the news, the captain's expression remained as blank as the desert on the day after a storm, when the windblown sand had scoured all tracks from its face.

Commissar Roshant, evidently satisfied with what he saw in the faces of the watching Kasrkin, turned back to Colonel Aruna.

'Should we find the general alive, it will be imperative to assess immediately whether he has been compromised. Should we find the general dead, the same question will arise. And should we fail to find the general, the question will become even more urgent. My father has given me the task of answering these questions.'

Colonel Aruna nodded. 'Very well, commissar. But, unless you have received new orders from the lord militant, operational command of this mission remains with Captain Obeysekera.' Colonel Aruna paused, making sure that all the men present were listening and would be able to hear the answer.

'Yes, that is correct.' The words sounded forced, as if Commissar Roshant said them against his will. Malick, face impassive, smiled inwardly at imagining the son pleading to his father for command of the mission and that permission being denied.

Colonel Aruna nodded. 'Thank you, commissar. So that there might be no misunderstanding, you will be attached to the mission as its commissar, with responsibility for the political and religious welfare of the men, but answerable to the mission commander, Captain Obeysekera. Is that clear?'

Commissar Roshant stared at Colonel Aruna, then glanced at Captain Obeysekera. 'Yes, it is clear,' he said through narrowed lips.

'Very well,' said Colonel Aruna. 'I am glad we have cleared that up before the mission begins.' The colonel began to turn away, but before he could do so, Roshant spoke again.

'While it is true that Captain Obeysekera has operational command of the mission, it is also true that Lord Militant Roshant has asked me to write a full report on this operation. I will of course note any instances where Captain Obeysekera fails to adhere to my advice – the advice of a commissar of the God-Emperor's Imperium.' Roshant looked from Aruna to Obeysekera. 'Is that clear, too?'

The colonel looked at the commissar. 'Perfectly clear.'

Roshant turned to Obeysekera. 'Captain?'

Sergeant Malick saw the danger light in the captain's eyes, a glint even in the deep shadow under the Valkyrie's wing.

'I understand, Commissar Roshant,' said Captain Obeysekera. His eyes broadened and he smiled. 'For my part, I am grateful that you will be writing a full report of the mission as that will save me the labour of filing my own account.' Obeysekera turned to the colonel. 'Now that is settled, shall I start the mission briefing, sir?'

'Yes, please do so.'

Captain Obeysekera paused and looked at each of the watching soldiers. His glance caught on something on Gunsur's uniform.

'Take off your campaign medals and kasr tags. That you fought in the Haetes Second Star campaign or which kasr you hail from is of no interest to me. For what it's worth, you are now part of First Squad, One Hundred and Fifty-Fifth. But I don't really care about that either.' Obeysekera looked round the waiting soldiers. 'All that matters is the mission.'

He waited.

Slowly, first in ones or twos, then followed by the rest, the Kasrkin removed their campaign medals, stowing them in pockets, and tucked their kasr tags away out of sight.

When they were all simply Kasrkin with no other identifying marks, Obeysekera nodded.

'Thank you. Uwais. Ha. Prater. Ensor. Chame. Quert. Lerin.'

Malick glanced at Lerin as her name was spoken. He had heard of her reputation with heavy weapons.

'Gunsur. Malick.'

As the captain called out each name, Malick realised that Obeysekera already knew who each soldier in the squad was.

'Sir,' he said.

Obeysekera paused, drawing the listening troopers in closer. 'This mission will test even the very best. For we will not only be facing the enemy, we will be fighting a planet.' Obeysekera gestured outwards, his arm taking in all the unseen expanses of Dasht i-Kevar. 'This world kills. All of it is deadly, but we will be going into the most dangerous area of Dasht i-Kevar, the Sand Sea. It kills with heat and exhaustion, it kills by blinding and wearing down, it kills the stupid with ease and the clever with indifference. Our survival on this mission, and its successful accomplishment, will rely upon exact attention to detail and an ability to maintain concentration under the most difficult conditions that you have ever known.'

Captain Obeysekera stepped forward. He looked at his squad, the Kasrkin gathered around him in the shade below the wing of the Valkyrie, and he smiled.

'I've got something to show you,' he said.

YOUR
NEXT READ

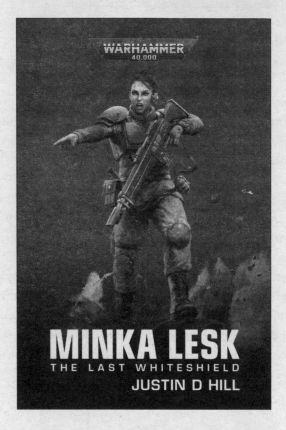

MINKA LESK: THE LAST WHITESHIELD
by Justin D Hill

Cadia has stood in grim defiance against the enemies of the Imperium for ten thousand years, an indomitable bulwark against the forces of Chaos… but now, the 13th Black Crusade has come, and there will be no victory. Here, Minka Lesk will be tested in the very fires of a world's destruction.